Black Tiger

Black Tiger

J.K. DRASKAU

MP Publishing

Black Tiger

First edition published in 2015 by
MP Publishing
12 Strathallan Crescent, Douglas, Isle of Man IM2 4NR British Isles
mppublishingusa.com

Copyright © 2015 by J.K. Draskau
All rights reserved.

This book is sold subject to the condition that it shall not, by way of trade or otherwise, be lent, resold, hired out, or otherwise circulated without the publisher's prior consent in any form of binding or cover other than that in which it is published and without a similar condition including this condition being imposed on the subsequent purchaser.

The scanning, uploading and distribution of this book via the internet or via any other means without the permission of the publisher is illegal and punishable by law. Please purchase only authorized electronic editions and do not participate in or encourage electronic piracy of copyrighted materials.

Your support of the author's rights is appreciated.

Jacket designed by Alison Graihagh Crellin.

Publisher's Cataloging-in-Publication data

Draskau, Jennifer.
   Black Tiger / J.K. Draskau.
   p. cm.
   ISBN 978-1-84982-155-1
1. Bangkok (Thailand) --History -- 1961-1969--Fiction. 2. Historical fiction. 3. Love stories --Fiction. I. Title.

PR6104.R3y B63 2015
823/.92 --dc23

ISBN 978-1-84982-155-1
10 9 8 7 6 5 4 3 2 1

Also available in eBook

For Jess, Olympic marathon runner and lioness.

*Tyger, tyger, burning bright
In the forests of the night
What immortal hand or eye
Could frame thy fearful symmetry?*

*In what distant deeps or skies
Burnt the fire of thine eyes?
On what wings dare he aspire?
What the hand dare seize the fire?*

*The Tyger
William Blake 1757-1828*

Starke, Florida, United States
1989

'Dr Raven?'

That lisping voice smooth as oil. The memories of the past I'd buried shot through me. The hairs on the back of my neck stood up. I almost dropped the phone.

'Prince Premsakul! *Sawasdee*, Your Highness!'

The prince chuckled. 'I see you have not entirely forgotten us, Dr Raven. Jolly flattering to have made such a lasting impression, I must say! Got an invitation for you—an execution, no less. You remember, of course, that Black Tiger's appeal has been denied? Would you like to be present as we bid goodbye to our good friend Colonel Sya?'

My teeth clenched in involuntary spasm. The memories were so strong as to be paralysing.

'It will not be an easy death.' The prince sighed. 'We are to witness Old Sparky in all his glory, I fear!'

My stomach churned. I'd thought the wretched saga was done and dusted. Naïvely I had imagined that the tedious process of depositions had been the last of it. I couldn't wait to get out of Florida, close the door on the whole wretched business.

'Tuesday. Seven a.m. sharp.' The voice was light with amusement, cordial, as though arranging an ambassadorial cocktail party. 'I will expect you at the State Prison, my friend! Toodle-oo!' He rang off.

'Chee Laan.' I found myself murmuring her name. The years fell away and I saw myself again, having just abandoned the Legion and the Service, telling myself I was finished with all that. Thoughts of settling down with my beautiful cousin Nancy, a rising star of the legal profession, and having a comfortable life as an obscure university don. A decent degree in politics, followed by a few years spent playing hide-and-seek with the angel of death in black holes and bomb craters, had qualified me to lecture the earnest young on terror, counterterror, and their moral implications. It wasn't a bad life, all told. Then, in a cliché blast from the past, who should show up but Angel Fleischer—sometime brother-in-arms, mercenary, and murderer—shouldering his way into my small campus office at Liverpool University. Unshaven, filthy, exuding the rank odour of sweat, testosterone, marijuana, and gun grease, Angel pleaded his case.

'Jesus, Raven!' He gazed round scornfully at the overflowing bookshelves, swept a stack of term papers off a chair, and sat down, his legs propped out in front of him like a cowboy. He picked his nose, snorted, and studied me scornfully. 'You're in a rut, man. You've sold your balls; the civilians have brainwashed you!' Soon I was listening to his new scheme for our partnership. 'Boot camp! I've been on a recce, found the perfect site. Normandy. Bocage country. Perfecto!' He rubbed his brown hands like a market trader and grinned.

'Boot camp for whom?'

'Well, mercenaries, and anti-terrorists—all government-sponsored, of course. And the civilians, rich adrenaline-junkies…'

'You're off your face, Fleischer.'

But all the same I followed him. And it worked well enough for a while, until they appeared: the three Thai girls, my eternal ghosts.

Salikaa, the Swallow, adopted daughter of a brigand; delicate Pim, Princess of the Blood, with her blazing revolutionary soul; and Chee Laan Lee, heiress to her grandmother's empire. At one time, a life I'd have given my own for.

'Little Miss Lee,' Fleischer boasted, 'personally recommended by the Black Tiger!' My notion of Thai society was unsubtle, based on technicolour tourist brochures, but I recognized the name of Thailand's first colonel. I might have known that Fleischer and the Black Tiger would be alert to each other's movements in the jungle. Little did I know, my eyes blinded by beauty, what that name would mean to me by the end.

Sya Dam, which means Black Tiger, the most powerful tribesman since Genghis Khan, had waded through guts and gore on his ascent to power, rivalling at his zenith any Prince of the Blood. Now it was his turn on the block—the execution he had escaped once could no longer be postponed.

We were instructed to arrive two hours before the execution, scheduled for seven a.m. Prince Premsakul smiled and joked as the driver helped him clamber into the white van. I followed in silence. We were transported to the briefing room, where an official explained the possible effects when 1800 volts at 7.5 amps flow through the human body for thirty seconds, followed by one minute of 240 volts at 1.5 amps. That cycle is repeated once.

Then I was told that, exceptionally, I was to be granted a two-minute interview with the condemned man. I don't know why he asked to see me—as if we had not already run that round, a lifetime ago. I was ushered into a small, drab room. Sya stood waiting between two hefty guards who stared stiffly into space.

I had rarely seen him out of uniform. Perhaps it was the informal denim shirt and trousers that created the illusion, but he appeared as young as in my memories, his handsome Mongol features unmarked by the passage of time. I noted that the right trouser leg had been cut off just above the knee. I averted my eyes from his pale, smooth lower leg. Asians are not hirsute, but the limb had clearly been shaved. He noted my unease and his eyebrows twitched in amusement. He greeted me with his old lazy grin.

'Raven! Black Bird! So. The fucking hounds finally caught up!' I grunted. 'No last requests, thanks for asking! Already ate my last meal—Starke strawberries, sweetest this side of heaven!' Sya patted his taut gut as he quoted the advertising slogan. His eyes gleamed. He prodded my chest. 'Got a going-away present, Raven: a slice of inscrutable Eastern philosophy for you. "We cannot prevent the black birds from flying over our heads. But we can prevent them from building their nests in our hair."' He stared at me for a long time, his eyes piercing straight through me, then grimaced and ran a hand over his skull, smooth-shaven for the metal cap and saline sponge. 'Showtime!' he bellowed, turning to the guards. They led him away. I stood staring after him.

Someone led me to the viewing chamber, where I took my place on one of the tiered plastic chairs and stared blankly into the brightly lit death chamber, already crowded with officials in dark suits. Sya was escorted in through a white door and was seated in the chair. Six correctional officers secured his limbs with big leather straps. I perched on the edge of my seat. The plastic rim dug into my thighs. My palms were sweating. My vision misted. Already steeling myself for the involuntary convulsions from the electric shock, I ached for the ritual to be over.

They started to drop the hood over his head, but he twisted away and grinned. The officers stood back. The warder asked Sya if he had any final words. Sya peered up at the glass through slitted eyes. Though I knew it was impossible, I felt his cold gaze settle on me. 'Are you there, Black Bird? Remember those black birds! Not only can we prevent them from building their fucking nests in our hair, we can also stop them crapping on our fucking faces! My life ends here, this time around. But I stole your life, too, didn't I? You never got to build any fucking nest, did you, Black Bird?' He chortled, shrugged his still massive shoulders, savouring his triumph. As I watched with mounting horror, I knew he was right. His death was not my victory. In embracing it, he remained unconquered.

The prince had been right, too. It was not an easy death. The big body convulsed, sinews straining; a scarlet shower erupted from the nose, and a plume of blue flame shot from his helmeted skull. At 7.07 a.m., Colonel Sya Dam, a.k.a. the Black Tiger, once essentially ruler of Thailand, was pronounced dead by the prison doctors.

The observers filed out in silence. I felt drained. Prince Premsakul pumped my hand in farewell. 'Hard-nosed bastards, these Akha tribal fellows, eh? No remorse, no priests, not even a bloody shaman! Well, toodle-pip!' He waggled his pudgy hand at me and hopped nimbly into the waiting limousine.

Still dazed, I found my hired car and motored up the freeway in the shadow of towering pink billboards proclaiming: *Starke strawberries! Sweetest this side of heaven.*

Changwat Chiang Rai District, Northern Thailand 1947

By the time he had seen seven rainy seasons, the Akha boy had made up his mind to run away. He knew he needed to get away from the tribe. He wanted more from life. He would have run away even earlier, but there was his sister. Their mother was dead, worn out with work, pregnancy, and casual violence. His sister, older than him by a handful of years, had cared for him and for their other two siblings until, neglected and malnourished, the younger ones had drifted into death. He had known this initiation day would dawn for his sister, as for all women, and that then he would fight for her. If he lost, he would have to die or flee the village, never to return.

Now it was time. She had been declared ripe for ritual deflowering by the appointed tribal stud. She had soft little hands, the memory of which would strike him sometimes later, after a life where there had been little softness, and in the course of which he himself had grown monstrous.

He hovered on the edge of the excited group that had gathered when they came to lead his sister away. She was shaking, the coins on her black and silver headdress jingling, her breath coming in sharp, shallow gasps. She cradled herself with thin arms while the tribal stud stood waiting for her. His nostrils flared and his white teeth flashed in a mocking grin as he savoured the girl's terror. She glanced up just once, darted a desperate look of appeal toward her brother. Just a snot-nosed, barefoot Akha brat, standing irresolute, inexperienced, but tense as a cobra poised to strike.

The boy made up his mind. His black topknot quivering like a coxcomb, he bent down and seized a sharp stone. He thrust it between his knuckles and squared up to the grinning bully. He knew his only chance was to strike first. He jabbed once, aiming the stone carefully. It was a good blow. He heard the nose-bone crack. The stud staggered back, howling with pain and outrage. Bright blood streamed from his shattered nose. Then he hurled himself upon the small boy, flailing with fists and feet.

A seven-year-old had no chance against his older, heavier opponent. Tearing himself free, the boy fled into the jungle, ignoring the yells of his tribesmen. He knew now: he could not save his sister from her fate. So long as he stayed in the tribe he would not escape his own. Destiny had forced his hand, and now it was time to break free. As he ran, spitting and grinding his teeth, he risked the vengeance of his savage gods and cursed his tribe. He sped fast, but not blindly, with a sense of purpose: he had heard of a temple, far to the west, where priests were reputed to teach orphan boys.

Akha knew better than anyone how to survive in the jungle. The boy gulped down rotten-sweet moisture from the boles of trees; from crumbling logs he prised fat white grubs. With his slingshot he killed frogs. He even tugged the wriggling leeches off his bare legs and sucked them. At night he curled up beneath the colonnades of a banyan trees, stuffing his fingers in his ears to shut out the twittering of evil spirits. At last he reached the temple and collapsed on the steps of the courtyard, feigning dead to outwit the pain. The scent of joss and jasmine stole into his pores like smoke. As he opened his eyes, he met the mild gaze of the monk. His saffron robe dragging in the dust, the monk rested his gentle hand on the boy's shoulder. He rose and hurried toward the temple, where the abbot was concluding his sacred chanting.

'Father, there's a boy,' the monk whispered, pointing. 'A face like a skull with yellow eyes.' Above the chanting of the other monks sounded an eerie wailing. 'Father, he howls like a wolf!'

The two holy men looked down at the half-dead boy. The abbot rubbed his chin. 'The boy may stay, for the moment,' he decided. 'It is written, despise no living thing, for all Life is one. He has the bones of a starved sparrow. He will soon die, no doubt. Perhaps in the next life his karma will be better.'

The boy fell upon the rice they brought him like a starving mongrel. 'Disgusting creature!' one monk muttered, regarding Sya's festering sores and running nose, the filth and blood that caked his feet and body.

The abbot beamed. 'The contemplation of ugliness is a valuable stage in the progress toward the State of Non-Being. But do not delay too long meditating on squalor. Bathe him.' The boy had to be dragged kicking and screaming to the river, convinced the water spirits would devour him. But to his own amazement he survived, after which he shovelled more rice into his mouth with both hands, then rolled over and dozed like a contented cat with a full belly for the first time in his life.

'It is time for you to return to your people,' the abbot said, when a week had passed. The boy leapt to his feet, ran at the bronze door of the temple and banged his head until oozing scarlet gashes appeared. Appalled, the monks dragged him away from the door. He flung off their hands, snatched up two stones and smashed them against his skull, spattering blood on the monks' bright robes as they rushed again to restrain him. In his basic Thai, he shrieked:

'*Mai mee baan allai!* I have no home!'

So the boy was allowed to stay. Having survived bathing, he now underwent the enforced removal of his pigtail, even though he fought like a demon because his tribe believed it spelled death. It took four monks to hold him down. When he stopped struggling, he waited, holding his breath, for fiends to appear and rush him off to hell, but nothing happened.

Later, when the abbot felt the process of taming him had progressed, he was given the duty of leading the monks on their dawn promenade. The monks were trained not to glance at the food the faithful placed in their bowls. Any morsel too delicious they plucked from their mouths. Quickly the boy learned not to grab these scraps.

A stony impassivity replaced his glare. Eventually, he was permitted to carry the sacred scrolls. This was acceptance.

The years passed in a cloud of joss and jasmine, the hours marked only by the tolling of the temple bell. He chanted with them. One day he ceased to be the Akha Boy.

'I will have a new name. I will be the Tiger,' he announced.

'Sya,' mused the abbot. 'A strange name for a temple boy.'

'I will not always be a temple boy, but from now on I will always be Sya, the Tiger.'

Chitr Lada Palace, Bangkok, Thailand
Memoirs of His Majesty King Rama

January 7, 1962
I write now of when I first set eyes on the young anagarika who would become my Akha officer, our faithful Sya Dam, the Black Tiger. Truly, he was an anagarika when I met him—a homeless person who had given up all worldly possessions to commit to Buddhist practice. I recall the occasion vividly. Our peaceful country was on the brink of a bloody civil war. With the unrest stirred up by those misguided Communist agitators in Vietnam and China, the trouble even threatened to spill over our borders from neighbouring Cambodia and Laos. In the light of these concerns, my politicians had entered into a 'gentleman's agreement' with our ally, the United States of America. The previous year the Americans had used five Thai airbases for reconnaissance flights. The bases remained under the command of my Thai air force to secure the defence of my realm. The political priority in these turbulent times was the Thai naturalization programme. The disaffected nomadic hill tribes were stubbornly refusing to be wooed.

Accompanied by an army of security personnel and journalists, I embarked on a journey to try and woo the hill tribes myself. Our itinerary took us to many parts of the country. We visited remote rural areas, making scheduled and spontaneous stops. We were on the road for the best part of two weeks. We roughed it, staying at temples and the homes of local dignitaries, even having roadside picnics at scenic spots, where the staff would set up trestle buffet tables under a silken canopy. We enjoyed feasts of noodles, fresh fruit, and refreshing iced tea. I quite enjoyed the break in routine, if the truth be told.

I could see how delighted everyone was. My people flocked to see me. Some had trekked for days through hills or jungle. Their devotion was most gratifying. They prostrated themselves in the red dust, some gabbling in excitement, many weeping for joy. I felt their eager eyes devour me; their hearts imbibed my essence as though they sucked the marrow from my venerable bones. By the time our travels were nearing their end, I was weak from happiness and exhaustion.

We had reached a remote jungle area in the north where the countryside was poor. Someone whispered, 'The temple here has a novelty that may interest Your Majesty. They have an Akha novice.'

This caught my attention at once, as I had never met a tame tribesman. It struck me that such a person could be useful in bringing other hill tribes to heel. Monks had lined up formally on the steps to greet us. My gaze was immediately caught by a figure looming in the background, larger than all the rest, in the white robes of an anagarika, a novice. The other monks dropped their eyes and stared respectfully at the ground, but this young man's eyes glared into mine before they looked away. I sensed the wariness of my attendants, but I stepped forward nonetheless, and examined the anagarika. He towered over me, not moving a muscle under my scrutiny, his stillness almost intimidating. Despite his tribal features, the young man was not only exceptionally impressive of build, but also distinguished of bearing. He did not grovel. Again he stared directly into my own myopic eyes. I could not penetrate his gaze but sensed some creature lurking in the depths. In an unworthy flash of superstition, I felt I had glimpsed a demon, and for a moment I was sick with dread.

'I think your studies have not yet freed you from ambition,' I chided gently, recovering my poise. 'Ambition chains us to the earth, like all desires.'

'Majesty,' he said, his yellow wolf's eyes still devouring mine, 'I have no ambition but to serve you. To die for you.'

Suddenly I was sharply focused. 'Well, one must hope the latter will not prove necessary,' I said lightly. 'But serve Us you shall.'

January 21, 1962

We were to return to Bangkok by helicopter. I had been looking forward to this flight after the exertions of the royal progress. As our helicopter took off with the usual deafening clatter, the Akha clapped his hands over his ears, shaking his head like a dog with a bee in its ear, but he soon adjusted and peered down at the green and red landscape, as though bidding it farewell.

In Bangkok I handed the young tribesman over to the charge of one of my many uncles, Worawong. The Akha was not the first of my acquisitions to be entrusted to his care. My uncle muttered irritably through his moustache that there was no such thing as an educated tribesman. My uncle further commented on the need to knock the nonsense out of him.

After distinguished basic training, Sya Dam was attached to the elite loyal Border Patrol Police, where a tame tribesman could certainly prove useful, but only if his allegiance were unshakeable. On the eve of his first assignment, I suggested my staff place him in Immigration, after which, if he proved loyal, to place him in Customs and Excise.

My uncle suggested I put him in Overseas Liaison, where the incentives were almost irresistible. Indeed, each successive post offered unlimited temptations. Those who sought favours brought limousines laden with sacks of money and opium and dumped the car keys on his desk. They left sapphire rings absentmindedly in his ashtray. They came to the interview room accompanied by nubile nieces and beautiful nephews; they brought title deeds to villas and apartment blocks, silver snuffboxes packed with snowy powder, and cufflinks set with rubies as big as pigeons' eggs.

Sya never gave in to temptation. The petitioners were rich and important; most were vindictive and all were ruthless. During the years of his temptation in the outposts, Sya Dam made many enemies. He remained invincible in his righteousness, pure as gold, hard as diamond. People began to call him The Incorruptible.

June 18, 1965

My dear Queen Benjawan is dead now. She died producing our only child, our Crown Prince, Vajah. Before our marriage, I had never thought much about ladies. I was slightly in awe of these fragile, volatile beings, complex as myths. As a young king I had been immersed in my pet projects—dams, nature reserves, literacy programmes and the like, and in my music and the life of the mind.

But it eventually dawned on me that an unmarried monarch is a disappointment. Benjawan was gentle and kindly, not terrifyingly beautiful or alarmingly haughty. Her death paralyzed me with guilt. All those sad attempts to produce an heir, all those false starts and dashed hopes—and her own life finally the price for our only son.

I miss her quiet good sense, her undemanding company. I wish she had been around longer for the boy's sake, too; while his servants and tutors are all excellent in their duties, they often display excessive adulation. I fear the boy will grow wilful and arrogant.

I also fear what might happen if I died, if the kingship were laid too soon upon his shoulders. My younger brother would be a conscientious regent. Still, I need to ensure, in the event of my demise, that my son has a stronger man at his side, one who will have the courage to make the hard decisions. My legacy to my son will be Sya Dam.

March 5, 1967
Sya's star continued to rise. He won promotion ahead of more experienced, and even better connected, contenders. There was resentment, but no one protested. His rivals never mounted a coup. His luck and his karma were good.

Even when promoted and recalled to Bangkok, he did not fall prey to its dubious attractions. (I fear our beautiful capital does not enjoy an entirely unblemished reputation.) He gave his enemies no opportunity to condemn him as a man given to perversity and excess. My faith in his ability increased. He became the youngest full colonel in our country's history, outside of our royal family.

My chancellor was clearly nervous when I told him of my plans for Sya, that I was creating a new post for him. I decided to give him the title of Director of Tribal Training Schemes and Information Dissemination. He would liaise with tribal headmen and promote centralization and a sense of nationhood.

The Chancellor disagreed with me, thinking it a mistake to give Sya carte blanche and worried at what his methods might be. It took some convincing to remind him that while Sya's carte blanche would certainly include and accept bribery and intimidation, they would be in our favour—in Sya's unquestioning loyalty, he would shun no means to further our goals. Any terror he inflicted would be in our interests. I was in no doubt that he possessed the fanatical ruthlessness of the terrorist. But he was my terrorist.

From Bangkok's military transmitter he broadcast in tribal languages. In the deepest jungles of the Northern Hills, his guttural tones pounded the message home to the communities within earshot of every Border Patrol post. During my official visits to outlying districts, I heard that familiar roar; the passion with which he thundered out those strange sounds was oddly unsettling. Since the Akha are the most savage of the tribes, moral recruitment of the Akha will make dealing with the Meo and the Yao and the Karen tribes mere child's play. If we win over the Akha, we will win everything.

March 5, 1968

Eventually it came to my attention that Sya Dam was perhaps going too far. I was told that he had made a brutal remark, something about burning down Chinatown and killing all the Chinese if any member of the Royal Family were assassinated.

Whims are the divine inspirations of monarchs. I happened to know that Sya Dam was inspecting the palace guard. I sent for him at once.

Under my questioning, Sya was unabashed. While he had no proof of any attempted assassination, he did comment openly on his desire to torch Chinatown.

'Somewhat drastic, Sya?' I murmured.

'Majesty.' He bowed low. 'Behind any attempt to overthrow the blessed Chakri dynasty, one would detect the hand of the murderous, unassimilated, bloodsucking Chinese!'

It might be true, but this kind of incautious and intemperate pronouncement contributed to the climate of hatred that was gathering around Sya. Jealousy festered. None but myself dared question him. People were afraid of who else he might blame.

I mulled it over for a couple of days and eventually decided it would be better for Sya to leave the country for a while. I sent my uncle General Worawong to approach the American director of the Southeast Asia Treaty Organization. Together we chose California.

June 24, 1969

It seems that Sya has studied obsessively, played certain Western sports with bravado, and dated intellectual sluts, my spies inform me. This year he returned, armed with an MBA and a racy vocabulary.

I am so happy with his return. Now educated and an expert in English, he is more useful than ever.

Sya quickly achieved yet another promotion. He was now a full colonel in the Border Patrol Police. He was too young, in reality, but I did not care about that. And because I did not care, nobody else dared raise objections. He now *spends much time at court, yet pays no respect to anyone, except myself.*

It is good to have my faithful Tiger back home. Sya is my talisman and my shield. I truly believe no ill will befall me on his watch.

Udon Thani, North of the Korat Plain, Eastern Thailand
January 1969

'Come!' Colonel Sya Dam stood with his back to the room, staring out at the cheerless compound. He did not turn, even at the staccato thud of three pairs of military boots on the wooden floor behind him, scraping to an abrupt halt.

'Prisoner, sir!'

He turned then, at the sergeant's bark, listening for any hint of resentment in the sergeant's voice, any rift in the unquestioning acceptance of his absolute authority. His hard gaze raked the face of the young soldier who stood between the two guards. On the youth's head, thrown back defiantly, Sya noted the black spikes where the cropped hair was starting to grow back. The chin was firm, the eyes steady. Only the clenched fists and unnaturally taut jawline betrayed his terror.

The boy's face expressed incredulity and indignation. His expression proclaimed that, had he dared, he would have yelled in protest that he had only been obeying orders, the incontestable commands of Colonel Sya himself, his fearsome, charismatic commanding officer, to whom the young man had demonstrated his doglike devotion over and above the call of duty. All this despite the fact that the commanding officer was not of his own people, not even a Black Thai or a Plains Thai, but an Akha.

One week ago, he'd been a trusted professional soldier at the start of a promising career. Or, rather, almost trusted. For it was well known that Colonel Sya Dam trusted nobody; his circumspection forestalled complications of just this unwelcome kind. Sya ensured that sensitive information, the kind that could too easily sow seeds of speculation and doubt, was withheld. He regarded the young prisoner with irritation tinged with regret.

'Read the charge, Sergeant,' Sya commanded tiredly.

'Boonchua, Corporal. Border Patrol Police number 10035. Mechanical support unit 306, airborne support division, Isaan. Suspected of collusion with insurgent terrorists, to the displeasure and jeopardy of the serenity and comfort of His Majesty King Rama and the security of His realm. Charge: treason, sir!'

'Defence?' Sya turned his heavy face once more toward the prisoner. The prisoner shied away from that cold eye. He shouted at the ceiling, hoarsely, without hope.

'Sir, just give me a few days to find witnesses to my innocence! I have important information for you, sir, concerning His Majesty. I have evidence His Majesty's life is in danger, sir! I work on the helicopters…'

'If His Majesty is in danger, it can only be from insurgent terrorists. With whom you, soldier, are accused of dealing.' Sya lowered his voice, exchanged the haranguing tone for a warmer, more intimate one. 'How did they trap you, boy? Was it drugs? Drink, women…little boys, perhaps?' Sya moved close, gazing into the boy's face.

'Sir, I am loyal! I would lay down my life for the king!' Sya nodded, wearily, as one who had heard the same thing many times. 'Sir, there are those who would kill the king!'

'You hope to be believed? What desperate plea is this?' Sya murmured contemptuously.

'I have witnesses to my loyalty, Colonel, sir. And witnesses who will swear they know of a plot against His Majesty. Please believe me! Just grant me a few days…'

'Request denied.' Sya shook his head. The condemned man shuddered. His eyes seemed to glaze, as though it were all over already, reminding Sya of the sudden resignation he had observed in animals at the point of slaughter.

'You seek to excuse yourself by incriminating others. This is the last resort of a desperate man. We must investigate these matters more closely. At all costs, the Chakri dynasty and the king's person must be protected. Take him away.'

The prisoner stared in disbelief. Sya lifted his hand as if in greeting, but it was a valediction, without compunction or regret. Sya looked hard at the sergeant.

'Take good care of this prisoner, Sergeant. I hope he will be too wise to attempt to flee. No one would be answerable for the consequences of such a rash action.'

The prisoner gave a great despairing cry and fell at Sya's feet. He clutched Sya's ankles and tugged at his boot, attempting to lift it and place it upon his own head as he grovelled. Sya did not move a muscle.

'Get up!' the sergeant snapped. The guards hauled the prisoner to his feet and dragged him outside.

Sya turned back to the window. He listened for the sharp, single bark of the service pistol. It came sooner than he had expected, and he drummed his finger on the window ledge, squashing, with efficient deliberation, a small blowfly crawling there. Small fry like Boonchua did not merit a full firing squad—a single shot to the back of the neck was all they deserved, just like a dog. Sometimes Sya fired the shot himself, in order to set a good example. A full firing squad would have entailed instigating a full-scale enquiry. Better by far, incomparably neater, for the fellow to be shot while resisting arrest. A full-scale inquiry must be avoided at all costs; whether the boy knew anything about a plot against the king or not, such a forum where he could blab his suspicions must be avoided.

Sya flexed his shoulders, feeling the damp uniform shirt lift from his skin and then reclaim it like a hot, clammy touch.

He felt confident that his own position was unassailable. His devotion to the dynasty and to King Rama's person was notoriously obsessive. He enjoyed a reputation as the scourge of insurgents, the hunter of terrorists. Diligently he scanned every shadow for possible royal assassins. When the moment came, the king would be removed from the scene, and none would mourn the popular monarch more vociferously. No one would pursue the investigations into possible treachery and sabotage more relentlessly than Sya Dam. Nobody would ever suspect that Colonel Sya, of the Border Patrol Police, the king's own creature, was not brokenhearted.

The members of the press, who privately called Sya the King's Blind Spot, publicly lauded him as the Incorruptible Black Tiger, the emblem of the tamed tribes. Sya knew they would have been less patronisingly complacent had they known that to the tribesmen he was much more than a contemptible emblem, a token tribesman among the Thai elite. Sya had carefully calculated the support he enjoyed among the tribes. Ostensibly wooing them in the national interest, he had instead established a useful power base among them. If the tribes had their way, Sya would rule the land as the reincarnation of their vengeful animistic gods—a savage, implacable deity after the Akhas' own hearts. Sya could now mobilise tribal resistance at will, following his successful campaign to bring wireless communication to them. 'Only through radio can we hope to centralise and educate the hill tribes, to channel their loyalties,' he had declared, addressing the tribes through that mass medium in the myriad variety of their own tongues. He spoke to the Meo, the Yao, the Tibetan, Burmese, South-Chinese hill people, and to his own people, the Akha, the last of the wild men, whose dread of civilisation had driven them deep into the northern jungles. Here, several days' march through bandit country, he knew they lived in primeval splendour and profound squalor, steeped in superstition, befuddled with the first fruits of their great cash crop, raw opium. Their annual yield of nubile village girls was still ritually deflowered by a handpicked village stud, with attendant brutality.

Since living in Bangkok and America, Sya had deliberately repudiated his fearsome inheritance. Once only had Sya revisited his tribe. It had been a semi-official visit, intended to win hearts and minds. They offered him the maiden crop. He recalled the dark gleam of frightened young faces, the crazy jangling of the silver coins in the black-and-scarlet pyramid headdresses that concealed their hair, the rustling of the heavy black-and-scarlet embroidered skirts. He remembered the muscular warm slithering of oiled skin smelling of blood and pork fat, the rank animal scent of pubic hair wiry as heather. He remembered his own readiness, and smiled. He had spoken true when he boasted to the shocked courtiers that, after the fierce taste of tribal fare, the refinements of civilisation seemed bland, anodyne, even tedious.

He sometimes wondered what he had become, away from his tribe. A white raven, a freak, walking among the Thai like a poodle tottering along on its hind legs. A savage pet, a pet savage. The Lady Asra, sometime Miss Universe, was known as Thailand's Smile, just as he, Sya, was the Black Tiger, or sometimes even Thailand's Conscience. She, too, must know what it was to be Thailand's pet.

The Thais seemed to him a soft people seduced by intricate fantasies. He wondered idly, as he waited for the sergeant's return, whether it was the influence of the Thai language that encouraged people into overdetermined symbolism. The language was richly metaphoric: a carburettor was 'nipples of mouse', an indicator was 'elephant's ear', to be naked was to be dressed in a 'garment of air'. *Overdetermined symbolism!* Sya rolled the syllables on his tongue. He had studied in America; he was a man of education. He could conjure with such terms. To understand these people was to destroy them.

The sergeant's polite cough recalled him to the present. He turned as the man re-entered the room and clicked his heels, saluting smartly.

'Beg to report, Colonel, sir. Prisoner shot while attempting escape, sir.'

'In order, Sergeant. Carry on.'

'Sir!'

'Boonchua. That was the name?'

'Sir!' the sergeant confirmed.

Sya snorted. 'Boonchua, formerly Boon, no doubt. Chinese. Bloody Jek!' He turned back to the window. 'There must be no hint of trouble in Isaan. His Majesty makes another official visit there tomorrow. His Majesty's safety is of paramount importance. We must all be ready to give our lives for the king, our father.'

'Sir!' agreed the sergeant heartily.

'Boon,' mused Sya. 'He would never have been able to afford proper witnesses on a corporal's salary,' he remarked casually, 'even supposing he managed to find any!'

'No, sir. Thank you, sir!'

As the sergeant turned on his heel he almost bumped into a soldier who immediately stood sideways, courteously, saluted at this awkward angle, and announced nervously, 'Please, sir, beg to report, foreign officer to see you, sir.'

Sya frowned. Expert as he was at the effective exploitation of the value of surprise, he himself was singularly averse to receiving surprises himself.

'Who?' he scowled.

'Please, sir, a Major Fleischer, sir. American person, sir!'

Sya gritted his teeth and forced his features into an expression of cordiality. Not a surprise visitor after all, but the long-awaited, recently promoted Major Angel Fleischer.

Sya had no wish to get off on the wrong foot with Major Fleischer, at least until they had explored one another's potential usefulness, so he hoped the sergeant had used what little initiative he had and tidied away the remains of the unhappy Boonchua.

Even battle-hardened Americans tended to find unexpected corpses off-putting so early in the morning.

Isaan, Eastern Thailand
1951

Young Tamnoon, his colleagues agreed, was never likely to become a successful police officer despite his enthusiasm for the job. His career would languish because he simply did not know how to make the best of a situation. He was too stubborn to ingratiate himself with his superiors, and too upright to take bribes and enrich himself in the usual way. And he was too pig-headed to refrain from open criticism of colleagues who did so.

Tamnoon, a poor but honest man, possessed only one treasure: his young wife, Sompong. She was a true Northern beauty, with skin pale and delicate as magnolia petals. She had the grace of the mythical hong bird, whose elegance is unsurpassed by any living creature. Tamnoon had bought her out of a house of entertainment within a week of her arrival, age fifteen, from the rice fields of Chiengrai, and never regretted it for a moment, even when his hell-raking old reprobate of a father, 'Python' Prasert, knocked his teeth out for marrying a Bad Girl. Tamnoon was accustomed to his father's intemperate reactions: upon learning of his son's intention to enter the police force, he had broken three of his ribs, yelling, 'Disgrace to the family! You will die a dog's death! You're too stupid even to be a policeman!' The Python had then gone on a bender that lasted three weeks, fully exercising the Thai capacity for drunkenness.

Tamnoon appeared to justify his father's misgivings. When his colonel cast lewd eyes upon the lovely Sompong as she strolled to market with her undulating stride, instead of turning a blind eye and accepting the inevitable promotion and favour, the young husband expressed his moral indignation. His reward was an immediate posting to the outback, the poverty-stricken far eastern district of Isaan on the Cambodian border.

In the meantime, his father, Python Prasert, had killed a man in a village brawl. This was not the first occasion, but this time, being too drunk to flee the scene, he was captured, fettered with leg-irons, and sentenced to life in Bang Saen prison. Here, Python lost little time in establishing his own social network. His fellow convicts considered him a straightforward sort of fellow, almost an aristocrat. It was widely felt that his crime, a brawl-killing, was a manly, clean-cut affair. There was nothing distasteful or premeditated about it, like the slow poisoning of an erring daughter or molesting temple boys. Besides, Nature had bestowed upon the Python disconcertingly crossed eyes, which to the superstitious convicts implied dealings with the black arts. Notwithstanding this blemish, the Python was a merry wag when sober, and had a great sense of humour and a kind word for everyone, even the blackest villains drug addicts. He even befriended Bang Saen's most notorious inmate, Crazy Archin, an acquaintance doomed to have disastrous consequences.

Crazy Archin, a shambling giant with the mental age of a toddler, had already dispatched fifteen people with his bare hands before the authorities caught up with him. Archin had once had a cellmate, but the experiment was not a success. One day, without apparent reason, he had shoved this unhappy cellmate's head through the bars and crushed his skull like an egg. After that he had nobody to share his cell but a chicken. He eventually ate the chicken alive, feet first.

But Archin took a great liking to Python Prasert. Whenever he caught sight of the Python's cross-eyed countenance, he pointed, shouting 'Witch-boy!' and laughing uproariously. As for the guards, they found the Python helpful and polite. Soon, his chains were struck off so that he could move freely and undertake the duties of a trusty.

'Life in prison' no longer meant 'until death', even in Thailand. Eventually the Python was released. While bloodthirsty in a drunken haze, in sobriety he waxed sentimental. Once free, he decided to look up his only blood relation, his son. Accordingly, he set out to the east, hitching rides on the back of trucks until he reached the Isaan village, where he enquired after the house of the village policeman.

Sompong opened the door, clutched her hair, and shrieked.

'Daughter!' cried the Python, saluting her. But Sompong went on shrieking.

She had started a new respectable life as the wife of a policeman. Besides, she had just discovered she was pregnant. The last thing she wanted was for her unborn child's disreputable old grandfather to turn up and claim a stake in the life of the law-abiding little family. She rushed about the tiny house like a terrified bird in a cage, hands fluttering helplessly, squeaking, 'Why did you have to come here? Leave us alone! We are decent people, respected. Jailbirds, felons, bad blood—how will this look? What about my husband's reputation?'

Tamnoon, alerted by a neighbour to the commotion at his home, rode up on his rusty bicycle. He was as displeased as his wife had been. But filial duty forbade him to exhibit his dismay in public, so he invited the old man in. Tamnoon produced a bottle of Mekhong whisky and some cigarettes, and ordered Sompong, in an unusually brusque tone, to prepare food. Grinding her teeth, she disappeared outside to her kitchen area. She resolved to make Tamnoon pay dearly for his rudeness to her. It would be easy, now that she knew she was pregnant. She didn't feel so inclined to vigorous demonstrations of affection these days. He would have to beg. Sompong smiled as she crushed the beetles for the red sauce.

'As you see, *Khun Paw*, honourable father,' Tamnoon indicated the modest shack, 'we have little room in our home.' The Python helped himself to a tumbler of whisky.

'Don't work up a sweat, son. I see how the wind blows.' He tapped the side of his nose and winked. 'I'll just look round for a place to put up a cabin and do a bit of fishing, a bit of farming, a bit of this and a bit of that.'

Sompong popped her lovely head through the bamboo fly-curtain. 'Where are you going to do all this, old man?' she demanded sharply. Tamnoon scowled in embarrassment, but his father grinned. He had lost three more teeth in jail, Tamnoon noted. Together with his creased, tobacco-coloured skin and his cross-eyes, he looked a consummate rogue, but his voice when he answered was mild and innocent.

'Why, hereabouts,' the Python made an expansive gesture toward the door. 'Lovely spot. Thought I'd build me a shack just there, on the riverbank. Close to my nearest and dearest!'

Sompong waved her kitchen chopper, making the bamboo curtain rattle like dried bones. 'Oh, no you don't!' she squealed. 'We don't want your type squatting on our doorstep!'

The Python looked hurt. 'I'm reformed. I'm as decent as anyone else these days,' he protested. 'You'll see. I'll be a credit to you!'

Soon, he had built himself a neat little cabin on the riverbank, just a few yards from his son's house. There he stayed on, doing a bit of this and a bit of that. It became clear, however, that prison had not entirely succeeded in reforming the old man, and his activities soon became a trial to his virtuous relatives. He got drunk, he chased low women and smoked opium, he played cards for drinks—Mekhong whisky on a good day and Singha beer the rest of the time. He bawled bawdy ditties at the top of his voice. He fell in the river, stole the odd chicken, and in general made himself an embarrassment. The hardest to bear was his choice in fellows.

The Python acquired a new best friend—no less a person than Vichai, the local bandit chief. Tamnoon thought this the most unsuitable choice possible. He was mortified. Sompong, her misgivings proven right, was bitterly triumphant and gave him no peace.

Vichai was a highly successful brigand. He ran an immensely profitable organisation from his fortress on the far shores of the great Isaan River. He maintained state-of-the-art battle firepower by trading opium for weapons with the American military bases at Udorn and Korat. Drugs, women, and terror were Vichai's stock-in-trade. Vichai abhorred problems; he had always been careful to ensure that the local policeman was on his payroll. But then Tamnoon arrived on the scene. Righteousness, a quality Vichai found tiresome in anybody, was intolerable in a policeman. To those engaged in free enterprise, an incorruptible policeman spelled no end of *lambaak*—as Tamnoon was to discover, to his cost.

Meanwhile, back at Bang Saen, Big Archin, lonely without his friend, had decided the time had come to make his escape. He could never have masterminded a jailbreak on his own, of course. His first act of freedom was to break the neck of the unfortunate who had helped him, for, limited though his mental powers were, Archin was nonetheless sufficiently astute to keep his life tidy. He tossed the dead body of his co-conspirator into a *khlong* and set off to find his good friend, the Python.

The Python had told Archin about the son who'd moved to a village in Isaan, to the northeast. He could not have remembered a name—Archin was not good at names—but luckily this village had no name, just a number.

Village thirteen. He plodded along the roads after nightfall, laughing aloud as trucks swerved and squealed past him, horns blaring, big lamps flashing. He stole food and drink from wayside stalls, bananas and papayas and Coca-Cola. When there were no wayside stalls, he ate insects and frogs. Sometimes, as he lumbered along, his big head wagging from side to side, he chuckled to himself, imagining the Python's delight at seeing him. They'd exchange a few backslaps and shoulder-thumps, a few laughs, a few beers, go look for a few girls—*bai theuw puying*. It would be happy days!

When Archin finally caught up with his friend, the Python, a sociable fellow, did welcome him. He took him into his cabin, offered him refreshments, let him doss down to wait out the hue and cry. He did not think it wise not to mention Archin to his son, nor did he tell Archin about his son's inconvenient profession.

It was unfortunate, therefore, that a couple of days later, Tamnoon received word from police headquarters that the monstrous serial killer known as Crazy Archin had escaped from Bang Saen and was rumoured to be making his way east. Tamnoon, realising his father and Archin had been fellow prisoners at Bang Saen, decided to stroll over to the riverside cabin for a chat. He thought his father might know something about the dangerous escaped prisoner's possible destination.

But there was another reason for this filial visit. Tamnoon now knew that his wife was expecting their first child. In Tamnoon, as in his father, such occasions brought out sentimental tendencies. He felt a grandfather's blessing and reconciliation would make for a more propitious atmosphere for the baby's birth.

He determined to speak to his father first, to make sure Archin was nowhere around, and then invite his father up to the house for a meal. Afterward, he decided recklessly, he would beard the notorious bandit chief in his den—for it was well known that Vichai would offer asylum to any useful antisocial elements. Tamnoon was determined to find out whether Vichai was harbouring Archin, or if he intended to do so, and warn him that this would not be tolerated. The authorities had promised a substantial reward for the recapture of Crazy Archin, and Sompong had warned Tamnoon that babies were very expensive.

As Tamnoon approached his father's shack, the Python saw him from the window and hurried out to greet him before he entered and discovered Archin. The Python had not told anyone in Bang Saen prison that his son was a policeman. So when Archin peered out and saw his host deep in conversation with a man in uniform, his instincts screamed, 'Treachery!' He waited until Tamnoon left, then did what he had to do.

The Python did not put up much of a fight; he wasn't expecting an attack from his guest. Meanwhile, Tamnoon set off across the river in a long-tail boat on his heroic mission into the heart of the bandit's lair.

Ironically, the Python, reluctant to take responsibility for his unpredictable companion, had already approached Vichai and tried to persuade him to take Archin in. But Vichai was no fool. He had stared at Archin and said, 'That psychopathic gorilla? When I need a thing like that I'll go to a zoo. Psychos are *lambaak*, and a man in my kind of business needs trouble like an extra hole in his ass. I can shit plenty with the one I have.'

Seeing the Python chatting jovially with a policeman had set the familiar anger demon dancing in Archin's brain. As he struck the unsuspecting man down and twisted the knife in his neck, he watched his friend's agonies through a red haze, as if he were looking through a film of blood. Killing the treacherous Python was not sufficient to placate the demon. So, growling and grumbling, Archin went up to the little wooden house, and when the stupid woman there opened the door and started screaming, it enraged him even more. He pushed her over and held her down and had her, right there on the wooden floor, in spite of her great girth and her bitter resistance. She scratched and spat, and Archin quite enjoyed that part, too. But she made too much noise, squawking like a chicken, and then there was nothing for it but to throttle her. He despatched her as easily as his feathered former cellmate. She no longer moved, but Archin felt his flesh stir again. This time he would take his pleasure slowly, revelling in the stillness and the silence.

Vichai's success as a chieftain was largely ascribable to his meticulous attention to detail. From the far bank of the river he had observed the police officer approaching his camp across the river in his long-tail boat. He had immediately sent one of his own men, in another, swifter long-tail boat, to watch the policeman's house, where he knew the policeman's pregnant wife was alone, in case assurances were needed. Vichai's spy, appalled by the carnage he found on the other side of the river, fled, sliding down the slippery bank to his boat and roaring across the river. As Tamnoon was getting slowly out of his boat, coolly watched by Vichai and his guards, and wondering if his courage would hold, Vichai's spy veered up behind him and crashed his long-tailed boat into the reeds. As he stumbled up the opposite bank, he yelled out that a monster was on the loose who would murder them all.

Once he understood what had happened, Tamnoon gave a howl, turned his craft around and headed back across the stream. Vichai barked out orders to his men to launch their boats, and with a roar of engines and a surge of bow waves they set off in pursuit. Vichai's face was black with rage. He would not countenance violence not of his own devising within his empire.

On the damp ground outside the shack, Vichai's men found the Python lying in a pool of his own blood. Archin had stabbed him a dozen times and then ripped his tongue out. There was nothing they could do for him. Hearing a sound from the nearby house, they started running again—but Tamnoon was swiftest, fired by terror. He stopped, peering into the dark interior, clinging to the doorpost. He thought at first some wild creature from the jungle had invaded his home, some lurching black bear or giant hog badger, rooting away, grunting rhythmically. But then, hideously, he saw. With a howl he hurled himself upon Archin. Archin shrugged him off and stood peering down at him as he lay helpless, struggling, wailing and weeping. Archin shook his head, picked up Tamnoon and threw him through the window, breaking his neck. Then he sped into the jungle.

The men fired a few shots after him but nobody was keen to follow.

Vichai now turned his attention to the woman lying lifeless at their feet, her neck twisted and her clothing disordered. He felt his men's eyes on him, waiting for his lead. He pushed Sompong's leg gently with his foot. He squatted down, big hands hanging loose, and studied her closely. He flicked up the cloth of her bright sarong and saw her swollen belly.

'I've heard this is possible,' he said, standing up and holding his hand out behind him.

Isaan was a land of hunters and trappers. Every man carried a skinning knife. A man slipped his knife into Vichai's hand. Vichai signalled to his henchmen to hold the dying woman's head, tugged aside her sarong, and with the razor-sharp blade slit open her belly. Someone shouted, 'There's the baby's leg!' and Vichai pulled the child into the light of day. He took one look at the furious bloody face and shuddered. 'Give it to the women. They'll deal with it. It'll probably die, anyway.'

He would never forget the rage on the child's face or the way the tiny fists pummelled the air. Even his strong stomach was upset. Steeped though he was in sex, blood, and torture, he had been at the death many times but never at the birth. It was revolting. He almost regretted succumbing to his curiosity and giving the child life.

The child stubbornly refused to die. Vichai's wives and concubines took over the duty of rearing it. At the moment of its birth, Vichai couldn't have cared if it had expired; later, however, he became possessive, almost obsessed. It was an unusually beautiful child, with its mother's fair features. Vichai's women took delight in spoiling the doll-like creature, dressing it like a princess in the off-cuts of bolts of smuggled silks. The child seemed to avoid the usual chubby, ungainly stages of toddlerhood; if it was ever pudgy, no one could recall it afterward. It grew up gracefully, and instead of crawling and stumbling into things, it danced, light as a leaf. It still had no name. The women called it 'Ugly' to fool any evil spirits who might be lurking and who would be attracted by a more flattering name. If they gave it a name too soon, especially after so inauspicious a birth, the name might prove unlucky. They did not want to bother changing it, which would be confusing not only to the spirits, but also to the child itself. Then one day Vichai, maudlin in his cups, watching the child dance to its inner music, said, 'Poor little motherless thing! It flits like a swallow. Call it after the long-tailed swallow. Call it Salikaa.'

Vichai never asked his wives about the gender of the baby. It was too beautiful to be anything but a girl.

By the time Salikaa reached puberty, Vichai's jealousy had grown intense. If a man ventured to speak to her, Vichai had him flogged. 'You're going to be a fine lady, Salikaa, little swallow. You're going to be Miss Thailand and marry a handsome prince!' he would say, dandling the giggling child.

'He wants Salikaa for himself,' some of the concubines whispered.

Others, more astute, ridiculed the notion. Salikaa, they argued, was an investment, a marketable asset. When the time came, Vichai would barter her to the highest bidder.

Still, some remained convinced. 'She is being groomed to sweeten his declining years.' Later, when Salikaa heard this, she said, 'He's going to be surprised, in that case. I want more from life than some fat old boar, stinking of whisky.'

But in her heart Salikaa felt Vichai, her adoptive father, was almost certainly the greatest man in the world, the only person who loved her, and under his protection, she grew up arrogant in her beauty.

Bangkok, Thailand
1956

Little Miss Chee Laan Lee danced along the pavement, swinging her Dior-pirated mini handbag and scuffing her scarlet sandals in the dust of Lumpini Park. Ah Lee, her *amah* or nurse, descended from Hakka fisherfolk, wrinkled and tough as smoke-cured buffalo hide, hissed irritably through betel-stained teeth. She was forced into an ungainly huddled posture as she struggled to keep the pink paper parasol over her little charge's sleek black head.

If any of the Thai kite sellers or the watermelon or noodle vendors lining the pathway thought, 'Jumped-up little Chink brat!' they kept such opinions to themselves. Little Chee Laan, exuding pampered wealth from every pore, clearly offered opportunities for enrichment.

One enterprising kite seller dashed forward, smiling and nodding, and thrust the string of a kite into the child's pudgy fist. Ah Lee pursed her lips and closed her eyes; she clicked her disapproval like a cross old owl. Then, grumbling, she set down the parasol on its spoked edge in the dusty grass and dug about in the folds of her voluminous black pants for the leather wallet. Manners now demanded that she pay the wretched kite seller twice the kite's worth, since it had come in the guise of an unsolicited gift.

This was Ah Lee's favourite route, past the towering edifices that testified to the aspirations and success of her millionaire employers and distant relatives, the Lee Family. But for once she failed to find solace in the reflected grandeur of the Lee Building and the nearly completed, already palatial Rachanee Hotel. Ah Lee waited until they were out of earshot; then, as soon as they turned the corner, she scolded: 'Wind no blow, kites no good!'

As though to spite her, a breeze arose, whirling the kite aloft. The child, eyes narrowed with laughter, gazed up in wonder. She gave a skip of triumph.

The kite had painted eyes and wings. It bobbed along above Chee Laan like an obedient celestial bird, a tamed Garuda.

At the corner by the great building site that represented the Lee family's latest, most stupendous project, the road deteriorated into a series of craters. The Rachanee Hotel was being thrown up floor by floor to catch the flood tide of Bangkok's increasing waves of tourists. Every rainy season carved out again the same ravines and pits that had been laboriously repaired during the cool season. Chee Laan, eyes turned skyward, neglected her feet, and she tripped. The kite shot up and out of her hand, snagging its string on the scaffolding. Chee Laan started to yell, then closed her mouth again, staring up in surprise. One of the work gang, a colt-legged girl with a man's discarded trilby perched jauntily on her head, grinned a gap-toothed grin.

'*Mai pen 'rai*, little miss! Never mind. Nit get kite.'

Many Thai girls were nicknamed Nit: 'Tiny', 'Midge', 'Titch'. But this girl wasn't small, only skinny from years of malnutrition and hard labour. Ah Lee's sharp eyes had noted her swollen abdomen and wondered how the girl had managed to conceal her condition from the foreman. Doubtless the brat she carried was his own get, she thought—that would explain why he generously permitted the girl to risk her life for eight baht a day, scrambling up the bamboo scaffolding, lugging the yoked buckets brimming with liquid cement.

'Go away!' Ah Lee muttered fiercely to the wall. She would not address the creature directly—she would not lower herself. Laughing, the girl slammed down her buckets. Cement slurped over the sides. She sprinted over to a ladder leaning against the scaffolding and started to climb, agile as a gibbon. The other women labourers paused to stare; some called to her in anxious fluted tones, like alarmed marsh birds, urging her to take care, but the girl just grinned and went on climbing. Chee Laan watched, forgetting, as always when excited, to draw breath. The old *amah* reached out for the child's hand and gripped it tight. More than any rage, the unexpected gesture struck a cold terror in the child. Although Ah Lee played a more central role in her young life than her own mother, a shadowy figure in the background, Ah Lee had never before taken her hand. Even when crossing a busy street, Ah Lee just gripped the neck of her frock, like a policeman arresting a felon.

Nearing the kite, the labour girl leaned out, almost at a right angle to the ladder, stretching, grasping. The ladder shuddered like a live thing waking, and started to slither sideways. The dancing kite imparted a festival air—an acrobat performing a trick for a gasping audience. The girl's body detached itself from the ladder slowly, like a raindrop dislodged from a palm leaf.

She was still smiling when she hit the ground, as though she didn't realise what was happening. She fell heavily, landing on her shoulders and the back of her skull, the ladder bouncing on top of her. She lay still. Some of the younger women started running, then, swooping and shrieking, cement slopping everywhere. The older ones, wary of disaster and its attendant *lambaak*—trouble—turned away silently.

All of Ah Lee's instincts screamed to her to follow suit, but the child broke free from her grip. When Ah Lee caught up with her, Chee Laan was already beside the girl, staring down.

'Come!' Ah Lee commanded, taking the child by the shoulders. At that moment a big Mercedes, driven hard and fast, screamed around the corner, bucketing and keeling over on two wheels. Ah Lee only just dragged the child out of its path. The driver never even hit the brakes. Both wheels on the left side of the car flybucked as they banked the labour girl's body: so slight was she, and the car's suspension such a triumph of German technology, that the passengers must have felt but the slightest jolt, scarcely more than striking a rock or mowing down some diseased pye-dog. Nonetheless, intrigued by the flustered little knot of people, the passengers peered through the tinted bulletproof glass to discover the source of the commotion. Those on the street glimpsed a slack-jowled, aging Chinese face, and a younger face, impassive behind its mask of make-up, glossy coils of blue-black hair. The younger face seemed too heavy for its pale, wiry ostrich neck. There was something ostrich-like, too, about the huge, cold eyes that glittered beneath green-painted lids, dominating the arrogant, sensual face. The two faces lurched close and were gone; the car powered away, bucketing through potholes, shrouded in choking dust clouds. But the child's eyes were sharp.

'*Khun Paw*,' Chee Laan shouted hoarsely. She started to run after the car. Ah Lee, chattering like a monkey, seized a handful of her skirt. 'That was father, in that car! Ah Lee, why didn't he order the chauffeur to stop?'

'Imagination and foolishness!' scolded Ah Lee. 'What use to stop? Girl dead, why stop?'

'She wasn't *all* dead! Not till *Khun Paw*'s car hit her. I heard her groan.

Before. Just like a ghost. "Oohh!"—like that. She *wasn't* all dead!'

'Girl dead. Maybe Little Miss hear ghost, maybe not. Hearing ghosts, seeing things, not good! Kites and low people, bringing *lambaak*. Forget about!' Ah Lee pawed fretfully at the dust on the child's clothing, shook out her flouncy underskirts.

Chee Laan pulled herself free. She stamped. 'I'm going to tell Grandmother!' She set off purposefully on her fat little legs.

'Little Miss! Honourable Old Lady busy! Not disturb!'

The child had inherited all her grandmother's determination, and, Ah Lee thought, a rash wild streak like her worthless father. Muttering and shaking her head, she followed her charge down the busy road toward the glass and chrome skyscraper that housed the headquarters of the family firm.

Chee Laan trotted briskly up the marble steps. The entrance was emblazoned with square *farang* letters, elegant ideograms and ornamental Thai, all proclaiming one identical message: THE LEE BUILDING.

Chee Laan darted past the uniformed guard and the white-robed watchman, ignoring their salutes, and dived like a questing terrier through the heavy carved teak door that led to her grandmother's private apartments. She did not even pause to remove her dusty sandals. Ah Lee, outraged and outmanoeuvred, glared at the dumbfounded attendants and shook her head.

'Worthless fellows, have you nothing better to do than stare?'

'*Tsu mu!* Grandmother!' Chee Laan stopped on the threshold and peered into the dark room. Her eyes were unaccustomed to the gloom after the bright glare of the street outside, and at first she thought the room was empty. But then she saw the slim figure before the shrine. Her grandmother, Sunii Lee, knelt, holding a lighted incense stick between her outstretched fingers. After the bustle of the street, the room was still and quiet. Sunii Lee, matriarch of the powerful Lee clan, was, as usual at this hour, at her devotions.

In Bangkok, Sunii Lee's piety and charity were famous. In Hong Kong, Shanghai, and Singapore, her business acumen and her ruthlessness in the high-finance marketplace had won her respect bordering on reverence. In appearance slight, in conduct modest, she possessed ageless beauty according to the Chinese ideal, and had through careful study attained timeless elegance. But these were adventitious attributes. Sunii's greatest assets were her entrepreneurial daring and her phenomenal skill with figures. Sunii habitually beat male competitors at their own game, while still affecting the retiring demeanour and soft voice of a traditional Oriental lady of good family. Yet she was not of good family, and there was nothing hide-bound about her approach to commerce. She was, in effect, a fragrant cutthroat. Many people hated Sunii Lee, and many more feared her; even her beloved granddaughter Chee Laan was a little afraid.

The child hesitated in the doorway, watching her grandmother, fascinated by the tiny lit incense stick that glowed like a firefly in the darkness of the shuttered room. She hardly dared to move until she heard behind her the tramp of the guard's heavy boots, and the rattle of chains and keys against his gun. At his side, breathless with outrage, Ah Lee huffed and clucked. With a howl, the excited child plunged into the room and threw herself to the ground beside her grandmother, who started and almost dropped her joss stick. Puffing, Ah Lee fell to her knees and squirmed forward as fast as she could, the knees of her chino pants squeaking on the wooden floor. The burly security guard hovered uncertainly in the doorway.

Sunii Lee took in the scene at a glance, and unhurriedly saluted the shrine. Then she turned, her delicate eyebrows arched in query and irritation.

'Worthless cement-girl steal Little Miss's kite!' panted Ah Lee swiftly, so as to establish matters. Chee Laan gasped in indignation at this barefaced lie. 'By Rachanee new building place. Coolie snatched kite. Ran away. Fell down, then car—*pam*!' Ah Lee struck her palm with her fist in illustration. 'Driver never stop. Foreigner, *farang*. Foreign devil, all time hurry hurry...' Ah Lee shrugged expressively, as if to say what more could one expect.

Chee Laan leapt to her feet and shouted, 'It isn't fair! She wasn't a thief— she was trying to help! And there were no foreign devils, it was *Khun Paw*, honourable father. I saw him!'

Sunii Lee's voice was cool as the dusk breeze. 'Granddaughter! Have you eaten rice yet?'

Deflated, the child hung her head. She muttered the traditional answer, 'Unworthy!' meaning that she had by her greed deprived her grandmother of her own meal.

Sunii rose in one fluid movement. 'The stupidity and ignorance of the labouring class can only be counteracted by education,' she said. Young as she was, Chee Laan recognised an official explanation when she heard one, and knew it to be immutable thereafter. But like a terrier, she persisted.

'But, Honourable *Tsu mu*, why didn't *Khun Paw* order the driver to stop? And who was that lady in the car, *Tsu mu*?'

Sunii's fine winged brows contracted as if in pain. She made an almost imperceptible gesture with her right hand. Ah Lee withdrew, reluctantly.

Sunii Lee turned to the black-and-gold lacquer writing desk; she withdrew a wickerwork basket lined with red silk and full of sweetmeats. With her long-nailed fingers she stuffed sweets into Chee Laan's mouth until the child, purple-faced, choking, felt the tears run from her eyes into the crevices of her jutting lips. The taste of the sweets mixed with the salt. Unable to speak, she gulped painfully. The sweets seemed huge as boulders. The pieces she managed to swallow bruised her gullet.

Sunii regarded her granddaughter's struggles thoughtfully. 'My precious one! Now we shall forget these bad things. We shall never speak of them again. We shall lift our thoughts to serious matters, Granddaughter, instead of bursting into rooms and racketing about like people unable to behave with dignity. A woman is never too young to acquire dignity. It takes a great deal of thought and skill to live successfully as a woman, especially a clever one. Fetch the calligraphy things.'

Still gasping and sobbing, Chee Laan brought the powdered inks and the bamboo brushes with their round covers, and set them carefully upon the glass top of the carved table. Beneath the glass, an inlaid wooden forest of fabulous leaves, flowers, and birds shimmered darkly.

They worked in silence. When at last some of the child's brushstrokes began to lose their awkwardness, sweeping across the page fluent and graceful, a smile like a wintry sunbeam touched the older woman's narrow lips.

'You are pleased, *Tsu mu*?' the child ventured timidly, glancing up.

'It is not forbidden to allow pleasure to appear on the face,' Sunii smiled. 'Sorrow, distress, these are unseemly. These are for the private heart.'

The child bowed her head, acknowledging the righteous reproof of her vulgar display. But she continued to wonder, nonetheless, about what she had seen. Her grandmother's disapproval had balked her investigation but not neutralised her curiosity, which was keener than ever.

———

The next day Chee Laan watched as Ah Lee rolled out her woven mat in the cool shade of the wattle tree and curled herself up with a grunt of satisfaction for her noontime nap. The wattle tree stood in the centre of the gated courtyard that was the heart of the Lee family compound, four pavilions separated by banks of bright flowers. Behind its tall walls and massive gate, guarded by dogs and watchmen, the atmosphere was secluded and serene. Bees hummed in the bougainvillea that spilled over the walls in a crimson cascade; twittering finches flitted in the large aviary along the far wall. Huge lazy koi circled endlessly in the pool, red and gold beneath the water, as a small fountain whispered a lullaby.

Chee Laan could easily have settled for a snooze herself. But she had something else on her mind. She waited until Ah Lee's grunts settled into a rhythmical pattern of snores. Then stealthily she rose from the old *amah*'s side and trotted across the courtyard to her father's pavilion, kicked off her shoes, and climbed up the wooden steps to the living area.

Her entrance awoke him. Her father had been slumped over a tabloid newspaper, a cigarette burning unheeded at his elbow, a glass of whisky tilting dangerously in his flaccid grasp. He bore little resemblance to his elegant mother. His father, Chee Laan's grandfather, was never spoken of. He had gone to join his ancestors so long ago that nobody appeared to remember him. His blunt features fly-blown, his slack, large-pored skin the same unhealthy yellowish-grey as his gold-edged teeth, Chee Laan's father yawned and belched. He reached out stubby fingers to pinch her, roaring with mirth and false bonhomie. A man who lusted after other people's children, on his forays into the city's seamy side, he was ill at ease with his own.

Squirming out of his reach, Chee Laan demanded straight out, brusque as a coolie, '*Khun Paw*, who was that lady in the car with you yesterday?'

With a roar of fury he snatched away his hand, which had strayed and was patting her bottom over the frilly knickers, in the lingering way she detested. He exploded: 'Shall a girlchild question her father?'

Accustomed though she was to the pendulum of his moods, between maudlin sentimentality and apoplectic rage, the force of his fury terrified her. She scuttled down the wooden staircase into the sunlit garden, saying nothing more. Her brother Pao was practising with his new badminton racquet on the gardener's blooming flower border. The severed heads of azaleas flew through the air like the bright feathers of dying birds.

These days Pao was more bloated than usual with notions of his own importance, having recently celebrated his fifteenth birthday with a visit to a brothel, sponsored by his father. Fuelled by his conquest of a couple of pathetic teenage addicts, Pao was now a man of the world in his own eyes.

'Oh, little mouse! Did the mouse make *Khun Paw* cross? What did it do?' he greeted his sister in mocking Thai, exaggerating the tones, slapping her with his racquet so her gold-lace skirt bunched around her bottom. A bee bumbled in a hibiscus near her face. The scent of the grass was sharp, hot as burning hay in her nostrils, and made her long for the cool of the evening, when the gardener would turn on the hose and the sprinklers.

'I just asked him about the lady in his car. All painted, like a film star, with dragon eyes. He got mad.'

Pao hooted derisively. He straddled the flowerbed, careless feet crushing the blooms. His tennis shoes had cost a fortune. 'So you thought that was a girl with *Khun Paw*!'

She stared. 'Of course. What else?'

He tweaked her ear hard. It brought tears to her eyes. 'What a flea-brained dim little mouse it is! That was Dad's *catoy*—a boy dressed in girls' clothes!'

She stared at him solemnly. 'You mean like the boys who dress up in women's clothes the day before they join the army, and run round the *sois* drunk, banging gongs and yelling?'

He cackled, swaggering with lewd knowledge.

'Why would a boy dress like a girl?' Chee Laan persisted. 'Confucius says being born a woman is the saddest fate in the world. You say women are cattle, only less valuable.'

'True!' he grinned. 'If there're too many girl babies, people put them out to die.'

She stared at her brother, horrified. 'But they aren't allowed to do that anymore! There's a law!'

He giggled, laying a finger alongside his broad nose and squinting down it cunningly. 'That's what you think. Dumb little mouse! Course they do it! Pity they didn't do it with you, pesky, chicken-brained *meimei*, little sister!'

'All right.' She swallowed hard. 'If it's so bad being a girl, why would a boy dress up and pretend to be a girl, then?' She glared at him, daring his answer.

He gave her a shove with his racquet. 'For kicks, stupid! Old guys like *Khun Paw* do it for kicks. The *catoys*—the lady-boys—do it for the money and the presents. You've the brain of a goldfish, *meimei*!'

She was unconvinced. 'But what do they *do*?'

Her pouting baby mouth engorged him. On a sensuous impulse, he lunged, hauled her close, whipped up her lace skirt and plunged his hand down, round the smooth firm curve, into the depths of her gold-frilled briefs. Despite their stubby plumpness, his fingers were surprisingly agile and hard. It felt disgusting, like having a big, determined insect with suckerpad feet crawl upon her, bore into her. She screamed and beat at him. He pushed her down among the azaleas. She sprawled there, humiliated and furious, her face plunged in the hot earth. He jabbed at her painfully with the end of his racquet.

'Up there! They shove it up there! One of these days I'll have to undertake your education, *meimei*!' he sniggered, eyes disappearing into his fat, round cheeks. He looked like a dimpled doughy bun, she thought. Brainless, flabby, and unappetising. Chee Laan scrambled to her feet and beat frantically at her clothes.

'Pigs!' she roared hoarsely. 'It's men that have no brains—pigs, all of you! I'm never going to have anything to do with any of you as long as I live!'

He laughed mockingly. 'You wait, mouse! Just wait till I catch up with you! I'll get you alone, and then…'

'I'll tell Ah Lee!' she shrieked, flailing her round little arms at his grinning face. 'I'll tell *Tsu mu*! I hate you, Pao!'

He was helpless with mirth now, shaking like jelly. 'Tell old Ah Lee, that old fleabag, that decrepit coolie! Ooh, I'm sooooo scared! And if you go blabbing to *Tsu mu* about her First Grandson, she will not choose to believe you!'

'I hope you die!' she roared.

Suddenly serious, he thrust his face close to hers. 'Before I die, I'll pull you down, you spoilt little brat! I'll make you eat dirt. I'll pump you full of dirt, little rat's shit. Just you wait!'

Bangkok, Thailand
1961

Pao's vengeance was to be delayed five years. His sister, watched over vigilantly, was rarely alone. Her schedule was hectic, crammed with studies, dance lessons, badminton, languages, and music. She was chauffeured everywhere, and everywhere Ah Lee accompanied her, clucking, bustling, and complaining. Pao watched, his jealousy and hatred simmering, as Chee Laan changed from a chubby pampered brat to a sleek, self-assured eleven-year-old on the brink of womanhood. She had begun already to take more interest in the family business. Pao saw with growing irritation how she began to model herself more consciously on their grandmother Sunii, toning down her own naturally ebullient spirits, her loud, cheerful voice, even restraining her young girl's inclination for exaggerated fashions in personal adornment. The more she came to resemble their clever, powerful grandmother, the more her poise and confidence stuck in his craw. Chee Laan, for her part, treated Pao with indifference bordering on contempt. She appeared to have forgotten his assault on her dignity and his furious threats, made so long ago.

    He was twenty years old, already raddled and disillusioned by too much money and too little responsibility. She was only eleven, infuriatingly intelligent, prim and proper, an award-winning paragon, a model student. At last he found an opportunity for that vengeance he had plotted and drooled over in secret. He caught her alone and off her guard in the summer house. Ah Lee, her ferocious watchdog, had taken a samlor to Chinatown to consult her astrologer; *Khun Paw* was at the singsong dive he favoured for boozy, sexy business lunches. *Khun Mee*, Honourable Mother, who, although she was the First Wife, had never bothered to be a mother to her children but instead had embraced religion and recrimination, was sobbing and praying somewhere down among the other women. The grandmother sat high in her steel-and-glass tower, manipulating millions and drinking tea. None of them were looking out for Chee Laan.

Barefoot, he approached softly across the lawn. He watched for a while, his infuriating, provoking sister, and noted how relaxed and happy she looked, humming, engrossed in her book. Her soft lips were parted round the expensive ironmongery that had been recently installed to correct her sexy, slightly protruding teeth. He pounced, taking her by surprise, knocking her half-unconscious, finally riding her like a toy rocking horse, grunting with triumph and pleasure as he felt her tender flesh rip and tear. He snatched up a striped cushion to muffle her screams.

Chee Laan never told; instinctively, she knew who would come off worse if she did. Perhaps *Tsu mu* and Ah Lee, those she loved most in the world, would have been outraged at first, even sympathetic. They would have condemned Pao. But later, after the initial shock had worn off, she knew that it would have been toward herself that they would change, not toward her brother. After all, everyone knew that Pao was a chip off the old block—a hell-raising, self-indulgent, irresponsible Bangkok male. Such behaviour, reprehensible though it might be, was only to be expected of a man like Pao.

But she would have been tainted. In their eyes, she would have lost her freshness. She had seen Sunii order the maids to throw away offertory flowers no longer fresh enough to grace the shrine. Inevitably, the stigma of depravity would have attached itself to her, subtly, like a faint odour of corruption.

Indeed, she thought, Pao was probably right, when he had warned her five years ago. *Tsu mu* would resort to revisionism. An attack on one grandchild by the other would be decreed never to have happened. As for Ah Lee, she always took her cue from Sunii.

That afternoon in the summerhouse, when Pao triumphed over his haughty little sister, was his last victory over her, and even that was short-lived. He watched keenly to see whether his despoiling had brought her down. He had plunged her in filth and humiliation; he expected her to accept her disgrace, as any decent girl would. He hoped she would walk small, skitter out of his way with downcast eyes, shrunk with shame. But Chee Laan strutted about as insufferably as ever—indeed, matters were now far worse than before, for she bullied and mocked him with a casual, bitter scorn.

Pao raged inwardly, burying his anger and frustrations in the frenzied pursuit of pleasure and surrounding himself with friends of similar character. Chee Laan, for her part, increased the distance between them. She threw herself wholeheartedly into her studies. Her delighted tutors praised her to Sunii with unfeigned enthusiasm. 'An old head on young shoulders, an old soul, the true granddaughter of Honourable Old Lady,' they murmured with increasing deference.

Sunii Lee, meanwhile, continued to expand her empire and watched her grandchildren develop. There could only ever be one hand on the tiller, and she herself would not live forever. Her son's First Wife, Pao and Chee Laan's mother, fell into the grips of Christian missionaries, as a distraction to her brutish husband's behaviour. Sunii Lee decided to turn the situation to her advantage.

'One religious maniac in the family is enough,' Sunii Lee decided. In matters of religion Chee Laan followed Sunii's pious but restrained example, but young minds were volatile. Assurance was all.

When she learned that the Premsakul family had announced that their daughter, the Princess Pim, was to attend a convent in Normandy for a year in order to improve her French, Sunii decided that her own granddaughter should follow suit. Her devout daughter-in-law, unsuspecting of Sunii's motives, sought a rare audience with her austere mother-in-law to offer her thanks. She greatly annoyed Sunii by clawing at her ankles and, to the older woman's intense repugnance, attempting to kiss her feet, blurting out her thanks her with tears in her eyes.

Pao sneered that Sunii's motives were political and calculated. He figured his grandmother wanted to show that Chinks were a match for Thai royalty any day. But Sunii reflected that a year with the religious would purge her granddaughter of any inherited fervour, and make her ready to respect her ancestors. She wanted Chee Laan to maintain that most desirable of attributes—the cool heart—and to undertake the task she had in mind for her. Besides, Sunii had learned that the Couvent de Ste Anne in Normandy was conveniently situated for a certain unorthodox training course.

This had been brought to her attention by a man who, despite their mutual wariness, promised to be an invaluable ally. His name was Sya Dam. Like Sunii herself, he trusted nobody. Unlike Sunii, apart from his steely loyalty to the king, he was entirely without scruples, and therein lay his usefulness. Their association was a closely guarded secret, even from those nearest to them.

Sunii did not mention Sya Dam's name in her last interview with Chee Laan on the eve of her departure. She sensed that the girl was tense with anticipation, straining at the leash. 'We live in a dangerous world, Granddaughter. A world requiring brutal tactics,' Sunii said. Chee Laan bowed her head, but her eyes were dancing with curiosity and excitement. Sunii regarded her thoughtfully. It was generally accounted lucky for a daughter to resemble her sire. But Chee Laan's father had been ugly from his ugly begetting. Fortunately, with her delicate arched brows and neatly modelled chin and cheekbones, Chee Laan's face already shared something of her grandmother's charm.

'We need to be prepared. The citadel of the mind and the citadel of the body, must develop defences. Your training will be rigorous, but you will emerge from it equipped to overcome all adversaries.' Chee Laan's brows contracted in puzzlement, but her grandmother continued: 'It will not be easy. But I have confidence in your abilities, Granddaughter.' Still, the thought of the challenge that, all too soon, the girl would face—and of which she was as yet unaware—made Sunii's own unshakeable heart quail.

Normandy
April 1968

'I shall not be able to sleep so close to other people,' Chee Laan informed the nun, dropping her suitcase on her narrow bed. Chee Laan had been obliged to carry the case upstairs herself. There was no sign of servants, so they were surely the lazy types who always hid when there was work to be done. Her first impressions of Ste Anne's Convent were no more encouraging than her impressions of Normandy itself: cold, grey, and shabbily down-at-heel. She surveyed the spartan dormitory, little suspecting that she would soon be longing for the comfort of that narrow bed as the height of luxury.

'I am accustomed to having my own room,' she explained patiently.

The nun stared at her. She had one of those faces Chee Laan had noticed before on deeply religious persons, such as Buddhist nuns at home in Thailand: a young-old face, unlined, innocent. Innocence in adults often seemed to be accompanied by simpleminded-ness. Nevertheless, the nun seemed a kindly soul, if a little garrulous. As the girls had struggled upstairs with their suitcases, she had kept up a constant chatter about how different things would be for them, how she hoped the cold would not bother them. Princess Pim, who possessed a kind heart and had had a private tutor in French, kept the conversation going. Chee Laan understood one word in twenty. The third Thai student was Salikaa, who had the glamorous sheen of a wealthy merchant's daughter. She was paying no attention, burdened as she was by her oversized Hermes suitcase, her glossy fashion magazines, and her leopard-skin coat. Teetering on her five-inch heels, it was all she could do to negotiate the narrow, twisty stairs.

Chee Laan's words seemed to depress the little nun, whose mouth turned down.

'But,' she protested, 'everything is modern! The young ladies have cubicles. Privacy!'

Rather ugly blue curtains separated their beds. But these did not block out the sounds and smells of other human beings nearby: the murmurs, grunts, prayers, expletives, and whispered confidences. The smells of talc, deodorant, unwashed hair, feral and acrid, the damp scent of young female skin, the odour of feet and recently worn shoes were overpowering. One might as well have lived under a sheet of corrugated iron in Thonburi's shantytown. And always the watching eyes of strangers, the creaking shoe-leather of the patrolling nun, the click of her beads running through her dry white fingers. Sometimes in those first days Chee Laan thought these repetitive noises would drive her mad.

They shared one bathroom, and its lock didn't work properly. So it was that, one evening, Chee Laan walked in on Salikaa. She stopped, surprised. Salikaa stood with her back to Chee Laan, studying her appearance in a hand mirror. Mirrors spelled vanity, and were forbidden; Chee Laan's had already been confiscated by the nuns. Salikaa had draped her towel round her neck like a kickboxer. Apart from that, she was naked. Chee Laan just had time to take in her long, muscular, golden back when the heavy wooden door groaned shut behind her and Salikaa spun round and found her staring. With a muttered curse, she tugged the towel from her neck and flung it over Chee Laan's head. She twisted it about her throat, hauling her around, manhandling her easily. Unable to see, Chee Laan lost her balance, thrust out her arms blindly—but now Salikaa was behind her, pulling the towel chokingly tight about her windpipe.

She growled close to Chee Laan's left ear, 'Knock next time, little shit-for-brains! Did no one teach you manners in your Chink school?' Chee Laan heard the door creak open, felt a rush of the cooler air of the corridor, and then a blow to the small of the back that sent her sprawling, still blindfolded.

'Next time I'll kill you!' Salikaa did not bother to lower her voice this time.

The hot, damp frotté material rubbed against Chee Laan's face. Gasping for air, she fell on her side on the wooden floor. She clawed off the towel and hurled it from her. She was lying in the corridor. The bathroom door was shut. She rubbed her bruises and sat for a while in the half darkness. As her anger subsided and her breathing and pulse returned to normal, she began to puzzle over the violence of Salikaa's reaction. Chee Laan knew she herself had the quick-flaring Chinese temper—*Tsu mu* had reproved her for it many times. Even so, Chee Laan felt she should not have been so enraged by a friend barging innocently into a bathroom. She had realised early on in their acquaintance that Salikaa was wild and farouche, one step above a savage in some respects. But even for Salikaa, Chee Laan found the extreme overreaction bizarre and alarming. Shaken, she made her way back to the dormitory.

Pim had drawn back the curtains of her cubicle and was sitting up in bed, studying her French grammar. She looked up from her book, smiling. Then she caught sight of the blood spreading over Chee Laan's forehead and the bruising on her neck. Her jaw dropped. She threw down her book. 'What on earth has happened to you? Have you been wrestling a crocodile, my dear?' She reached out a hand and touched Chee Laan's face.

'That crazy bitch,' Chee Laan said, rubbing her face. She studied her hand, saw the blood, and grimaced. She told Pim what had happened.

Pim covered her mouth with her hand. 'Oh, Chee Laan,' she whispered, 'you mean you didn't know?'

'Know what?'

'Salikaa didn't want you to see her naked! It's—it's a phobia.'

'She's just crazy!' Chee Laan said.

'You mustn't ever, ever say anything about her attacking you!' Pim urged. 'Promise?' She took Chee Laan's face between her hands. 'She is capable of anything, you know. You could get hurt. And her family, if that's what they are…I mean, did you see them, at Don Muang airport, when we left? They're lowlife thugs, Chee Laan, but they're rolling in money. They have a long reach and plenty of friends.'

Chee Laan shook her head free.

'Don't worry about me,' she said. 'My own family have a couple of baht to rub together and a few ugly friends of our own!' Her face softened as she looked at Pim. 'But thanks for looking out for me, Pim.'

She never mentioned the incident again. She felt sure Salikaa had expected her to tattle to the nuns. When she did not, she earned grudging respect. Chee Laan was still angry, but she had been brought up to believe that anger diminishes one and is a sign of poor breeding. She fought her anger for a practical reason as well: she remembered her grandmother's teaching, that anger impairs the judgment and weakens the power of argument. It hands the advantage to the adversary. She sensed that in the future, she and Salikaa might well stand on different sides.

And yet, while trust did not flourish between them, the unusual experience the three of them shared made of them co-conspirators. Chee Laan realised that, left to their own devices, she and Salikaa might well have allowed their mutual suspicion to escalate into open antipathy, but as the weeks went by they found themselves increasingly bound in the web of Pim's generous affection for them both, and theirs for her. All three young women had previously led somewhat isolated existences, shielded by wealth or birth, and by vigilant attendants, from the world of their peers. While their characters and backgrounds were poles apart, thrown together in this strange land had deepened their loyalties to one another. Despite Chee Laan's natural reserve, and Salikaa's pathological secrecy, the alien environment in which they found themselves drew them together.

Chee Laan's special childhood horrors still haunted her, even here in this cold, grey land: her brother's assault, and sometimes the memory of the kite girl, falling, ever falling. Once she cried out in her sleep, and awoke to find Pim kneeling by her bed. Pim was shaking her arm and stroking her face with soft fingers, as a mother might have done. Chee Laan's mother had never comforted her so.

Chee Laan shot bolt upright, feeling ashamed and vulnerable at the thought that she had woken Pim from her own sleep. But when she switched on the bedside lamp and looked into Pim's sweet face, puckered with concern, Chee Laan felt she owed her friend an explanation, so she recounted her nightmare. 'It's strange it should still disturb me so. I was just a child,' she concluded, her terror lessened now that she was wide awake.

'There is something unresolved in your life, Chee Laan,' Pim said. 'Dreams are like ghosts. They return to haunt one because they seek solutions.'

'But she was just a coolie.' Chee Laan shook her head, trembling still from the vividness of the dream and puzzled by the strength of her reactions.

Pim frowned and drew back a little. 'What do you mean, "just a coolie"? You think, therefore, that she is unworthy of consideration? Rousseau says there is no such thing as natural inferiority. When we Thais call others low-class, or of dirty blood, these are ignorant prejudices, which successive ruling parties have cynically exploited to oppress the people and maintain the status quo.'

She used the language of the revolutionary. It did not surprise Chee Laan. Pim had already hinted that her royal parents had sent her to France in the hope that she would not only improve her French but would forget all of her socialist inclinations.

'Power has only one duty: to secure the welfare of the people,' Pim continued.

'For my people, the first duty is to the family,' Chee Laan said. With a stab of irritation, she realised that her tone was almost apologetic, as though she were suddenly ashamed of being Chinese. Trained since earliest childhood to recognise that she belonged to the oldest civilisation in the world, with the longest-surviving traditions, Chee Laan had never felt ashamed before.

'Don't pay any attention to me, Chee Laan! My father calls me a pinko hothead!' Pim swept back her long, soft switch of hair and laughed softly. She squatted back on her heels and gently smoothed Chee Laan's pillowcase. Then, to Chee Laan's surprise, she climbed onto the bed, lay down beside her, and stared at the ceiling. Chee Laan had never shared a bed with anyone else. She edged toward the outer side of the mattress and copied Pim's posture, lying flat on her back, staring at the ceiling, too. She tried to adjust her breathing pattern to Pim's.

'The only person who understands how I feel is my brother,' Pim mused. 'Toom.'

'I saw him at the airport,' Chee Laan remembered. The two girls, wearing their new, specially selected travelling outfits, each surrounded by a bustle of chattering attendants, had been observing each other surreptitiously. Chee Laan remembered the fine-featured, studious-looking young man who held Pim's hand the whole time and whispered to her, as though they were all alone. She had found him attractive, despite his rather long hair and the huge spectacles. 'Is he your twin brother? You're very alike.'

'Twin souls, not biological twins. He is a year older. But we share a birthday, so many of our astrological elements are similar. Except, of course, that Toom is brilliant. He studies science at Cambridge—my father's old college. Although Father, unlike Toom, was not really clever enough for Cambridge.'

Chee Laan grunted, reflecting that if you were a prince, or your father had a fat chequebook, it was not so necessary to be clever, perhaps. Even though her family was not of royal blood, they certainly belonged to the Bangkok plutocracy. Had not her own ignorant brother Pao been awarded a scholarship to Taiwan, financed by Bangkok's Chinese business community, where he was to study calligraphy and classical Mandarin? The Lee Family had put up most of the money, much of which went into the pockets of university officials, and the rest, his generous allowance, into Taipei's thriving entertainment industry. Pao greatly enjoyed his time in Taipei, but to this day, his calligraphy remained inferior to that of his sister.

'My father adored Cambridge,' Pim mused. 'He loved the life. Intellectually, it hardly made a dent on him. It certainly did not affect his politics. But he realised sending me there too would hardly cure me of my socialism, especially as Toom is there. And he holds old-fashioned views about the education of women. So I was packed off to this backwater.' She made a vague gesture toward the blue curtains and the worn floorboards.

'And thanks to you,' Salikaa's harsh voice suddenly sprang up from the other side of the curtain, 'I ended up here, too!' She thrust the curtain roughly aside, stepped up close to the bed and stood gazing down at them, her eyes gleaming with mockery. 'Remember the headlines in the Bangkok papers: "Princess to study in France!" Vichai, my stepfather, saw it as an opportunity.'

Pim looked so mystified that Chee Laan took pity on her. 'Let's face it, Pim,' Chee Laan said, hauling herself up onto her elbow and looking down into her pale, puzzled face. 'It's all your fault. My grandmother saw the same headline. Our families hope that, being thrown together here, we'll become bosom pals. They see our friendship as a potential social advantage.'

Pim threw back her head and began to laugh. 'They must be mad! Surely everybody in Bangkok knows I'm Red Pim, the black sheep of the Premsakuls. If they dared, my family would throw me into the gutter! They already despair of finding a decent husband willing to take me on.'

Chee Laan stared at Pim in surprise, and with new respect. She had never heard her speak so forcefully, hadn't thought her capable of it. Despite her obvious, and somewhat tedious, overactive social conscience, she had always seemed to Chee Laan to represent the ideal of Buddhist womanhood: mild, modest, just a touch mealy-mouthed. Pim was the very antithesis of Salikaa, whatever Salikaa was.

Chee Laan had encountered women of Salikaa's type before, of course, tangentially—loud-mouthed fishwives bargaining raucously in the market at Pratumwan, or brawling with noodle sellers outside bars—but none of them had possessed Salikaa's electrifying beauty, and Chee Laan had certainly never known their names or met any such person in the proper circles.

Salikaa, unable to bear someone else stealing centre stage for more than two minutes, now dragged the attention back to herself. She yawned like a lazy cat, closing her eyes and showing the inside of her wide red mouth, even the little vibrating tongue at the back of her throat, shameless as a young animal.

'At least you two have families,' she said with a provoking casualness.

'Why, haven't you?' Chee Laan obligingly took the bait.

'Me? I was brought up by a bandit chief after he and his gang murdered my parents,' she said, watching their faces for the effect of her announcement. After years of experience with her brother Pao, Chee Laan had learned not to react when people sought to shock her. Pim, on the other hand, did nothing to conceal her horror.

'How terrible!' she murmured sympathetically. 'Kidnapped by bandits! Why didn't you run away?'

'Why on earth should I do that?' Salikaa laughed scornfully. 'My own folks were pathetic losers. I'm better off without them. Besides, when I return, I'm going to be the next Miss Thailand. I'm going to follow in Lady Asra's footsteps.'

Chee Laan, like everyone in Thailand, knew all about Lady Asra, the Siamese Cinderella. A very beautiful girl of undistinguished origins, who had become Miss Thailand and later Miss Universe, and went on to marry a Prince of the Blood. Every bargirl and waitress in Bangkok dreamed of becoming the next Lady Asra. Chee Laan cocked a sceptical eyebrow at this ludicrous ambition.

'Salikaa, surely you wouldn't want to become part of the beauty circus? It is demeaning to women. It reinforces stereotypes!' Pim frowned in her solemn way.

Salikaa laughed. 'Demeaning? When I win, princes will beg to drink champagne out of my shoes! Perhaps even the Crown Prince himself.'

'The Crown Prince is fourteen years old, Salikaa.' Chee Laan rolled on her back and kicked her foot in the air, wearying of this conversation. 'He is a baby. A child.'

'You could never get near the Crown Prince, anyway,' Pim pointed out reasonably, shaking her head. 'You've no idea what court security is like. The old king's favourite, the Black Tiger himself, is in charge of it.'

Salikaa delicately lifted the hem of her white nightgown. The nightlight glanced off her thighs, toned and sinewy, glossy as polished cherrywood. Buckled round her inner thigh was a long skinning knife in a leather sheath. Before her companions could recover from their surprise, she had pulled it out and itched herself luxuriously between the shoulder blades, arching her back like a cat. 'I know about Sya Dam, but I also know what bandit security is like,' she said. 'And, if one were to be received at court, gain an entrée through a dear school friend, so many possibilities would open up!' She looked at Pim and her smile seemed to harden. 'Thanks to you, Pim dear, I've already met my first prince—your handsome, intellectual brother.'

Pim stiffened. She looked down at her hands. Chee Laan suddenly noticed that her eyelashes were like dark fur, spiky and glossy, owing nothing to art and all to nature—unlike Salikaa's, which lived in a sequined case concealed beneath her mattress and were glued on every morning. Chee Laan had caught her in the act of applying them once. There had almost been another flare-up.

Now, for the first time since they had known her, it was Pim who was offended. Silently she rose and went back to her own bed, without so much as a murmured goodnight. Salikaa laughed again, tossed her black mane, and was gone, throwing the curtain closed behind her. Chee Laan lay for some time staring into the dark. She did not sleep for many hours—and when at last sleep did come to her, it was dreamless and deep.

In the cool, watery moonlight, Sister Marie-Hélène paced the creaking boards, her rosary beads sliding softly through her fingers. She peeked in on the three sleeping foreign students, their heads dark against the snowy starched linen. The young princess lay still and straight as a medieval martyr in a vault, her hair spreading out in a dark cloud. The Chinese girl lay curled knees to chin, clutching a pillow, muttering occasionally. The wild girl, who so alarmed gentle Sister Marie-Hélène, tossed and turned restlessly in the tangled bedclothes, making little clicking noises and sometimes grinding her teeth. The nun watched for moment, then crossed herself.

'A restless spirit,' she murmured. *'Une âme inquiète!'*

The thought crossed her mind that these three dark-haired girls had the air of beautiful lost children, stolen away by some creature in a fairy tale. Far from home, outside the faith, they seemed to her creatures of legend. She clacked her tongue at herself for a fanciful old woman. The sound was loud in the silent dormitory, but the girls did not stir. Sister Marie-Hélène seized another bead and embarked upon another Ave. Tomorrow she would speak to them of St Theresa. Surely that would touch their hearts.

Bangkok, Thailand
From the diary of General Blaze van Hooten, United States Army, Director General, South East Asia Treaty Organization [SEATO]

March 14, 1968
I knew it was more than a social visit when King Rama's uncle, General Worawong, said he wished to see me. He gave no notion of his agenda, but I had my suspicions, which turned out to be correct. There was no question of refusing or postponing the meeting, even though I needed this royal visit like a hole in the head.

I had a lot on my mind at the time. The unfortunate My Lai 'massacre' episode was a fresh wound that continued to fester. It had caused acute embarrassment to the United States, and the issue was still sensitive. Public consciousness is never even-handed, especially when manipulated by the left-wing propaganda of the prejudiced media. They seemed intent on promulgating the concept that our involvement in Vietnam was foolhardy and doomed to disaster. The media did their best to ensure that My Lai was remembered, while the atrocities of Hue, where Viet Cong terrorists massacred several thousand Vietnamese, were forgotten.

If I had my way, I would line those pinko hacks against a wall and blast them to kingdom come.

This is not happy time. The U.S. military engagement in Vietnam has developed unforeseen complexities. Every objective achieved, every substantive gain, is followed by setbacks. Like the mythological hydra, it seems that, where we succeed in chopping off one head, ten more spring up in its place.

In the course of my posting to Thailand, I have met with many members of the Thai royal family, including this old rascal General Worawong. They tend to wheel the old guy out on official occasions with a military flavour. He is a *frail older gentleman with wispy grey hair and beard, exquisite manners, and the wise, mild face of an ancient saint. My sources informed me that in his time he had been one of the most bloodthirsty butchers in the history of the country. Still, I knew that there was a man capable of surpassing the blood-stained general's colourful record. I was fairly sure that this new figure was the subject of my meeting with General Worawong.*

After we had exchanged the usual courtesies, the general accepted the chair I offered. He looked so fragile that I fancied the icy blast from the air conditioner might have lifted him like a leaf and sent him whirling about the room. A Marine brought our tea. The general went on about the key to Thailand's future success being education, not the presence of military bases belonging to foreign powers. I nodded eagerly, as though in complete agreement, adding that the United States maintains military bases in Thailand for the protection of our allies, the Thai people, against the communist threat. After a pause he continued about the importance of non-fragmentation. He tried to convince me of the need to ensure the loyalty of hill tribes. I sensed a wave of disapproval and disgust. His eyes met mine with a veiled accusation; we both knew that was a bumpy road, which I was not prepared to go down at this time. I said that I was aware of the concern that the hill tribes' lifestyle might constitute a threat to national security, though inwardly I was wondering how much further we had to go. I've always found such delicate circumlocutions tedious.

He nodded again, and I nodded too, and we sat there nodding silently, like two Chinese mandarin dolls.

Then his face lit up as though he'd had a sudden inspiration, and I knew we had reached the point in our discussion where he was going to reveal his intentions, or at least twitch the veil aside and allow me a glimpse.

'A Western-educated tribesman!' he exclaimed. 'Imagine what a weapon against ignorance and depravity that would be. What a potential power for good!' He fell silent. The ball was in my court.

I decided to put him out of his misery. It wasn't a bad idea: a king's favourite, a tame tribesman, sympathetic to American aims and aspirations, familiar with the American way of life. I asked if it was Sya Dam he spoke of. He nodded almost imperceptibly in agreement. Then I reminded the general that the aims of the South East Asia Treaty Organization are not military. He was nodding again, this time with a gleam in his beady slanting eye.

'As an indication of the good relations that exist between our two great nations, it is intended that scholarships to American institutes of learning will form a major part of our new programme,' I said. 'Any candidate put forward for such an award would come, I take it, with the best credentials, highly recommended?'

'Oh, yes, recommendations from the very highest source. You may rest absolutely assured of it.' He paused, making sure of me. 'May I ask, General van Hooten, when SEATO's new educational programme was proposed?'

'It is of comparatively recent date—a week or so,' I lied. 'I have been intending to announce it. Somehow it slipped my mind...'

General Worawong nodded graciously, and his lips parted in a real smile, revealing the ochre-coloured tips of rodential teeth.

April 7, 1968

Even before this meeting with the general, I already had a passing acquaintance with Colonel Sya. I found him to be an impressive man, both in respect of his superb physique and obvious mental powers. But he never assumed in my mind the mythical, almost cult-like status that many people accorded him. Still, he was a force to be reckoned with: Sya Dam, the Black Tiger.

It always struck me as strangely incongruous that such a man should have assumed this absurdly romantic nickname. It had to be an exercise in irony—certainly a nom de guerre. Ordinarily, I'd have said nom de plume like any other poor ignorant soldier. But I had the inestimable privilege of being married to Mrs Taylor van Hooten, nee van der Lies, of the Cape Cod van der Lies, whose continuous presence in this stinking, teeming, pulsating city had severely curtailed my personal acquaintance with the more lurid aspects of Bangkok life. I knew more about the Royal Family than about Patpong song-and dance dives. I rigorously repressed any notion that this ignorance was regrettable.

Despite my own democratic convictions, I had a soft spot for dear old King Rama. Nor did I for one moment give credence to the scurrilous rumour that either he or his mother had gained the throne for him by having his feeble-witted teenage half-brother drowned in his bathtub. This affectionate response of mine had very little to do with the fact that my wife Taylor was employed by the king to teach English and French to his son, the young Crown Prince, a post of inestimable value to me and the U.S.

This princeling was the darling of the nation, born to Their Majesties in his father's late middle life, after a decade and a half of disappointments. The devoted king broke with tradition and remained monogamous throughout his marriage despite his wife's failure to provide an heir. When she finally did have a son, Queen Benjawan did not survive the birth. Since his queen's death the king remained celibate, spending several months wearing the robes of a monk. Perhaps he sublimated more earthly urges through meditation, or maybe his zest for life died with the queen.

My wife Taylor takes her tutoring of His Royal Highness extremely seriously, and is not flattered when the ignorant refer to her as a 'latter-day Anna,' recalling some Victorian English lady called Mrs Leonowens who worked as a royal governess and claimed to have romanced King Chulalongkhorn's papa.

You don't mention 'Anna and the King of Siam' in Thai society. The marine band once struck up 'March of the Siamese Children' in the royal presence and it went down like a lead balloon. Taylor herself dismissed the entire Anna thing as 'the epitome of vulgarity and gross lèse-majesté.' Taylor also pointed out that, in any event, a mere governess, a glorified nursemaid, such as Anna, was not to be compared with a tutor such as herself. Asperity is very much part of who Taylor is. Needless to say, her own academic credentials are unimpeachable, pure Ivy League gold.

No, King Rama was no assassin in my book, just a mild gentleman. If he hadn't had a throne more or less shoved under his ass when he was too young to protest, he'd have been much happier as a musician. Not solo artist calibre, but a decent cocktail lounge ensemble player, toting a nifty clarinet. Easy-listening stuff, forties and fifties swing. Within the confines of his position, the king was modest, full of good intentions, and, I believe, genuinely concerned for his people.

The Thai monarchy had finally changed from being absolute to constitutional, after several uneasy decades following its original collapse during the revolution of 1932. There ensued various counterrevolutions, bloodless coups and the like, alternating with intermittent periods of experimental democracy. The monarchy was ultimately restored, but it was no longer absolute. Technically, constitutional monarchy means that Thailand can play at the democracy game while retaining as a useful rallying point a popular king who is no longer celestial—no longer a god—probably not a murderer, and very keen to stay out of trouble. So no more of those apocryphal stories the tourists love about royal aunts drowning in khlongs (Bangkok's urban waterways, most of them putrid) in full view of helpless onlookers unwilling to lay hands upon a divine personage, hence obliged to stand by and watch said royal personage drown.

Notwithstanding their tumble from divinity, the royals retained atavistic quirks of absolutism. Perhaps that was inevitable with monarchs—I wouldn't know. King Rama was the only monarch I'd been around. One of those habits appeared to be the urge to pluck some hitherto unrecognised talent from obscurity, creating unexpected favourites, presumably to ensure loyalty unto death. Mild monarchs need a Cerberus, a pitiless flesh-eating guard dog. Throughout history this tendency may be observed—the Czarina's Rasputin springs to mind. For his personal Rasputin, King Rama had handpicked Sya Dam, a mystery man.

When I realised I did not know nearly enough about Sya Dam, the thought struck me that the sooner young Fleischer took up his post as Assistant Military Attaché at the U.S. Embassy in Bangkok, the better. There was no more devious, cold-hearted bastard than Fleischer, possibly a contributory factor to the truth that, in my experience, there was no better intelligence officer, either.

I first met up with Lieutenant Fleischer at Fort Gullick at the School of the Americas: a Spanish-language training facility set up some two decades ago, at the U.S. taxpayer's expense, in the Panama Canal Zone. The U.S. trains more foreign military and security personnel than any other country in the world. SOA Fort Gullick was one of its most secret and efficient establishments. At the time, I was a logistics instructor at the facility, and Fleischer proved a godsend.

There are those who call the SOA the School of Assassins, claiming it's a place where human rights exist at the point of a gun and folks use the Geneva Convention to wipe their ass. The School's official aim was to provide 'professional training' for military personnel from Latin America, and to inculcate in such personnel American notions of genuine democracy. The freebies included membership to exclusive golf clubs, tickets to sporting events, and trips to Disneyland, the infrastructure of the American dream.

Our students would routinely arrive with suitcases stuffed with thousands of dollar bills, which they'd use for luxury purchases—cars and household durables—that they shipped back home. Our alumni included a few bad eggs that spat on human rights and would go down in history as the perpetrators of major atrocities—but these were statistically insignificant.

Congress wouldn't have voted to continue supporting the SOA if all these overblown stories had been true, would they? The nurturing of terrorists, the kidnapping of homeless people for human guinea pigs and organ transplants—the usual conspiracy theories invented by bleeding-hearts liberals with more imagination than sense.

Fleischer was in his element at SOA, but he always had his sights set on greater things. He had run off to join the French Foreign Legion when he was but a boy, but he was now bona fide U.S. military. He'd made lieutenant and was, at the time we became acquainted, on loan to the SOA because, despite his Teutonic-sounding name, he had a Guatemalan mother and spoke good Spanish. His first name was Angel, pronounced the Spanish way, An-hell. Mostly, he was called Fleischer, or Lieutenant. At SOA he taught counterintelligence and the handling of sources. Much of the training material he created, including source-handling manuals, later found a place in counterintelligence instruction in Vietnam, and would later be dubbed 'the torture manuals.' Presently he was running some boot camp, in France, I think. He'd picked up sufficient French in the Legion to bawl orders and scare the crap out of his students, anyway—God help them.

His future appointment as Assistant Military Attaché had been broadcast on the grapevine. I need Fleischer in Bangkok, but still I felt wary. At any rate, he would not be joining us for another year. I wonder what Fleischer will make of the Black Tiger—what they will make of each other. Already I sense an affinity between them. Had Fleischer already been in place, I am sure Sya Dam would not have seemed such an insufferably enigmatic and inscrutable entity.

Inevitably, when the king began to display such marked favour toward Sya, there had been rumours, jealousy, and the usual unpleasantness. At such times, even removed from the theatre of war, the situation was volatile, like sitting on a powder keg. One never can tell what spark will set it off. Bangkok was already seething with unrest, and the king was a monarch concerned for his own and his people's peace of mind—a man who valued a life of gentle contemplation, devoted to philosophy, music, and good works.

I am not sure whether Sya Dam still enjoys the royal favour. If he does, in the light of the attention he's attracting, I imagine that it could be considered useful to send him off-stage for a while.

May 24, 1968

So Sya and Fleischer will not meet—in the immediate future, anyway. I am not sure whether that is an advantage or not. Sya's absence will give Fleischer a chance to gather and collate information without interference, but, on the other hand, he always had a maverick, opportunistic way of working, which thrived on confrontation and the manipulation of incident.

I had begun speculating about how and when Fleischer would appear on the scene when his posting finally came through. He has a tiresome habit of turning up ahead of schedule, fuelling his rather sadistic enjoyment of creating alarm and astonishment by catching folks on the hop. It's a calculated way of embellishing his legend, though I regard it as somewhat juvenile, like something out of a childish comic strip. However, it can't be denied that in many quarters it's had a considerable impact.

Fleischer, as AMA, would rightly expect to be wined and dined at the residence of the Director General of SEATO. These domestic arrangements would necessarily entail the involvement and cooperation of my wife, Taylor. My wife is a woman of impeccable taste and extremely high standards. I hardly imagine she and Fleischer will turn out to be soul mates. Fleischer has his uses, but he comes at a price.

I am dying for a cup of decent American coffee. I never drink coffee at home. My wife frowns upon it, saying that it produces palpitations. But there are days where palpitations are a blessed respite.

London, England
October 1968

Nat Raven burst into the Trattoria twenty minutes late, cursing English rain and London traffic, but blaming nobody but himself for his tardiness. As usual, he had allowed himself to be buttonholed after his seminar by students too timid to ask questions in front of their peers, preferring to waylay their tutor as he hurled overheads and lecture notes into his battered brown leather briefcase. Raven preferred this honest artisan's accoutrement to the costly Hermes model brought to him from Paris by the beautiful woman he lived with.

Raven paused to get his bearings and let his eyes adjust to the pink-shaded gloom designed to create instant cosiness and boost sales of indifferent Chianti. He was wearing his characteristic scowl, and lowered his head and glowered about him with the intensity of a bull released into a *plaza de toros*. A waiter danced toward him, then stopped in his tracks, abashed. Raven's muscular intensity, the bulky shoulders pitched forward, as if poised to charge, often unnerved those encountering him for the first time. Dark and fierce as a gypsy, a throwback to his dour, grim-featured ancestors, Raven knew his battle-axe face hardly embodied the popular concept of a university don. Still sun-tanned from his summer in France, he would have looked more at home in Sicily—Don Corvo Nero, padrone. Or as the Legionnaire he had once been.

By now Raven had spotted two men, grey and unremarkable, seated in a booth against the wall. Raven recognised Professor Robin Bellwether, who was covertly watching the entrance; upon perceiving Raven, he smiled faintly. He looked relieved, Raven thought. Droplets of rain pearling off his long leather coat, Raven steamed through the tables, moving with agility for a man of his size.

By way of welcome, Professor Robin Bellwether, the Chair of Oriental Studies, dragged over a nearby stool, placed it at the end of the small wooden table, and patted its seat. 'Ah, Raven,' Bellwether confirmed, in his precise, faintly surprised Edinburgh voice. 'This is Dr Raven!' he announced, adopting the high-pitched tones of feigned astonishment, like a conjuror producing a white rabbit from a hat. His companion, whose thin grey hair and face matched his sober city suit, inclined his head formally, then offered his hand. His grasp was decisive yet cool. His eyes studied Raven. Raven found the appraisal of this entirely unexceptional middle-aged, middle-class Englishman oddly disquieting.

'James Smith,' the man said firmly. 'Hello.'

'Yes, well.' Professor Bellwether stood up, leaning on the table, a napkin scrunched in his hand. He appeared in a hurry. Words poured from him in an unaccustomed spate. 'Must be pushing off, I have a meeting with the dean at one thirty. The queen bee! Female deans, nowadays, the monstrous regiment, the mind boggles. Well, duty done, you two have met. Amen! Leave you to your own devices. Told Mr Smith something about you, Raven. He'll explain, I'm sure. By the way, don't touch the prosciutto—like litmus paper. God knows what ill-starred beast it came from. Stick to pasta and you'll be all right, I shouldn't wonder!'

With this he departed. Raven set the stool back where it belonged and slid himself into the seat vacated by the professor, opposite Mr James Smith, whose stare he now returned with interest. He wondered what exactly Robin Bellwether had been telling Mr James Smith, and why his august colleague should suppose Mr Smith would be interested in a fairly insignificant university lecturer. His natural impatience urged him to demand bluntly what the hell this was all about, but he curbed it, and sat in silence. Too long the prisoner of cities, Raven savoured silence. In silence he studied first the wine list that lay open on the table, and then the open bottle of Italian red, turning it in his hand, reflecting that one day he really had to learn more about vintages.

'An interesting CV.' Smith leaned back and studied Raven with a half smile. A waiter hovered, laden with menus. Another glass was brought, pasta was ordered, the waiter's effusions gently but firmly curtailed. Smith spoke, musingly, without haste, as though there had been no interruption. 'Nathaniel Dane Raven. Age thirty-four. Marital status, single. Only child. Born on the West Coast. Father a fisherman, lost at sea.'

Raven braced himself to acknowledge the obligatory expression of regret. None came. The grey man barely paused, continuing imperturbably: 'Scholarship to Marlborough. Performed with distinction. Athletics and rugby football. Exhibition to Trinity College, Cambridge. Holds degrees in zoology, politics, and environmental science. Rowing blue. Left England abruptly after graduation to join the French Foreign Legion.' He paused, cocked his head on one side, and asked, 'Why? Romantic leanings, Dr Raven?'

Raven shrugged. 'Obstinate, more like. In my cups at a family wedding, the class of function that lasts for a week and never a sober breath drawn. Proposed to my cousin. Swore I'd join the Legion if she refused—which, of course, she promptly did, sensible girl! Trying me out, probably. So I called her bluff. She should have known; cussedness runs in the family.'

Smith nodded and continued, 'And now you two are "an item", as they say. Ms Raven capitulated and surrendered to your importunities when you made earnest of your threats. Interesting creatures, women!' He wiped the corner of his mouth fastidiously with the edge of his napkin, then folded it carefully. 'You served five years, mostly in North Africa. Upon return to Britain, embarked on career in documentary filmmaking. Outstanding pieces include *Legion of the Lost*, subject self-explanatory; *Whose Apron Strings?*, Freemasonry; and *Lion's Share in the Lion Port*, politics and economics in Singapore. Considerable critical acclaim. Most recent career moves: university associate lecturer, and collaborator in survival training school.'

'You're very well informed,' Raven conceded.

'Bear with me.' His companion ran his finger round the base of his untouched wine glass. 'The list of your achievements is revealing, Dr Raven: you are not easily discouraged; you possess discretion, as well as talent and determination. Your work has been controversial; as well as national awards, it has attracted death threats, to which you have proved indifferent. You've never collected a single award; you've consistently refused police protection. Why?'

Raven shrugged. 'Mostly, with awards, you don't win. So it's no good setting too much store by awards. Entails too much wailing and gnashing of teeth for my taste. As for police protection—agh, the police have more important things to do than play nanny to pampered media folk.'

Smith nodded, but Raven felt he had extracted the gist instantly, and that, by the end of Raven's speech, his attention had wandered back to what he himself would say next, and he was selecting his words with fastidious care.

'Oh, you're a driven man, Dr Raven. Despite this façade of *laissez-faire*, there's a touch of the crusader. You have the urge to uncloak corruption and exploitation; moreover, Dr Raven, you are a patriot.'

'How do you make that out?' Raven asked, trying to keep his voice from betraying his resentment. This catalogue of his qualities and achievements, recited by a stranger, was highly irritating.

James Smith sighed theatrically, as Raven himself might sigh over the obtuseness of a student. 'Why did you leave the Legion, Dr Raven?'

Raven knew the question was rhetorical, designed to force him to an acknowledgement of Smith's own conclusion regarding Raven's patriotism, or lack of it. Amused, he decided to play along. 'My mother became ill. I decided not to re-enlist.'

The mild-mannered gentleman swooped forward, bringing his face startlingly close to Raven's. 'Ah! I mistook disenchantment for truth!'

Raven, despite his intentions, found himself answering, 'Grapevine suggested our next undertaking might well run contrary to the interests of this country.'

Smith smiled, as if an unpromising pupil had at last come up with the goods. 'Precisely. And now, Dr Raven, you continue to make meteoric forays into the media limelight from the ivory towers. However, your recent documentaries have been concerned with subjects more closely related to your real fields, zoology and environmental science. The plight of mountain gorillas, the return of the wolf and brown bear to parts of Western Europe, and the consequent implications for local farmers. Playing it safe these days, Dr Raven?'

Now it was Raven's turn to smile. 'You'd be surprised. People are more passionate about animals than anything else except sex and football. You get more death threats for suggesting a wolf cull than for denying the

Holocaust.' He paused, looking Smith straight in the eye. 'I still don't understand your interest.'

'I liked your work on Singapore.'

Raven nodded noncommittally. Many people had liked his work on Singapore. He hoped he was not needy enough to treasure compliments.

'You're considered something of an Asia specialist, Dr Raven.'

'Hardly that.' Raven had started on his pasta, and now glanced up at the other man over a fork wreathed in what looked like golden knitting. He set it down, feeling the need to explain. 'Asia presents an infinitely complex picture in every respect. Coming to grips with the Asian reality—*any* Asian reality—is like grappling with a bag of eels in the bilges of a leaky rowboat. Contradictions, revocations, disavowals, *voltes-faces*. Besides, Asia's a big place. There are many Asias.'

'Siam.'

Smith's use of the old-fashioned name jolted Raven off balance. The loss of equilibrium bothered him. He hoped it didn't show.

'Nothing's going on in Siam,' he said slowly. 'Enlightened constitutional monarchy. The occasional bloodless coup, skirmishes on the borders, but a relatively stable society for decades. Amazingly so, when you think of the situation in contiguous countries—Burma, Cambodia, China, not to mention the Vietnam mess.'

'Precisely. Siamese stability is vital to the Western interest. It gives us a foothold in the area. Thailand's never been colonised, but it is friendly to the West. Not only do the Americans have airbases there—essential to the engagement in Vietnam—but, despite Southeast Asia's bad memories of World War II, Japanese businesses function there, too. Thailand's usefulness as gateway, as neutral meeting place, can hardly be overestimated. The Thais remain responsible for their own administration and running their own affairs to their own satisfaction, and with a popular monarch, Thailand's stability is vital to many international interests.'

'So all is for the best in the best of all possible worlds?' Raven provoked.

Smith blinked tolerantly. 'So long as nothing rocks the boat. The world… or rather, we cannot afford any untoward events to jeopardise that stability. Any developments tending to point that way must be nipped in the bud. We would need to know well in advance and not allow it to happen.'

'*We* being who, exactly?' Raven interrupted impatiently.

The other man waved this aside. 'Let us say interested parties close to the bridge—people concerned with world progress and the fate of nations.' His tone was ironic. Seeing his response only partially satisfied Raven, James Smith leaned forward, pushed his half-empty plate aside, and rested both elbows on the table. 'We need someone on the spot for a while, Dr Raven—someone capable of forecasting the weather. Someone with political insight, linguistic ability—we know you speak French, Arabic, and German, and you have some Malay—someone for whom no implausible cover story need be devised. As a reputable academic and acclaimed investigative journalist, your own cover, for example, would be ideal: you are investigating the decline of the great hornbill, assessing the long-term effects of slash-and-burn agricultural policies, and, if need be, the opium cash crop in the Golden Triangle.'

He touched the cloth napkin to the corners of his mouth, delicately as a cat, his eyes never leaving Raven's face.

'There'll be formalities: signing the usual papers, proper briefings from those better informed.'

'And who might they be?' Raven tried to control his truculence.

Smith simpered, eyebrows arching like circumflexes above his expressionless eyes. 'I am merely Ganymede, cup-bearer to the gods.' He bowed in mock reverence. 'The gods who will reveal themselves in their own time. Oh, and get Bellwether's Thai experts to give you a few lessons in the lingo. Officially, you'll be on a cultural exchange—give a few lectures, make a few studies, hand out a bit of free expertise to a worthy local project or two. Your full salary plus emoluments will be paid into your local account as usual. And you'll not find us ungrateful. This assignment is not entirely devoid of potential hazards.'

'Danger money?' Raven's lip curled in a half grin.

Smith, totally unfazed, allowed his simper to appear once more. 'From what one hears of the Legion, hardly more hazardous than you are accustomed to—but yes, it would be unrealistic to exclude some small element of risk.'

Raven interrupted him. 'And how are the Thais going to feel about it?'

'Take it from me, they will be delighted. In exchange for you, a Thai student will attend our business school. Business! That's all they want these days: commerce and technology. A mercenary and mechanical age we live in, Dr Raven! Distressing for an old Luddite like myself.'

The self-deprecating smile implied that Smith did not allow much to distress him.

'Why me?' Raven demanded, suddenly weary of playing games.

The grey man's eyes widened innocently. 'But, my dear Raven, I've just told you. You've the right background and qualifications. Moreover, we've established that you are a patriot.'

'And why should I agree?' Raven suppressed a cold shiver of anger.

'Have I misjudged you?' Smith sighed softly. 'Curiosity. Boredom. Oh, yes, Dr Raven.' The grey eyes glittered mockingly. 'Or let us consider the lovely Ms Nancy Raven, whose biological clock is ticking loudly.' He paused, fixing Raven with a beady eye. 'That sound equates, in the minds of many men of your age, to the ringing of alarm bells. A signal to evacuate the building.'

'I don't have to listen to this.' Raven started to get to his feet. He could feel the flush of anger flooding his cheeks.

'Sit down!' Smith snapped softly. 'Behave yourself, man!'

Despite himself, Raven obeyed.

'You'll accept, Raven. You won't be able to help yourself. Simply because, if you refuse, you will always wonder, if developments take an interesting turn, what part you might have played. The reason we selected you is because we knew that you would not refuse us, could not refuse us. You will accept, because the temptation to be on the inside is irresistible to a man of your sort. Inquisitive, restless, pig-headed, you are a driven man. Am I right?'

Raven's silent fury escalated with the knowledge that the man before him spoke the truth.

Taking his silence as consent, Smith continued blandly, 'One more thing: I said we should be grateful, but elastic expense accounts are guaranteed to bring out the beast in people. All too frequently, one observes that they foster delusions of grandeur. So, no soaring above the heads of men. We don't just want the bird's-eye view; we want the worm's view of the grass roots.' He clicked his fingers. The waiter appeared.

'*Due espressi, per favore.*' The grey man cocked an eyebrow at Raven. 'I'm assuming you drink yours black. One never quite trusts a man who drinks it white at this time of day.'

Raven nodded resentfully. For once, he had been outmanoeuvred. God only knew what Nancy would say! 'You were sounding me out just now. Why did you decide I was the man?' he rephrased his earlier query, other unasked questions buzzing inside his head like disturbed wasps.

'The way you spoke of Britain as "this country", Dr Raven,' James Smith said, sipping his mediocre wine gingerly, as though it were an unpalatable cough mixture and only a genteel upbringing prevented him from spitting it out on the red-chequered tablecloth. 'Only those Britons who experience a genuine sense of national identity and social responsibility say "this country" in just the way you did a few minutes ago.'

Raven choked with outrage.

Smith, smiling broadly at last, tapped the stem of his wine glass, then, as if making up his mind to an unappealing duty, drained it in one and stood up, not waiting for the ordered espresso. 'I'll leave you to reflect, Dr Raven. But not for long. You'll be back in your room at the Faculty this afternoon? Excellent! Someone will be in touch later today.'

He walked purposefully over to the bar. Raven watched him pay the bill and leave, acknowledging the waiter's 'Please come again, signore!' with a backward wave, courteous yet indolent, like the flipper of some basking seal. It was obvious that for Mr James Smith the outcome of the discussion had never been in doubt. Someone, somewhere, knew more about Nat Raven than he was comfortable with.

'Holy shit!' grunted Raven under his breath, his anger mixed with a curious exhilaration and the first creeping sensation of apprehension.

London, England
November 1968

Raven
On the steep staircase leading to the annex of the East Asiatic Languages Department, I came upon the Worzel Gummidge figure that could only be Iolo Ellis, lecturer in Thai Studies, hunched like a wounded bird on the window ledge. The building was a picturesque inner-city firetrap, scheduling preventing its long overdue demolition. We students never grumbled over the climb, because it was worse for Iolo. He was asthmatic, and lame. Mysteriously so: the young amanuensis variously ascribed his gammy leg to encounters of a personal kind with landmines, the Khmer Rouge, drug smugglers, the CIA, and unfriendly Burmese border guards.

'Raven.' Iolo squinted at me, his newest recruit. 'Hello, Raven, how are you? You'll be Slightly More Advanced, you will,' he diagnosed, running a freckled hand through tawny pot-scrub curls. 'Reckon we'll skip Beginners altogether. I've had my instructions, see. Speed, of the essence, isn' it?'

Iolo's South Welsh singsong touched everything he said with whimsy, imparting to Thai, a tonal language, an innocent, quirky malapropism that I was to discover, too late, could occasion great offence, as when, imitating Iolo, I found I'd addressed Buddhist dignitaries as dogs or horses.

The Thai language classes were scheduled too early in the day for my and Iolo's tastes, but suited my fellow students. One was a Buddhist convert, a retired train-driver who habitually rose before dawn in order to complete his meditations before his wife began her daily recrimination. 'Heathen idols! Give you the creeps! What's the matter with St Effin Thomas?'

The other mature student was a butcher who had purchased a catalogue bride. Their brief honeymoon a distant memory, he now wanted to be able to argue with the grasping little madam in her own language.

Iolo was soon exasperated by our clumsy attempts to reproduce the four-tone melody of Thai sentences. He attempted to interpret the elegant curlicues that constituted the Thai graphic system, 'devised not by qualified linguists but by a king, so no wonder it's such sheer bloody mayhem!' He hobbled about the room, striking at the sparse furnishings with his crutch for emphasis. 'Rigid class system, birth and wealth. That's their long suit. Inevitable, where you've got inequality of opportunity and an inadequate social safety net. But there are a couple of jokers in the pack. Holiness. Holy is good. And there's pretty. Pretty is even better—for any sex. Like prowess in a medieval tournament, where any plucky nobody could batter his way to stardom. Snakes and ladders, Thai society is. One unlucky throw, you land in the bear pit. One lucky break could catapult you to fame and fortune. Look at Asra, case in point!'

'New model Toyota?' I provoked. The butcher, Dave, self-confessed connoisseur of Thai pulchritude, bent on me a look of aggressive scorn.

'Only won Miss Universe, didn't she? What a looker!'

'Right you are,' agreed Iolo. 'Captivated the eye of a Prince of the Blood. Beauty was her passport. There wasn't a murmur; everyone was delighted. She came from the wrong side of the river, but not a raised eyebrow. If anything happens to old King Rama, they'll be regents, Asra and her prince—he's just a kid, the other guy, the Crown Prince. Fair play to him,' Iolo warmed to his theme, abandoning for once the sardonic tone of righteous censure which discussions of the aristocratic and moneyed classes normally brought up in him like acidosis, 'the old system of concubinage meant any Thai with a title was automatically a Prince of the Blood; but Asra's fellow's the real McCoy: the king's full brother.'

'They call Asra "Thailand's Smile,"' interposed Dave, not to be outdone. 'Only made the list of the world's ten best-dressed women, didn't she? Bloody gorgeous, she is, I tell you. Thai women, they're something else. The cream de la cream! Ask one who knows…' His voice trailed off suggestively. His wife's appearance, despite her duplicitous nature, remained a source of pride.

Pictures flashed through my mind then of the three Thai girls on the survival course I'd helped Fleischer devise during the last long summer vacation. I had agreed to help Fleischer with his project out of boredom, curiosity, cupidity—who knew? Nancy and I had been at each other's throats toward the end of the university semester, stressed and impatient with each other. The sixties' flower-power revolution had had little impact on Nancy, but it had benefited her professionally. Cool and ambitious, Nancy would have climbed over dead bodies to achieve promotion. As, by the sixties, many of those bodies were semi-comatose, drained of all ambition by a surfeit of sex, drugs, and rock and roll, her ascent to the top of her profession had been meteoric. She had blasted through the glass ceiling like a surface-to-air missile. I was happy for her. That did not mean I liked the person she had become. Personally, I'd had enough of clambering over corpses in the service of ambition. I'd grown comfortable and lazy, and I knew it. Perhaps in some perverted way I imagined a shot in the arm of the old cocktail of testosterone and adrenaline would render me a more worthy partner for Nancy. Beautiful, predatory, razor-sharp Nancy.

And so, without telling her, I'd driven over to Normandy, met up with Fleischer and his half-dozen students, passed on a few key skills—bushcraft, self-defence, and so on—and come away both fitter and wealthier than I had expected. It was unlikely our paths would cross again, or that I would ever see the Thai girls again, either. If by any chance we did meet, I thought they would have difficulty recognising me. Out of a perverse need to register my detachment from Fleischer's monstrous theatre of the absurd, I'd insisted on wearing a balaclava at all times except in private. The students never knew my face. I had also disguised my voice, addressing them in barks and growls, like the caricature of a drill sergeant.

I told myself sternly that that was just as well. The effect of those Thai women on me had been stupefying; I'd never met women like them in a long and misspent life. I'd fancied myself inured against the lure of the exotic, but their beauty, their tenacity and courage in spite of all Fleischer's sadistic invention could throw at them, fascinated me. They were so different, yet the strength of their friendship meant that thoughts of one inevitably brought the others to mind. Salikaa, tempestuous, dazzling, dangerous; Pim, the Royal Princess, fiercely committed, fragrant, strangely vulnerable; and Chee Laan, the Chinese girl, the biggest threat of all to my efforts to gather up the shreds of my disreputable rackety existence and forge a grounded life for myself.

'Yes, well,' Iolo was saying, 'to Thais, we're not worth spit. Bloody *farangs*, we are. *Farang*. Derived from *français*. The first European the Thais were aware of was the king's French favourite. They even adopted a French legal system—imagine the trouble *that* caused! So you remember, boy'—here he bent his sombre dark gaze on me—'two facts: in Thailand, you're guilty until proven innocent. The burden of proof is on the accused. And,' he admonished the Buddhist convert, slumped stolidly on his chair, clutching on his lap a yellow plastic bag containing his books with the portentous dignity of an ill-favoured matron of honour holding a bouquet, 'you can shave your head, don the saffron robe, spout Thai as well as the Patriarch himself. But don't delude yourself. Kipling was right, the old fascist: never the twain shall meet. Once a *farang*, always a *farang*!'

'Where did you learn your Thai?' I asked.

'Ah!' Iolo tapped the side of his beak, miming peasant cunning. 'That'd be telling, now. Compromise my mystique, see?' He rubbed his hands, beaming sadistically. 'Now, let's see what you made of the homework. You go first!' He pointed at me.

In spite of myself, and much to my surprise, I enjoyed Iolo's classes. It was odd to find myself on the other side of the fence for once, regressing to irresponsibility and inventing excuses for inadequate preparation. I was childishly pleased when Iolo, in an unguarded moment, uttered a word of commendation for my efforts. There was an eccentricity, a colourful, off-beat quality about the entire chaotic proceeding that was very much in tune with the late sixties Zeitgeist. The atmosphere was paradoxically both laid back and charged with passion, a euphoric combination that few of us will ever experience again. I was impatient to encounter firsthand the society he described, eager for my intriguing mission to begin.

I'm pretty sure, looking back, that Iolo was high half the time. He was certainly suspiciously devoted to the plants growing on the windowsill of his tiny flat, to which I half-carried him on that last evening many months later, when I'd got my marching orders and Iolo and I got royally drunk to celebrate the end of our association.

I had happily drifted along, feeling the new language and the distant alien society gradually taking shape in my imagination. I was conscious that, from the moment I plunged into that society head first, the contours

I had drawn up would shift, perhaps violently, before they settled into a recognizable pattern.

There's nothing like a shrilling telephone startling you out of sleep for creating resentment and disorientation. Cursing, I fumbled for the instrument and growled into it like a disturbed hibernating bear. Nor was my humour improved when I recognised the smooth tones of Mr James Smith.

'Dr Raven? Hope I didn't wake you.'

'What?' Irritated, I forgot to keep my voice down. Beside me, Nancy groaned and flounced, dragging the pillow over her ears in a way that boded trouble.

Smith tut-tutted in mild rebuke at my intemperance. 'Meet you at eleven. Redfern Art Gallery—you know it?'

'Oddly enough, I do.' I smouldered, as though accused of philistinism, and added childishly, 'Though I mainly just use its website, of course. That's where I buy stuff to cover the damp patches on my walls.'

'Splendid,' returned Smith impassively, and rang off. I sat glaring at the telephone, one of Nancy's impulse purchases. Right now, it struck me as self-conscious rather than an ironic fashion statement. Squatting on the desk like a pale plastic toad, its pallid lustre reminded me of Smith's smug imperiousness. I wondered what the hell the bloody man wanted. He couldn't just state his business on the phone, there and then—all the cloak-and-dagger rigmarole. Art galleries indeed! Just playacting again.

On my way to the meeting, slumped in the Tube, idly scanning the back of a fellow passenger's tabloid and still speculating resentfully, I found my answer.

A banner headline proclaimed: KING OF SIAM DIES IN CRASH.

There were two pictures: one long-lens shot of tangled wreckage, helicopter blades and palm trees. Another other, smaller shot of a slim, elaborately coiffed woman, whom I recognized as the most beautiful woman I'd ever seen. The smaller headline read: NOW SHE'S QUEEN FOR REAL. I knew this was the Princess Asra, ex-Miss Universe, whose husband would now be Prince Regent.

The possessor of the newspaper, discovering my interest, shook his paper angrily, folded it small, and shifted in his seat so as to study it in a position inaccessible to my eyes. I had seen enough. I folded my arms and whistled silently, staring with unseeing eyes at the underwear adverts on the carriage walls.

I burst through the doors of the Redfern Gallery. Smith appeared to be engrossed in the appraisal of a Bryan Kneale sculpture, his head cocked like an inquisitive robin. The majestic bronze structure was stark and forbidding, like the skeleton of some prehistoric predator. As he straightened up to meet my eye, Smith was nothing if not matter-of-fact.

'Ah, Raven. Whole new ball game, my dear fellow! New developments. Seen the papers? Now the king's out of the game, we need you there yesterday. This could be just the chance they're waiting for. That's if they didn't engineer it in the first place…'

'They? Who are they?' I snarled. Hunching my shoulders crossly, I began a restless circumambulation of the sculpture.

Smith merely continued, as if I had not spoken. 'The king was too popular. That could be perceived as a threat. And now, of course, the whole region could flare up at any moment.'

I stopped prowling, turned and faced him. 'If you tell me you're concerned for the Americans' military bases…'

Smith met my eyes coldly. 'I shall not tell you that.'

'It's something to do with the Yanks, though, isn't it?' I persisted. 'But why don't they send their own spook? The place is rotten with them as it is. Why me?'

Smith sighed. He bent to study the brass plate at the base of the sculpture. As he straightened up, nostrils curving with mild reproof, as though I had farted, he answered casually, 'Unthinkable. That would not do at all.'

'A third national, then. A Frenchman or a German, or even a naturalised American, someone like…'

'Like our mutual acquaintance, the valiant Lieutenant Fleischer,' Smith intercepted smoothly. Refusing to show how taken aback I was, I scowled, feigning puzzlement. Even when you both knew a fellow Legionnaire's real name, the code dictated that you did not bandy it about art galleries, or betray recognition in the presence of mysterious and infuriating characters calling themselves Smith.

Smith smiled as though he understood all this. 'I rather fancy your friend and mine, Lieutenant Fleischer, will soon tire of his current occupation.

Yuppies learning assertiveness by stabbing cushions and abseiling down cliffs.' He sniffed fastidiously. 'Poodle-fakery and parlour tricks. Fleischer's stock-in-trade involves torture, terror, and death by stealth. But you know that, of course.'

Smith sighed and turned to walk out, forcing me to follow him.

'Apparently there is a market for such skills as Lieutenant Fleischer's in this naughty world of ours, Dr Raven. Your flight has been booked for Thursday. Ten p.m. check-in. Trust your shots are up to date? Everything else has been taken care of.' He extended his hand. In it there was a small, black lizard-skin wallet. 'Local currency and U.S. dollars. Also the number of your new bank account. You will find it, I trust, in an agreeably healthy condition. I do hope my telephone call last night did not disturb Ms Raven. Take her to dinner, but resist the temptation to confide. The less she knows, the better. For her own protection.' Before I could explode, Smith patted my arm cheerily. 'Siam's chock-full of pretty things. Oh, dear, yes!' The mask dropped for a second. His rain-grey eyes misted with yearning. 'While you're there, get her a nice pair of star sapphire earrings. Remember to keep in touch, there's a good chap. Little and often, that's the ticket. Like feeding fledglings. We're relying on you, you know.'

I was too furious to reply.

Iolo had read the newspapers, too. When I arrived in the classroom I was surprised to find him perched on the windowsill staring glumly out at the rain. Despite his oft-trumpeted socialism, he appeared quite upset by the news of King Rama's death. 'Not a bad old sod, really,' he grunted. I regarded his beaky Welsh profile silhouetted against the grimy pane.

'Fancy a pint?' I suggested. He snorted.

'A pint or bloody three,' he said, reaching for his crutches.

It was an undistinguished watering hole, the Mitre, but conveniently adjacent.

'So you're finally off, then?' Iolo asked, leaning back on his barstool. He eyed me with speculation and envy. 'Jammy bugger! Well, you can get the beers in.'

Meekly, I complied. After several libations, Iolo waxed conversational. 'You watch your back, Raven, my man. There are bad people where you're headed. They play hardball.' I cocked an enquiring eyebrow but forbore to verbalise the query. Questions made Iolo clam up.

'You were asking where I learned my Thai. VSO. Four years ago. Building schools, teaching. That sort of thing. Northeast. Isaan. Then further north. Akha country.'

'Akha?'

'Hill tribe. Savage, gorgeous, doped out of their skulls. Poppy growers. Outsiders. Only one of them ever made it big in Thai society. His Excellency Colonel Sya Dam. The Black Tiger. Chief of Royal Security.' Iolo pronounced the title with an emotion impossible to fathom, with an expression both portentous and deadpan.

I laughed. 'Chief of Security! He seems to have screwed up big-time, letting the Royal Family board dodgy helicopters.'

Iolo now snorted with laughter, causing beer foam to appear on his lip. 'He probably arranged it,' he said. 'Never, ever try to second-guess them—him especially.' He wiped his lip with the back of his hand and rolled up his trouser leg, revealing the back of his calf. I gazed in horrified fascination. 'Sya gave me this.' Iolo's left calf gleamed purple and grey, like a plate of diseased liver, painful-looking, although the injury was old. The skin graft shone with a bronze lustre.

'God! Why would he do something like that?' I knew better than to ask whether Iolo had sued for compensation or accused the general of assault.

Iolo shrugged. He let his trouser leg drop again. 'I insulted the Akha. Or Sya thought I did. I was high. We were both high. Stupid, it was. Plain stupid!' Iolo contemplated his ruined leg reflectively, but without rancour or even regret.

'What did he do it with?'

'A meat hook. For slinging dead dogs on the village gates. The Akha hang carcasses there to discourage evil spirits.'

'You must really hate the guy.'

Iolo eyed me strangely. 'No. Why should I hate him? He was my friend.'

'A fine friend!'

Iolo sipped his ale. 'Raven, somehow I don't think you and the East are going to get along. You're too logical.'

'You're subtly telling me I lack subtlety?'

'No. Not subtlety. Obliqueness. You must forget your obsession with the obvious.'

He refused to be drawn after that, and we devoted ourselves to the serious business of drinking and the serious topic of rugby football.

Yet beneath the surface, several different streams of thought flowed through my consciousness, combining into a broad, fast-running river. There was Nancy; in our trendy arrogance, we had not played it right, Nancy and I. I think we both realised this. We were neither courageously committed, nor free; too close for comfort, yet no longer close in any way that mattered. Possessiveness had outlived passion. She dismissed my female students as 'your worshipful prepubescents.' I pettishly referred to her head of chambers, a perfectly amiable, inoffensive man who had long idolised Nancy with a hopeless adoration, as 'that reactionary dinosaur.' She disapproved of my association with Fleischer—'that Fascist thug,' she called him. I had told her I'd gone to France to write a book but I was only too aware that she suspected that was a front. If she knew about the Thai girls…

Then, there was my barely suppressed fury with Smith and all his ilk, the grey-faced, pen-pushing widowmakers of the world.

These two names kept cropping up, the one familiar, the other alien; both slightly exotic, both, it seemed to my drink-fuddled mind, faintly absurd. Lieutenant Angel Fleischer, of North Africa, Panama, and now, of all places, Normandy; and that other name, Colonel Sya Dam, the Black Tiger of Bangkok. I wondered how the hell I was going to play the strange hand life had dealt me. I felt very sorry for myself.

'I tell you, boy.' Iolo, breaking into my thoughts, leaned forward and thumped the table, making the glasses skitter and swash. 'We'll bloody hammer 'em next time they show their faces in Cardiff!' He took a gulp of ale, raised his glass to me, slightly askew, and intoned with patriotic solemnity, '*Y Ddraig goch am byth! Cymru am byth!*'

I grinned idiotically. For a moment, I believe I actually imagined Iolo was speaking Thai, and that I understood it perfectly—but it was Welsh, after all. *The Red Dragon and the Welcome in the Hillside.*

London, England
April 13, 1969

Raven
Sourly I watched my fellow passengers manhandling their bulky hand luggage down the aisles. Royal Thai Orchid Flight 245 to Bangkok, via Zurich, Rome, Tehran, Calcutta, threatened to be packed. Nancy, thrusting her silver Porsche through the early morning traffic with cold fury, had tipped me out at Heathrow in sufficient time to secure a window seat. We Celts are not noted for our pragmatic optimism; nonetheless, as soon as I located my seat, I immediately dropped my well-travelled Zeiss Ikon with its ungainly lens attachment into the central seat. Repelling boarders. A black mood was upon me, and I was not eager for company, debilitated by the wrangling through a long, loveless night.

'You get yourself into these things,' Nancy had railed. 'It's the bloody Legion all over again. I bet that bloody Fleischer's involved somewhere, too. I know you, Nat!' She glared, her blue eyes glistening with anger. 'Just don't expect me to put my life on hold again while you fart about playing James Bond!'

'All that's dead and buried. And it's nothing to do with Fleischer, Nance!' I moved to kiss her but she turned her face aside.

'Don't call me that!' she snapped.

One way or another, Nancy and I had made our farewells on terms worse than bad—terms of indifference. Foolishly confiding in my cups, I'd admitted my partnership with Fleischer during the previous summer. As I had feared, his name was a red rag to the proverbial bull. 'He's a rogue and a murderer!' she'd screamed. Even I had to admit that his reputation was tainted. That was why, in the end, I'd terminated our association.

The morning dawned chilly, the atmosphere still bitter.

My bags stood ready by the door. She'd dressed without a word. I watched, fascinated, despite long custom and present rancour, as she deftly swept her blue-black hair clear of the collar of her cashmere coat. She looked exactly what she was, one of a frightening new breed, an independent alpha-female, a sharp, Bond Street–wise high-flier, exuding ambition and assertive sexuality. Nancy was a successful City dealer. My own modest salary hardly kept the Porsche in windscreen-wiper fluid. Most of the time, that suited both of us just fine. But not always.

Shrugging the strap of her black leather bag over her shoulder, she bent on me a withering glance.

'You'll never get a cab now!'

The Porsche squealed to a bone-racking halt in the drop-off lane, and I leapt out, slamming the door with unnecessary force, and collected my cases from the boot. The loaded atmosphere between us had robbed me of the buzz of anticipation. I stood stiffly beside my cases on the kerb, waiting for her to drive away.

The automatic window slid down. Through it, Nancy extended a small, expensively wrapped package.

'What's this?' I moved out from under the overhang, and stood in the sooty drizzle, staring stupidly.

'Bon voyage! Happy landings!' The window slid up silently between us again. Nancy wiggled her gloved fingers teasingly, her eyes already on the driving mirror, then swerved out in front of a savagely honking taxi and was gone, my best beloved, into the clover-leaf-junction jungle. For a moment I forgot where I was and what lay before me, and clutching my farewell gift, I gazed after her with regret.

Now, seated, obediently harnessed, I tore open the flimsy gold designer wrapping paper and stared in disbelief at Nancy's Parthian gift: a solid-gold Kit Kat holder, the chocolate-covered biscuit in its gaudy red-and-white wrapper already in place, the bauble still bearing its Asprey & Goddard price tag: £395 sterling. If I'd not been travelling by plane, but by bicycle or bullock-cart, I'd have hurled the idiotic object into the nearest ditch. I stuffed it into the back of the seat in front of me, along with the menus and the sick bag. I stared out at the rain-washed tarmac, remembering it was

April 13. My mother's birthday.

The overpriced trinket recalled to my mind my mother's obsessive frugality; she considered electric light a wicked indulgence. This ironic extravagance of Nancy's would have appalled her. She'd never said so, but I sensed that she did not care for Nancy.

When pressed for an opinion, she would say, 'Such a smart lass.'

I shook myself free of my recollections and watched as the stewardess greeted each passenger. If I'd been a sociologist, I'd have gotten a whole thesis out of the Thai greeting ritual alone. Smiling, the stewardess pressed her palms together, placing her fingertips to her nose; foreigners all received the same degree of reverence, I noted, but, when the passengers were Asian, a lightning assessment of their social standing dictated the precise grade of respect they commanded, to be reflected in the angle of her graceful *wai*.

Three elegant young Asian women boarded; I jumped as if shot, recognizing the trio from Fleischer's boot camp, though they looked so different without their army fatigues, spattered with mud, camouflage paint, and blood. I hunched in my seat, having no desire to be recognized myself, and studied them covertly.

Chee Laan Lee entered first, wrapped in a tangerine-coloured coat of soft wool, its collar raised, her round, smooth head protruding like a pistil from the corolla of a lily. Her hair could have been painted on, in one sweep of blue-black model paint; two more daubs for the merrily sparkling black eyes. The flame coat shrieked 'couture', though I could not have conjured a name; despite Nancy's attempts to educate me, I still couldn't tell my Balenciaga from my Christian Espiritu. I was surprised that she rated only a rather perfunctory salute from the stewardess.

Behind her, at the head of the queue, a shimmer of wolfskins quivered with impatience. Salikaa's small booted foot, adorned with golden spurs, tapped the floor.

'*Vous permettez?*' she demanded in a grating tone, for the benefit of the onlookers. I chuckled at the stage-French mimicry, the shrug and imperious nasal whine, so incongruous in Salikaa, with her dazzling dark-gold face, her slanting eyes, the cascade of hair so black it had the greenish sheen of a rook's wing when, as now, she swung it imperiously.

The stewardess bit her lip. I sympathized with the poor woman's dilemma.

I recalled Iolo Ellis's briefings on Thai society, about the potential upward mobility of the beautiful. Looking now at Salikaa, I knew she would raise high stakes on her single ace, what poker players call holding the tiger by the tail. She flung her furs into the outstretched arms of the waiting hostess like a bundle of rags and struck a pose in her blood-red dress.

The stewardess, staggering under her load, struggled to greet Princess Pim, making deep reverence. Pim's face, as she returned the greeting, was gentle. She wore a sober garment of pale lemon wool, without ornament of any kind, but the stewardess had recognised her status. This was the genuine article, a Princess of the Blood—as Iolo would say, 'The real bloody McCoy or I'm Shirley Bloody Temple, boy!' Much later, the curious coincidence of the colours—lemon, crimson, and flame—would strike me.

Salikaa oozed past the stewardess. With her extravagant make-up, one might be fooled into thinking she was a *poule de luxe*. Bangkok's awash with them. It would certainly have explained the stewardess's lack of enthusiasm. While I was gradually regaining the will to live, Salikaa flashed a provocative gap-toothed grin around the cabin, her gaze caressing the male passengers. She took her time looking me over. Last time my face had been smeared black and green, I'd worn a balaclava, a helmet and shades. I realized none of them had recognized me, and that suited me just fine. The fascinating trio were a complication I didn't need.

'Sit down, Salikaa!' I heard her companions hiss disapprovingly. Her only response was to grin more wickedly than ever, while her eyes continued to rake the cabin, challenging. She caught my eye again and smiled, her tongue flickering over her pearly lipstick.

After she sat down, I realised she was still studying me, holding a compact at an angle through the gap between the seats. She saw I'd noticed, but she continued her appraisal for a moment unabashed, then snapped the compact shut and leaned over to Chee Laan, and said in English, loud enough for me to hear over the noise of the engine: 'That *farang*. The big one. Behind. You think how old?' The glossy furry eyelashes, her sharp little nose and glistening teeth, reminded me of a mink, released by sentimentalists on an unsuspecting countryside.

Chee Laan shrugged. 'Who knows? *Farang* faces all alike. Same-same chickens.'

Farang. It was fortunate I did not need to blend discreetly into the background on this assignment. I was branded an outsider from the outset. In North Africa, my natural swarthiness, plus my fluent Arabic, afforded some camouflage. But this was not North Africa. This was a new undertaking, unfamiliar territory. Now at last I began to feel it, the old heady tug of excitement, like the second before you jump. I was startled out of my thoughts by an arrogant nasal whine.

'Pardon *me*! I take it that this seat is not presently occupied?'

Glancing up, I encountered the eyes of an idol, glittering coldly within a mask.

Scalpels had slit and lifted skin; syringes had pumped liquid silicone and pops of poison. The woman was a triumph of artifice; the nose girlishly pert, the enhanced cheekbones smooth as new apples—they hadn't been able to soften the stony eyes, though, nor prevent the hair, meticulously fluffed and glued, from appearing dead, coarse, dry and reddish as a wind-singed conifer. She scooped up my Zeiss and dropped it in my lap. Seating herself briskly, she established territorial rights, deploying hat, gloves and journals.

'You like me take your purse, ma'am? Put overhead locker?' the little stewardess invited. The woman curtly flipped a hand in dismissal, a gesture of colonial hauteur that surprised me. I had never before encountered a Yankee Memsahib. I removed the plastic from my headset and adjusted it. Out of the corner of my eye I noticed how the red-haired Memsahib clutched the bulky crocodile purse to her breast as though it were her firstborn, or as if it were stuffed with rubies. She accepted a newspaper from the stewardess and spread it out. Now, I'm a compulsive reader, a back of-the-cornflake-packet man. I was struck, centre page, by the same picture of tangled wreckage I had first glimpsed illicitly in the Tube. Above it a 72-point black banner headline proclaimed: A NATION MOURNS! Beneath a portrait of a muscular man in uniform, a subheading proclaimed: "'Vengeance on Assassins!" swears Colonel Sya.'

I studied the face of the man who was to become my enemy. It was an alert, intelligent face, with strong bones and remarkable Mongoloid eyes. It reminded me, with the broad flat nose and prominent cheekbones, the lazy yet intense gaze, of a tiger, his namesake.

With an unfriendly glare in my direction, the woman turned the paper over, folding Colonel Sya's face up and crushing him brutally into the pocket beneath her table.

I fiddled the dial on my headset. Mozart flowed over me like aromatic oil, smoothing my brow quicker than Botox. I pulled the eyeshade from my flight bag and, turning my head away from my unwelcome companion, drifted into the easy light slumber of the seasoned traveller. Just before I nodded off, I noticed that it was Chee Laan who now held the compact, observing me in its little gold-rimmed mirror with an unblinking gaze, which I might have found unsettling, had sleep not blotted it out.

Salikaa

I had a good look at him, the *farang*. He reminded me of somebody. In the small mirror of my compact I studied him feature by feature like a painting, and found to my surprise the result was not entirely repulsive. There was the big beaky Western nose, of course, a firm chin too, but I quite liked that, and the sexy dark blue eyes. I caught them watching me and snapped the compact shut. I passed it over to Chee Laan. I saw with amusement that she was intrigued by the big foreigner also. I can sense that sort of thing. My instinct never fails. He wouldn't get any change out of Chee Laan, though. She'd been practising that basilisk stare of hers for too long. She even practised it on Lieutenant Fleischer. Not that it made any impact there. Nothing had any effect on him, the crazy bastard.

Thinking of the lieutenant made me remember my bruises, and my anger.

'Shit,' I grumbled to Pim. 'I still feel like I've been run over by a truck! My ass is black and blue!'

'We learned a lot, though,' Pim replied. 'We should be grateful. But I will be glad never to see that man again!' She'd told us that when they learned of her father's plans to send her to Normandy, her secret political organisation, SWORD, had arranged for her to join Fleischer's training course. SWORD stood for Students and Workers Organising Revolutionary Development. I don't have time for that sort of thing myself; it's every girl for herself as far as I'm concerned.

Chee Laan's grandmother, the property tycoon Sunii Lee, had arranged for her to go on the course, too. All Chinese are twitchy, especially the ones with money. Always scared someone's going to come along and take it off them. Fleischer seemed to know of old lady Sunii, and my guardian, Vichai, as well. 'The famous drug baron,' he called him. I just flashed my teeth at him. Fleischer was a sinewy blond animal with mad blue eyes. He smelled of sweat and grass. Good-quality grass. Even before we got to the training camp, when he stopped that filthy jeep of his to expose us to the first icy blast of his personality, I was provoked by his indifference. I dropped my hand on his thigh and awaited developments. I didn't have to wait long.

'I'm going to give you thirty seconds,' he hissed through his teeth without looking at me, 'and then I will break your fingers.'

I snatched my hand back. I was seething, but I smiled.

Then, in that gritty voice of his that ground out the words, he warned us what to expect. We'd be hurt and humiliated, we'd crawl on our bellies, kill our own food, eat rats and slugs, jump off cliffs, and pee into a pit in front of fifteen men. He warned us, and it all came true, just as he said, even the rats and the pissing. And when he was done warning us, and Pim was white and gasping, and Chee Laan's eyes had narrowed to two slits above her waxy pale cheekbones, he turned to me at last and said: 'Meantime, you will address me as Lieutenant Fleischer, sir, and you will never touch me again. Not until I put my hand on your ass.'

I leaned back and closed my eyes. 'Oh, happy day!' I murmured dreamily. He did not reply but I sensed his irritation, and I grinned into the darkness.

We all suffered under Fleischer, Chee Laan the most. That girl was lucky not to end up crippled for life or dead from blood poisoning or lockjaw, according to Pim. The nails in her boot pierced the sole and she marched on like that, saying nothing, biting her lip. When she pulled her boot off in the evening, squatting on the floor of our tent, groaning with agony, we crowded round her. Her foot looked like chopped liver. Pim examined Chee Laan's foot and offered to bathe it. Pim is a nice girl, but she certainly is eccentric. Who ever heard of a Princess bathing a Jek girl's foot? As for me, I turned away, nauseated. It was a disgusting sight. When Fleischer looked in, Chee Laan asked him for a hammer. With it she beat the nails down, and the next day she marched on. Say what you like about the Jeks, they don't give up easy.

That night it rained. Not warm rain, like at home, but icy needles of rain than stung your eyes and chilled you to the marrow. It was still raining buckets when Fleischer followed me out into the night. I'd nipped out for a quick joint. I was leaning against a gnarled old apple tree, trying to relax, but just feeling drained and filthy, and longing for fresh linen and my own bed. Then Fleischer came up and just stood there in the rain, staring at me. I looked back, and I saw he knew what I was, and wanted me anyway, and I laughed in his face. He moved quickly. Most of my nails were broken by then, but the ends were jagged. I raked his cheek. He lunged at me.

I still have the mark on my neck where he bit me. His teeth almost met through my flesh. I wanted to kill him. One day I will.

Bangkok, Thailand
April 1969

Raven

I awoke when the engine note changed to the higher pitch of reverse thrust and peered down at the city. Such beautiful sights: the jumble of houses interlaced by waterways, the brilliant, artificial-looking emerald green of tropical vegetation, the massive golden chedi of a temple gleaming in the distance.

When I stepped onto the baking tarmac at Bangkok's Don Muang airport, the air rippled and wrapped itself about me like a hot perfumed bath. From the airport roof, massed brown and golden faces watched with interest as we passengers stumbled through the heat haze like people wading ashore through a boiling sea. I felt my sweat glands explode, soaking my clothes; my breath became laboured, as if the air were burning. It was the climax of the hot season. The whole dusty central Southeast Asian plain lay gasping like a landed flounder.

Ahead of me, the three young Thai girls walked, together and yet each keeping her distance. Salikaa, the arrogant beauty, carelessly dragged her wolfskin coat through the dust by its designer label. The little princess, smiling, returned the wave of an excited urchin in a pink jockey cap, hopping excitedly among the sea of faces. Chee Laan in her flame-coloured coat acknowledged no urchins, but strode briskly, eyes front, high heels clacking a tattoo. I wondered how she could stand the weight of the cashmere coat. I felt oddly regretful that I should certainly never see any of them again.

Inside the airport building, an official, sere and brown as an ant, extended a languid hand without looking up. 'You come Bangkok Lecture tour?' It sounded like 'lecher tour', and, judging by the lively demeanour of the group of Hawaiian-shirted Economy-class travellers crowding into the terminal building, the inadvertent malapropism seemed curiously apt.

'Lecturing, that's right,' I said. 'Conservation.'

'Politics, ne'er min' talk too much,' the official reproved gently; his air of weariness deepened. On the desk beside him lay a huge, used syringe, resembling a veterinary instrument rather than one intended for human ministrations. 'Vassination?' the official invited.

I had no intention of submitting to an on-the-spot immunization. I was relieved when my papers were handed back with a curt nod; no chirpy formulaic 'There you go, sir!' or 'Have a nice day now!' Preferring this restraint, I returned the tired little man's nod and made for the arrivals lounge. The scene was familiar, unpleasantly reminiscent of overcrowded transit refugee camps, the air soured with enforced inactivity and thick with resentment. Exhausted people sacrificed dignity for comfort, sprawling listlessly amongst their baggage.

About the exit jostled a noisy throng of touts, porters, tour operators and company chauffeurs. A handsome hawk-nosed woman, towering above most of the Asians, pushed her way forward, impervious to the curious glances excited by her naked shoulders and unfeminine determination. Her copper mane was tied back with a pink band that closer examination revealed to be the missing belt of her skimpy gingham sundress. A streak of oil paint barred her high cheekbone and another smeared her hair, giving her the appearance of an Apache warrior. 'Raven!' she bellowed in a husky contralto. I elbowed my way toward her, grinning. I'd met Laila Drinkwater, Iranian-born wife of the British Council Representative, only once, but she was not a woman easily forgotten.

Laila grabbed at my bag, and I resisted, and nearly compromised by handing it to a third party who suddenly appeared at her elbow, a diminutive dark man whom I at first took for a garden boy or very youthful chauffeur.

'No, no!' cried Laila in horrified protest. 'This is Siegfried!'

I realised my mistake. Siegfried was clearly not a man who carried burdens for others. He was lithe and graceful, but the initial impression of youthfulness was subsequently revealed as a careful illusion. I'd been deceived by a certain quickness of gesture, the neatness of the exquisite ebony skull, shaven clean as a novice priest's. A second glance showed that this spectacular black man was certainly older than either Laila Drinkwater or myself, but marvellously well preserved. And what a peacock he was. His pink shirt split to the navel across the sculpted, slightly glistening pectorals and glinted with golden chains. As my hand was grasped in a double-handed shake, my eye was drawn to the impressive Pathek Philippe watch half-covered by his gold bracelets. No speck of Bangkok dirt marred the dazzling white trousers moulded onto Siegfried's body. His shirt bore a small, exclusive monogram that even I, self-confessed fashion illiterate, recognised. As he turned his head, a single massive pearl glinted in the curve of his neat-pointed ear, like a raindrop on a copper beech leaf. Siegfried returned my appraisal, nodded, and murmured softly, as though satisfied by what he saw, 'Oh, yes! Yes, indeed!' He bared a row of perfect teeth, startlingly white against his chocolate skin.

'Laila will tell you,' he purred, 'that Siegfried does not carry things. But I have other talents. *N'est-ce pas*, Laila, *cherie*?' His purr was sweetened by a slight lisp and a strong French accent.

'Siegfried is artist.' Laila waved an arm vaguely above her head, leading the way to her car. 'Oh, and, of course, also baron! I hope you screw your courage, as Poet says, to sticking place, Dr Nathaniel Raven. Siegfried is wickedest girl in Bangkok, and I am worst driver!'

I chortled dutifully. Siegfried rolled his eyes affectedly and said, 'Whatever makes you think she jokes?'

Don Muang Airport, Bangkok, Thailand
April 1969

Ah Lee's dislike of airports was overwhelming, as she watched the departure of the heavy-shouldered dark foreigner and his colourful companions. Scowling at their loudness and louche eccentricity, she shuddered. Unsatisfactory, open-ended places, where people disappeared out of sight to a destiny beyond comprehension. At a certain time, on a certain day, according to the meaningless marks in the foreigners' almanacs, people dropped out of the sky and back into real life again.

The years had eroded the old lady's features. Eyes and nose had gotten mislaid somewhere among the wrinkles. Yet for one brief moment, catching sight of the girl in her bright tangerine coat, the battered old face exploded in a sunburst of delight. The next moment the girl caught sight of her. The beam was smartly extinguished, the mask fell back into place. The girl stood before her, tall on her fashionable Western shoes.

'Ah Lee!' Chee Laan felt her own eyes brimming. The old woman, scowling now, gave a perfunctory Chinese salutation, hands folded to one side, and launched into a vehement diatribe. All her grievances surfaced: her hatred of crowds, of foreigners, of wearing shoes, of being stared at by rude strangers. These people had no idea of her dignity, and did not recognize that she was not a worthless old woman, a small person, but the trusted servant of a noble house.

'Unsuitable shoes!' spluttered Ah Lee, the harsh Hakka coming in short bursts like machine-gun fire. 'How does Little Miss hope to bow before Honourable Old Lady on stilts like clown? Perhaps...' For a second her true fear revealed itself, the terror of finding herself, the old nursemaid, outgrown and discarded. 'Little Miss has forgotten the Way? For doubtless, in France-country, England-country, elders are nothing, ancestors, nothing! Face paints, lewd scents, self-indulgences, shoes like heron's legs, these are for French persons and modern young misses. Ah Lee's teaching, blown away, wind on the water's face. Honourable Old Lady, shamed in the flower of her age! Ah, indeed it is a bitter thing to be an old woman tossed aside!'

Chee Laan laughed delightedly. 'Your tongue has not grown blunter with the years, Ah Lee! It's good to see you! Now, I must just say goodbye to my friends.' She looked round and spotted Pim at once. The crowd had parted instinctively to allow the Premsakul party space, and now watched respectfully as Prince Toom Premsakul, the Prime Minister's son, greeted his sister. Handsome, slightly built and delicate of feature, Chee Laan thought yet again that he seemed Pim's mirror image, except for the large round glasses that enhanced his mild and studious air. Secretaries and servants surrounded them, but Prince Toom himself reached out for his sister's case. Pim's hand was still on the handle. Their hands touched and they stood looking into each other's eyes, and then at the same moment smiled identical secret, intimate smiles. Their eyes embraced, though their bodies did not.

'Welcome home, sister,' Toom said quietly, still holding her eyes with his own. 'How was France?'

'France was still there. How was Cambridge?'

She sensed the fever of excitement in him. He dropped the case and made a large, gauche gesture with both hands, as though trying to catch two watermelons in the air. 'Amazing!' he said. 'Just amazing—you can't imagine! Oh, Pim! I've got so much to tell you; it's a miracle, we're on the brink of a major breakthrough!'

'You are tipped for the Nobel Prize, I suppose?' she teased mildly, touched by his enthusiasm.

'More important than that—much more! We could save the world!' He seemed to shimmer and twitch like a buzzing hive. His father cut in, commanding gruffly,

'We cannot stand here chattering, Toom! Give the servant your sister's hand luggage, make yourself useful!' Those about them drew back respectfully. Toom flinched as though he had been whipped across the face at his father's brutal public rebuke.

Elsewhere, the crowd had also withdrawn from the reception party surrounding Salikaa, but the respect here was of a different quality. 'Goodbye, Comrade Highness! Goodbye, China Doll!' Salikaa ran back to bump cheeks with each of them, her fall of straight black hair whirling lashlike, stinging their faces. *She could not resist a taunt, even in farewell,* thought Chee Laan. Closet socialist princess, poor little Jek rich girl. Trust Salikaa!

Young Prince Toom's eyes left his sister and fastened on Salikaa. The hurt in them was replaced by wonder. Pim followed his gaze, frowning slightly. Salikaa flicked her dark mane again, gripping Chee Laan and Pim and swinging their hands, ignoring the stony faces of the three reception committees.

'I thought at first you two were a pair of stuck-up bitches. I admit I was wrong. We had some good times, eh! Remember that sexy Lieutenant Fleischer?' The small knot of men tightened around Salikaa in a manner both protective and oddly threatening. Chee Laan saw that they were the same sinister-looking crew that had accompanied Salikaa's departure months ago: swarthy faces, opaque sunglasses with the sheen of insect wings, their identical dark suits straining over hard-pumped muscles, their arrogance edgy. Now they rammed a pathway through the crowds, keeping the tall girl in their midst, like a military escort. Salikaa grinned back over her shoulder. 'Next time we meet, I'll be a star! Watch out!' she called, flirting a kiss along her fingers toward Prince Toom, who stood like a statue, wide-eyed, blinking through his glasses. As the group reached the exit, a late-model Cadillac squealed round the corner and bucked to a halt. Doors were flung open. Salikaa's companions bundled her inside. She was only a blurred shadow behind bulletproof glass hazy with cigar smoke.

All the while Chee Laan, Pim, and Toom Premsakul watched. At Chee Laan's elbow Ah Lee cleared her throat. 'Bandits, camoys, no-good people. And Little Miss, staring like coolie. Like foreign devil. Pah!'

'High-born Thais stare too, Ah Lee.'

Ah Lee squinted disapprovingly at the royal Premsakul siblings. 'Lose too much face.'

Chee Laan smiled and looked at the floor. 'You are right, Ah Lee. Minding one's own business is a virtue. I've been away too long. I must just say goodbye.' She stepped over to Pim. 'I hope we'll meet again. I'm glad you were at school. That terrible bland foreign food—you saved our lives, all that *nam pla* and *nam prik* you got sent up from the Paris Embassy for us!'

Before Pim could reply her brother stepped between the two young women, frowning, wearing an air of abstraction. 'We should hurry, Pim. Father is growing impatient. Excuse us!' he *wai*'ed Chee Laan hastily, then, taking his sister's elbow, he steered her firmly toward the exit. Pim tried to look back and wave but her brother was moving too fast. A chauffeur in the uniform of the Prime Minister's Office sprang out and saluted. Chee Laan smiled, tight-lipped. The public snub stung.

Ah Lee waddled toward the exit as though nothing had happened.

Behind the Prime Minister's Mercedes stood another, newer, cream-coloured Mercedes, just as highly polished. Ah Lee compared the two vehicles with evident satisfaction. 'New car Honourable Old Lady,' she announced, as the chauffeur jumped out. Ah Lee sniffed. 'Same-same worthless no-good driving boy, anyhow, ne'er mind.'

Chee Laan settled herself into the red-leather upholstery of the back seat. 'How is Father's mother?' she asked.

Ah Lee grunted. 'Honourable Old Lady very old. Very old woman.' Through the car window she watched impassively as the Prime Minister's Mercedes pulled away from the curb.

'Great is the face of Honourable Old Lady!' chanted the chauffeur, seeking their eyes in the driving mirror.

Ah Lee lurched forward and boxed his ears. 'Drive car, rat!'

Bulletproof windows and the air conditioner's hum could not blot out the fumes, odours, and cries of the street. A battered red Ford shot out in front of them. A foreign devil-woman was driving, waving her hands, honking loudly. A big *farang* with a long nose and a smaller black one clung to its window frames.

Ah Lee snorted. 'Hurry, hurry, all time hurry. Low people.' It was a veiled rebuke to the arrogant Thai prince who had publicly insulted her Little Miss. Not much escaped Ah Lee. The Lee Mercedes hurried without the appearance of vulgar haste, rocked smoothly across the humpbacked bridges over the khlongs. At last the congestion slackened. In the residential quarter there was suddenly more space, more sky. The chauffeur turned into the narrow *soi* between ditches lined with long *hai* grass. Ignoring Ah Lee's muttered disapproval, Chee Laan leaned forward, peering about her eagerly.

Hedges and walls blazed with scarlet hibiscus and swathes of bougainvillea—puce, mauve, snowy white.

Beside a high forbidding wall, three and a half metres of featureless pink stone, the Mercedes halted. Chee Laan could not see the top of the wall, but she remembered it well, deadly with broken bottle glass and bristling with rolls of barbed wire. The Lee family valued its privacy. The defences of the Lee compound, which contained four mansions, had been increased in her absence. The garden gate, with its six-foot-high dancing wrought-iron *dephanon* angels, had been backed with steel plates. At one corner she glimpsed brown hands wrestling with slobbering black and tan jaws, blood-red gums, foam-flecked crocodile teeth.

Ah Lee sniffed. 'Do-Ber-Man. Honourable Old Lady she say no-good people too much. Do-Ber-Man come. Do-Ber-Man bite all people, good, no good, all same-same for Do-Ber-Man, never mind. Bite cookee. Bite Muna old garden-boy.'

'I hope it didn't bite you, Ah Lee?' Chee Laan asked, amused.

The old woman cackled evilly, shaking her head. 'Ah Lee, too much tough old woman!' She folded her hands primly and rocked back and forth on the edge of the red leather seat in secret delight. Chee Laan knew very well that the guard dog had recognised the indomitableness of Ah Lee's character.

Presently, the raging animal was brought under control and dragged off by the frantic efforts of the unseen garden boy. From the stone sentry box, which sheltered him from sun and rain, Old Muna saluted the car, searching its dark windows with blank, short-sighted eyes, grinning his toothless grimace.

'Muna, too much old man,' pronounced Ah Lee.

They swept through the gates and into the circular drive before the main house.

On the steps of the largest house, Chee Laan's father's mother, Sunii Lee, had emerged to greet them. 'Honourable Old Lady!' stammered the young chauffeur, awed. It was indeed a supreme honour. A Western grandmother might have waved or wept; but Sunii was Chinese.

Chee Laan noticed a new frailty in the slender, fine-boned figure; but though she might appear to be carved from one single piece of ivory, Sunii Lee's iron will and ramrod dignity still radiated power. She wore a crimson silk tunic with a floating foulard of the same shining material over a narrow black skirt with slits at the calf. Chee Laan studied her fiercely, if not protectively. Dreading to see deterioration, she could see with satisfaction that there was no hint of grey on the neat dark head, no tremor in the delicate hands. Now Sunii was smiling, her rather long upper incisors pressing into the lower lip. A fine network of lines spread over her prominent cheekbones. The magnolia complexion was innocent of liver spots; the eyebrows still swept upward and outward like wings.

To grow old like you, Chee Laan thought. *As strong as you, beautiful as you.* There was something profoundly depressing about such perfection.

'Granddaughter. Have you eaten rice? Are you well?' Despite a hint of tension, the voice was quick and soft as always; the hands were steady, the cool gaze of the almond eyes unwavering as ever. Then Chee Laan saw the trembling lips. This excess of emotion was profoundly shocking. Chee Laan forced herself to stare at the marble steps to conceal her own disgraceful tears of joy. The older woman reached out and touched her hand, tentatively, as if apologising for untoward intrusion. The touch of Sunii's hand was cool, like a flower—'lily hands', as Chinese poets called such hands. Chee Laan followed her through the tall gilded doors into the altar room. They paused briefly before the family deities, and then passed through the French salon, furnished with antiques imported from Paris, then through a succession of rooms, spacious, impersonal as museum exhibits, lined with antique cabinets of priceless porcelain, the walls hung with Chinese tapestries and scroll paintings, with old photographs and sketches of members of the Lee family. The Lees were Sunii's family. No one could recall her husband's name.

Of Chee Laan's grandfather there was not one single portrait. For the first time, this struck her as odd. Before, she had just accepted that it was so.

The two women came at last to the inner courtyard.

Beneath the flame tree, a maid squatted on her haunches, peeling and carving fruit for the table. Sunii Lee stopped. She studied the flame tree.

'My mother,' she said with a kind of wonder, 'she planted that tree. Now my mother is dead. Yet the tree lives on.' She shook her head.

Chee Laan waited just long enough for respect. Then she said, just above a whisper:

'How strange

That these white bones beside the river
Once were living men.'

She glanced at her grandmother's face quickly enough to catch the brief flicker of pleasure.

'My granddaughter has not forgotten her classical Chinese poetry.' Sunii nodded. They walked in silence through the courtyard toward the kitchens, whose vast charcoal ovens had remained unchanged since the house was built. Now they entered the cool dark room at the heart of the house, and memory opened before Chee Laan like a tunnel. Her childhood lay at the end of its dark shaft.

The carved screen still stood in the corner. As a small child, driven by a precocious urge to know, to be able to categorise and dispose, it had been her hiding place—eavesdropping on her elders, hearing much that she did not understand, and more that she should not have heard.

In the darkness, the pale moon-glow of porcelain and the shimmer of mother-of-pearl made milky pools among the ornately carved wood.

'Sit!' Sunii motioned her to one of the high-backed dragon chairs, taking the other herself. 'Drink tea!' She clapped her hands. Ah Lee appeared immediately. She had hurried from the car to the kitchen. The delays before the deities and the flame tree had been calculated to save Ah Lee face, so she did not appear flustered or out of breath. Chee Laan noted with awe her grandmother's meticulous, all-seeing eye.

Now, in her element, bossy and barefoot once more, the old servant woman bustled in with tea and mooncakes. Chee Laan set out her homecoming gifts on the table. Ah Lee lit a candle before the ancestor shrine.

'See that we are not disturbed,' Sunii said. The old *amah* shuffled off into the darkness.

'Now, Chee Laan. What have you learned, after your year in Europe?'

Chee Laan spoke of the convent curriculum, of contacts made. She spoke pragmatically, curbing any gush of girlish anecdote. This was a serious auditing of accounts. Sunii Lee was assessing the return on her investment. And as she spoke, Chee Laan felt Europe receding, becoming unreal. Chee Laan explained that she had decided, once and for all, against a life dominated by religion, like her mother's, and that she had learned self-discipline and how to endure hardship and insults.

At last, Sunii raised her hand. 'It is well. Here in Bangkok, too, we move with the times. The Rachanee is to be expanded and refurbished...' She paused, glancing at Chee Laan reprovingly. 'Grimaces are unbecoming, Granddaughter. You must conquer this childish aversion. The Rachanee is a five-star hotel, recommended by the Chaîne des Rotisseries—one of the finest hotels in the Far East, the flagship of Lee Enterprises. I have moved my office there.' She looked into Chee Laan's face. Her tone became softer. 'What odd tricks memory plays! You were a tiny child when that unfortunate business occurred. Odd that you should remember, after all these years!'

Odder still, thought Chee Laan, smiling now, *if I should ever forget. Forget the girl who tried to help me, and was killed for it. Forget the sound she made. Forget my father's face, bloated and staring, the hideous catoy at his side, the lies they all told. They all lied, the grown-ups, lied through their teeth; even you, adored and fearsome grandmother!*

'It is time for you to enter the family business.' Sunii switched without warning to French, which she had mastered with the assistance of tutors sent by the Alliance Francaise. She had never set foot in France. 'The Rachanee is much improved. The new pool has fountains and wave machines. At night the fountains change colour as the organ changes key. There is a water ballet to entertain diners in the sub-aquarian dining area. A pool with live sharks, the spice of danger.' She laughed. 'Our new penthouse floor is unique. My architect has recreated the hanging gardens of Babylon. We also have aviaries with rare birds. Conservationists have recommended them, threatened species are breeding—excellent international publicity! In the new ballroom, three thousand people will dance. Fashionable *farang* artists, Madame Laila Drinkwater and the Baron Siegfried du Bas, are supervising decór.' She gave a small sigh of satisfaction.

'What do you have in mind for me?' Chee Laan asked.

Sunii paused in silent rebuke at this impatience. Then she said, 'Raising the profile. Advertisement. Television reaches only the Thai population. Resident *farangs* and big firms, tour operators, PR folk—they like radio. Their own chat, their own noisy music. They have local English-language networks here now. I have purchased airtime. You will be a "disc jockey".'

She switched to English and pronounced this exotic term with care and a tinge of pride, or perhaps, Chee Laan thought, disdain.

'The announcer for the Rachanee must speak *farang*. Be loyal to the family. Become the voice, then the face, of Lee Enterprises to the English-speaking world.' She switched to Thai. 'The Rachanee represents a major investment. It has to succeed. A large part of this success will depend upon you, Chee Laan.'

Chee Laan bowed. Recognising with some relief that she had passed all initial tests, however narrowly, she reverted with pleasure to speaking Chinese, as though she had won the right to return home. 'Honourable Father's Mother, I shall do my best.'

Sunii smiled. 'Social commitments do not grow easier for a business-woman alone, especially as the years pass. You will be my eyes and ears, you will go about in society, see and be seen where it matters.'

An objection would have been unthinkable. Chee Laan said mildly, 'For me, life in Bangkok has been this house, ancestors, the wall hangings for summer and winter. Once the main gate is closed, the other world does not exist.'

Sunii nodded, not displeased. 'It is good to honour the family. Yet outside contacts are vital. They are the lifeblood of business. To mix business and pleasure, as foreign devils do, is foolish. One's business should become one's pleasure. That is the Chinese way.'

She took a stiff white card from a side table and read, 'The British Council Representative and Mrs J Drinkwater…request the pleasure…to meet Dr Nathaniel Raven. You will attend, Granddaughter. Every such occasion, you will represent us. Next week, you start your radio show. Granddaughter disc jockey!'

'Unworthy,' gasped Chee Laan. 'I've never done anything like that before.'

Sunii Lee raised one eyebrow. 'You forget your manners, Granddaughter. These outbursts are intolerable! I have arranged for you to have training from an experienced announcer. We shall draft the commercial texts together, in the beginning, but you will make your own choice of music from the station library, give the programmes a personal character, build up an audience. One more thing: you will not use your Chinese name. One's Chinese name should be reserved for special occasions.'

'In Europe, they—the *farangs*—called me Julie.'

'Chu-lee. Infantile. Cute. Chu-lee. Yes. That will serve very well.'

'Who is to be my instructor?' Chee Laan asked.

'Colonel Sya Dam. An experienced broadcaster.'

Chee Laan recalled what she had heard about Sya Dam, and frowned in the dark room. 'What kind of man is he, *Tsu mu*? Do you know him?'

'Drink tea,' replied Sunii Lee. Rebuffed, Chee Laan felt, not for the first time, that she had been in danger of crossing an unseen line into forbidden territory. Conversations with her grandmother had always taken this course, governed by arcane and unknowable rules, taking one unawares with unsuspected twists and dead ends, like a maze. The tea tasted of smoke and jasmine; in her mouth the mooncakes melted like new snow. Sunii rose and walked to the cabinet. She unlocked a drawer and removed an object wrapped in silk. She handed it to Chee Laan, who saw to her surprise that it was a small revolver.

'You were not only at the convent with those religious women.'

'I was not.'

'Show me now what that man Fly-schurr taught you.'

Chee Laan weighed the gun in her hand. 'Where?'

'I will show you. Are you accustomed to live targets?'

'Some.'

'Then it is time.' Sunii was walking back toward the courtyard.

Chee Laan had a lump in her throat. She swallowed painfully. 'Shoot what?'

Sunii paused, reflecting. 'The target must be expendable, maybe the dog. It annoyed me by biting the cook; an intelligent animal should have more discernment. Though a brute, it has its uses.' She walked on, unhurried. They were almost at the steps leading down into the courtyard. 'But I have a more suitable target. I have become increasingly weary of your elder brother's antics. It is time to recall him to the path of duty.'

Chee Laan thought the yard was empty at first. Then she saw the maidservant leaning against the flame tree. The bowl of fruit and the knife lay on the ground where she had dropped them. A stocky figure was leaning over the girl. His right arm braced against the tree trunk, his left hand groped brutally under the girl's sarong. His leering face was thrust close to the girl's, clearly relishing the spectacle of her pain and fear. Her neck twisted up and backward, like a calf at the slaughterer's; she rolled her eyes to avoid meeting his gaze. From her parted lips came a low keening. It was not a moan of pleasure.

'There is your target, Granddaughter. A rat. It is not necessary to kill it,' Sunii whispered close to Chee Laan's ear, 'unless, of course, you wish to.' She glided silently away toward the house.

Chee Laan took careful aim, two-handed. At that range, she was sure of her control. Lieutenant Fleischer had been uncharacteristically complimentary of her accuracy. 'Shoot the eyes out of a fucking wasp, China Doll!'

The report racketed deafeningly around the courtyard. Chee Laan's brother Pao leapt backward and spun round wildly, as if the bullet had done more than pass harmlessly through his sleeve. He stared about, eyes bulging. *Truly, he looks demented,* thought Chee Laan. Shrieking, the maid fled toward the servants' quarters, sobbing and wringing her hands. Pao Lee's glazed eyes focused; catching sight of his sister, he lumbered toward her. He was no longer a figure of fun. His heavy shoulders hunched menacingly. Chee Laan stood her ground, swinging in her hand the heavy gun, its ugly black mouth pointing into the ground.

'What you do that for? Crazy fucking bitch, back in town two seconds and already do something like that!' he bellowed, fury fanned by his own shame and terror, the desperate loss of face burning a hole in his head. Through his broad, upturned porcine nose and open mouth, the breath came in noisy puffs, sickly and sour-smelling. Sweat glistened on his chubby, pallid cheeks, green-tinged now with delayed shock, his fat legs beginning to tremble uncontrollably.

Coolly Chee Laan returned his stare. 'Well, hello, Brother. Still the same old Pao. Calm yourself!' She patted his cheek tauntingly.

He wrenched his head away. 'Don't tell me to calm myself, bitch! I do not choose to calm myself! You could have killed me!'

She blew imaginary smoke from the mouth of the gun as she had seen cowboys do in Western films. 'You are quite right. I could have killed you,' she said, looking him straight in the eye. 'I chose not to.'

Rage rendered him speechless. Chee Laan laughed.

From the cool depths of the big house they both heard, like the ripple of a distant stream, merry, fey, and entirely ladylike, their grandmother's laughter, echoing Chee Laan's own.

'Listen, brother. Do you hear that?' And as Pao shuddered uncontrollably with shock and dawning comprehension, she smiled.

The Drinkwater Residence, Bangkok, Thailand
April 1969

Raven
After my shower, I felt cooped up in the air-conditioned cocoon of the shuttered guest suite. I was powered by an adrenaline high. Even though my talk on environmental issues was merely a cover, I'd worked on it, tried my best to make it interesting. Once you're up there, confronting your audience, pride enters the picture. Even with the icy blast from the air conditioner, it felt like I was talking in a sauna. But there was a large, well-behaved audience. The speeches of introduction and thanks, professionally delivered by Laila's pleasant husband, were suitably effusive. The applause was respectful if not ecstatic. All in all, I felt that it had gone well.

Restless, I hurried back downstairs, although I was too early for the evening's reception. I padded about the pool, nursing the lime and water the silent attendant brought in a long, mercifully ice-filled glass, as I remembered the faces of my audience, politely interested, speculative, or cynical. I wondered where they all fit into this alien, heterogeneous community I'd been sent to analyse, for reasons that struck me, the more I thought about it, as increasingly implausible. What had induced these worthy citizens to sit patiently in uncomfortable clothes in the enervating heat, even with the incentive of free booze? I sensed that some of my audience were motivated not by a fascination with my subject, nor by the attractions of a prestigious social gathering offering copious liquid refreshment, but by an interest in myself—an interest possibly linked with the tiresome machinations that had brought me to this place against my will. The thought was unsettling.

Now Bangkok's beautiful people, dressed to impress and avid for sensation, would demand their pound of flesh. Eager to shake paws and be photographed with the visiting celebrity, whether he is a hellfire prophet, sword-swallower, or serial killer. One or two might ask intelligent questions; gossip columnists would solicit my views on Thai women, Thai boxing, Thai food. Everyone would ask about the latest European fashions, the prices in Bond Street shops, what music and restaurants were 'in', and who was currently holding the 'must-be-seen-at' parties.

They'd find me a disappointment. Nancy, on the other hand, would have been a fountain of information. On an impulse, I had slipped my favourite snapshot of her into the ridiculous Kit Kat holder, back to front and upside down. This childish action seemed to express my current feelings about our relationship. Perhaps later, when I was mellow, I'd contemplate her picture with maudlin sentimentality. Or, again, perhaps not.

Standing in the shadows, I allowed my gaze to follow the movements of the girl placing lighted mosquito coils, her bare feet gliding silently over the teak decking, the only sound the rustling of her long black sarong. As she placed each glowing coil beneath the low, ornately carved tables, her graceful swooping soothed my jaded eye.

My hostess, Laila Drinkwater, shattered the idyllic scene with her abrupt entrance. Shrieking, she leapt from the stairwell, loud and bright as a parakeet clattering out of a gum tree. She rushed at the maid and plucked at her clothing. 'Where is the new blouse I am buying you?'

The girl straightened up; her expression was mulish. 'New blouse, *mai dai*, no go, madame,' she declared boldly. 'Holes in. Can see my meat. Same-same bad low woman.'

'Low women do not wear best Swiss broderie anglaise!' Laila plucked a hibiscus from a bush near the veranda and thrust it behind the girl's ear. She took out a small cut-glass atomizer and sprayed the girl's arm. 'Lavender,' Laila said. 'Very calming.'

The girl backed away as if burnt. 'Smell like low woman!' she protested, rubbing her arm.

Now from the drive, where flaring torches flickered among the palm fronds, the first cars could be heard, sweeping into the drive, crunching over the gravel. Car doors slammed. The girl took up a tray with an ornate silver cigarette lighter and box and stalked toward the sound. 'Nee!' Laila stared after her receding back, rigid with indignation.

The Royal Thai Navy musicians were taking up position on a platform in the garden. After some preliminary squawks and hoots, they struck up 'Wienerblut'. As they gained in confidence, something of the decadent elegance of Alt Wien pervaded the dark garden. The glow of hanging lanterns and flares glanced off their gleaming brass instruments in the velvet blackness, reminding me of an open-air performance of Don Giovanni in the grounds of Schönbrunn. Here, at least, there were no Japanese tourists to sabotage the magic with their sheet-lightning flashbulbs. A theatrical blood-red moon hung large on the horizon. My sense of unreality deepened.

'Chinese!' Laila murmured, scowling after the grumpy maidservant. 'One always can tell. Clever, but mutinous. This Nee, she trusts nobody! See how she carries personally the cigar box, the lighter? You think this is a sense of duty? Pah! She fears guests pocket them and she gets the blame! Always three moves ahead, the Chinese!' The first wave of elegant guests surged in, clearly miscast as pilferers. 'I wonder who she's spying for?' Laila mused. 'No point to fire her before I find out!' She hurried off toward her guests.

Amid air-kissing, squeals of delight, and jovial braying, I recognised my disagreeable fellow passenger, the American matron. She had draped a spangled net over her foxy hair. I longed for the refuge once offered me by Mozart. This time she had a kid in tow, and a square, bull-necked purple man in the dust-coloured tropical dress uniform of a general of the United States Army. In his squashed snub face, liquid brown eyes brimmed innocently with good humour, like a pug pup. Seizing my hand, he pumped it vigorously, crying, 'Proud to know you, Dr Raven, sir! That was a fine talk, just fine! You surely brought nature alive! Blaze van Hooten, call me Blaze, this is my wife Taylor...'

The red-haired Mrs van Hooten and I eyed one another coolly. Neither of us referred to our previous meeting, as if by mutual consent. I felt an uncomfortable sense of complicity. She inclined her head stiffly, without speaking. The general continued unabashed, his speech punctuated by palpable italics and the occasional disconcerting exclamation mark mid-sentence.

'I hope you'll believe, Dr Raven, that I speak with the *utmost* sincerity when I say there's nothing to beat *culture*! Our country, the United States of America, for example!—currently conducts a *major* ongoing cultural operation—such bodies as the American Alumni Association, USIS, SEATO—and, let me preempt any questioning of my inclusion of SEATO by assuring you that the civil and military wings of the South East Asian Treaty Organisation have long since been integrated, with the emphasis *firmly* upon civilian and cultural activities!'

The general's lady cut in, with that imperious nasal whinny I remembered. 'The general is deeply committed to this adopted land of ours!' When she smiled, the masklike effect was startling. Her lips stretched around the words. 'These people are childlike. Delightfully so.' I remembered her curt dismissal of the young Thai stewardess, which had surprised me by its brusqueness. Until then, I had always found the ready courtesy of Americans impressive. Perhaps she read my thoughts, for she went on quickly, 'I consider helping these people as my duty. They are, by and large, entirely irresponsible; they display a terrifying disregard for human life. Lilies of the field, Dr Raven, frolicking away with no thought of the morrow, improvident.' The general watched his wife with unfeigned admiration, breathing heavily, his mouth slightly open.

'Taylor can command any platform, Dr Raven! Comes to fundraising, she's dynamite!'

'Entire villages,' Mrs van Hooten declared didactically, raising her eyebrows slightly. 'The American Ladies' Circle, of which I have the honour to be president, raised the funding to provide state-of-the-art sanitation to an entire upcountry community. Similarly, we financed the acquisition of a mobile ambulance unit to service rural areas.' She paused for the applause, but was distracted as she stared, deeply affronted, at Siegfried. He was descending the staircase, seraph, clad from head to toe in cloth-of-silver, twirling a silver-headed cane, and paused to pose provocatively at the foot of the stair. Laila embraced him, took his hand, and dragged him through the guests toward me. It became apparent, silhouetted against the torches, that Laila's diaphanous shift dress had no lining, and that her underclothes were skimpy, if, indeed, she were wearing any at all.

General van Hooten cleared his throat and fiddled with his collar as if it suddenly choked him. 'The Queen of Spades approaches,' he rumbled like a baited bear. 'Baron, my *arm*! Bought his title in Hong Kong, so I hear!'

His lady intercepted silkily, 'I do believe I see His Highness the prince right over there; come, Blaze! Excuse us!' The multicoloured throng absorbed the van Hootens. Siegfried, now at my elbow, beaming ingenuously, showed all his teeth, like a dog who had successfully routed a postman. He delicately plucked the glass from my hand, deposited it on the tray of a passing attendant, and replaced it with a full glass of peat-coloured liquid.

'Have no fear,' he murmured, close to my ear, 'it's the good stuff—and I should know! Nasty tongues will tell you I was once a waiter in a Hong Kong gay bar!'

He laid his index finger alongside his nose and cocked his head, as if waiting for me to ask if the rumour were true. But I merely attempted an expression of unconcerned gratitude.

Siegfried watched me. 'You do not betray curiosity,' he pronounced. 'This is good, especially here. The key to health and long life.' He moved closer. 'Whatever will make your stay among us more agreeable, I am at your disposition! See, already I deliver you from the clutches of *la générale*. She told you, no doubt, of her privies and her ambulance?'

I nodded, amused. Siegfried smirked like a satisfied cat.

'That precious ambulance. It stayed an ambulance for exactly three days— for the photo opportunities!'

'And then?' This time, obligingly, I prompted.

Siegfried closed his eyes and yawned, showing a marshmallow-pink tongue. 'They painted it pink, staffed it with floozies, and turned it into a mobile brothel. They say it paid for itself three times over the first month, touring the bases—and it was American money that purchased the facility in the first place! A sweet deal for somebody, eh?' He licked his lips appreciatively.

I studied the dark, exquisite face, seeking clues. 'You know someone who could verify that?'

Siegfried shrugged, suddenly bored by this intrusion of pragmatism. 'Many who could, not one who would. Everyone knows. How did it happen?' He shrugged, skilfully avoiding spilling his drink. 'Stolen, borrowed, hired out, handed over to the wrong general—who knows? The American knows it; he is CIA, he should know everything. But he will not tell Madame!' He giggled. 'These good ladies. They make the adventurous trip upcountry, and what do they find? The primitives rejoice in illiteracy and squalor! So, the good ladies, they collect money and they donate the toilettes of porcelain that flush. The village headman accepts, a photogenic child is photographed making pis-pis into the porcelain, too cute, everyone is content! Alas! Later, an observer visits the village, and there are the primitives all about as usual, making pis-pis and kaka behind the trees and in the river, in the most splendid naturalness. You see, none of the villages in this area have running water. So the flushing toilettes, it is an impracticality!'

'Why did no one think to mention that fact?'

Siegfried opened his eyes so the whites glistened all round the protruding dark irises, like licorice all-sorts. He clicked disapprovingly. 'What? Disappoint the charitable ladies? Too ungracious! Besides, although her dear little daughter Genty is a hophead tart, Madame has become a great lady. She is tutor to the young king.'

'What does she teach him?'

Siegfried shrugged. 'What you think, *chéri*? How to be an American. In case he ever needs to know. I must fetch Cedric. He will pout so if he misses the party, and Laila will not forgive me. Laila collects exotica. Cedric is part of her menagerie. Like me!'

He waggled his fingertips mischievously and was gone.

'Sir!' The van Hooten girl stood before me, clutching her glass in both hands, like a good child. Her demure Biba granny-print dress covered her ankles. The unfocussed gaze of her dilated pupils was unsettling. I recalled Siegfried's words, wondering how much was accurate, how much sheer malice.

'I did admire your talk,' she said breathlessly. 'I admire educated people. My mom...' She glanced furtively across the room. 'She's *fixated* on getting me educated. She was just in Switzerland, checking out schools. Do you know Switzerland, sir? What's it like?' The vague eyes ransacked my face. Her voice trailed off in an enervating fretful whine.

'Cute as a cuckoo clock, pretty as a chocolate box, runs on time.' In lazy clichés I dismissed Switzerland. The mother signaled imperiously to the girl across the room, and she drifted away listlessly. The woman was lecturing what Angel Fleischer and I, in our wicked old unreconstructed pre-PC days, would once have called a Slaphead—a rotund, stocky Siamese with a hairless skull and the inward, self-satisfied smirk of a carved idol. This was my first sight of Prince Premsakul, Pim's father. He now extricated himself from the group and tapped his way through the partygoers, forging a path for himself with the righteous self-absorption of a blind man, striking with his cane at skirts and legs, ignoring the winces and squeaks. But he was not blind. The eyes that fastened on mine had the liquorice darkness of leeches that would suck my blood and brains out through my own eye sockets. Then, mercifully, heavy lids dropped over his eyes like curtains, and I almost breathed a sigh of relief. He stood smiling up into my face.

'Phra Om Chaaw Premsakul,' he announced. 'Prince. In the old days, you'd have had to bang your head on the ground three times before addressing me. What larks, eh?' The vowels were vintage Oxford, the phatic elements old-world county. 'Jolly interesting talk, old boy, good show! Quite an honour, you clever young chaps taking an interest in our country.' He invested no attempt at sincerity in this conventional statement.

'Yours is an extremely fascinating country, Highness,' I countered as gamely as I could.

The prince sniffed, feigning deprecation. 'It has certainly inspired many poets. You are interested in poetry, Dr Raven, besides hard scientific facts?'

'Considerably, Excellency.' I've found these two words useful in many ambiguous situations. The prince's smile broadened; I was reminded of the glee of a toad watching a fat insect flit within range.

'Always delighted to meet a fellow scholar. Chance me arm at the odd spot of translation and composition meself—hardly what you might call a dab hand.' I tried to imagine circumstances under which I would wish to call anyone, anywhere, a dab hand. 'I fear me Siamese isn't really up to snuff, what?' The prince waved a golden paw. 'Drawback of a Western education, dontcha know? Still, I've turned out one or two trifles in me time that have been tolerably well received among the cognoscenti.'

I cocked an eyebrow, feigning fascination with this information.

'Oh, yes, indeed!' the prince simpered modestly. 'Transposition of early Thai poetry into contemporary English. My especial forte!' He beamed expectantly at me.

'Impressive!' This was the inadequate best I could come up with.

'Oh, I dunno. More of a knack than anything. Now, how does this strike you?' The prince, with lofty indifference to the circumstances—the rising hubbub of voices, the chink of glasses, the whoosh of strings and whirl of woodwind from the garden—now adopted a recitative pose, leaned backward, placed his feet more securely on the polished teak floor. Recognising the imminent rendition of a literary quotation, I braced myself. Even so, I was unprepared for what followed.

The Prince elocuted portentously:
'What ere be yon spot 'pon my Beloved's cheek?
What winsome gnat, naughty mosquito or merest midge
Did it there wantonly plant?'

'Course,' the prince added modestly, abandoning the declamatory mode for his own soft, lisping tones, as though forestalling my rapturous acclamation, 'you lose a lot in translation—rhythms of Thai poetry, inordinately complex. But you're a young academic with international contacts. No sense beating about the jolly old mulberry bush, what? Bit of a hobby-horse of mine, I'm afraid. Our great Thai poets deserve wider recognition in translation. Can't expect other poor beggars to learn Thai in order to appreciate 'em, what?' He giggled, then grew serious again. 'Now, if one's own poor efforts were deemed worthy of a wider audience…a word to the wise, pull a few strings…'

So that was the way the wind blew! The compulsion of fortune's darlings, the well-born and wealthy, to be valued for their achievement also.

The prince went on. 'Come to tea. Always appreciate a chance to chat with one's fellow literati.' He lowered his voice and pushed his round head closer to my ear. 'You would not find me ungrateful…'

'Father!'

It was then that I first noticed them, Princess Pim and Chee Laan Lee. They stood watching me and the fat little prince expectantly. I doubted they had recognised me on the plane, or that they did so now. Slender, sweet-faced Pim, with her cloud of soft flyaway hair, looked more European than Asian. Her face was long and her features straight and fine. Whereas all the other women were dressed to amaze in transparent gowns, sequins, and rich brocades, her dress was sober as a nun's habit, misty dark blue, its neck modest, the sleeves long. She wore no jewellery, and her long sweeping eyelashes and dusky golden complexion owed nothing to art.

'M'daughter, Pim,' said the prince with an airy wafture of the hand. His darting gaze glanced off his daughter's companion, and his glistening smile suddenly acquired a harder edge.

The princess was undeterred. 'Father, this is my friend Chee Laan Lee. We were in France together. You know her grandmother, Madame Sunii Lee.'

I looked at Chee Laan Lee and caught my breath. Her emerald green cheong sam poured over her shapely body like water, its gold-edged seams and frogs catching the light as she bowed her glossy black head, which rose from the high collar like a dark poppy. The defiance with which she paraded her traditional garment was not lost on me, nor was the irony of her deep obeisance for the prince. I observed, I admired, and I speculated.

'Charmed,' murmured Prince Premsakul without moving his lips, as if he were practising for a new career as a ventriloquist. 'Well, time one was making a going noise,' he turned to me, grinning jovially. 'Seen that brother of yours, Pim?'

But the young princess, taken aback by her father's brusque lack of cordiality, was staring toward the other side of the room, and what she saw caused her narrow lips to tighten into a grim expression of disapproval. People were moving aside, pointing, exclaiming. Around the edge of darkness a young leopard padded with its rolling gait, blinking in the lights, its jewelled collar flickering in the candlelight. On the end of the leopard's plaited buffalo-leather leash strolled Siegfried, looking insufferably smug.

'Meet Cedric!' he announced, and made a little bow.

The leopard stared round haughtily. Conversation ceased. Princess Pim spoke loudly into the sudden silence. Her voice was sharp with accusation. 'And how did you acquire Cedric, Baron? Did you commission poachers to kill his mother, or did you perhaps bribe a game warden in the Khow Yai Nature Reserve?' She stepped up to him, ignoring the leopard, consumed by anger. 'What will you do when he grows too strong, or you become tired of him? Try to palm him off on a zoo? Or will you simply put a bullet through his brain?' The leopard, disliking the sudden attention, gave a low growl, tentative but increasing in volume.

There was a silence. Then in quick succession came three sounds: Laila Drinkwater's high-pitched laughter, the leopard's growl, and the tapping of Prince Premsakul's cane on the polished floor. 'My daughter,' he turned his professional smile on the astonished guests, 'suffers from the effects of a Western education. Destabilises 'em. She's a little hothead! I'm convinced the fair sex is ill-suited by Dame Nature to cerebral challenge! Ah, the ladies!

How they keep us on our toes, with their sudden enthusiasms!' He sighed indulgently. His eyes glittered black.

The girl stamped her little foot. Ignoring the murmurs, she went on, undaunted, 'Stability! The situation in this country is not stable; it is restless. Everyone knows it. Especially since His Majesty King Rama's tragic death. So what do we do? We drink cocktails, we keep tame leopards, and we appoint yet another field marshal! How many field marshals does Thailand need to achieve stability? Four? Ten? A thousand? A thousand like Sya Dam?' She strode up to the astonished Siegfried and snatched the leopard's leash out of his hand.

Chee Laan Lee moved to the princess's side. I was just close enough to hear her say to the other girl, in low, urgent French, 'Don't mention his name. Not here, among so many. You know what can happen. They are everywhere.'

The leopard's head was between them, but he seemed to have calmed down. Pim reached out a trembling hand and rubbed his ear and he tilted his head like a domestic cat. She looked at the other girl. 'The time for caution is past, Chee Laan; someone has to speak out before it's too late.'

I moved closer and caught the note of urgency in the Chinese girl's voice as she laid her small hand over the princess's. 'Pim, you are putting yourself in danger.' The princess laughed lightly.

'From this leopard? He's not dangerous.'

Anger flashed in Chee Laan's eyes. 'You know that is not my meaning!'

'I know. You mean Sya Dam. But Chee Laan, my dear, I can take care of myself. In part thanks to that wretched bully Fleischer. And I have good comrades.'

'We are leaving,' her father commanded. He took the leash from his daughter and handed it ceremoniously back to Siegfried. The leopard looked from one to the other and lazily licked its lips. It occurred to me that it was drugged. Pim turned away from her father.

'Leave when you like,' she said. 'I will go home with Chee Laan.'

The prince's tone remained soft and lubricious, but he seemed ready to burst with rage. 'You return home with your family. Now!'

Siegfried laughed gaily. 'I think Cedric has enjoyed sufficient excitement for one day,' he said. 'Come, Cedric, say goodnight to the ladies and gentlemen.' The big cat looked at the people sleepily with his green-gold eyes. He had lost interest, and padded after Siegfried as docilely as a tabby cat up the carved teak stairs, his powerful haunches and barred golden tail swinging contemptuously.

Chee Laan looked up at me. I could see her wrestling with some familiar element, distracted from placing me by questions of how much I had overheard, and how much I might have understood. Then she smiled suddenly, a disarming social smile. She greeted me with a graceful *wai*, holding the glass between her slim fingers as she bowed her head. '*Khun Ajaan*, honourable teacher! A warmest welcome.' She half turned toward her friend. 'You must excuse us. Pim has high principles. She has been up all night, picketing the university to demonstrate against the sacking of liberal professors. She disapproves of keeping wild animals as pets. Siegfried's pet pussycat was the last straw for her.'

'Her father seems a little out of sorts, too,' I fished. Chee Laan held her glass of iced water against her cheek and looked up at me through her lashes.

'How strange, the death of all ambition,' she said. Even I, with my negligible knowledge of Chinese poetry, recognised the quote. 'But his ambition is far from dead. So. I think it is time I left. Pim and I will slink off together in disgrace.'

I did not want her to slink off. I wanted her to stay there, on the rim of that noisy festive gathering, on the edge of the dark garden where torches flickered here and there on the palm trees and the night creatures chirped and sang. I wanted her to stand looking at me, with her head tilted like a flower on a slender stem, and I wondered what the hell had gotten hold of me. I had admired her spirit and her grim tenacity in boot camp, grimy, bruised, humiliated, oozing blood and sweat in that hostile and unaccustomed environment. She was a poor little rich girl, bent on proving she could face a challenge, a spoiled but gutsy kid giving Fleischer's sadistic circus her best shot. This was different. She was different. Her poise and the ironic slant of her dark eyes mesmerised me. I loomed there like an ox and could think of nothing more intelligent to say than to ask:

'Are you in disgrace, too?'

She smiled, a dizzying smile, eyes disappearing behind their black-kohled lids, her cheeks blushing like a dark double dahlia. 'The Chinese are permanently in disgrace,' she said. 'Surely you noted how ecstatic His Highness was to make my acquaintance? Don't worry, my family are equally racist! This is an extremely complex society, despite its accommodating outward face!' Intrigued, on an impulse I set my drink down on a low table and escorted her to the exit. Laila stood, delaying the guests' departure with her laughter and vivacity, while her husband puffed on his pipe and managed to convey an impression both patient and congenial. As they passed the buffet tables, I stopped to stare. A little square woman was stuffing crab rolls into a crumpled brown paper bag held by a respectful servant boy. The crone peered at Chee Laan through bloodshot eyes behind pebble-thick glasses; her brow wrinkled like a Shar Pei puppy.

'Huh!' she grunted. 'Sunii Lee's First Granddaughter. So this is how you spend your time, with these social butterflies? Nothing like your grandmother to look at. Remarkably handsome woman, your grandmother...still, if you've an ounce of her brains, you'll do.' She rattled the bag. 'For my children.'

'You must have a lot of children,' I said, for something to say.

The old woman grunted again. 'Eighty-seven, at last count. Varies. Rapid falloff. Riddled with syph. Can't always save 'em, poor little brutes. Come and see my new clinic, if you've the stomach, Dr Raven. You might find it of interest. Change from gadding about at cocktail parties. Regards to honourable grandmother, daughter. Remarkably sound mind, for an old woman. Come on, useless boy, fresh fruit, that's what we need next. Over there.' She waddled off.

'Dr Pien. Our first woman doctor. Social reformer, professional pain in the side of the authorities,' Chee Laan said to me. 'She works with prostitutes.' She looked at me sideways, assessing my reaction.

'I'll bet she keeps pretty busy,' I said.

Chee Laan nodded. 'There are a hundred thousand prostitutes in this city, but no science museum.'

'I guess we all have our priorities.'

'Oh, they did intend to have a science museum. Under Pibul Songgram, the then-Minister of Education, General Luang Mangkornpromyothi collected five million ticals a year to build one. But then the general decided Thailand could not afford the luxury of a science museum. So he spent the money setting up a dance hall in Lumpini Park. He explained that the dance hall was, in fact, the projected museum. It was an interim arrangement to top up funding for the museum.'

'When was this?'

'Oh, about fifteen years ago. There's still no museum, but the dance hall's going strong.' Chee Laan smiled. Laila's Chinese servant was hovering nearby. Chee Laan placed her empty glass on the girl's tray. 'Honourable Nee,' she said courteously, 'I should like one more glass of *nam manaw*. Please make it yourself—you know so well how I like it.' The girl glided away obediently.

'I'd like to see that clinic,' I said. 'Would you show me?'

Chee Laan tilted her head, considering. 'Maybe. National mourning for the king ends tomorrow. People are still paying respects to his embalmed body in the temple, of course. That will go on for some time yet. But they haven't cancelled the Songkran procession.'

'Miss Lee,' I said impulsively, 'I couldn't help overhearing. Why did you warn the princess not to mention Colonel Sya?'

Her eyes were suddenly opaque as adamite.

'You know him, don't you?' I persisted. She nodded almost imperceptibly. 'Could you introduce me to him?' I was fully alert now, powered by the old urgency.

She stepped very close to me and smiled her secret smile into my face. 'No promises,' she said softly. But I felt some contract had been sealed between us.

'I'll see you to your car,' I said, reluctant to let her out of my sight. She nodded. I waited while she thanked her hosts. A white Mercedes, summoned by the attendant to the steps of the mansion, was purring in the driveway.

'I will send the car for you,' she said. 'At ten. I will show you the Songkran festival. Many foreigners find it picturesque. Goodnight.'

Genty van Hooten sprawled on the steps, displaying her bare brown legs. The attendants looked at her curiously from time to time but she ignored them, snorting with private mirth. A spliff glowed in her hand, and the scent of new-mown hay drifted upward against the colonnades. Seeing Chee Laan, she giggled. 'Hi, Missee Lee! Give my love to your bro. Sweet Pow-pow!'

Chee Laan stopped on the step, staring. 'You know my brother?'

Genty arched her back against the colonnade and rubbed her shoulders sensuously like a cat. 'Your brother, your dad…I know *everyone*!' She giggled.

'And everyone knows little Genty!'

Chee Laan Lee gave a tight little smile and walked to the car with her chin up. She moved with the dignity of a queen, but I had noticed the flash of anger and contempt in her eyes before the serene mask dropped once more.

Thoughts rattled round in my brain as I watched the big car glide away between the lighted flares and the ghostly palm trees. I felt something had broken loose inside my head. Despite her obvious intelligence, and maturity beyond her years, Chee Laan was a child. It was not merely a question of age. Her wealth and cultural background placed her in a different orbit. Besides, my life held enough complications as it was; this was one more I could certainly do without. But I rationalized swiftly: she could prove an invaluable contact. She knew Colonel Sya Dam, and she clearly suspected something of his ambitions. She spoke Thai and Chinese, and she had offered to take me out and about. It was an opportunity too good to miss. I could only guess at her motives. While I longed to impart to them a flattering interpretation, such as a dawning interest in me, the realist in me sternly rejected this. The girl must have some other agenda. Even so, the thought that I should see her again in less than a dozen hours' time filled me with an unreasoning and quite unreasonable happiness.

I breakfasted alone on the veranda, on fresh pineapple and good coffee. My host had already left for his office, after a friendly exchange of greetings. Laila was, I assumed, still enjoying her beauty sleep. After the guests had left, she and Siegfried had made a night of it, fetching out the chessboard and another bottle of champagne, squabbling animatedly into the small hours. The servant brought me a couple of English-language newspapers. I picked up the *Bangkok Herald* and began to read:

Traditional Festival Presages Year of Bloodshed and Strife

Despite the recent tragedy, which plunged the nation into sorrow, the Land of the Free this week celebrates the Annual Rains Festival of Songkran with the traditional Queen of Songkran's procession. Even the current official disapproval of beauty contests exempts the Queen of Songkran. She is not a luxury, but a necessity to ensure the nation's continued prosperity. This year, Songkran is even more significant than usual. For not only is this the dreaded Year of the Tiger, but all the omens are inauspicious, and Brahmins predict a stormy year of trouble and unrest.

Today in Parliament, Field Marshal Praphan declared that the relationship between omens and events was all a matter of interpretation. He went on to say...

I heard the creak of the compound gates and the stealthy crunch of wheels on the drive. I folded the *Bangkok Herald* neatly, leaving it on the teak table, and went out to the car. Chee Laan Lee had been as good as her word; it was a few minutes before ten. As I eased myself into the cream leather seat next to her, she flashed a brief smile and uttered a brief staccato command. The chauffeur nodded and swung the big car out into the traffic.

'Happy Year of the Tiger,' I said. 'Do you believe in omens?'

She frowned. Instead of replying, she tapped her index finger on the smoked glass window. I realised that this deflection of attention would henceforth be her method of dealing with questions she had no intention of answering.

'We are now passing the Ministry of Industry. See that seal? It represents the god Vishnu. You will note that he has four arms. They chose him because he is more grasping than any other god.' Outside the Ministry, street vendors had encamped with portable kitchens.

'One half of the city lives by selling food to the other half.' Chee Laan glanced quickly through the rear window, then looked at me with her head on one side, a gesture at once innocent and provocative. 'It's a Thai thing. You can be hungry for noodles even after a five-course dinner.'

She addressed the driver in rapid Chinese, and he swerved violently into the kerb, ignoring the hoots and shrieks of other road users. For a brief second his eyes met Chee Laan's in the rearview mirror. I could not read the expression, but felt the manoeuvre had more to it than a sudden whim.

People crowded around the charcoal braziers: a couple of kids on their way to school, smart in their blue and white uniforms, servants in black sarongs and white blouses, samlor drivers, coolies, and housewives were all there to eat. The other customers stepped aside for Chee Laan. She jumped the queue as by right, haggled, handed over satang coins, and plied me with delicacies. Banana fritters in fried rice jackets, sizzling paper-thin wafers of pork, sweetmeats in palm-leaf platters held together by paper clips. There was pink coconut jelly with lotus seeds, coconut ice cream, and sweet rice cakes, fluffy globes that melted in the mouth. We washed it all down with cold black tea out of a triangular plastic bag, from which a drinking straw protruded rakishly. I tasted every delicacy, telling myself it was in the interests of research, and thanking my stars my breakfast had been frugal. While I was thus occupied, she spoke briefly and urgently to the noodles vendor, and I saw her slip him a high-denomination note. He was a jovially cackling ogygian, gnarled and toothless, with ragged khaki Bermudas clothing his knobbly legs; upon his misshapen feet flapped green rubber flip-flops.

'Here you go, friend.' I handed over a pocketful of small change. The old man laid his crooked hands to his nose in salutation.

'That man's kerbside business,' Chee Laan remarked, 'has put his two sons through medical school in Australia. In the East, things are not always what they seem.'

'You seemed to be paying over the odds for a bowl of noodles,' I suggested, reflecting that I had in my Western arrogance patronisingly tipped someone I mistook for a pauper, and who could certainly buy me out. Chee Laan smiled.

'He hears everything.' Without warning, inexplicably to me, her eyes flashed black anger, before the smile was pinned in place. 'Now, this festival.' She launched into her professional voice, a smooth, fluent purr. 'In Thailand we celebrate many festivals. Festivals to mark the birth, enlightenment, and ascension of the Buddha. Festivals to mark the donning or putting away of the Buddha's seasonal robes, festivals of kites and of ploughing, festival of the giant swing. Now it is April; the rains are due, and we celebrate Songkran, which is today. Tuesday. Most inauspicious day.'

'What happens?'

She looked at me coolly, and replied, in her normal voice, 'If the day is auspicious, the Queen of Songkran dines on butterfat. But Tuesday means she gets to drink blood. She has to ride on a tiger. Also, the appearance of the god was ill-omened'

I was puzzled.

'At Songkran, the god appears in a form revealed only to the priests,' she explained. 'If he comes as a bowl of water, he comes in peace. There will be good rain and good harvests.'

'But he didn't come as a bowl of water?'

She shook her head. 'No. He came as a lighted lamp.'

'So that means?'

'Bloodshed.'

'Whose blood?'

She met my eyes impassively. 'Who knows? Gods are not required to be specific.'

She rubbed the corners of her lips with a fingernail to rid them of coconut crumbs. 'In the old days, they would ask the priest's blessing on jasmine flowers floating on water in a silver bowl; then the holy water was sprinkled on the hands and faces of the people you loved, to bring luck. Nowadays things tend to get a little livelier.'

The driver, who had eaten his own noodles squatting on the kerb a few discreet paces away, began polishing the wing mirror of the Mercedes to indicate his readiness to drive. A gaggle of giggling massage parlour girls clattered out of the red horseshoe door of a Chinese nightclub, then vanished again, carrying steaming bowls. The driver watched them speculatively.

'Good. Now we take a boat.'

Bangkok's canals were the arteries and the alimentary canal of the city's millions of inhabitants. Throughout history, the Thais would relocate their capital city to foil their traditional enemies, the Burmese and the Khmers. When the French made a bid for Ayudhaya in the seventeenth century, the Thais shifted their power centre to the swamplands of the central plain. Despite the lack of a proper port, this straggle of huts crouched on the tidal mud banks of the mighty Chao Phraya River grew into Bangkok, Village of the Olives, later nicknamed Krungtheep, City of Angels. Bangkok's network of khlongs comprised both arterial waterways, pulsating with every variety of river craft, and narrow capillaries that faded into lotus ponds and stagnant backyard pools. To the riverside dwellers, the khlongs were livelihood and leisure centre, drinking fountain, toothmug, washing machine, bathtub, garbage disposal, and lavatory pan.

As we alighted from the car, the helmsman of a wallowing tourist tub, sighting my foreign face, yelled excitedly: 'Heh heh Sirmadame! You like Floating Market Tour, Sirmadame? Khlong tour, number-one good price?'

Chee Laan signalled our lack of interest. The man spat contemptuously and shouted something I didn't catch but judged to be insulting. Chee Laan's face was closed and tight with anger as she led the way over a crumbling wooden bridge.

'What did he say?' I asked. 'You seem upset.'

She shook her head. 'I shouldn't be. Or at least I should not show it. I am sorry.'

'Well, what was it?'

'Oh, he just said you must be a poor man, with little face, if all you could afford was a Chinese mud turtle.' She laughed bitterly, and, as if that had released some poison, her features relaxed and she was, once more, dazzlingly beautiful. 'You'd think I'd be used to it by now, wouldn't you? After all, I've lived here forever.' She gave a wry, lopsided smile. 'These loveable Thais, with their funny little ways!'

She turned on her heel and set off along the road beside the water. I followed her. She hailed a prowling water taxi, and it swooped toward the bank, a slim craft dwarfed by its huge outboard motor. After a brief discussion between Chee Laan and the piratical boatman, we stepped aboard. Electric dragonflies hovered and flashed over the water. From the jetties of villas, servants fished for lunch. The scene shimmered in the heat, exotic yet tranquil. Here I was, going boating with a beautiful girl, yet I felt hot, irritated, and a rising anxiety arose within me, for which I had no good reason. But I soon found myself lost in fascinated contemplation of the scenes that unrolled before my eyes as we chugged up the waterway.

That boat trip up Khlong Bangkok Noi was an anthropological excursion. Colonies of khlong-dwellers lived their lives in full view of the busy canal. Handsome, fiery-eyed Persian Muslims challenged our scrutiny; Malay Muslims were too busy stuffing mattresses; Cambodians squatted among their fishhooks. The boat headed into a smaller tributary; from mud huts, flat-faced Central Plains Thais peered at us suspiciously. The Chinese villages hummed with activity: paler gold people, wiry as whipcord, were building boats, hawking sides of beef from sampans, twisting cord from banana fibre, and from wharf booths and chophouses the click of the abacus bounced clearly over the brown water. On the jetties trousered grandmothers batted resentfully at the torpid air with rattan fans.

We swept past temples, each one forming the hub of a community, their parking posts crowded with sampans. From the glassless windows of the temple schoolrooms young voices rose in chorus, chanting their lessons like mantras.

But not all the children were in school.

The first dishful of warm, brackish water, smelling of earth and rotten vegetation and universal putrefaction, took me full in the face, robbing me of breath. A shoal of riverside urchins mobbed the boat, some grabbing the tailboard, skinny arms inches away from the churning knives of the propellers. The toffee-coloured water streamed over their naked bodies. Many clutched a makeshift utensil—bowl, buffalo horn, hat, balloon, plastic bag—anything that could be made to squirt water with satisfying force at the big *farang* and the Jek girl in the boat. They swam, wriggling through the tawny water like tadpoles, and shrieked with hyena laughter and there wasn't a thing to do about it except join in, especially when Chee Laan stowed her handbag under the thwart and the boatman lashed the tiller, and both retaliated with the baler and an empty petrol tin. At one point we almost overbalanced and we fell against each other, wet, helpless with laughter. I wondered if she felt the electric charge. She disengaged herself quickly, without meeting my eyes.

As we left the boat, steam arose in clouds from the soaking clothes drying on our backs. I felt I had taken some kind of test. I was unsure whether or not I'd passed, but following the girl's small figure down the dusty lane, I sincerely hoped I had.

We turned a corner and were plunged instantly into bedlam. Terrifying cacophony made our eardrums ring. Shouts, whistles, drums and tambourines—we were swallowed up in a heaving throng of people who jumped, shrieked, whirled, danced, and ran on the spot, clapping their hands, waving, jeering, cheering. A full-blown procession was in progress.

The central figure was an enormous painted tiger created from plywood and papier-mâché, with dripping blood-red jaws. Perched on the creature's back, glorious in glitter and sequins, her head thrown back to balance her massy gold crown and her blue-black mane rippling to her waist, the queen waved in acknowledgement of the crowd's frenetic acclamation. I'd have known her anywhere.

'Salikaa!' Chee Laan exclaimed. She spat a single monosyllable. I did not need to understand Chinese to know it for an expletive. She turned and stalked away to the street corner. The big Mercedes was waiting. Looking at the seething mass of humanity that blocked the thoroughfare, I felt respect for the driver's skill in reaching the rendezvous on time. We got into the vehicle without attempting to speak against the din. As the driver eased in the gear lever, curiosity got the better of me.

'What's wrong?' I asked.

'The Queen of Songkran is usually chosen well in advance.' Despite her smooth, even tone, I could see she was angry. Her fingers drummed a beat on the upholstery. She kept her face averted, staring fixedly at the stragglers who frolicked in the procession's wake. 'Until last week, we were all in France.'

'Your friend must have made some speedy moves.'

Chee Laan shrugged, but her body was rigid with disapproval, and with the need to prevent any part of herself from touching any part of me as we shared the soft leather seat. She tucked herself into the corner, taking up no more room than a child.

'Salikaa's bandit cronies have powerful friends and much money. Beauty contest judges all have price tags in their eyes. Well, Salikaa's on her way.' She paused. 'Queen of Songkran is only the first step in Salikaa's battle plan. Power through beauty.' She shook herself, closing her eyes, then smiled, turning to face me again. 'Well, Bangkok is famous for its pretty girls. Now we visit the flipside. We call on the good doctor. I hope you are not easily upset by not-so-nice sights.' She looked at me, sizing me up.

'I'll endeavour not to faint,' I countered dryly, meeting her quizzical gaze.

'This car,' Chee Laan stated, 'it belongs to my grandmother. We must take it, because Asian girls who go about alone with a *farang* lose much face. But because it is Grandmother's car, for certain places it is not suitable. The driver has orders to wait two blocks away from the clinic.'

'Why?'

She shrugged. 'Dr Pien is a controversial figure. Some call her a saint, but by others she is shunned. All her life it was so. She had to tell lies to her family and run away to Europe and live by scrubbing steps in order to study medicine.'

'Yet now she has an official position?'

'When she came back, qualified, she waved her degrees in their faces and demanded a job. So they offered her only what no decent woman would accept. The VD clinics. Nine dollars a week. If she'd turned it down they'd have triumphed. She accepted.'

'A woman of rare courage! And the official reaction?'

'What you'd expect. Denounced as a national disgrace—obscene, unwomanly, a freak.'

'Women doctors encountered hostility in Britain, too, you know,' I suggested.

She shrugged again. 'Perhaps so. But long ago.'

The doctor's clinic looked like an ordinary house. The doctor, that diminutive bulldog, met us and led the way up a flight of wooden stairs to her surgery, which was painted bright turquoise and smelled strongly of powerful industrial disinfectant. 'Make like at home.' She nodded at chairs. Obediently, we sat, and awaited developments.

There was a knock at the door. A uniformed policeman entered, prodding before him three teenage girls, giggling with embarrassment. They squeaked and hid their faces when they saw Chee Laan and me. The policeman pulled a card from his pocket, cleared his throat and read aloud. Chee Laan translated: 'Charged with soliciting.' The doctor clapped her hands briskly and gestured to the girls, barking staccato commands. In turn, with bovine docility, they climbed onto the table and rolled their skirts up about their hips, uninhibited by notions of false modesty. Dr Pien performed her examinations with dispassionate brutality, as if drawing and stuffing chickens for the oven. 'Come, see!' She invited us to view the overt symptoms of disease for ourselves. We had to pretend to comply, but avoided looking, either at the organs displayed or at each other. The policeman rolled his eyes and slipped quietly out of the room. The doctor snorted. She positioned the three girls on low stools in front of her desk like kindergarten miscreants. From behind the desk she produced her educational graphics, large charts featuring pictures of deformed babies, middle-aged cripples, demented old people. No lurid detail had been omitted.

'Progress and effects of syphilis,' Chee Laan whispered helpfully. The girls giggled and hid their eyes, peeping at each other through their fingers.

'They do not believe me,' sighed the doctor. Leaning forward, she snatched the youngest girl's hands away from her face, a pretty, heavy face with dull brown eyes. 'Why do you do it, you silly girl?'

'Please, Honourable Doctor, Mama-san is good to us, and lying on our backs is easier than planting rice,' the girl bleated.

The doctor grunted. She said to me: 'These are young. Sixteen, fifteen maybe. They may have a chance. So long as the arresting officer stands by his testimony.' She clapped her hands twice. 'Now I ask the policeman to prefer formal charges. Then I can have them officially transferred to the rehab centre, I can cure them, they can learn a trade...'

The door opened. But instead of the policeman, a mountainous woman waddled into the room, beaming sociably. The girls flung themselves on her, clinging to her beefy arms, stroking her hands and face with small glad cries like pet gibbons.

The policeman sidled in. The Mama-san spread her hands. 'This policeman was mistaken. He never saw these girls before. He was on duty in quite another part of town.'

Dr Pien flashed a laser-sharp glare at the policemen. He seemed to shrivel, shuffling, then bent his head almost to the desk in salutation and shot out the door like a scared jackrabbit.

'I shall remember this,' the doctor said icily. The Mama-san bowed, as if complimented. She heaved her bulk out of the chair. The girls made graceful reverences to the doctor. She caught the youngest girl's wrist. 'What's your name, child?'

'Pawn, honourable doctor!' She scuttled out of the room, tittering shrilly.

'Fifteen years old,' Dr Pien sighed. 'Riddled with syph.'

We witnessed other things at the clinic: teenagers wearing the blazers of an expensive school, carrying their textbooks in leather straps, each boy holding a sheaf of yellow admission cards bound together with a thick brown elastic band. Each card represented a course of treatment for venereal disease. The doctor rapped their knuckles with a ruler and harangued them in Taechew. 'Sixteen years old! A disgrace! I don't want to see you here again!'

One boy whined, 'But if I miss my Friday night at the brothel, Honourable Father teases me—he tells the whole family I'm a sissy!'

'Huh!' scoffed another. 'I'm going to stop shagging Thai girls. They're all poxed; it's the GIs' fault. I'm going to get me one of their women instead. A yellow-haired round-eye. A real young fresh one. They're expensive, but they're worth it. I'm going to ask my dad where he gets them.'

On the way out we passed through the women-only waiting room. One lone old man sat there beside a dignified old lady, hiding her shame, her head enveloped in a shawl. The old man stared fixedly at his feet as though he expected them to disappear. Dr Pien clapped him on the shoulder and shouted in Thai: 'Why is Grandfather among the ladies? Has he not seen enough of ladies?'

There was a ripple of ribald tittering. The old lady, shrinking within her shroud, peered out with the sad eyes of a caged monkey.

'The old pig has been on the razzle and infected his poor wife. Now his grandson has ordered him to bring Granny to be cured. I can cure the poor old girl, but him, with his sick head, only the gods can cure!'

Another patient, a young girl, also hid her head in a green scarf, with an oddly incongruous design of horses' heads. A blonde lock sneaked out and she hooked it back behind an ear. She glanced up and then quickly turned away. Startled to see a Caucasian child in such surroundings, I stared at the familiar wide, unfocused grey eyes.

'My God, that's...'

Chee Laan nodded me to silence.

The little doctor shouted jovially, 'Well, my friends, I hope you enjoyed your sightseeing in our City of Angels!' She bustled off, harrying the ranks of the diseased.

We walked in silence to Chee Laan's Mercedes. With exaggerated nonchalance, the driver lolled in his buff uniform against the wing, polishing a headlamp with his handkerchief. Then I saw someone was sitting in the car. As we approached, a slim girl in the sober uniform of a house servant slid from the seat and saluted us. I recognized the hard narrow eyes, the mulish jaw. Chee Laan issued a spate of instructions in rapid Taechew, a language of which I knew nothing. Listening intently, I managed to pick up the Thai expression *Rachanee Songkran*, the Queen of Songkran; and a name, Salikaa.

Having observed Chee Laan's disgust at her friend Salikaa's antics, I was surprised that she should discuss the matter with a servant. All of a sudden the recollection came to me, and I knew where I had seen this girl before. She was the stroppy one who had defied Laila Drinkwater—she who suspected the social bigwigs of coveting their hostess's silver.

The girl nodded, saluted, and slipped away in the crowded street. Questions plagued me again. I risked a asking a few, those most likely to receive an answer.

'Those girls—Pawn, there's a name to conjure with! Young Genty! They're just kids. What will happen to them?'

Chee Laan shrugged. 'Carry on, of course. Until too old, too sick, too pockmarked. Maybe die of disease, maybe the abortionist kills them.' She looked up at me reprovingly. 'It is not worthwhile to learn the names of such people.'

The callousness was chilling. I swallowed hard before trying another tack.

'Those young lads…so the father was actively encouraging them to visit brothels?'

She laughed at my innocence. 'Naturally. Who do you imagine gave them the money?' She regarded me coolly. These things happen in the best of families. In my own, for instance.'

'What about young Genty van Hooten?' Seeing the young American girl in such circumstances had filled me with an astonished helplessness. It seemed both incongruous and profoundly sad. But why should her plight affect me more than the plight of the other sufferers who sought the doctor's help? I bit my lip. Was my response innately racist?

Chee Laan was less sentimental. 'How do you think Miss Gen-tee van Hooten'—she pronounced the name in an exaggerated tonal singsong, some obscure racial joke that escaped me—'finances her drug habit? She and her friends run an underage sex service. Much patronised by Chinese businessmen'

'God! But she can't be more than fourteen!'

She nodded. 'Caucasian juveniles are regarded as exotic.'

'Do her parents know?'

'I am sure her mother does not know. Is it not strange, how people from republican countries are entranced by royalty? Madame van Hooten cares for nobody but the Princess Regent. She is obsessed with her. '

'How about the general? Does he know?'

'He is CIA, so he knows many things. But not, I think, about his daughter.' She beamed again, her head tipping sideways, the dark eyes dancing. 'We have had a useful day, yes?'

Interesting, I thought. Not useful, in the sense that it seemed to have brought me no nearer to meeting Sya Dam. I was wondering how to mention this tactfully, when she said:

'I will be in touch.'

Whatever deals she had conducted as she shepherded the *farang* visitor, struck dumb with wonder at the mysterious East, her good humour was apparently restored.

As I changed for dinner that night, I could not get the Chinese girl's dazzling smile out of my thoughts. Cursing myself for a middle-aged fool, I decided it was high time to get Nancy's picture out. Nothing so crass as comparisons. Nor did I need a photograph to revive my memory of Nancy—always vivid, although clouded with the unhappiness of our parting. I wanted to get a bearing on my life again. I rummaged in the drawer where I had stowed it. The picture still lay in the Kit Kat holder, still back to front. But something was different. I stared at it, puzzled. Then, suddenly, I knew. I felt cold and slightly sick.

The picture was no longer upside down.

Old, once-honed instincts arose, stiffening the fine hairs on my neck like hackles. I proceeded, in a frenzy, to investigate my belongings, my papers, my clothes.

Superficially, everything seemed just as before. But someone had been going through my possessions with great precision, and, except for the careless mistake with the photograph, fairly professionally. I lifted up my folded clothing, sniffing for the alien scent of the searcher. The photograph must have been removed, then replaced hastily. Perhaps the intruder had been disturbed. I cursed; had I slipped up, attracted attention through carelessness? Or had I changed the photograph myself and forgotten?

Fortunately, with a practical caution, I had purposefully left nothing to link me with anything but my cover story. It was natural that Dr Raven, visiting lecturer, should have a picture of his beloved. As I removed the snapshot, smoothed it out, and was about to replace it in my wallet—where, until the rift, I had carried it—I studied Nancy's elegant, spare features and realised with a shock that it seemed the face of a stranger. I seemed a stranger to myself at that moment, a stranger in a strange land.

I closed my wallet and slipped the photograph into the pocket of my suitcase. I sat down on the bed among my scattered possessions, dropped my head into my hands, and took stock of my position.

Someone had been in my room. Perhaps the same person who had straightened my bed, laid out fresh towels, placed orchids and foil-wrapped chocolates on my pillow and a newspaper on the bedside table. My thoughts were going round in circles. Chee Laan. Nancy. My undercover mission. The fact that someone had thought it worthwhile to snoop through my few possessions.

If a text is in front of my eyes, I feel compelled to read it. It is in most circumstances a fairly innocuous neurosis. I took up the newspaper and I read the article on the front page.

Thailand's Conscience Slates Beauty Circuses

This week Thailand's most delectable young misses gather in the City of Angels for the annual Miss Thailand contest.

Yet, if the country's most glamorous military personality, Colonel Sya Dam, has his way, it may soon be farewell to beauty contests as a way of life.

The 29-year-old colonel, who is of tribal origin, has been dubbed Thailand's Conscience for his courageous moral stance, including the denunciation of his own officers for corruption.

Now the righteous colonel has protested, in an open letter to the Minister of the Interior, that the current situation calls for austerity and self-sacrifice.

'How can a country ravaged by insurgents, flooded with refugees and agitators by its disloyal neighbours, its borders violated by infiltrators and terrorists payrolled by our communist foes, justify dissipating energy dallying with frivolous beauty pageants? This pandering to the light-minded exploiters of the vanity of foolish young girls must stop! It is a national disgrace. It is an insult to our gallant soldiers!' fulminates the fiery colonel.

> *Unofficial sources predict that in the light of such powerful opposition, the city's most exclusive venues may find themselves suddenly 'unavailable'. The Miss Thailand competition may find itself homeless.*
> *Colonel Sya Dam is not a man to be trifled with. Few care to risk his displeasure.*
>
> Siam Rath News

The blurred newsprint photo was captioned: *Colonel Sya Dam calls pageant a disgrace.*

I peered at the photograph. The uniform cap was pulled so far down that his eyes were concealed. Only the mighty square jawbone, the steel trap of the tightly closed lips, betrayed the character of the man. I was mildly surprised by the tone of the piece. Nothing I had heard about Sya Dam so far had suggested a role for him as moral crusader. A weariness flooded my veins. Everything seemed bewilderingly chimeric. Perhaps I was slowly learning about layered Asian subtleties. Or, more probably, I was enervated by the realisation that I never would. Like so many before me, I should flounder in this morass. Kipling got it right. 'East is east,' I murmured to myself. I had to learn the work by heart in school. Nowadays, of course, it would be deemed politically incorrect.

In a sudden attack of lassitude, I dropped the newspaper to the floor and lay back against the silk cushions and the carved teak headboard. I began to wonder when I would see Chee Laan again, what I would do when we met. How she would bring about a meeting with Sya Dam, and how that would play out. My head buzzing with conflicting impressions and desires, lulled by the hum of the air conditioner and the scent of the purple orchids I had placed in my tooth glass, I dropped off and snoozed.

Lee Residence, Bangkok

As Ah Lee listened to the account of Chee Laan and Raven's outing from her nephew the Lee chauffeur, her eyes grew hard and bright as abacus beads. She hissed her disapproval through the scarlet stubs of her remaining teeth.

When she brought Chee Laan her morning jasmine tea, she set the cup down with unnecessary force on the ebony table, her whole person rigid with outrage. A lifetime of subjugating her hair, now at last fading to battleship grey, had dragged her loose banana-coloured skin upward to her skull, pulling her eyes open in a permanent expression of childlike surprise. There seemed hardly enough skin left to afford decent coverage to her long mare's teeth, but she managed to purse her lips and avoided Chee Laan's eyes.

Ah Lee came from the old world and was proud of it. She no longer fled shrieking upon hearing Chee Laan's voice on the radio, hands over her ears, crying out that the girl's spirit had been stolen and put in a box. But she still regarded it as against nature. Sometimes Chee Laan caught the old woman studying her, as if assessing how much of her soul had been lost in her involvement with this newfangled medium.

"Thank you, Ah Lee." Chee Laan sipped her hot tea sedately and studied the old woman through the steam.

'Heap bad joss!' Ah Lee mumbled. 'Paint, scent, same-same low woman. Ride about all day in Honourable Old Lady's car with foreign devil. Eat foreign devil food—ice cream, coffee with cream, *cheese*.' She grimaced in disgust at this ultimate proof of depravity. 'Stink like foreign devil. Maybe now Little Miss ride in cage-go-up-and-down with *farang*, not gag at foreign-devil-cheese-eating-dead-man-decaying stink!'

Chee Laan remembered Raven's big sunburned hands hurling the water at the river urchins, the deep hearty ring of his laughter. Even the smell of him, musky-sweet, had not been so bad at all, once she was used to it.

'Something upset Ah Lee,' Chee Laan soothed. 'Will she tell her loving precious one?'

'Who cares for the troubles of an old woman? *Lambaak*, bad joss. Honourable Father and Honourable Old Lady,' panted Ah Lee, kneeling to retrieve Chee Laan's red silk slippers from beneath the bed.

Chee Laan set the tea on her little round inlaid table. 'I saw Father sent a whole carload of gold leaf to the Pratumwam temple.'

'Gold leaf, plump chickens, joss sticks,' Ah Lee recited, shaking her head, bedazzled by such extravagance. 'Honourable Father, mighty fierce, beat up on kitchen girl very bad. Doctor come. Much money for doctor to mend kitchen girl, more money for make doctor forget. Doctor, very clever man. Honourable Old Lady say fetch priests.'

'What did the priests say?'

'Priests, what do they ever say?' Ah Lee mimicked in singsong, '"Is your conscience clear?" Honourable Father shouts,' here she nodded vehemently, her topknot wobbling, '"I honour the gods. My spirit house is better furnished than my own. The spirits want for nothing, slaves, horses, cattle I give them—even elephants! Every year I burn Kitchen God, so He can take record of my good life, my well-conducted household to Heaven."'

Chee Laan smiled sceptically. Ah Lee noted the smile, and continued, this time in an elevated tone, with a certain grandeur. 'Honourable Old Lady say, "Well, Number One Son, I hope you smear plenty honey on that Kitchen God's lips so he speaks sweet words to the chairman of the gods."' She clapped her hands and rolled her eyes to the ceiling, reverting to her own hoarse staccato. 'Oh, the anger devil entered that man then. How he roared! Like a dragon, breathing foul fumes! But Honourable Old Lady, she fears neither dragons nor devils!' Ah Lee closed her eyes and spoke again in that soft, commanding tone quite unlike her natural voice. '"Are your accountants honest?"'

'What did he say to that?' Chee Laan snuggled down into the bed and regarded Ah Lee with fascination. Ah Lee, with the indelible memory of the illiterate, enjoyed recreating for an interested audience scenes she had witnessed as an invisible observer. Now the old servant slumped dramatically like a discarded puppet. She squinted up at Chee Laan and shrugged convulsively, with an air of aggravation. 'Who knows?' She clapped her hands loudly. Sound effects were important. 'Screen fall over. Honourable Old Lady says, "Ah Lee, worthless old skin, skulking behind screen? Shake carcass, go fetch tea!"'

'So you heard nothing more?' Chee Laan was disappointed.

Ah Lee refused to lose face by admitting to this defeat. She pattered over to the shuttered window and stooped to peek through the slats into the sunlit courtyard beyond. She clicked disapprovingly. 'No-good useless maid come now.'

'Nee?' Chee Laan sat bolt upright in the big carved bed. 'Send her up. She brings back my calligraphy books. I lent them to that foreign devil-woman with paint in her hair. Madame Drinkwater.'

Once admitted, Nee knelt by the bed and placed the books on the stool, squaring them delicately with a tap of her fingernail. Chee Laan regarded her with annoyance.

'Well?' she demanded. To show impatience was degrading. But, she reflected, she had fifty years to gain composure to equal *Tsu mu*'s.

Nee murmured tonelessly, 'I saw Queen of Songkran.'

'Where?'

'Riding Tiger, glittering crowns.' Nee rolled her eyes. Chee Laan swooped from her silk pillows and struck the girl's truculent face, her eyes narrowed into two black slits of rage.

'Don't talk nonsense! Tigers, crown! All Bangkok has seen that! That's not what I sent you to find out! Where is Salikaa living? I know you followed her as I told you; you were watched!' She forbore to mention the old noodles vendor.

Nee rubbed her cheek. Her hard eyes regarded Chee Laan calculatingly. 'Bad place, bad people,' she muttered. 'I know more, too. First Grandson…'

'Pao? My brother? What of him?'

'He visits Black Tiger. I have seen him. He takes messages. He thinks nobody knows.' She smiled evilly. The Lee servants held the self-indulgent youth in no high esteem.

'Pao? That's absurd! Who would trust him as a go-between? He's a donkey.'

Nee remained obstinately silent. Infuriated, Chee Laan leapt off the bed, seized the girl's hand and twisted the fingers upward so the joints cracked and the girl fell to the floor, screaming. Chee Laan clapped a hand over her mouth. 'Tell me,' she said.

At first she could make no sense of the spluttered syllables. Then she was incredulous, angry. She prodded the girl with her bare toe.

'Well, you found Salikaa. You will take me to her—but first I have business to attend to.'

Fifteen minutes later Chee Laan knocked on her grandmother's door. Sunii Lee, resplendent in a crimson *cheong sam* embroidered with golden dragons, was changing the joss sticks and jasmine of her shrine. She smiled at her granddaughter but her face showed strain.

It had taken Chee Laan five minutes of blackmail and intimidation to extract her father's accounts from his chief clerk, a toffee-complexioned, respectable-looking bureaucrat with a penchant for sexual exotica. Saved from prison by the powerful Lee family's intervention, he laid his professional talents at their disposal for minimal remuneration. He had not realized Little Miss was so well informed about his past. He left the office in shock, aiming for the nearest singsong house and a stiff Mekhong whisky.

The calculations took Chee Laan precisely eight minutes. She noted the figures down solely for the purposes of evidence. She was comfortable with figures; people posed more problems. 'My granddaughter calculates quicker than an abacus,' her grandmother often proudly exclaimed.

Now Chee Laan brandished the books accusingly. 'I expected to find irregularities, but not on this scale,' she said tightly. 'My own father! How could he?'

'Your father has no head for business,' Sunii sighed.

Chee Laan could not keep calm. 'And who has altered this entry, and this, to protect him? Who cares so much?'

'He is my son.' The admission was almost inaudible.

The enormity of the crime against the family washed over Chee Laan like a wave of nausea. 'He abandoned his filial rights when he set out to defraud the family!' she stormed. Her voice grew dark and harsh; even her grandmother's raised eyebrows could not deter her. 'He is just a puppet-man, a painted bird for whom you have created a gilded cage. Worse than a criminal, he is a fool.'

'He is your father!' The rebuke was sharp.

'The thought sickens me!' Chee Laan laughed mirthlessly. 'I know why he did it—his little pleasures, his whores and *catoys*, his opium and whisky and gambling, and every other damned thing. Selfish, self-indulgent... but how could you condone it?' Her voice was bitter. The older woman was silent, her face in shadow; Chee Laan thought perhaps she had finally overstepped the mark.

When Sunii spoke, not turning her head but still arranging her votive offerings, her voice was soft and threatening.

'You are quick-witted, Granddaughter. I did not tell you because parents must be respected. I expected you to discover this for yourself, and so you did. I am disappointed in my son.' She moved over to the shrine, and shook the jasmine and rose wreath gently. The heavy scent lay on the air like a tint of purple. 'Do not let me be disappointed in my granddaughter. Yesterday,' Sunii said, watching Chee Laan, 'a *farang* visited me. He sniffed these offertory flowers like a bird dog, great snuffs! So sacrilegious! Now, of course, I must throw them all away. These *farangs* are primitive brutes. No respect for ancestors. No dignity, no discipline.'

Her voice held a note of warning. She sat on her silk couch; Chee Laan, with the habit of childhood, crouched at her feet. Sunii took out the sweetmeat box. Its red lacquer was flaking a little now, since that day long ago when she had crammed Chee Laan's mouth until she could not breathe, the day of the kite girl's death. Chee Laan recognised its role as a ritual accessory to debate. She murmured thanks in their secret language. The sharp, guttural Hakka dialect so closely resembled classical Mandarin that Sunii Lee had been able to engage a Mandarin tutor for Chee Laan. She alone was permitted to address Sunii in comparatively direct terms, a unique privilege.

'If you had attended an ordinary Chinese school here in Mang-ko, Granddaughter, with state-produced, state-controlled textbooks, you would not have achieved such proficiency in Mandarin. They are so fearful of "racial glorification."'

They were silent, remembering. The Hakka, the Chinese Guest people, were accustomed to a turbulent existence characterised by extremes.

'My granddaughter has neither been brought up to be disrespectful nor to gallivant about the city with foreign devils like a low woman of no family.'

Chee Laan gasped at the suddenness of the attack. But Sunii Lee continued mercilessly:

'Remember the family's origins. We were once small, insignificant people in the eyes of the world; we are not Yip-in-Tsois, longtime shipping owners. We are Lees of Mang-ko; we carry knowledge of our own value in our hearts, but to others we always need to prove it. Beware of this foreigner, Granddaughter. Tell him nothing, put no trust in him. They are very charming in their rough-and-ready way, no doubt, but make no mistake. Not one of them is to be trusted. This one will get what he wants from the East. Then he will return to his devil-woman. They are cunning...'

'What devil-woman?'

Tsu mu took from her pocket book a photo. Chee Laan stared at it. Nancy Raven stared back, her high-cheekboned face and delicate aquiline nose perfectly matched with the craggy landscape in the background.

Chee Laan, forgetting to speak in a low tone to indicate respect and good breeding, demanded sharply, 'Who is this woman? Where did you get this?'

Sunii Lee did not deign to acknowledge the ill-bred insistence. Suddenly links and connections clicked into place. Without being told, Chee Laan knew instinctively that she was looking at some young woman who was important to Raven, and that the copied photo had been stolen, possibly by the servant Nee. But on whose orders? Nee's initiatives were invariably mercenary. Chee Laan baulked at the notion that her grandmother had taken such a dishonourable course.

Then with chilling certainty she knew who was to blame. Loathing for the Black Tiger swelled her breast. The relationship between her grandmother and General Sya had already puzzled and alarmed her. Now she thought of a possible way to cause a rift between them. She handed the photo back politely, cradling her right hand in her left as if it were a salver. She shrugged, and said with careful casualness, 'Who is this foreign devil-woman? Why are you showing her to me? I am not interested in these pale ghost women—I am interested only in business.'

Sunii Lee closed her eyes and inclined her head faintly in acknowledgement.

Chee Laan continued, 'We need good publicity, all we can get, for damage limitation. Such things cost money. You promised me a major say in all decisions regarding the Rachanee?'

'I did.' Sunii nodded gravely, but her gaze was watchful.

'I want to host the Miss Thailand competition at the Rachanee. '

'And invite the enmity of Sya Dam,' Sunii pondered. 'Every leading hotel has refused.'

'And they will all regret it. All the more publicity for the Rachanee.'

Sunii still looked thoughtful. 'Sya Dam will be a powerful enemy.'

Chee Laan shook her head. 'Power goes before a fall. The wise man does not attempt to appease the earthquake. He moves his house. We should be ready to cut loose.'

Sunii sighed. 'The responsibility is yours, Granddaughter. You run the Rachanee. But take care. Sya Dam is dangerous.'

Chee Laan looked her straight in the eye. 'I know he is. But I think he has powerful friends.' One glance at her grandmother's shocked face told her all she needed to know. She rose, bowing. 'Thank you, Grandmother.'

'Where are you going?'

Chee Laan smiled. 'To meet an old school chum. Catch up.'

Chee Laan dismissed the hired boat at the landing stage of the tiny house. She called softly, and Salikaa shrieked in reply, flashing out of the door like the bright bird for which she was named. 'Chee Laan! Welcome!' She clapped her hands frenziedly at the squat servant who stared, open-mouthed. 'Bring sweetmeats, imbecile, don't you see we have an honoured guest? Hurry, hurry!'

Chee Laan kicked off her Charles Jourdain pumps. The friends curled up on mats, the shocking-pink silk of the triangular cushions exactly matching Salikaa's miniskirt.

'Your Majesty the Queen of Songkran!' Chee Laan smiled. 'We—that is, I saw you. Very glam. Is it what you wanted?'

Salikaa laughed throatily. 'This is just the start! Vichai wanted to drag me off to the fortress, of course! But I refused. I said if I was buried alive down there, without ever trying my wings, I'd be discontented the rest of my life. I said, "You only accept into the Organisation warriors who've proved themselves, Vichai! A woman needs to prove herself too." Of course, he trotted out that old argument: "A good woman is supportive, she stays in the background; she is like the hind legs of the elephant!" Huh! What kind of a dumbum would waste foreign travel, schooling, clothes, on a Jumbo's arse, I said! So he said he'd give me one chance. Just one. It'll be enough to get me launched. I've been noticed—you saw the pictures?'

She dived under the low carved dining table. The well beneath was littered with newspaper cuttings and professional proofs. Salikaa scattered them on the floor like the falling leaves of some vast deciduous tree. Her smile was smug.

'Vichai sent two of his lieutenants to fix the rental of this place and hire the maid. She's a stupid cow, but too dumb to ask awkward questions.' Salikaa scooped up a handful of sunflower seeds from a nielloware bowl before pushing the bowl toward Chee Laan. She spoke indistinctly, her mouth full. 'And he appointed darling Tamsin, my personal bodyguard, who shatters butterflies for kicks and has a weakness for sequined bustiers!'

'Charming!'

Salikaa's eyes flashed. 'Tamsin is the sword of my vengeance.'

'How theatrical!' Chee Laan scoffed, but Salikaa's intensity was chilling.

A water taxi roared up, its bow wave surging against the bank. Like a heavy panther in a bad humour, a figure leapt ashore, landing on the wooden jetty, hurling some coins and an inventive obscenity at the boatman. Salikaa's bodyguard booted aside the mosquito screen. Seeing Chee Laan, he posed in a caricature of astonishment, open-mouthed, thrusting out his padded chest. Under the spiky jelled crest of black hair, his false eyelashes waved like the furry legs of tarantulas. Chee Laan glimpsed the gun strapped to the garter belt, momentarily exposed by a flick of his miniskirt. Tamsin inclined his head at Chee Laan and grunted an acknowledgement, unrolled the newspaper he was carrying, and jabbed a finger at the screaming headline. 'Read this, darling!'

Salikaa did not attempt introductions, but pounced on the newspaper and pored over it. As she read the article she emitted shrieks of rage. She hurled the newspaper away from her and kneeled, hunched on the cushions like a hyena at bay.

'Who is this priggish little swine? This Sya—a filthy Akha! A dog-eating, pig-fucking tribesman! They ought to lock them all up in reservations! They're nothing but animals!'

Tamsin smiled lazily. He lit a spliff and drew deep, leaning his head against the triangular cushion, his long golden legs stretched out before him. 'Reservations, darling? We'd have to feed them. No, extermination's the answer. Kinder, in the long run. Come on, darling, smile for Tamsin, you'll get lines on your pretty forehead. Let's all have a nice drink—Tamsin will fix it, then we needn't bother the Fat Sow! Besides, you haven't read the next bit. Pim's father, the dirty old dog.'

Salikaa retrieved the paper and read:

> 'Prince Premsakul, Minister of the Interior, told this reporter today, "Beauty contests are a harmless form of relaxation. Good fun for everyone, and they give these young girls an aim in life." Asked whether we could look forward to His Highness's own lovely daughter, Princess Pim, taking part in Miss Thailand, the prince replied that his daughter had other life aims. "She is the studious type, like myself." His Highness was immediately invited by the organisers of Miss Thailand Incorporated to join the selection committee, and graciously accepted. The event's venue remains undecided. The Oriental Hotel, the original venue, has reluctantly declared itself unable to stage the competition this year, owing to structural alterations to the ballroom...'

Salikaa's eyes were speculative. 'I wonder if the old pals act will count for anything, whether Pim would put in a word for me...supposing they can find a location, if all these yellow curs of hotel-keepers aren't scared off.' She broke off, biting the fuchsia lipstick off her curling lip and darting a glance at Chee Laan, but the scion of the Lee family hoteliers merely shrugged.

'Not a hope! Pim despises nepotism, and beauty contests are incompatible with her feminist ideals. Besides, Pim hates her father.'

'Well, he is a sly old snake.' Salikaa grinned, rising to her feet. 'I guess I'll just have to give him the glad eye, see if I can kindle a spark...that is, if there is a contest at all. If the grand hotels don't all close ranks like geese scenting the wild cat. They're all shit-scared of Sya Dam; they've all got closets bulging with skeletons they can't afford to have dragged into daylight. He'll stop at nothing to get his own way. I doubt if any hotelier would have the balls to risk confrontation with the Black Tiger!'

Chee Laan stretched luxuriously. 'Don't bet on it.'

Salikaa swung round and stared at her. 'What do you mean?'

Chee Laan smiled lazily. 'I'll offer them the Rachanee.'

Pat Pong Red Light District, Bangkok

Nee, the Chinese servant girl, had been thrilled to be summoned to meet with the great Colonel Sya Dam himself. She had made her way to the address that had been whispered to her by the street noodles seller. The address was not in a good part of town, Nee thought, but perhaps the great colonel had many small offices scattered around so he could keep an eye on things all over the city. The man who showed her up to the small room had been rougher than she had expected, and had looked her up and down in an unpleasant and familiar way. But she had been invited to sit, and a silent woman who did not greet her or meet her eye had brought tea.

Still dressed in the modest garb of a house servant, Nee perched awkwardly upon the sofa, knowing her true place was squatting beside the table on the wooden floor. A bamboo curtain separated the small room from an inner alcove where she could hear the great colonel speaking on the telephone.

Sya Dam listened to the harsh foreign voice on the other end of the line, and grunted with satisfaction. He held all the cards now, and could bide his time until the moment came for the one masterly play.

'Good,' he murmured into the phone. 'You know what has to be done.'

He put the phone down so softly that the girl seated in the next room, screened by the bamboo curtain, did not even look up from her tea. In consequence she was startled when Sya thrust the curtain aside and considered her with, despite himself, a tinge of regret. She was young, she had been loyal, and, more importantly, useful to himself and his secret ally, Sunii Lee. Certainly more so than that degenerate bladder of lard, Honourable First Grandson Pao. Not that she was pretty, this peasant; too dark, too coarse-complexioned, her wiry hair hacked too short to appeal to him, a man whose delight was winding long silken tresses around his hands, jerking mercilessly, exciting screams of pain.

It was unfortunate that Sunii's insufferable, meddling, *farang*-loving First Granddaughter was now alerted to the girl's activities, and also her Brother Pao's role. Sya needed to cut his losses fast, before this spying, tiresome fellow Raven got involved. Sunii Lee had told him about Raven. The bumbling professor act didn't have either of them fooled. Raven was heavy-duty goods, and Sya knew it. He also knew of Raven's association with Major Angel Fleischer. Perhaps an adversary worthy his steel at last! The thought excited him.

Pao Lee might meet with an accident later. For now, it was the servant girl's turn. To kill her here would leave him with the tiresome problem of disposal. He smiled as the perfect solution occurred to him.

'You are a good girl. It was right to tell me that Miss Lee has discovered that her grandmother and I are…friends, and that Master Pao has been of some use to us. Let us drink to the downfall of traitors,' he said. He poured a generous portion of liquor into the glass and held it out. Seeing the doubt in her eyes, he smiled reassuringly. He towered over her, a powerful, affable, irresistible presence. He raised his own glass and touched hers, and, obediently, as if mesmerised, she drank.

She was unaccustomed to strong liquor, but to her relief it didn't taste nearly as bad as she'd feared, and in a few moments she drained the glass. The effects were dramatic. She felt the floor lift and sway and buck, and she was too dizzy to protest when he filled the glass again. He leaned toward her.

'Nee,' he growled softly, his deep voice making her temples throb, setting up a buzzing echo in her brain. 'Nee, little one, mouse, do you know your letters? Can the little mouse read and write?' His face was very close now, blocking everything out, enormous. It was smooth and hairless; the shaven skull was smooth and clean and streamlined. He loomed in her vision like a great golden idol. In his face she read infinite wisdom and a godlike kindliness. His eyes were lazy yet calculating. What was he asking, whether she could read letters? Those meaningless pothooks and squiggles and whorls, like ferns or flying birds? Who did he take her for? Some rich Miss who had been to school? Perhaps he was offering to teach her, to help her rise in the world, to open up for her the treasure house of riches that education would bring. Slowly she shook her head from side to side, gazing at him in wonder and anticipation. He held her head in his hands, which looked soft but were strong as a bear's paws, and she knew now what he wanted. It would be an honour, so long as his love did not consume her in his divine fire.

She only began to struggle when he thrust his hand into her mouth and seized her tongue. Pulling it out between her teeth, he reached for the knife and plunged. To his annoyance he found a human tongue was so much larger than one expected. Before he had finished plunging and sawing, they were both drenched in blood.

He left the mutilated girl slumped unconscious across the blood-spattered sofa, washed his hands, and lifted the telephone receiver. Without announcing his name, he said, 'I have a plump young bird for you, one whose squawking will not disturb your rest.'

'How much?'

'Consider it a gift. For services rendered.'

'Young and voiceless. A valuable bird indeed,' replied the Mama-san. 'I shall remember your generosity. Someone will collect the precious fowl.'

'Tonight,' he said, adding, 'I know you will remember.' He opened the slatted door and walked down the dingy teak stairway into the night, whistling softly between his teeth.

Premsakul Residence, Bangkok

Across town, Prince Prem Premsakul was having the most serious conversation he had ever had with his only son. Neither of them was enjoying the experience.

The prince liked to keep busy, but his plans rarely included his children. His son Toom had requested a father-and-son chat about his future plans. After pointing out the inconvenience, the prince had summoned the young man to the spacious dressing room of the Premsakul mansion on the outskirts of Bangkok while he dressed for dinner. He had dismissed his valet with a wave of the hand and was now standing before his cheval glass, studying himself in profile, turning this way and that, and sucking in his spreading gut. Toom, still in his awe of his parent, hovered hesitantly in the doorway. As he outlined his future plans, he realised his hateful stammer had come back. Silently he cursed it, flushed with anger at his own inadequacy.

'Half-baked poppycock!' snapped the prince, pausing in his assessment of the three ties he was holding to glare at his son. 'Not another word!' He wagged his spherical head from side to side. 'Do you imagine that is why I sent you to Cambridge? To strike out on your own with these maverick johnnies? Scholarship boys, pack of ne'er-do-wells, Reds! All fancying yourselves Madame Curie!'

'But Honourable Father!' Prince Toom blurted out, then stopped, biting his lip. His soft dark hair flopped into his eyes, slipping under his glasses. He flicked it impatiently.

Prince Toom realised he must present a sorry spectacle. He had forgotten how easily his father could reduce him to the knock-kneed, short-sighted, asthmatic little boy he had once been, a boy who stuttered and snivelled, and frequently wet the bed. As he stood before his father in the attitude of a penitent, the bitter thought struck him that his Cambridge friends would not recognise him in this pathetic weakling. He had been the Prince of Cool to them, a nickname becoming for him. In his Cambridge laboratory Toom was skilled and decisive. With his friends and fellow scientists he was lighthearted and relaxed. His tutors, who had at first found his deferential manner cloying, had come to appreciate his dedication. Once success reinforced his self-confidence, they openly acknowledged his brilliance. It had come as a surprise to nobody at Cambridge when Toom and his colleague Jim Tompkins, a 'scholarship boy' who, moreover, had won additional research sponsorship from a minor but forward-looking pharmaceutical company, had made their great breakthrough. Naïvely, Toom had looked forward to this moment, when he would announce the marvellous news to his father. He had been convinced the prince would be delighted and proud, and, most importantly, supportive.

That morning he had shared his triumph with his sister, Pim, who had received it with delight, kissing him warmly. 'That's splendid, Toom! I'm so proud of you!'

'I'm going to tell *Khun Paw* now. Tonight, before we go out!' He grinned happily.

To his surprise, her face clouded. 'I don't know how he'll react, Toom. This discovery of yours could have all sorts of implications, commercial and political. Father's got a finger in lots of pies. Far more than we know.'

He stared at her. 'How do you mean?'

'Just tread carefully. Father may not be as overjoyed at your news as you hope.'

'That's crazy!' he'd cried, incredulous. 'You know how important this could be, Pim!'

'Yes. I do.' She'd stroked his cheek, gazing up at him with worried dark eyes.

'So how do I persuade Father? I want him to be proud of me. I want that, even more than I want—and need—his support!'

She'd gripped his hands, shaking them gently. 'Just take control, Toom. Let him see you as a rational, mature person. If he is discouraging, stand up for yourself. Be assertive, but keep calm. Don't let him upset you.' That was what Pim always tried to do, what both of Prince Premsakul's children strove to do, but they did not often succeed. Despite his suave exterior, their father was a determined man with a ruthless streak.

Now Toom focused on speaking slowly and clearly, fighting for control. 'Do you understand what I am telling you, Honourable Father? Jim and I have done it! We have found a cure, not only for hepatitis B, but potentially for a whole range of new lentiviruses, diseases we've just begun to research; it's a broad-spectrum drug and one that can be produced cheaply!'

'Most interesting, I am sure. Why exactly are you telling me this?' his father drawled with casual arrogance, raising his eyebrows.

'We need funding. This is a humanitarian project, not just another profit-making venture, extorting money from the desperate! The effects will be unimaginable!' In his excitement, overactive saliva glands caused a fine spray to start out of Toom's mouth. His father's brow contracted fastidiously, but Toom continued, his voice rising. 'I must go back to Cambridge as soon as possible! We think we've made a revolutionary discovery—another sexually transmitted condition that suppresses the immune system. It is potentially more virulent than anything we know!'

'I always supposed...' Prince Prem gazed into the distance, raising his eyebrows, his tone musing, '...that scientists dealt in hard facts, not sensationalism!'

'We have hard facts!' Toom countered, his words spilling over one another in his enthusiasm. He continued recklessly: 'There's been a death in St Louis, a black teenager. Jim's in contact with the path lab there, and they've analysed frozen tissue samples from the body. They've found something extraordinary, possibly a retrovirus, transmitted through zoonotic transfer. It may have been deliberately created, a biological weapon aimed against specific sectors of the community.'

'My dear boy! What are these ravings? Have you become a lunatic? Who on Earth would do such a thing?'

'The CIA, for example.'

'Oh, pishtush! To destroy whom?' The prince's tone was scornful.

Toom spread his hands wide and shrugged. His glasses trembled on his nose.

'I don't know!' he said impatiently. 'Blacks, for instance. Never mind—if we're right, this condition suggests what we call a "starburst phylogeny"—it undergoes rapid genetic variation. The implications are...' He struggled for control. 'It could assume pandemic proportions in next to no time. We're talking about the future of the world!'

His father studied him coolly, then considered again the ties still gripped in his plump hand. 'Let me explain something to you, Toom, my dear old chap.' He smoothed exasperation out of his voice. 'In your eyes I may not, perhaps, qualify as a humanitarian. But I am a realist. His Majesty King Rama is dead. There is, it is true, His Royal Highness the Crown Prince. But he is only fifteen. A child. And you, Toom, are his cousin. Older, more intelligent, with an unblemished record.'

Toom stared at his father. 'What do you mean?'

Prince Premsakul sighed, as if dealing with a wilfully obtuse servant. 'In such cases, elections are not unheard of. You are a Prince of the Blood, you are personable, you could be popular if you exerted yourself. Your prospects are spectacular.'

'I don't care!'

His father dropped two rejected ties on the floor for the valet to retrieve. He turned to face his son, stung by the young man's lack of respect. He spoke sharply. 'Don't give yourself airs, boy! Such elevation appears unlikely in the extreme, given your present behaviour! Spouting nonsense, prating on about "wonder drugs" to save the lives of worthless addicts, gutter dregs! It was a gross error of judgment, permitting you to study science. Science, pah! Stinks and alchemy and a lot of mumbo-jumbo; it's overheated your brain. I should have packed you off to do an MBA in the States.'

'I'm to take that as a no, then?' Toom asked dejectedly.

'I should put the whole thing right out of your mind, dear boy.' Prince Premsakul made a sweeping movement with his hand. His smooth, smiling face belied the forcefulness of the gesture. 'In any event, your student days are over. You will not be returning to Cambridge.' He glanced at his son's stunned expression and continued blandly, 'Your destiny lies here, in your own country. One cannot argue with destiny. To do so is presumptuous.'

Toom stared at him, uncomprehending. 'But, Father...the lives we could save!'

'My dear boy,' the prince interposed, 'one must retain one's sense of proportion. There are certain afflictions to which those who lead a base life are prey—unfortunate, perhaps, but it is so. Survival of the fittest, weakest go to the wall, isn't that the scientific view?'

'Th-that is bl-blatant cynicism!' Toom slammed his hand against the doorjamb in frustration, both with his father and with his own unshakeable stutter.

When he was a child, his father had him whipped when he stuttered, considering the speech impediment a sign of weak-mindedness. By the time he was five years old, Toom had come to share this negative view of himself. He had struggled to overcome both his low self-esteem and the stammer, which now ambushed him only rarely, in heated moments such as this, when he felt he was being deliberately misunderstood.

Prince Prem frowned. 'All is preordained by fate, my son. Those who lead a blameless life will have no fear.'

He raised his hands in smug fatalism, and turned away in dismissal. He sat down heavily in the silk-covered armchair, humming a little tune. His son stared at him, then shook his head, the big glasses dwarfing his slender face. Suddenly aware that his own chin was, disrespectfully, higher than his father's head, he squatted like a coolie on the Oriental rug before the prince's chair, and gazed up, his dark eyes burning in his pale face, pleading. His father patted his shoulder.

'You're a clever chap, Toom, old son. Jolly clever, in your way. Unfortunately, you have little understanding of political realities. Now go and dress yourself, or we shall be late. Punctuality is the politeness of princes,' he added virtuously, although he himself was often more than three hours late for his engagements, and both of them knew it.

Toom rose, threw up his arms in despair and left the room. His stomach was taut, his shoulders tense. 'I won't!' he muttered to himself furiously. 'I won't give it all up!'

When the sound of his son's departing footsteps died away, Prince Premsakul padded over to the door on his stockinged feet and locked it securely. Then he returned to the armchair, his face thoughtful. He lifted the telephone.

Bangkok, Thailand
1969

General Blaze van Hooten
When I put the phone down, my dignity and repose, as well as my digestion, had been demolished by a jackhammer. Prince Prem had hinted over the secure line at problems. I did not need problems. Clearly, we needed to thrash it out face to face. He had suggested we meet in a lunchtime dive favoured by local businessmen, off Rajdamnern Avenue. I felt the prince had to shoulder some of the blame for this tiresome boy of his. Giving a kid a chemistry set to play with is asking for trouble. Any growing boy is better off with a gun licence. Purges them of cockamamie notions like inventing cut-price cures for social diseases. Although, I mused, with three hundred American military personnel arriving in Bangkok every day for a five-day R&R break from Nam, and a hundred thousand hospitable ladies, social disease needed factoring in. We addressed it with sergeants' pep talks and the issuing of high-quality prophylactics. Everything was done to ensure that the men's visit was culturally enriching and educational.

As I got out of the car and raised my hand to greet the rotund figure of the prince, I recalled one grizzled sergeant telling me, 'Ain't nobody believe that shit anyway, Colonel! Besides, our boys are straight out of the tabernacle choir.' Then he added confidentially: 'This one guy I met, down from Nam, he hired four massage parlour girls, took 'em everywhere for five days—wined 'em, dined 'em, took 'em on the goddamn Floating Market Tour for godssakes. Spent a thousand bucks on 'em and borrowed another thousand from the R&R centre and flew back to Nam wearing a grin as wide as the Mississippi, and all he could say was, "Man, it was worth every damn cent!" Let's face it, Colonel: if you had to choose between that and five days in Hawaii with the missus, griping about the mortgage and junior's dental work, which would you choose?' He had me there!

Thailand's industrious sex workers and their problems were on my mind now as we walked out of the blazing sun into the underworld murk of the 'day-night-club'. Prince Premsakul instructed our chauffeurs to drive three times round the block. The way the city traffic was, even during the lunch hour, it gave us a good ninety minutes. It's not always sensible for recognisable vehicles to be seen parked around this city, especially official vehicles.

The club was so dim that even with the waiter's pencil torch guiding us to the table, we groped about blindly. I signalled to a hovering hostess and ordered a couple of beers, holding up two fingers. '*Song yaj!*'

I was aware the old prince despised beer, especially the local brew. I ordered it just to see how the royal courtesy would stand the irritation, hoping to glean more from our conversation by tipping him off balance at the outset. I also reckoned fetching our beers, tottering through the gloom on six-inch heels, would distract our transvestite attendant for a while. You never know who's listening in these joints, but you can bet your sweet ass somebody is.

On the small stage, in a pool of sickly light, what looked like a girl squealed an inappropriately sexual interpretation of one of the unsexiest hit songs ever, 'Born Free'.

'Bored flea,' the artist squeaked, 'flea at the window. Bored flea to furrow you hot.'

This made me laugh. The performer flashed a mean glare toward our table. I turned to my companion.

'There are millions of 'em, you know.' The prince's affected tone of deep concern didn't have me fooled for a minute.

I sighed. 'Forget them. In the unlikely event of a pandemic, the infected sector of the population must just be jettisoned. Believe you me, it's for your country's good, Prince. Any attempt at individual treatment would be futile. A criminal waste of resources.'

'But this young man who came to me—son of a faithful old retainer, clever chap, studied science and all that…'

Old retainer, my eye and Betty Martin, but it's somewhat difficult to say 'bullshit' to a Prince of the Blood. That is, if you want to stay on the right side of him, and I did. For now, anyway.

'He swears they can produce a miracle drug at a giveaway cost, in sufficient quantities to cure millions…'

I leaned forward, trying to gauge his expression. 'Sounds to me like a young man who's too clever for his own good,' I suggested. But my companion appeared preoccupied, eyeing the singer's short, rotating golden legs in their fishnet tights. I'm a leg man myself, but give me a long-stemmed Vegas showgirl any day. I returned to the attack. 'I suppose, Prince, you yourself financed this lad's education, and now you're regretting your generosity, huh?'

He stretched out his hand in a gesture expressing modesty and helplessness. 'One does what one can. *Noblesse oblige*, and all that, dontcha know?' If I hadn't known better, the old rogue would have had me fooled. 'Anyhow, this young chap claims he and his associates can produce this miracle drug at an affordable price. And more importantly, there's this new disease he claims to have discovered. Says it appears incurable, could decimate the world population…' He hesitated. 'Would you believe, he even suggested it could be man-made. Deliberately engineered.' He paused, his pensive gaze glued to the stage. ''Straordinary notion, don't you think, General? Few organizations would have either the foresight or the power…'

'Well, Prince,' I said, and I let a hard edge creep into my voice so he knew I meant business, 'I'd suggest your son forgets all about that. With all possible despatch. Pronto!'

He was mumbling now, and I had to strain to catch his drift over the whining singer. 'Young hothead…only hope no harm comes to him. His only crime the naïve enthusiasm of youth…'

I shifted my weight and tapped the ash off my cigarette. 'Harm? No call to dramatise the situation. But there are corporate interests to be protected. That's something you'll readily appreciate, Prince.' We sat in momentary silence. The girl on stage removed her sequined blouse and writhed around the microphone. It was a girl, after all, or else those were great implants. Impassively we watched the jiggling of her round, vulnerable breasts.

I decided to lay it on the line for him. 'What proportion of Thailand's foreign income is represented by wooden goods and jewellery?' I asked, and, without pausing for a reply, I supplied the answer. 'Some thirty per cent, I guess, a rough estimate. It's never advisable to compromise major interests. Now, if word of this got out—if American drug companies were to perceive some cheap wonder drug as a threat, and if, by the same token, it were to emanate from Thailand, we'd be looking at a massive tariff increase on Thai exports. Massive, potentially prohibitive.' I paused for a moment to let this sink in. The Asian mind is so devious it does not always recognise the beauty of a straightforward threat. 'It would cripple the economy. It would be much better to forget all about miracle cures and pandemics and all that jazz. It's hardly worth compromising Thailand's GNP, to say nothing of international goodwill, for the sake of a handful of deadbeat junkies.' I paused judiciously, and added, on a warmer, friendlier note, 'We've got our own junkies, back home, you know. We shovel them up off the streets like debris. They made their choices, they're stuck with 'em. After all, *que sera, sera*, eh? If you get sick from fooling around, you get sick. Divine retribution.'

The beer arrived.

'Can't fuck with karma, Your Highness!' I said. I scooped up a handful of the peanuts that accompanied our beer and tossed them one by one into my open mouth. The prince watched, though I sensed he disliked this small exhibition of vulgarity as much as he disliked the taste of beer. He appeared preoccupied, as though he were considering whether to speak out or bide his time. When he spoke, at last, I had the distinct impression it was not what he had originally intended, but it was sufficiently interesting for me to stop my clowning and give him my full attention.

'This Dr Raven,' he remarked conversationally. 'Jolly interesting chap. Wonderfully well-read Johnny, actually,' and I swear he smirked, though it could have been the lighting, or rather the lack of it, that created the illusion. 'He seemed rather taken with me own piffling labourings in the poetic vineyard!'

'Well, now, how d'ye like that?' I muttered encouragingly. Dr Nathaniel Raven had interested me, too. I felt there was more going on there than met the eye, but his story had checked out. He'd had a brief romantic fling with the French Foreign Legion in his youth. Oddly enough, he'd met up with Angel Fleischer there. Fleischer, now promoted to major and installed as AMA, informed me Raven had gone into documentary filmmaking, done

one or two interesting pieces, and now appeared to have sunk into academic obscurity as a university don.

'Dabbled in investigative journalism, you know,' the prince continued, moving the beer glass a little further away, but showing no more distaste than if it had been a chess piece in an undecided match. 'Fascinating stuff! Thailand.' Prince Premsakul sighed, feigning a fond self-deprecation. 'It's a funny, complex old place, and Dr Raven is rather the innocent abroad, what? Wouldn't you agree? One wouldn't want a chap like that to go poking his nose where it wasn't wanted, falling foul of undesirable elements…or worse, getting the wrong end of the stick. Wouldn't do at all.'

I decided that he was right about Raven. Innocence is dangerous, and if Raven got to know too much, he might shoot his mouth off to the wrong people. And the trouble with former investigative journalists is they never lose that nosy newshound's fatal curiosity. They can never leave things alone. If Raven got what the prince called the 'wrong end of the stick,' he could screw everything up, including the major developments I had been primed to expect—and would be held responsible for.

Moreover, although sending our friend Colonel Sya Dam to the States seemed to have achieved the desired result, I remained unconvinced, as I think many others did, of the colonel's true motives and allegiances. You'd have been publicly lynched if you'd dared to suggest it, in the face of the colonel's apparent obsessive loyalty to the Thai crown. Still, there was much about the late king's fatal accident that remained unexplained, at least to an old cynic like myself. On the face of it, there would appear to be no earthly reason for Sya Dam to wish his patron out of the way. But I reckoned old King Rama had known Sya too well. Intimate knowledge is always perceived as a threat by an ambitious man. I did not trust Sya Dam. But if some Limey freelancer were to have the ill luck, through stumbling into something that didn't concern him, to attract the unwanted attention of Sya Dam, he might just wake up dead. And such a contingency could have unfortunate, not to say catastrophic, consequences for all of us. So, upon mature consideration of all these factors in the course of sipping my beer, I decided the moment had come for me to make an executive decision. However reluctantly, I must take Raven under my wing and save him from himself. For the moment, anyway.

I had that very morning been ordered to investigate certain remote locations for their operational feasibility. The operation in question was top secret, and all I knew was that it was big—big enough to transform the entire international situation. My field study would take me upcountry, and I was looking forward to being on the open road between the jungle and the paddy fields under a blue, unpolluted sky.

'I'm going upcountry soon. Maybe I'll invite the good professor along. Spot of sightseeing. He can meet the interesting character who runs the American Mission, and see a little more of your wonderful country. Keep him out of Bangkok.'

The Northwest American Mission is on the Burmese border, in the heart of the Golden Triangle. Western hacks and paparazzi, superannuated hippies, aspiring drug mules, hopeful hopheads, and goggling gawpers from many nations regard this area with fascination. If Raven shared this universal curiosity, it would be better for everyone, including Raven himself, if he explored it under supervision.

Prince Premsakul smiled. The light on the stage was now a bilious violet colour, and his small pointed teeth glittered in his dark face like amethysts. 'I am sure Dr Raven would find such an excursion both enjoyable and informative. You Americans are so hospitable. It is a noble quality! As for that other business, I take your point entirely. There will be no trouble about it.'

'Excellent!' I grinned, swilled down my beer, and paid. That was how we left it.

Rajdamnern Avenue, Bangkok, Thailand

The prince's car was waiting outside the lunchtime club. The air conditioner was on full blast, and the interior was pleasantly cool. The chauffeur closed the door and Prince Premsakul settled back into the leather seat with a sigh of satisfaction. As the big car nosed out into the almost stationary traffic, he reflected on his meeting with the American. He hoped that he had, by alerting van Hooten, ensured support for his discouragement of Toom's rash endeavours, as well as ensuring protection for his son, if that foolish young man were to let anything slip about his groundbreaking discoveries. It would be convenient to have Raven removed from the scene for a while.

But, he mused, what would the general and his fox-haired lady say when they found out about their dear little daughter? Would the revelation alter the general's views on divine retribution? Miss Genty, that little cutie, Prince Premsakul reflected. Such an unlikely product of the unimaginable union of those two ugly *farangs*, the hairy pink peanut-chomping pig and the bony vixen with the waxwork face.

Genty was such a naughty little schoolgirl, such a tireless, inventive little minx, this all-American gum-chewing daughter, with braces on her teeth and the Mickey Mouse hair bobbles! She deserved her jolly good spankings! Such a pity, he thought wistfully, that pert little Genty, like all the others, would be used up so soon. That she could not continue forever young, healthy, and enthusiastic. Momentarily depressed by this reflection, he cheered himself up by speculating maliciously on the reactions of her fond parents when little Genty's luck ran out. If Toom were right, how would the gallant general react, the one who had so blithely written off millions of Thailand's indigenous sex workers?

Prince Premsakul smiled more widely than ever. How interesting life was! However, he reflected soberly, children were a trial, even one's own. Toom and Pim needed a sharp reminder. So difficult, rearing children in modern times, he mused, especially with a wife who was incapacitated by migraines so much of the time. No wonder a poor harassed father had to seek his diversions where he could find them.

He dabbed fastidiously at his lips with a small square of silk to rid them of the foul taste of Thai beer. The American had no doubt meant well, had intended his offering as a tribute to local products—but, like so much of what foreigners did, it was clumsy and misplaced. 'Not the faintest idea of what's what!' he murmured to himself. 'Not an inkling, poor dear chaps!' He tapped on the glass. The chauffeur had worked for the prince for many years. He nodded and swerved to the left, plunging the big car into the narrow backstreets, clearing coolies off the road with its blaring horn as it sped toward a familiar establishment.

Asian Highway, Northbound

Raven
I flipped the sunblind down, shielding my eyes from the white glare. Beside me, General Blaze van Hooten spun the wheel of his big black Chevrolet Impala expertly. He had dispensed with the services of his chauffeur for this trip of ours upcountry, and appeared to relish sitting behind the wheel himself. Plainly exhilarated, he radiated energy and bonhomie. When we finally emerged from the chaos of Bangkok and found ourselves on the open road, rushing eastward between brilliant green paddy fields, he thumped the wheel and emitted a cheery yell, like a Hollywood cowboy, and I grinned.

I was still mystified by his invitation. Was it just typical American friendliness, or was there more behind it? I was conscious that Sya Dam, the focus of my interest, remained in Bangkok. But I was curious to learn more about the country, both for my own interest and the purposes of Smith and his ilk. I needed to get away from Bangkok for a while, to consider my confused feelings about Nancy, and my new, unlikely awareness of Chee Laan Lee. I was haunted by thoughts of her, and in grave danger of making a first-class idiot of myself.

The general settled his bulk more comfortably behind the wheel. 'So long, Sin City!' he crowed. 'Sin City, ha! They all lay the blame on us, par for the course. Let me tell you, Raven, both the Chinese and the Thais have created Bangkok's reputation themselves. All the American presence ever did was inject hard currency into the situation. Hey—bastard!'

He broke off, cursing. A top-heavy truck, emblazoned with painted eyes and dangling jasmine leis, swerved halfway across the highway, shouldering the Chevrolet toward the deep bank down to the roadside khlong, where the buffalo wallowed and the snowy egrets stalked among the corpses of abandoned or burnt-out vehicles. Fortunately, like many Americans, van Hooten seemed to have been born clutching a steering wheel.

We made our first rest stop where a row of spikes marked the 450-mile-long frontier with Kampuchea. I studied them for a moment, pondering the gleaming white sphere that topped each spike. Realisation dawned on me slowly. They were human skulls, bleached white in the sun. Nausea made my head buzz in the heat, and bittersweet bile surged into my throat. Van Hooten glanced over his shoulder and nodded. 'Yup. Fugitives, gunned down by the frontier guards. There are hundreds who try, but the Khmer Rouge've got every inch of the frontier booby-trapped.'

'How many make it?'

'Maybe sixty a month.'

In the fierce sun, I was suddenly cold.

We returned to the car in silence and drove on, northwest now. I was still contemplating the haunting fence of skulls sometime later when, as if telepathically, van Hooten grunted.

'The Thais never used to be afraid of the Khmer,' he began. 'Traditionally, they got their slaves from Cambodia. These days, they've got a bad case of insurgency paranoia.'

'How come?' I still wondered what his game was, and where I fit in. But the more he talked, the more he would relax.

'You want the official version? Thailand discovered her insurgency problem in the early sixties.' His tone was conversational. 'Wheels were set in motion—economic and political—making counterinsurgency high priority, and rightly so. The threat to the Thai Constitution was openly sponsored by hostile powers outside the country. Communist infiltration had the express aim of undermining security and eroding Thai culture, including the freedom of the individual. Nowadays, every two-bit noodle seller is a dragonslayer, defending the fatherland from the Red Threat.' He paused, then added quickly, 'The whole situation has been inflamed by the fanaticism of one individual.' Correctly reading my silence as curiosity, he spat out the name: 'Sya Dam!'

'I gather refugees are hardly welcomed with open arms here,' I prompted.

He nodded emphatically. 'Right. Officially, "refugee" is read as "infiltrator or spy". After the French defeat at Dien Bien Phu in 1954, Thailand took in fifty thousand Viet refugees. Many are still active in the northeast today. Communist agitators, taking orders direct from Hanoi. Even before the boat people gave the whole world a headache, the UN maintained sixteen camps for more than one hundred thousand refugees from Indochina. The camps cost the UN eleven million a year. The Thais are better businessmen: they fine refugees as illegal immigrants. If they can't pay, they lock 'em up and throw away the key.'

'Lock them up where?'

'Why, right here!' the general declared, with the timing of a showman, hauling the Chevrolet violently off the highway and onto a red dirt track leading straight to the camp. Here, on the frontier between Thailand and Laos, an open-air cage held a listless horde of sad-looking people staring into space.

'Laotians. They're the lucky ones,' van Hooten said. 'The Thais don't mind Laotians in general. They call them "Black Thais", regard them as somewhat inferior ethnic cousins. They rob them blind while they're in the camp, of course—nothing personal, just business. When they need cheap labour for their own factories, they hire refugees. Refugees are less trouble than Thai labourers. Thais are wising up to their rights, getting uppity, the usual things: trade unions, social security, paid vacations. Whereas refugees are grateful. Everyone wins.'

I studied the Laotians. They didn't look as if they appreciated their good fortune. There was a commotion at the Border Patrol Police point. Van Hooten shrugged into his uniform jacket as we left the car and strolled over. A few police officers stood around, watching an emaciated Thai clad only in a ragged vest and greyish tattered pants. He was telling a dramatic tale with much gesticulation. The burly Thai police captain introduced himself to us. He pointed at the storyteller with his baton, proudly, as one exhibiting a rare and valuable animal. 'This man, Thai soldier, escape Pathet Lao. Pathet Lao, very bad people. This man work all-same pack animal. Human buffalo. Long time long time ne'er mind this man, drink only rice water.'

The man, following the exposition of his story with hot, dark eyes, nodded violently, and demonstrated vividly how sick he'd gotten of rice water. 'Only way not to be sick, this man pretend drinking Ovaltine,' the police captain concluded triumphantly.

It was a surreal moment. In Bangkok, every pig-iron fence around a new building site is plastered with posters featuring those curiously old-fashioned, Janet-and-John Ovaltine ads, red-cheeked kids with hair slides and Fairisle sweaters. Clearly, this nursery goodnight drink, in the Thai consciousness, rivalled Tiger Balm as a universal panacea.

'Fight again,' declared the Human Buffalo suddenly. He walked close to van Hooten and examined his uniform meticulously. 'But not side by side with American. American not understand war. American think off duty, boots off, gun down. Think only bad sportsman kills unarmed man eating ice cream. But guerrilla, very bad people, shoot plenty American with mouth full ice cream!'

'I think this man does not mean rudeness,' interjected the police captain anxiously.

'Sure, son,' van Hooten beamed. 'Well, men, *tempus fugit*, as the man said. Gotta hit the trail.'

As we drove off, van Hooten said, 'He's got a point—that Human Buffalo guy. There's an element of complacency. I guess many Americans are just too comfortable.' He laughed, a fat, rich, deep chuckle that suggested he was pretty comfortable himself.

We slept that night—uncomfortably—in a Chinese village hotel, its damp walls green with slime. Awakened at dawn by the screeching of jungle roosters, we breakfasted at the coffee shop in the dusty street: greasy cold rice saturated with putrid fish sauce, coffee like liquid varnish. An old man played plaintively on a three-stringed fiddle, and among the poultry and goats a group of saffron-robed monks walked in silent file, impassively accepting food in their bowls from the devout. In the opposite direction strode an elephant in silent majesty toward his day's work in the teak forest, his newly washed hide gleaming copper and blue.

'Poor Pastor Waddle, now.' Van Hooten rocked a little on his chair, regarding without enthusiasm the raw eggs served in two streaked glasses. The café owner, a toothless sage with betel-stained teeth, had set the eggs before us with pride. 'Preaching to the La-wa's no walk in the park, even for a dedicated man. The La-wa always ate missionaries, until the fulfilment of the prophecy.'

My uneasiness deepened. I shut my eyes and downed an egg, doing my best to pretend it was an oyster and I was in New Orleans after a long night, the bloodsong of the drums still throbbing in my ears. I failed dismally. 'Prophecy?' I repeated.

'The La-wa were deserted by their gods. Much like the rest of us.' Van Hooten sighed and fell silent for a moment. 'Difference was, they foretold a god would return, as a white man, mounted on a white mule, with a book in his hand, who would show no fear. So when a Caucasian doctor, riding a white mule, fell into one of their animal traps, they were about to terminate him until some smartass recalled the prophecy. So they fell down and worshipped him instead. Man hadn't shown fear because he was drunk as a skunk at the time. Much later, some busybody told the La-wa the truth, and they were sore as hell. That's why I need to check up on old Waddle. Make sure they haven't eaten him out of orneriness!' He grinned boyishly. 'Shattering illusions is dangerous, Raven; folks get mighty upset.'

We left the Chevrolet, guarded by locals after negotiations conducted by van Hooten in a mixture of pidgin Thai and sign language, and took to the water in a long-tail boat manned by a betel-chewing skeleton. As our boat roared up the river, I was struck by the deathly stillness of the landscape. I had expected the jungles of Thailand to teem with exotic wildlife. Brilliant tatters of bright blue snagged on the reeds. Seeing it, I cried, 'A kingfisher!' against the noise of the engine, only to be disappointed when it was just a rag. But there were more turquoise rags, and these had chestnut heads and moved independently of the breeze, and I realised that there were kingfishers after all. A few white herons and egrets flapped furiously, creating momentum to slip the water's muddy face. A flock of great hornbills clattered into the bamboo thicket on huge piebald wings. Rabid bats infested the cave shrines, jungle bees as big as birds, and bee-eater birds smaller than butterflies. Except for one curious squirrel, we saw no mammals, not even a rat. I'd seen more wildlife in Hyde Park.

'Locals like to hunt between rice harvests,' van Hooten shouted to my unspoken question. 'Any source of protein, and pow!' he mimicked, pointing his finger first at my stomach, lingering just too long for comfort, and then, grinning lazily, across the turgid stream at the peering squirrel. 'I think you're going to find Mae Sod interesting,' he said.

'Interesting how?' I asked. But he just put on one of those jovial, impenetrable smiles of his.

In Mae Sod, a market town on the banks of the Myawaddy River, which marks the border with Burma, people were going about their affairs casually, without curiosity. Down the gravel pathway leading to the riverside, an incongruous figure approached on a wavering course.

'Ah, behold, the man of God cometh,' van Hooten boomed, stepping from the river craft onto the muddy shore. The missionary was riding an old-fashioned lady's push-bike. He pedalled inexpertly and extremely slowly, wobbling to a degree that caused his sun helmet to bob up and down. Beneath the sun helmet his face gleamed with a rigid pinkness, like week-old ham. 'Well, Pastor? How goes it?' boomed the general.

'Welcome in the Lord's name, friends!' the pastor cried, dropping his bicycle in the dust. He seized our hands as though he would have dragged us to our knees there and then to offer up a prayer. 'Isn't this delightful? Come, my treasure has prepared refreshment!' I contemplated him in silence as, wheeling his cycle now, he walked slightly ahead of us through the narrow street. As if piqued by this scrutiny, he declared: 'My treasure, Patsri. She keeps house for me. The only soul I can be quite confident of having won for Jesus amongst the La-wa, I'm afraid. Historically, they are a people responsible for much mistreatment of God's servants. Most lamentably resistant to the Word.' He shook his head disconsolately. Van Hooten grunted and slapped the missionary's bony shoulder in a bracing manner.

Patsri, a vast dark woman, scorned us and refused to offer a respectful Thai greeting. In keeping with her status as one of the Saved, she shook our hands in a crippling grip and pointed imperiously to three bamboo chairs. 'I bring drink,' she announced.

'Tea?' Waddle suggested, smiling anxiously.

The woman clicked her teeth. 'No tea. Forget.'

'Oh, dear. You forgot to buy tea? But you know how I like my tea, Patsri,' he whined like a disappointed child.

'Ghost steal my shopping list.' She stared down at him implacably.

Waddle grew pinker than ever about the gills. He removed his sun helmet, setting it upon a glass-topped table. 'Now, Patsri, sheer superstitious nonsense! There are no ghosts!'

'No ghost, no Holy Ghost!' As we three men appeared silenced by this casuistry, she continued: 'Maybe Holy Ghost Himsef steal shopping list.' Waddle continued to glare as she placed tall, rough-edged glasses before us and filled them with 7-Up. No alternative was offered. I gritted my teeth and let the sickly fizz swill around them.

'So, how's life, Pastor?' the general asked, wiping his mouth.

Waddle looked depressed. 'Challenging. I wrestle constantly with Satan for the souls of these people, steeped in ignorance and superstition, and yet the Lord sees fit to visit other trials upon me. Prickly heat. Such a pestilence!'

'You always contrive to wring my heart, Waddle! Last time you were dying of gut-ache!'

The missionary winced. 'Ah, yes. I fear that affliction still recurs.' He wrinkled his pink nose, reminding me incongruously of a rabbit. Much later, I would discover that even as a corpse, Waddle, with his pink nose, his air of perplexed anxiety frozen in death, would resemble a white rabbit.

'Soon you'll have the diversion of the Asia rally,' van Hooten remarked.

Waddle's forehead contracted as in pain. 'All that dust, that loudness!'

'But you will be here for it?' van Hooten asked sharply.

Waddle groaned. 'Unfortunately. Now, let us break bread together.' He brightened. 'I warn you, I live simply—I share the people's deprivations.' Patsri now clattered noisily onto the table a selection of Thai hors d'oeuvres: toad mun, fried fish paste, the pink labia-shaped roots of ginger, and *kai yu maa*, black petrified eggs.

'Horse-piss eggs,' van Hooten translated, to Waddle's discomfort. 'Notice that special mouldy-leather consistency? Cure 'em in horse piss!'

Patsri, who, when not watching us eat, stared out of the window, now proclaimed: 'Ong he come! You want Patsri tell him you busy, *Nai*, huh?' Waddle jumped guiltily.

'Ong? Who in hell is Ong?' demanded van Hooten testily.

'Numbah ten lazy Burma-man,' the big woman said contemptuously. 'Bring ruby, *Nai* like. *Nai* like plenty!' She chuckled. The sound was fat but not cosy. She looked at Waddle. 'You want Patsri tell Ong, *Nai* got plenty satang, now friends come?' At his look of indecision she shook her large head from side to side derisively and stalked with massive dignity through the mosquito screen.

'Twinings. That's right, isn't it?' Van Hooten took from his pocket a small, square tea canister. He handed it to Waddle, who cheered up, but said cautiously, 'Never can tell till you get the lid off.' I half-expected the missionary to open his gift there and then, in view of the old-maidish fuss he had kicked up about tea earlier. I wondered about the canister, and would have liked to examine it more closely. I also wondered what it was van Hooten wanted to show me, and why he couldn't just spit it right out and have done with it.

The woman came back. She shook her head. 'Ong say frontier guards more tougher. Pick up de-fec-tor and pang!' She illustrated gunfire. 'Pigeon blood more rare.' I was surprised to find Burmese refugees and ruby smugglers so openly discussed.

'Ong is a prey to the sin of covetousness,' Waddle reproved pettishly. 'I shall not be held to ransom. Tell him he'll have to peddle his wares elsewhere, if he can't be reasonable.'

'Tell him he no-good greedy heathen bugger,' Patsri nodded complicity. Waddle flinched.

When she had gone again, sighing mightily, he opened a small writing desk with a key, removed a sheaf of letters, and handed them to van Hooten. 'Post these for me when you get back to town. Up here, one might as well be sending despatches in a cleft stick!' He batted his eyelids, his mouth twitching with disapproval of godless inefficiency.

'You got it!' The big man threw a heavy arm about his neck. 'I'll leave you to your precious gems! I've got something Dr Raven ought to see.'

At last! I was suddenly reminded of the Mad Tea Party in Wonderland, where Alice exclaims: 'I'm glad they've begun asking riddles!' Except that there had already been too many riddles asked and unanswered. I rose and followed van Hooten through the looking glass.

The local police station in Mae Sod resembled a shack. We perched uncomfortably on tin folding chairs, which the officers had set out for us with many courteous gestures. We were witnessing the statement of a young Burmese defector. He was darker than the Thais, scrawnier too, but he stood his ground as he declared his reasons for fleeing a totalitarian regime.

'In Thailand, the Land of the Free, human rights are safeguarded! I renounce communism and all running dogs of Peking!' he recited confidently. He had been taken into custody, but he had not yet been chained. Indeed, he had been offered a chair, a rather grubby towel, and a cigarette, which he had prudently tucked behind his ear. He now sat dabbing his damp face and scanning the faces of his Siamese interrogators, occasionally darting covert glances at van Hooten and myself. His papers he had thoughtfully preserved from the waters of the Myawaddy in a waterproof tobacco pouch tied around his head.

'Good man!' van Hooten breezed. 'Now, there's an interesting story, eh, Raven? I guess you'd like to stick around, get the lowdown straight from the mule's mouth?' He gave a quirky smile, as if pleased with his attempt at irony, and left.

I knew he had his own agenda for the afternoon. So the Thai police were to babysit me while they interviewed the defector! However, I'd heard my fill of coached recitations of well-rehearsed statements in my time; I planned to embark on a few investigations of my own.

'Most interesting.' I stopped scribbling and waved my notebook at the Burmese and his guards. They nodded cordially. They had removed their caps and belts and sent out for noodles. They had ordered a bowl for the defector, too. Outside the station stood an army jeep, the key still in the ignition. Smiling, waving my notebook, and nodding toward the wooden guardhouse as if I were taking the vehicle by arrangement with the authorities within, I leapt into the driving seat, fired the engine, and set off along the single dirt road in what I hoped was the direction taken by van Hooten ten minutes previously.

The road ran red through the jungle like an open wound. The jeep jumped about the uneven track, roaring and skipping like a speedboat breasting a heavy swell. Suddenly the trees and road came to an abrupt stop. I slammed on the brakes just in time.

There was a tarmac landing strip, an incongruous scar across the bumpy clearing—sufficiently wide to accommodate a light aircraft, or the bulky helicopter that now occupied centre stage. I was congratulating myself on finding the jungle airfield when the blow came from behind, out of my line of vision. It was professional, a blow intended to incapacitate, not kill. It felt as if it cracked my skull like an eggshell and drove the sharp edges of bone into the soft centre of my brain. I pitched face-forward into the grass and lay still.

For several minutes I thought the darkness had swallowed the sun. I was sure the back of my head had caved in. Only later did I put an exploratory hand up to my nose. I felt it had been torn off my face in the fall, but when, eventually, I tweaked it gingerly, it appeared to be all in one piece. I lay motionless, the pain pulsating through my head, and feigned unconsciousness as I thought out my next move. From a dizzying height came the sound of van Hooten's voice, no longer lazy and cordial, but sharp with anger.

'Who in hell's responsible for this? This is not what I wanted.'

'But, sir…'

'Are you arguing the toss with me, soldier? Now help me get this man on his feet. And if he's sustained serious damage, you will wish your momma had remained intacta all her life, you hear me?'

His voice was close to my ear now. The tone was social, concerned.

'Raven! Dr Raven! Are you okay? What happened? Did you trip?'

Trip, hell! I was mugged! By some goon that did your bidding. But if an accident was to be the storyline, I would follow the script. I sat up slowly—very slowly—and put a hand to my head. I gazed up in the direction of the general's voice, straining my eyes, looking puzzled, which was not difficult, under the circumstances.

'I-I guess I must have done!'

'Well, you surely did not fall on your feet this time! Let's get you aboard, then. Can't leave you here!' Strong arms assisted me, not ungently.

The Chinook's rotors were already whipping up a gale; it was heavily armed and painted in camouflage. The uniformed Thai military escort stood by impassively as I was helped aboard. Van Hooten followed. The Thais were armed. The olive green of jungle fatigues seemed to my dazed eyes to echo their complexions. I must have been looking pretty green myself. They laid me facedown with my head half out the open door. They could have tipped me out like a bale of cloth without much effort, and this fact was not lost on me. As the helicopter roared and swung, parting the jungle's hair with its bluster, I ran through what I knew of the Golden Triangle. As well as practising my squiggles and singsong tones for Iolo's Thai language class, I had read up on the area. I knew its chief cash crop provided 12,000 tons of opium a year. It was cultivated by the tribesmen:

the Meo, the Lahu, and the Akha, and across the Burmese border, by the Shan, at altitudes of over 3,000 feet. Even at 4,500 feet, where no other crop would grow, the Meo could coax poppies from the dead earth. The semi-nomadic Meo were gypsies and, like gypsies the world over, traditionalists at the same time; they still cultivated the land by the immediately effective but ultimately wasteful *ray* method—slash, burn, and move on. The ashes of the ruined forests, relentlessly cleared and set alight, provide ideal fertiliser for the next opium crop. The bulk of the opium was intended for export to the American market, systematically expanded by enlisting the bargirls of Asian cities, who encouraged their soldier clients to opt for a little skullpop in place of bourbon and rye.

In the area's half-dozen processing plants, the base morphine and acetic acid bubbled away for six hours in a double boiler at 85 degrees centigrade. Base morphine was obtained by allowing the raw opium to simmer in water. After separation, processes utilizing quicklime isolated the morphine and codeine. Any impurities visible to the naked eye were eliminated by straining, then ammonium chloride was added, and presto—base morphine, crystallized powder the colour of milk chocolate.

The processing plants were rigorously supervised. Accidents might trigger explosions, resulting in loss of life, or worse, the destruction of valuable equipment—or, worst of all, the loss of valuable heroin. Besides, the American market accepted only eighty per cent pure products.

I scrambled to a sitting position. As they had not yet thrown me out of the helicopter, I assumed I was safe for now. I estimated we were flying some twelve miles inside Thailand, west of the Burmese border. Van Hooten pointed down at a cluster of rooftops. We circled above a small village. 'Know who lives down there?' the colonel yelled, his face straining manically against the noise and the vibration. 'Remnants of Chiang Kai-shek's gallant counterrevolutionary forces. Settled here back in 1949, after they were kicked out of Red China. Overpowered the local chieftains, took their women, settled the place.'

I wondered how much more he would confide, confirming what I knew already. Surely not how the warlords-turned-businessmen had been offered, and gratefully snatched, a sponsored airlift, relieving their major headache: the safeguarding, difficult even with five hundred men, of the ponderous trains which began their progress down from the mountains in March and June, transporting twenty tons of opium. Those twenty tons represented a mere seventh of the Meos' total crop. Now, the finished product could be flown to Vientiane in Laos by a special subdivision of Air America, and thence to Saigon aboard military aircraft. American aid programmes promoted the traffic by providing Thailand with ninety-one new airstrips. All arrangements for the financing, processing, and collection of the crop lay in the hands of Chinese racketeers, whose activities were protected by the shadow of the eagle's wing—the American military command.

If the public conscience pricked a little, the ritual offering of symbolic victims was periodically arranged: pawns in the game, drug mules, scapegoats, gullible, greedy Western backpackers—easy sacrifices. The lucky ones had their fifteen minutes of fame when their executions were broadcast on national television. The others…

The helicopter swung south again. Van Hooten wanted me to think he really trusted me. But the Agency didn't trust its own shadow. The less reassuring alternative was that it no longer mattered what I knew. I would never be able to tell; I had become expendable.

Van Hooten and I grinned at each other without cordiality.

Whatever the reason, someone didn't want there to be any waves in Northwest Thailand. Suddenly, and with absolute certainty, I knew there was more afoot than the opium trade.

The helicopter landed in a clearing and van Hooten and I climbed out and walked to where he had left the Chevrolet. I saw that in our absence it had been polished, the red dust scraped off hubcaps and radiator grill. A small group of men stood round it, grinning proudly in anticipation. Van Hooten duly brought out his wallet and dispersed largesse, received with many bows and expressions of appreciation, and we got in. Before he fired up the engine, van Hooten rooted around under the dashboard and produced a large cigar, which he lit. Its aroma was chokingly powerful in the closed car. I coughed pointedly.

Van Hooten laughed. 'How's the head?' he asked.

'I'll live.'

He grunted, not wasting his time on sympathy. 'Get that Waddle!' He shook his head. 'Him and his precious letters! You know what'll be so all-fire important? A strongbox rental for the precious rubies he's salting away. And, no doubt, one to our mutual friend Siegfried, the Queen of Spades. Siegfried arranges special entertainments for his pals. Nice little side line.' He began to croon a sentimental country ditty.

Neither of us saw the car coming before it slewed across our path. We almost hit it before the big Chevrolet fishtailed off the road and into the scrub, coming to a halt with its bonnet rocking over the canal.

'Ambush!' shouted van Hooten. 'Run for cover!' He threw open his door and tumbled out with more haste than dignity, and disappeared from view. Before I could follow suit, my own door was flung open and I found myself staring down the ugly, businesslike barrel of a gun I recognised and identified as the assassin's favourite, the Hecht 567. The gunman wore a rally driver's crash helmet and an orange flameproof suit, but I knew who it was. A pale blue eye glared through the goggles.

I trawled deep for some conciliatory words and came up gasping and empty. I steeled myself in anticipation of the gun's report, but a blind man couldn't have missed at that distance, so it was ridiculous to worry about the report—I'd never hear it. I shut my eyes. The gunman grunted, as if in surprise. I heard the car door slam, and as the security of the enclosed space cradled me, I opened my eyes warily. The gunman had disappeared. Behind the scrub I heard the full-throated scream of a highly tuned engine, the squeal of tyres.

I became aware of a thud against the window. A groping hand appeared, and then van Hooten's face, mouthing inaudibly. He forced the door open, thrust his head in, and shouted: 'Jeez, Raven—you okay? I thought you were dead!' He heaved his bulk into the seat and leaned back, breathing heavily. 'Fucking bandits!'

He punched the steering wheel several times, repeating his words. I sensed in him, however, the tension of frustration, rather than the jangling nerves of relief.

'What a relief, old buddy—I can't tell you!' Van Hooten eased the car into gear. 'Who knows what he wanted—the car radio, your change, your watch, anything that's not nailed down. No sense even going after the bastard— that's the trouble with this entire continent. Everything's so haphazard!'

I drew a deep breath and settled down to watch the road. I conjured up the fierce blue eye of the so-called bandit, but forbore to mention to my companion that, amongst a million men, even if they'd all been blue-eyed, I'd have recognised the mad stare of Angel Fleischer.

Afterward, van Hooten concentrated fiercely on the road. Thankfully, he had lost his cigar in the attack, and made no move to find another. His feigned bonhomie had evaporated. We travelled in silence. For all of these blessings I felt grateful. My head was pounding and I felt nauseated as well as bewildered by the ambush, the presence of Fleischer, and other unforeseen complexities.

Van Hooten brought the car to a squealing stop on the outskirts of the city by a public post box, leapt out and dropped the missionary's letters into it, and got back into the car. I felt sure this was not what Waddle had intended, and I wondered at the preacher's naïve faith in entrusting them to the colonel. He had surely expected his letters to be despatched through more secure military channels. But then, I reflected, all military mail was date-stamped as a matter of routine. The official stamp would establish a connection that Waddle might well be reluctant to broadcast.

I had to rally my waning forces, pull myself together and keep a promise to a lady. Seldom had I felt less like donning the motley, but I did want to see Chee Laan again.

Bangkok, Thailand

If only Thai journalists had a bit of style and less obvious modes of expression, thought Chee Laan Lee. She read out the article to her grandmother, assuming a scornful high voice to express her distaste. They were seated side by side in Sunii's sitting room. As Chee Laan read, the older woman watched her face. The tea was getting cold on the inlaid ebony table. They both ignored it.

> **Miss Thailand Contest Inaugurates Rachanee Ballroom**
> *His Highness Prince Premsakul has graciously consented to judge the year's most glamorous event. Co-judges will be movie prince Vilas Petchandra, Madame Laila Drinkwater, and Madame Sunii Lee, owner of the Rachanee Queen Hotel and doyenne of Bangkok's business community. Madame Lee's talented granddaughter, Miss Chee Laan Lee, will compere the dazzling show. Recently returned from her studies in Europe, Chee Laan's double life as PR girl for Lee Enterprises and popular disc jockey 'Julie' (catch her show on Radio Tor Tor Tor) makes full use of this attractive young lady's sparkling personality, sexy voice, and scintillating wit.*
>
> *Bangkok Post, Sanita's Social Diary*

'Absurd puff!' Chee Laan scowled. 'Scintillating!' She snorted indecorously. 'Still, as the lady said, I shouldn't care what they say about me as long as they keep talking about me.'

Her grandmother graciously ignored the snort. 'You quote who, Granddaughter?'

'Talullah Bankhead. An old *farang* lady.' Chee Laan shook the newspaper straight and folded it.

'Not all *farang* are stupid,' murmured Sunii.

'No,' Chee Laan said slowly. She was thinking of Raven. It seemed strange that she should ever have longed to be *farang*. She had yearned for Western freedom, but now knew that it was just another kind of servitude. And yet this *farang* had impressed her. At the thought that she would see Raven that evening, her heart sang. These new feelings were most confusing, and rather unwelcome. Chee Laan had always considered it great foolishness to invest one's happiness in another person. Foolish and dangerous. But she was happy, for now.

She jabbed a finger at the article again. 'I'm glad they didn't rake up my friendship with Salikaa, anyway. If she wins, everyone will say it was rigged. Unsuccessful "Miss" contestants have a nasty habit of hawking their hard-luck tales round the gutter-press.'

'Usually when the winner has granted favours to members of the judging panel.' *Tsu mu* nodded. 'If your friend does not win, I hope you will not be sad for her.'

'Oh, she'll win,' Chee Laan said. 'Unless the judges are blind, she'll win. Salikaa always gets what she wants. And she'd walk over dead bodies to get this.'

She rose and placed the newspaper on the table within her grandmother's reach, so that when Chee Laan had gone Sunii might check the article for herself.

'Excuse me, *Tsu mu*. I'll just go check on the arrival of the Kobe steaks. It's all very well having them flown in specially from Japan, as long as they make it to their destination and don't take detours into undesignated freezers.'

Sunii Lee smiled her concurrence.

Rachanee Hotel
Bangkok, Thailand

The Miss Thailand competition was in full swing. Raven had looked round in vain, hoping to see Chee Laan, but he assumed she was busy behind the scenes. Now he sat at table with the Drinkwater party, seduced, despite himself and his still-aching head, by the whole tasteless Saturnalia. He had to admit that the Rachanee had put on a good show.

The Kobe steaks tasted of the beer the industrious Japanese had massaged into the hides of the young cattle. The lobster *Pattaya* was served in the form of lotus blossoms; the butter and ice were carved in the shape of swans. The tables groaned under the weight of crystal, orchid bouquets, and towering ice sculptures of Garuda birds. Between each of the six courses, the twenty aspirants for the Miss Thailand crown strutted down the raised catwalk above the diners, sporting day outfits, then swimsuits, then evening dresses, each apparition more spectacular than the last. Each appearance was greeted by a storm of clapping and the clash of silver and glass as people dropped their cutlery and abandoned their drinks to applaud. Those with their mouths not crammed with food whistled and hooted. Others stamped their feet or hammered on the tables, making the ornaments jump. The contestants simpered and tittered and fluttered their false eyelashes. Only one of them swaggered arrogantly, swinging her hips in challenge.

From the moment she stepped forward, her eyes flashing, her blue-black mane tumbling free unlike the tortured coils of the other girls, Salikaa's victory was a foregone conclusion. She was more than beautiful. She was annihilating—she blazed like a torch. As her defeated rivals applauded dutifully, some with tears smudging their make-up, the crown was placed upon her head and the absurd crimson velvet mantle draped about her shoulders. Raven glimpsed for one second the blaze of triumph in the fierce black eyes. Then Salikaa dropped her head, covering her eyes as though overcome by emotion. When she raised her eyes, the modest smirk was tacked firmly in place. An awed child in a sequinned dress presented Salikaa with a bouquet of orchids. Prince Premsakul, the senior judge, took her hand and led her forward in triumph. Another storm of cheering and clapping erupted.

Seated at a nearby table, Raven saw Princess Pim shoot a worried glance at her brother. Prince Toom was leaning forward, breathing heavily, nostrils flaring. His glasses had slipped to the end of his nose. Previously, Raven had thought the young man appeared sulkily preoccupied; now he looked half mad. As he watched, he saw the young prince's sister nudge him sharply. When Toom turned to glare at her, she arched her eyebrows at him in query. He mouthed something that looked like 'She's amazing! A goddess!' Toom's eyes glazed over. Pim shook his arm, but he shrugged her off. He continued to devour Salikaa with his eyes, as though he had seen a vision.

Salikaa stood on the edge of the stage and surveyed her worshippers. Her searching gaze fell on Pim and Toom. In one fluid movement she stepped down and moved to their table. She plucked a white orchid from her bouquet. She *wai*'ed the siblings, then handed the orchid to Toom. She pressed his hand to her cheek and he snatched it back as though burnt, his eyes boring into hers. Prince Premsakul, his face rigid with controlled fury, waddled purposefully up behind Salikaa, took her arm and led her back to the stage. Pim looked down at her hands, folded in her lap; she was pale with embarrassment. Toom half rose and made as if to follow Salikaa, but Pim laid a restraining hand on his arm.

Salikaa looked back over her shoulder as she allowed herself to be led away, and she smiled. Scandalously, she blew a kiss to Toom, and then extended it to the whole shrieking audience.

Raven was not sure what he had witnessed. But he knew Salikaa had triumphed.

Tor Tor Tor Radio Studio
Royal Thai Army Base, Bangkok

Chee Laan Lee

Across the studio table of Tor Tor Tor Radio, I faced Salikaa. Once, we had been comrades—not long ago, though it seemed a lifetime. There was not a trace of affection in the way we looked at each other now. The green baize tabletop was bare except for my notebook, with a few scribbled questions listeners would be burning to ask the newly crowned Miss Thailand, who had just announced her engagement to a Prince of the Blood: Pim's brother, Toom.

Our initial mutual wariness had returned. The friendship forged in exceptional circumstances had evaporated. I might have regretted it, but life is too short for regrets. I have not been close to many people outside the family. Even within it, only *Tsu mu*, and she was a very private person. She kept her feelings in check. Even I did not know her thoughts, or why she secretly associated with Sya Dam.

Above us loomed the bulbous overhead microphone in its fuzzy covering. I drew a deep breath, then began to speak in the quick, breathless, girly voice I adopted for broadcasts. It wasn't a bit like my day voice, which was quite sharp and incisive, especially when speaking Mandarin or Hakka. But listeners expected female announcers to be ultra-feminine, eager to please, kittenish. Cute and unthreatening.

'Welcome to the programme, *Khun* Salikaa—whom we must soon call *Mom* Salikaa, as befits the bride of a Prince of the Blood,' I fawned.

Salikaa inclined her head regally. She'd probably been practising before a mirror. I continued smoothly,

'Queen of Songkran, then Miss Thailand—crowned, of course, at the magnificent Napalai Ballroom at the Rachanee Hotel.' There was our subliminal plug, deftly slipped in. 'And soon to be a princess—most young women would think you were living a fairy tale, a dream come true! Are you overwhelmed by your good fortune?'

I looked down at the table, unwilling to let her see that I knew how ruthlessly she had schemed and clawed and manipulated her way to success. I couldn't condemn her, because business is business, after all, but I felt bad for Pim and her brother. This engagement was proof of her heartlessness. Toom had no more chance of protecting himself against Salikaa than a mouse in a boa constrictor's cage. He was besotted with her, but I knew she would have no compunction about throwing him away when he ceased to be useful.

Salikaa purred huskily. 'Destiny has indeed smiled on me.' She smirked sweetly toward the microphone. I stifled the impulse to remind her tartly that this wasn't television; she could spare the simpers. She kept twisting the huge square-cut sapphire ring she'd boasted that Prince Toom had set upon her finger.

'Remind our listeners of how you and the prince first met. Are you an old friend of the family?' I cooed innocently. I knew that would annoy her. Upstart bandit brats don't move in court circles, and we both knew it. It was sheer malice. Pim would not have done it. But I wasn't Pim, and when I saw the angry tightening of Salikaa's sculpted jawline, I was glad.

'My fiancé's sister, the princess Pim, is my dearest friend,' Salikaa countered icily. 'We first met in France.' Pim, an eccentric royal revolutionary; my comrade in blood, sweat, and tears, and co-survivor of a thousand humiliations. She was my friend, too—more than Salikaa's.

'In France?' I prompted encouragingly, thinking of France, and Lieutenant Fleischer, and the mud. Oh, gods, how I recalled the mud! And that sadistic bully—how we loathed him, Pim and I. Although I had often wondered how Salikaa genuinely felt about Fleischer. Now her eyes challenged me boldly to mention any of this.

'Yes, in Paris, actually,' she drawled, 'when I was working as a fashion model.'

'Really?' I was so surprised by this bold fiction my eyebrows shot up.

'Yes. For Balmain—you have heard of the maestro? Even our dear Princess Regent patronises his salon.' Salikaa sighed wistfully. 'Monsieur Pierre was desperate for me to turn professional, to travel all over the world for private showings of his collection.'

I started to laugh appreciatively. Her talent for invention certainly made good radio. I effused admiringly. 'Most girls would have leapt at such a fabulous chance. But not you?'

Salikaa sighed even more histrionically. 'Ah, Julie, you know how it is. I was homesick. What are fame and fortune beside happiness? I am just a home girl at heart.' Salikaa flashed her perfect teeth in that healthy animal grin. Her right hand caressed the sapphire, tracing its contours like a blind person reading the beauty of a face.

'What beautiful sentiments, ladies and gentlemen, dear listeners! Truly, *Khun* Salikaa represents the ideal of Thai womanhood: modest and home-loving, despite her glamorous Cinderella story! Listeners will join me, *Khun* Salikaa, in wishing you every happiness, and congratulations!'

I'd got enough. Anything more would have been gilding the lily. Besides, another minute spent enduring her pretentious flummery would have severely compromised my professional equilibrium. I already felt like slapping her very hard. What the French call an *aller et retour*. I wrapped up the interview with my usual formula. My technicians, who had been shamelessly ogling Salikaa, crowded about us, murmuring, saluting Salikaa adoringly. She smiled and purred and tossed her mane, then flitted away through the studio door, kissing her hand and flicking her fingers at them like a movie star. I caught up with her in the corridor.

'How long do you intend to keep up this ridiculous charade?' I demanded.

She stared at me, all wide-eyed and innocent. 'I don't know what you mean.'

'Oh, yes, you do, Salikaa! Marrying Toom! Modelling in Paris—for Balmain! What made you say a thing like that?'

Salikaa threw her head back and laughed, no longer Salikaa the future princess, but the old, reckless Salikaa. Her hair, falling straight as a blue-black river from the upswept crown, cracked like a whip. 'You don't think the old toad would deny it, now I'm going to be a princess, and a potential customer. I'm going to buy a thousand gowns! That Philippine woman, Imelda Marcos, she's got a thousand pairs of shoes. I'll have ten thousand!' She grinned, eyes gleaming with ambition. 'I'm to be presented at court! Toom's snotty old family will have to accept me; they must sponsor my presentation, whether they like it or not. Toom is the heir. And I'm going to be his princess.' Her sensuous voice throbbed with excitement.

We'd reached the door. I paused in the doorway, looking hard at Salikaa, shielding my eyes from the white-hot sun with my Hermes document case. 'Pride goes before a fall, *Princess*!' I warned. There was something desperate about her triumphant attitude, as if she were seeking revenge for a lifetime of slights. I understood her, at that moment, better than ever before. Both of us had our catalogue of insults to avenge; both had experienced a peculiar upbringing, lacking no material comfort, but feeling ourselves outcasts. I shook my head. 'You're flying too near the sun, Salikaa, believe me!'

Salikaa gave her short, hard snort of derisive laughter. She was entranced by the glorious prospects before her. 'Toom's old man, old Prince Premsakul, thinks the Princess Regent might well appoint me to her entourage. They say she likes having pretty girls about her. Even,' Salikaa beamed smugly, 'ones prettier than herself.'

She clattered down the wooden steps on her high heels, and I followed her out into the dusty compound where our car waited. I felt helpless. I could not advise her about what went on at court. It's not a circle in which our people have ever been welcome. 'Take things calmly, just at first,' I suggested. 'Feel your way—ask Pim how to go about things. She knows how to behave in those circles, even if it goes against the grain.'

Without bothering to turn her head, Salikaa replied, 'Now, Chee Laan, dear, you know caution has never been my way. Where I come from, life itself is a dangerous game. You have to grab it by the balls.' She half turned, grasping my arm in a gesture apparently affectionate and spontaneous. 'As Fleischer is going to discover,' she hissed, 'if he stands in my way.'

'Fleischer?' I was staggered. 'What's Fleischer got to do with anything?'

'If I have my way, absolutely nothing,' she said through gritted teeth. I looked at her in surprise and I saw she meant it. Salikaa's stepfather probably knew many people who arranged unpleasant accidents for others, I reflected.

'Have you seen Fleischer? I heard he was here, in Bangkok, but…'

She cut short my astonishment. 'Now, Chee Laan, dear, those ghastly Americans are hosting an engagement party for us tonight. At the Baan Thai. Your family are invited. Also your long-nose round-eye friend, Raven. Toom's old man has taken him up in a big way, probably sniffing after some favour. I'd as soon trust a crocodile as Toom's darling dad.'

I was to attend the engagement dinner. The thought struck me that I could arrange to drive Raven there. I made up my mind to do that.

I suddenly became aware of the attention we were attracting. Soldiers, mechanics, and coolies, many clad in shorts and sandals, stood about in little groups, observing our every move, eyes gleaming, mouths open. 'Get in the car, Salikaa—people are staring,' I urged.

Tsu mu's Chinese chauffeur was looking tense, anxious at being at the centre of a crowd of Thais and burdened with responsibility for two young ladies and an expensive vehicle. Rigid with disapproval of Salikaa, whose presence appeared to make him instinctively uneasy, he saluted and flung the door wide. Salikaa swung round, blazing her smile at her audience.

'Get in the car, Salikaa!' I snapped with greater emphasis. I gave her a push in the small of the back. Not a gentle one.

Bangkok, Thailand

Raven

Despite the powerful air conditioner in Chee Laan's new sports car, I was sweating already—and unpleasantly conscious of the fact that beside me this girl, cool as a slice of lime and subtly fragrant as lilies, was not suffering as I was.

'Aren't we early?' I tugged at my bow tie, silently cursing the Western man's absurd dress code. How much happier I'd have felt in *burnous* or *pakomah*, so much more suitable for that brutal climate, so much more dignified than this penguin suit.

'Early is good manners.' Chee Laan swung the wheel smartly.

'Arriving before the appointed hour would be counted as a discourtesy in Europe.'

Chee Laan wriggled her shoulders in the short-sleeved green *cheong sam*.

'But we are not in Europe.' She laughed coolly. 'I am *over* Europe! Now it is as if I had never been away.' The casual response was a challenge I intended to take up.

We unfolded ourselves from the low-slung Lotus and entered the enchanted garden. At first sight, the Baan Thai looked like any other theatre restaurant beloved of the package tour operators. But I knew there was a subtle difference, and not only in the price. The Baan Thai was discreet, coyly concealed deep in a side *soi* off the clogged and choking main residential thoroughfare, Sukhumvit. The food was sufficiently bland not to offend delicate aristocratic or unaccustomed Western palates. The lovely hostess was no turbocharged call-girl, but a titled, Western-educated aristocrat, competent to explain the mysteries of the traditional dances and dishes in impeccable French and English. The restaurant was a favourite neutral venue of the royal family's for the entertainment of official guests. Small wonder that van Hooten had chosen it.

A scarlet-shirted stripling greeted us with a professional smiling *wai*. He raised his lantern to light our way through the flare-lit garden. From behind his ear a hibiscus blossom bloomed, its long stamens dancing like the feet of a red spider in tiny yellow shoes. The twin wooden houses, with their graceful sweeping roofs and the sharp, carved prows of their eaves, seemed to float like Viking longships at anchor, moored between the dark water of the lotus pool and the starless sky. I paused to survey the magical sight.

At my elbow, Chee Laan said: 'Replicas. These are from the Sukothai Kingdom period, thirteenth to fourteenth century. They call it the Dawn of Happiness.'

'How long did it last?'

'About one hundred years.'

'Not bad.'

'For a dawn? Or for happiness?'

'Either.' Her coolness inflamed me. Devil knows what I thought I was doing as I grasped her hand and swung her round against me. I felt a surge of power, and immediately afterward, unmanned by the flower scent of her hair and the fragility of her bones, a protective tenderness.

'You are right.' She extricated herself gently, but I sensed she was not offended. 'All is transient. Happiness is merely less pain. Change is the only permanence.' She seemed to make up her mind about something. 'Raven, Sya pretends to hate the Chinese. Yet I think he and my grandmother…'

'Yes?' I prompted, suddenly alert.

'Oh, I don't know. Just be careful, that's all. Don't believe all you hear. Shall we go?' She slipped her arm through mine, forgiving my earlier temerity.

At the top of the carved wooden staircase, Salikaa, who had observed everything, posed, gowned in a shimmering rose-pink *barong pimarn*, the full-length, clinging garment combining regal refinement with spectacular glamour. Slashed diagonally across the neck, it left one smooth coppery arm and shoulder bare. A heavily decorated silver belt girdled her slender waist. She glided back into the lighted room, smiling secretively.

I sensed Chee Laan's momentary reluctance to enter the lighted rooms, as if she shared my longing to linger in the shadow, canopied by the rain trees and the great spreading flame-of-the-forest, by night dark and anonymous as its less flamboyant fellows, with little shrines built in their trunks to the resident hamadryads. She let go my arm, and our two hands brushed by chance, trembled, clutched and held fast. I was conscious of her heavier breathing, as she must have been of mine. Pale lotuses starred the pool's face, and from nesting huts on the rafts Chinese geese, disturbed by the activity and the lights, burbled softly. A breeze stirred the reeds. I gasped at the tremor of quickening consciousness. The longing to pull her again into my arms, to cover her upturned face with kisses, was overwhelming. I tightened my grip on her small hand.

'Chee Laan,' I murmured. She removed her hand from mine gracefully, without reproof, and moved away toward the patiently waiting usher, into the light. After a moment I recovered my wits and followed her up the wooden staircase.

Apart from the humming air conditioners, the decor inside was authentic upper-class Thai. Fragrant teak, worked slippery-soft as red-tinged sandalwood; triangular lotus-patterned silk cushions for elbow and back. The knee-high tables of carved teak were set for six with bronzeware cutlery, *dephanon* angels dancing on their horn handles. They'd thoughtfully cut wells under the tables for Westerners unaccustomed to reclining. I watched van Hooten, grunting, manoeuvre his bulk, swinging his bulging thighs beneath the table. He raised a welcoming hand, booming cordially: 'Hi there, Raven! Glad you could make it!'

But we had unfinished business, he and I, despite his apparent frankness in the Golden Triangle. There was something more at stake. The opium had been a decoy, a blind, to distract my attention from some more important issue. But what?

The hostess began to explain culinary and artistic traditions. As I listened, I surreptitiously studied my fellow guests. 'Celadon is the direct descendant of the opaque jade stoneware of Imperial China. The craft of high-fired stoneware died out seven generations ago in China, but was revived in Thailand.' Pim and Salikaa had been standing with members of the royal family, and now broke away, fluttering over like beautiful butterflies to embrace Chee Laan with small cries, bumping cheeks, touching her hands, holding her arms. 'When victorious kings divided the battle spoils, they bargained as fiercely for master potters as for young concubines, flawless rubies, and war elephants.'

I lifted a lotus-shaped bowl from the table and turned it in my hand. Its glaze, from the wood-ash of slender Northern trees, gleamed with a dark, soft lustre which owed nothing to synthetic dyes. It reminded me of Chee Laan. I looked at her now as I listened politely, all the while absently caressing the smooth, glossy celadon. The stoneware felt like the touch of her skin, cool, firm, slippery-smooth. It seemed to me incomprehensible that, moments ago, my own bony, callused hand had held hers prisoner.

'Look!' Salikaa squealed in triumph, thrusting her wrist under Chee Laan's nose. 'Look at my betrothal gift from Vichai, my adoptive father!' She shook her arm, spinning the massive gold bracelet so its cabochon rubies and sapphires caught the candlelight. 'You can't begin to guess what it cost!' She lowered her voice, drawing them close. 'Vichai said if I was determined to marry some popinjay princeling, I should not go to his bed a beggar—he'd endow me richly as a queen, if he had to bleed his whole territory white to do it.'

Pim stared at her, pale with fury. 'I would not boast so loudly, Salikaa.'

Chee Laan took Pim's hand. 'Come, Pim,' she said. 'Leave it! Salikaa, you'd do better to welcome your guests than brag about your baubles.'

Now it was Salikaa's turn to glare. 'You sing a different tune now from the one on the radio, Julie dear!' she retorted. Assuming a high-pitched, breathless voice and an exaggerated simper, she mimicked savagely: 'Ooh, *Khun* Salikaa, you're the Thai Cinderella!'

Chee Laan said shortly, 'That was business!' She stalked over to our table and sat down without a word.

Salikaa turned her attention to Pim. 'Why are you so angry, Pim?' she said. 'Is it because you are jealous?'

'Of course not! I'm angry you should flaunt that—that disgusting monstrosity,' she indicated Salikaa's bracelet, 'that has been paid for with the blood of innocent peasants! Vichai is nothing more than a terrorist who intimidates and exploits people!'

Salikaa blazed back. 'Where do you think your royal family fortunes came from, if not terror and exploitation, Princess?'

The cheerful hum of well-bred voices ceased. All eyes were on the young women now. Prince Toom, intense and anxious, hurried over to lead his bride back to the family group. He was smiling determinedly, but sweat beaded his pale brow beneath the floppy fringe.

The silence was broken by a thunderous sound outside as heavy footsteps approached up the wooden staircase, followed by the scuffling of boots impatiently kicked off at the threshold. I saw Colonel Sya enter unceremoniously through the screened door like a whirlwind. At last I was in the presence of the Black Tiger, the most powerful man in the country. His hooded eyes swept the crowded room, reconnoitring the gathering. He made the essential reverences and slid into the empty seat at the high table, setting his radio against a carved table leg. Taking a hot towel from the pretty attendant, he mopped his face and neck, insolently taking his time about it. Meanwhile, everyone present—guests, restaurant staff, and dancers peeking round the carved screen—solemnly watched Colonel Sya wipe the sweat off his brow, as though witnessing a unique event. Finally, he dropped the used towel on the tray, gesturing indifferently in dismissal to the beautiful attendant.

'How would a girl set about making an impression on the incorruptible colonel?' I muttered, under cover of the murmured conversation that had resumed.

Chee Laan wriggled her shoulders impatiently, as if the question were beneath contempt. Her black eyes were unfriendly. 'He is Akha. For Akha, women are less than pigs.'

The last important guest having arrived, the atonal music struck up. Dancers, glittering in jewel-encrusted crowns and costumes, drifted barefoot like shimmering phantoms. Briefly I surrendered myself to the magical experience, momentarily blotting everything out, from my sore head to the confused, hopeless lust and longing for the girl at my side and my anxieties about my increasingly dangerous, irritatingly mysterious mission. Sya Dam was seated at a table behind me. I had no option for the moment but to address my attention to the feast. On the crowded table there now reposed a central dish of boiled rice, and before each diner a semicircle of celadon lotus cups, lidded to retain heat, containing Tom Yang Kung soup redolent of makrut herbs, lemongrass, prawns and *nam pla*, the sharp sauce made from rotting fish. There followed Kaeng Khiao Wan chicken curry, with sweet basil and makhun, chillies both green and red, and coconut cream made by pounding coconut milk in a pestle; duck boiled with water chestnuts; a side dish of beef, flavoured with palm sugar and garlic, the semi-aquatic creeper *phak bung*, and the *kha* tuber added for piquancy.

Chee Laan pointed to this dish. 'They call this "the Lord Rama descending into his bathwater." Charming, no?'

The dancers swayed and shivered like leaves in a breeze; their hands, with the foot-long false fingernails, wove their fatalistic tales of hope, love, and despair. Only the smiles never wavered. Then the lights went out, and they danced on, bearing lighted tapers on their fingers, a love dance of fireflies that drew gasps of wonder even from the supercilious Mrs van Hooten.

As for myself, battle-hardened and generally spell-resistant, I found myself reaching for Chee Laan's hand in the darkened room, imprisoning it firmly yet carefully, as if it were a butterfly I intended to release into the air without crushing its wings. She made no protest, watching the dance while I watched her neat, feline profile; when the house lights came on again, I regretfully released my grip and set her hand free.

There were murmurs of appreciation for the entertainment. Celadon trays with delicate serrated edges appeared, piled high with desserts, coconut, mung beans, and bananas in various guises, with fairytale names: *khanom thin fon tong*, rice and coconut milk slabs, decorated with a flake of edible gold leaf; *khanom lep mu nang*, lady's fingernails; *kanom khai hia*, alligator eggs peppered in mung beans and lard; and *kluey buay chi*, bananas stewed in coconut cream, sprinkled with pounded and roasted mung beans.

'They call these Nun Bananas. Thai nuns wear white robes,' Chee Laan explained.

Mountains of carved fruits were now set before us: rose apples and rambutans, pearly *ngo* and *lamyai*, mangosteens, fuzzy red globes of melon, golden durian stinking of ripe cheese. Salikaa was in high spirits, squealing with laughter, offering her bridegroom titbits from her plate as if he were a pet spaniel. The smiles of the Premsakuls and the van Hootens grew glassier by the minute as they attempted to ignore this vulgar display. Then Salikaa's voice rang out above the conversation, shrill with irritation: 'What are you staring at?'

Conversation ceased. Ears strained to hear, although few were willing to lose face by staring.

Prince Toom was in an agony of embarrassment. 'Your lips. They are so beautiful.'

'Please do not watch me eat. Watch the dancers.'

Toom devoured her with his eyes. 'You are more beautiful than any dancer in the world, Salikaa!'

Salikaa seemed about to snap a harsh reply when Pim leaned forward and stared right into her eyes. Salikaa dropped her gaze. Then she tilted her head sideways toward Prince Toom and smiled into his face. She reached out her arm weighed down by the huge golden bangle and patted his cheek like a cat playing with a mouse. 'Of course I am, darling!' she said. Without warning she sharpened her fingers and pinched his cheek hard. She sat up very straight then and flashed her radiant smile around the room. Toom stared at her, mystified and hurt, rubbing his cheek where a red mark was spreading. Pim sat back, shaking her head imperceptibly. Glancing at Chee Laan, I saw her lips, too, had tightened disapprovingly.

With a burst of noisy good cheer, van Hooten raised his glass to the diners at our table. He leant toward Chee Laan's elegant grandmother, Sunii Lee, straight-backed and exquisite in black and gold. 'Miz Lee, your lovely granddaughter surely resembles her daddy!'

Sunii inclined her head graciously. 'It is considered good luck for a girl to resemble her father,' she said, acknowledging the compliment.

Colonel Sya Dam gave a snort, wiped his mouth and dropped the napkin in the centre of his plate. His voice was mocking. 'And do you know why? The Chinese exposed girl children. Reckoned they weren't worth feeding. A girl baby who resembled her old man had a chance of touching his heart and getting herself saved.'

'Ah, the bad old days, eh, Miz Lee!' van Hooten interposed swiftly, anxious to avoid offence to his distinguished guest.

'They've still got a society in Hong Kong today taking care of unwanted female infants,' Sya continued complacently in a faint American accent. Chee Laan shot me a meaningful glance.

Her father now created a diversion. He was very drunk. He seemed to me a man who was thoroughly spoiled, the sort who resents having to make the effort of good manners and civil conversation. I was sure, from what Chee Laan let slip, that he was happier with his paramours and his gambling cronies. As though suddenly recalling the presence of his daughter, he bawled out roughly in Taechew: 'First daughter! Come!'

I sensed her sudden resentful rigidity. But she scrambled up from my side, smiling obediently, and crossed the room to kneel before the fat slob.

I watched helplessly as Sya, noting this pantomime of filial duty, began to laugh.

Baan Thai Restaurant, Bangkok

Raven was shocked when, without warning, Chee Laan's father, who had been drinking steadily, leaned over and shouted at his daughter in the ugly Taechew dialect of the street. 'Want to talk to turtle-turd barbarian thinks he gains face by setting pigswill before Lee family and pushing our noses in the trough! You translate, first daughter!'

'Has Honourable Father forgotten his foreign-devil talk, then?' smiled Chee Laan. He caught her by the wrist in a play of rough affection. Raven saw her wince with pain, though her smile never faltered. Too low for anyone to hear, he hissed, 'Do not quiz me, rat! I expend a fortune on your education, pour my gold down a worthless hole. Show me some return on my money!'

'*Your* money!' Chee Laan smiled bitterly into his eyes, which were glazed now with rage and drink, deeply sunken into bloated rolls of fat. 'Family money! Grandmother's money!'

The fat man belched and released her arm with a vicious little shove. 'Translate. Give time for think. Keep you busy, besides, stop you rubbing your whore's body against that long-nose devil who looks at you with eyes of baboon in rut!' He tugged her down to the seat beside him. 'Now. Ask this foreign red-hair devil how many helicopters he got. I want helicopter!'

When van Hooten heard the question, duly translated, he grimaced ruefully, scratched his head like a yokel and looked up at the carved ceiling. 'Aw, shucks, Mr Lee, now I confess you got me there! I don't know that I'm in a position to give you an exact figure. But America has a full complement of materiel, optimally deployed for the defence of our valued ally, the great Thai nation, and the preservation of her traditional freedoms.'

Lee narrowed his eyes to slits. His face twisted with malevolence. Crossing his bronzeware fork and spoon, he dive-bombed his messy plate, scattering rice and shreds of shrimp. With a burping roar, like a toddler imitating a plane, he cried 'Heli-copter!' Seeing the havoc he had caused on the polished teak table, he creased his face in a demonic grin and roared with laughter. Remnants of food clung to his chin; scraps were caught in his gums and gold teeth. His mother's black onyx eyes flickered over him thoughtfully and as quickly away, as though he were someone else's badly behaved toddler and she wished they would have the social grace to remove him. Once again, conversation ceased. Then a babble of voices broke out as people resumed animated conversation to cover the embarrassing moment.

Just as it seemed the feast was getting back on track, there was a sudden deafening roar. Stunned again into silence, people stared around wildly. In the sudden quiet, a male voice, unnaturally high, shrieking in Thai, bounced off the walls. Colonel Sya was on his feet, swift and agile as a hunting cheetah breaking cover. He seized his radio, listened, then shouted, 'Robbery at the Lee Bank!'

'Whassay?' bellowed Mr Lee, suddenly alert and apparently sober.

Amused, Sya Dam turned and looked at him. 'Afraid so. They broke into your vault, Mr Lee!' he said. The two men, both powerfully built, one bulky with muscle, the other with blubber, stared at one another. Lee had turned a sickly butter-yellow colour. Outrage and disbelief struggled on his features. Sya, straight-backed, authoritative, stared him down with a challenge in his eyes. Then he turned and was gone. The mosquito screen clattered shut behind him.

A babble of shocked voices burst out. Chee Laan had moved quickly to her grandmother's side. The formal dignity of the occasion was shattered. People rose, collecting their possessions, asking each other excited questions. Chee Laan's father crashed his balled fist into the table, scattering tableware and food.

'Rob my Walt!' he yelled, his competence in English miraculously restored. 'You tell me how in bloody hell no-good shit-eating turtle-egg come in my Walt?'

'Dynamite, maybe?' suggested van Hooten helpfully. 'Maybe blasted their way in—it's been done before.' Lee blew a raspberry of contempt. His saliva contaminated Mrs van Hooten, who maintained a stony reserve.

'Diana-mite? Using diana-mite, that not some two-satang dogshit Thai *catoy*. Diana-mite, that organised stuff, maybe Commie terrorist. Saboteur, maybe!'

'Political motives can never be entirely ruled out.' Van Hooten composed his features in a mask of statesmanlike gravitas. 'Your robbers could be small fry, with bigger fish in the background.'

'I'm sure you can safely leave everything in the capable hands of the authorities, Mr Lee,' Mrs van Hooten said, discreetly dabbing sauce spots off her silk evening skirt.

'Petty criminals! Scum!' Prince Premsakul demonstrated his good breeding by sipping his drink unperturbed. 'Chuck 'em in the chokey! Only solution. These antisocial elements. All pinkos, what? Cool their heels and cool their heads.'

'No doubt Honourable Father would reintroduce the third degree,' Pim challenged. Ignoring his scowling offspring, the prince smiled imperturbably, cradling his drink in one plump paw. Merriment shook his rotund body.

'No need for accidents at the police station. With Buddhists, all is so much easier; one can rely upon the sensitive conscience.'

'How reassuring! It would be uncomfortable to take a fall in leg-irons,' Pim retorted. 'What if the robbers are not Buddhists? What if they are foreigners?'

After another tense silence, Lee shouted, 'Need to break heads, go break heads! But catch me dogpiss *catoy* blow hole in my Walt, get me his ass pretty damn quick! *Farang, catoy*, commie, ne'er mind, all same, break head!' He lurched unsteadily to his feet.

'I hardly think, little lady,' the American colonel said, looking hard at Pim, 'that we need seriously entertain any notion the perpetrators would be Caucasians.'

Raven was aware, catching van Hooten's eye, that he knew not only that the bank robbers were not locals, but that he knew who they were, and more besides. Urgency seized Raven. Sya already had a head start. He needed to get after him, fast.

Fortunately, the party was dead in the water. The guests made their farewells as swiftly as convention allowed, although Raven was seething with impatience. Prince Prem decorously waddled over to him and shook his hand. The touch of his plump fingers was soft as a pampered woman's. His good humour was undisturbed.

'Shockin' business, what?' The prince beamed up at Raven. 'Look here, old chap. Had a bit of a rummage, managed to come up with one or two poetic doodles. Thai lyric poetry. Poor things, but mine own. Done in the style of the Immortal Bard. Cast an eye, old chap, if you've a spare moment.' He nodded and wandered back to collect the rest of his party.

'His wretched sonnets! Some timing!' Chee Laan whispered as they queued to take their leave. 'I hope you're not fond of poetry? I've seen some of the prince's efforts!'

Raven murmured an absent reply. Suddenly he made up his mind. He was certain the highwaymen had been sent to kill him—and possibly van Hooten as well, if the American's alarm and bewilderment were genuine. Yet the killer had backed off, recognising Raven. That hired assassin was Angel Fleischer. He remembered, blindingly, Fleischer's expertise with explosives. He decided he had to gamble on Chee Laan. How would she react when he asked her help in a venture that had nothing to do with romance but everything to do with Angel Fleischer, and whatever he was up to? A venture that could set both their lives at risk?

He leaned close and murmured urgently, 'Chee Laan, I need your car. Now.'

She darted a quick, unnervingly comprehending look at him and shook her head. 'Only comes with a chauffeuse.'

'No!' Raven protested sharply. 'You don't understand. It could be dangerous.'

She laid a hand on his arm. 'You are the one not understanding. But then, what can one expect of a foreign devil? I was trained by the best. By Fleischer. Let's go!'

He saw she was smiling. Her eyes sparkled, like a little girl honoured by inclusion in her big brother's gang's adventure. They made their farewells. She looked very small between the tall Westerners, doll-like, achingly vulnerable. He felt an intense compulsion to protect her, and at the same time a profound sense of unease.

Asian Highway, Southbound, Toward Bangkok

Helmut Boeckel, the rally driver, was a beer-barrel Bavarian competing in his third Asian Rally. His co-driver had sickened mysteriously in the sticks, in Northern Thailand. It must have been a dodgy curry, because the only other refreshment they'd taken had been tea, served by the Yankee God-botherer. The replacement co-driver slipped aboard seamlessly. Boeckel knew Fleischer had his own agenda, but the guy could navigate, and drive, too, almost like a pro. He looked at Fleischer's hard lantern jaw and the jutting cheekbone, and recalled, rather anxiously, his legend.

The slogans plastering the rally car's sides were covered in mud and dust, turning to sludge in the downpour. The powerful headlamps carved the night open. A glistening horde of nocturnal insects encrusted the lamps and windscreens in messy death as inconsequential to Fleischer as the men he'd killed. Fleischer had come up hard: a petty juvenile offender in his mother's native Guatemala, he'd graduated to adult penitentiary for armed robbery and safe-breaking, and escaped to join the Legion; ill-advisedly revisiting his native shores, not from sentimentality so much as to settle old scores, and recaptured, he'd emigrated to his father's country, the United States, under a Prisoners' Aid Scheme in time to catch the draft. He was posted to Vietnam.

Vietnam did not suit many people, but it suited Angel Fleischer. He went in a disturbed, unruly youth and came out a disciplined psychopath. His peculiar talents won recognition. After his tour in Vietnam he was assigned to special duties at the School of the Americas. Prior to his promotion to major and his 'respectable' posting to Bangkok as Assistant Military Attaché, he had been briefly seconded to run elite survival training camps in Northern France. Here Fleischer operated under the guise of private enterprise. This arrangement permitted his masters to simultaneously unofficially train their own experts while keeping an eye on terrorists sent from other nations to acquire the skills of murder and mayhem. Fleischer took pride in his expertise. It had brought him the best of both worlds: gotten him a passport to the Land of Opportunity, and saved him from ending up, in Nam, as what he described as either 'jungle hamburger' or 'chicken-in-a-basket.'

As he spun the wheel and the car bucked through craters, rocks bouncing off its sides, Boeckel thought Fleischer looked like a madman.

'You my nanny, Kraut, or what?' Fleischer yelled over the engine's scream. 'Or are you just another Expendable? '

'What the hell eats you, man?' Boeckel bawled back.

'I work alone! I *always* work alone!'

But he had failed to carry out his last assignment. Fleischer raged internally. He must be going soft. Why had his hand faltered when he realised his target was Nat Raven? Sentimentality? The Old Comrades' fogbound, undiscriminating loyalty? This was an inconvenient time for Fleischer to experience failure. He had several lucrative ventures underway. Working for van Hooten, such as the present operation, came under the heading of official commitments, but there were other profitable sources of income. The pleasant possibility of blackmailing Salikaa, for instance, was a prospect whose attractions had increased a thousandfold with the announcement of her engagement to a member of the royal family. At the thought of Salikaa's fury and wild threats, Fleischer bared his teeth in amused derision. Salikaa didn't have a prayer!

Then his grin faded. He had failed the terrifying Colonel Sya. What was happening to him? More importantly, what *would* happen to him? He contemplated an explanation for his momentary and uncharacteristic lapse that might satisfy Sya Dam.

Fleischer muttered a stream of obscenities inside his helmet, fogged with sweating plastic and perspiration, that uniquely personal scent. He brought the car to a halt outside the Lee Bank. The Indian watchman approached them, walking softly on the balls of his bare black feet, his spotless white dhoti giving him an air of saintliness. He radiated helpfulness and a desire for foreign conversation. Boeckel waved the chart at him, crisscrossed and scarred with rally navigator's notations. Fleischer slipped out quietly on the other side and struck a single blow. Together they bundled the old man up in his robes and left him swinging in his own white hammock, slung between the Doric pillars of the bank's ornate portal.

Fleischer pulled off his fireproof gloves, adjusted his night-sight goggles. Thirty minutes later, Waddle's account with the bank—his safety deposit box, his rubies earned for poisoning inconvenient people and surveilling airstrips, had ceased to exist, as had all documentation recording funds deposited by the Bangkok Chinese for transfer to more appropriate destinations. Not too difficult. There were not many records of such transactions in any case, for the Lee Bank conducted much of its business on the principles of honour, reciprocity, and tribalism, combined with a Druidical distrust of the written word. What records existed were expunged. Fleischer's loyalty belonged to anyone who could pay the price, but, as he enjoyed a little free enterprise, he casually blew a hole in the vault, extracted a few gold bars, and beat an orderly retreat.

They threw themselves and their booty into the car. Fleischer kicked the motor into noisy life. The throbbing snarl of the twin carbs rumbled satisfactorily in the sultry night. The car smeared 500 centimetres of tyre on the grit and tarmac, hurtling toward the Bang Pa In Highway. Fleischer flicked a laconic finger at two packages propped on the dashboard. Boeckel pushed back his visor, licked his fingers, and started counting. The old 100-baht bills, tenderised by years of filth and fondling, were tattered and cellotaped in places.

Boeckel grunted, satisfied, and tucked the money away somewhere under his belly with a seismic upheaval.

'Keep bloody still, you'll have us in the fucking ditch!' Fleischer bellowed, aware of lights on the road ahead. 'Some fucking truck broken down...no. Sweet Jesus, it's a fucking roadblock.'

'Drive on, drive on!' yelled Boeckel, panicking. 'It's maybe demonstration! In India, last rally, peebles demonstrate, shout, throw rocks. Some drivers they have pulled out the cars, some they have killed! Drive on, Fleischer, man! Drive them over! Don't stop!'

But the warning came too late. Handheld torches flashed them down. The dark bulk of the truck blocked the carriageway. Fleischer, cursing, slammed the brakes home, and the car bucked to a stomach-jerking halt. Outside, lit by questing torches, the muzzles of service revolvers butted at the windows.

Uniformed police signalled to them to get out of the car, menacing them with swinging barrels. Fleischer snatched up the unopened envelope, ripped it open, revealing the banknotes. He thrust it out of the window. Gently but firmly it was pushed aside, and at that moment a finger of cold dread traced Fleischer's spine, as if an icicle had been thrust inside his shirt.

Prodded by the muzzles of the guns, they staggered before the policemen into a small wooden shed. Through a grimy window they watched as khaki-clad police swarmed over the rally car. Helmut Boeckel seized one of the policemen by the lapels and shook him.

'Get your damned apes out of my car! Let us go, *ihr Scheisskerle*! Immediately I am back in town I complain to German Embassy. *Kapierst du, Idiot?*'

'Very sorry, Sirmadame, cannot,' the policeman spluttered, teeth rattling. Boeckel let go and took to banging his fist against the wall, bellowing. The Thais watched him with polite interest. He struck a nail and cursed. He thrust his shredded fist into his mouth and tasted the salty blood on his tongue.

'You please waiting Colonel Sya,' the policeman pleaded, as one soothing the ravings of a lunatic. Boeckel turned to Fleischer, throwing his arms wide.

'What in hell he means?' he demanded, helplessly.

Fleischer's face was steely. 'How the fucking hell should I know? He can't mean Sya's coming here in person.' He snapped at the policeman, 'Get me a telephone! That's an order!'

'So sorry, heartbroken,' said the policeman as though with genuine regret. 'Cannot. Telephone no good. You wait. Maybe,' he brightened, adopting a wheedling tone, 'you like tea?'

'Fuck your tea,' said Fleischer, 'and fuck you too!' He sat down beside Boeckel on a wooden bench, his mind racing. He was trapped like a rat. There must be a way out. There had always been a way out before, and Angel Fleischer always found it. Boeckel had begun rocking himself like a huge disconsolate infant, the consciousness of impending disaster finally penetrating his fleshy head.

Fleischer snapped out of his urgent pondering, thinking he heard a noise outside. He sprang to his feet and leapt to the small window, peering out. It was raining heavily. The rally car was parked just beyond his line of vision.

By squinting, head pressed close to the pane, he could see the radiator grill. A slim figure moved round the car like a shadow—perhaps a young recruit, sent to guard it. If so, his movements were oddly surreptitious. Then Fleischer's attention was caught by the sound of an approaching engine. A jeep roared up and jerked to a halt, spraying the hut with mud and pebbles. The driver jumped out and saluted, as another uniformed figure sprang smartly down without touching the step. Through the downpour, the scene had the mesmeric unreality of an underwater ballet. The Thais' waterproof jungle greens glistened in the headlights. Boots stamped heavily outside the hut and the door was flung wide. Silhouetted against the bright sheets of rain caught in the jeep's headlamps, and the soft darkness beyond, Colonel Sya Dam stood staring at the captured rally drivers. They stared back in silence. Fleischer's face was astonished, Boeckel's apprehensive.

Sya smiled broadly. This did nothing to reassure the prisoners. 'Sorry for the inconvenience, gentlemen. These men confused your car with the getaway vehicle from a bank robbery that occurred this evening in Bangkok. My apologies. They will be disciplined.' He looked around appraisingly. 'Somewhat basic, this place. Maybe we should get them to bring us some tea. Or some whisky? Huh?'

His very calmness, the uncanny lack of emotion, made Fleischer sweat. He took a step forward, then stopped in his tracks.

'Colonel,' Fleischer said. 'It was a glitch. The other business…' He could not bring himself to name it. He should have blown Nat Raven's head off. For the life of him he could not think why he had not. 'It won't happen again,' he added lamely.

Sya regarded him coolly. 'No,' he said at length, 'I do not think it will happen again.' Fleischer experienced then a sensation he had thought he had left behind, in the early days in Nam. The twist in his guts of the icy hand of fear.

'Colonel,' he said, and he caught the pleading bleat in his own voice, and was sickened. Sya Dam continued to smile. He gestured toward the door.

'If you do not wish to take refreshment with me, then you are free to go. No hard feelings, eh?' He shook their hands in the Western manner, a gesture Fleischer recognised for more than a hint of solidarity. His grip was firm. He met Fleischer's eyes candidly. 'Have a good race, Major!' Boeckel's heartfelt relief appeared to afford him some amusement, for he smiled good-humouredly.

Fleischer grunted a farewell. As he made his way out toward the rally car, he imagined at every step a heavy hand laid on his shoulder, yanking him back to face some terrible retribution. He winced inwardly, even while he forced his steps to be firm. *March, you old skeleton*, he told himself grimly. *Tremble if you will, but march, damn you.*

Nothing happened. No heavy arresting hand, no cold gun barrel thrust into the cheekbone, no angry yells of pursuit. Outside, the jungle night was still going about its business; insects chirruped and whirred, leaves whispered. The car stood there as he had left it. He got in, leaned back in the driver's seat, and drew a hand down his face, clawing at his skin as relief flooded his veins and he felt his heart judder back to a normal rate. 'Phew!' said Boeckel, heaving his bulk into the passenger seat beside him. 'These guys, they sure give me the creepies! What you think?'

'Shut up, Boeckel!' Fleischer snapped. He started the engine with a vicious twist and kick, as if the car were to blame for the delay, and for their humiliation. The engine roared into life and the car throbbed and trembled as they shot off along the dark road. He was still feeling jumpy and confused.

It had been too easy. He could not believe, after a mistake like that, that he had got away with it. That was Asians for you. Impossible to second-guess, even though he knew them as well as any man, or fancied he did. Perhaps, he reflected, his pragmatic nature gradually reasserting itself, Colonel Sya still needed him. He was in the clear for now. There must be no more dumb mistakes.

He knew this road: there was a monster turn coming up, a great sweep to the left, with a punishing gradient, just the kind of obstacle he delighted in negotiating, rejoicing in his own skill and the vehicle's fine-tuned engineering, the wide lock and powerful road-holding ability. He was almost enjoying himself. Exultant. Always the winner, Angel!

As the road plunged downhill, as usual, he left it to the very last minute before he slammed the brakes home. Boeckel was clinging on. He emitted a guttural squeak of protest. Fleischer grinned malevolently and floored the brake pedal. Nothing! He yanked the handbrake back and felt terror as the brake cable sagged, powerless and flaccid. The car rocketed on, unchecked. Fleischer, cursing, crashed down the gears, but the camber had caught the speeding wheels. Now both men were yelling. The car hurtled sideways in a flying buck and left the road. It bumped violently down the steep scree, doors flung wide like the wings of a night beetle tumbling down a screen. It hit the huge boulder head on. The petrol tank, topped up for the rally and the getaway, exploded into orange flame. Blazing like a torch, the car plunged one last time; then the slow, muddy wallows of the river extinguished it. A vehicle moved slowly out of the scrub on the other side of the road: a large black American car, with a lone driver. The sedan paused for a moment beside the tyre tracks Fleischer's car had left, then sped away into the night.

Sya stood on the bank, keeping his polished boots just out of the mud, and surveyed the charred wreck beached in the shallow water. Fleischer's dead hands still gripped the wheel, which the Thais called 'the wreath of jasmine.' Across the windscreen, miraculously preserved, a leaping tiger and the legend 'Tiger Balm' gleamed briefly as the policeman moved his torch beam, giving a momentary illusion of life.

'Both *farangs* dead, please, Colonel,' the officer reported.

'The ground rises higher,' Sya sighed. Another officer marched up, prodding before him a slim figure with its arms twisted behind its back. He saluted and shoved the prisoner to the ground.

'Please, sir, this person, sir, tried to run the roadblock. The vehicle crashed, and we apprehended the driver. We also recovered this from the vehicle, sir!' He handed a plastic-wrapped packet to the colonel.

The prisoner sat on the wet ground, glaring at Sya through the rain. Sya looked at the flattened cockscomb of hair and the burning black eyes. 'Take him inside,' he said wearily, weighing the heavy packet in his hand, his fingers tracing the outline of the calipers within. He glanced over his shoulder at the river. 'Rally driving is a very dangerous sport. Only for foreigners with too much money and no brains. Remember that, Sergeant.'

'Sir!'

The sound of a car approaching fast reached them from the highway. Sya swung around in the direction of the sound.

Raven had driven hard.

Once they had had established which road their quarry had taken out of the city, they had exchanged few words. Seeing the little group in the roadway, Raven hit the brakes and the Lotus slithered to a stop. Raven leapt out and, ignoring Sya and his men, ran to the riverbank. Chee Laan followed. Raven seized a torch from one of the soldiers and pointed it at the wrecked rally car. At the sight of the tiger and the distinctive white helmet with the bold navy stripes, he let out a groan. Sya was at his side immediately, leaving his men to bully the young prisoner into the hut.

'Most regrettable. Fatal accidents are of course common in the Great Asian Rally. Alas, brave young men. You knew them? Perhaps that is why you are here?'

'Miss Lee and I followed you—Miss Lee thought you were on the trail of the people who robbed her father's bank. This, however, is unexpected.' Raven gestured toward the river, where the water lapped indolently against the half-sunken vehicle.

'Indeed. It is a great shock,' Sya replied formally.

Suddenly conscious of Chee Laan's presence at his side, Raven put an arm around her and moved her away, dropping his torch beam from the desolate scene.

'We shall send people to recover the bodies,' Sya said, walking beside them. 'I am sorry you had to see this, Miss Lee.' In deference to Raven's presence, he used the European form of address. 'Now you must excuse me. I have an interrogation to conduct.' He nodded in a friendly way and moved off toward the hut. Muffled cries were heard as Sya's men encouraged the unfortunate prisoner to talk.

Wordlessly, Raven and Chee Laan returned to the car. Raven circled the car around and headed back up the highway. He felt her critical gaze. There was no escape.

'You knew them!'

'Knew them? Who?' he hedged, playing for time.

'Stop the car! Pull over!' He did so, and turned to face her. 'Those dead people in the wreck.'

Her black eyes, boring into his, demanded an answer. He knew she would detect a lie immediately if he attempted to fob her off, so he didn't even try.

'Yes. One of them, anyway.'

'Who was he?' she pursued mercilessly.

'A guy called Fleischer.'

'Fleischer?' She was tense now, her tone sharper. 'Fleischer. What was the rest of his name? How did you know him?'

He had no intention of relating any of it—the Legion years, the heady dreams shattered by confrontation with sordid realities, the old ridiculous yet binding loyalties, the manifold regrets. He felt reluctant to reveal that side of himself, as though it tarnished whatever little lustre was left to him.

'I knew him in the old days. I was in the French Foreign Legion for a while. His name is Angel Fleischer. He was a lieutenant then; he's been promoted to major.'

'Describe him, this Lieutenant or Major Fleischer!' she demanded with great deliberation, scowling.

'Fleischer was one of the most genuinely wicked men I've ever met. Quite without conscience. But I saved his life once, and he repaid me.'

'How?' she snapped out the monosyllable tersely.

'By sparing mine.'

Her eyes widened. 'That happened recently, didn't it? It happened here, in Thailand.'

There was no hiding place now. He told her the miserably few facts he had figured out. 'I think Fleischer was sent to murder me.'

As he had expected, she scoffed. 'That's ridiculous! You are a professor. People don't go round murdering professors! Why should anyone want to kill you? What is all this, Raven—these mysteries, rushing off into the night, car accidents and hitmen? What is it you're not telling me?' Then she added quietly, 'I too knew Lieutenant Fleischer.' She paused, her eyes challenging him. 'He was our instructor in France. On that awful survival course. Pim and Salikaa and I. He was a sadistic beast.' She sighed. 'A horrible man. But very efficient.'

Raven realized then that none of them had recognised him as Fleischer's partner. He decided to conceal that fact a little longer. 'Fleischer was efficient, all right,' he conceded. 'As an operative, he was one of the best.'

'Which means,' Chee Laan thought aloud, 'that he wouldn't be there, in that riverbed, the very efficient Fleischer, unless someone wanted him dead very badly.' She was quiet for a moment, and when she spoke again her voice was thoughtful. 'I am sure many people will be glad Fleischer is dead. Do you think he robbed our bank?'

'Quite possibly. The question is, why? Why the robbery? Why are two men dead?'

'The deaths may not be connected with the bank robbery,' Chee Laan said.

'Perhaps the driver lost control and they simply skidded off the road,' Raven suggested.

'You don't believe that.'

'No,' he agreed, 'I don't. For one thing, Fleischer drove like the devil. And Colonel Sya's presence suggests sabotage. He may even have arranged it.'

There was silence except for the engine. Chee Laan thought of her grandmother's relationship with the Black Tiger. The air between herself and Raven was heavy with shared longing, and thick with unshared secrets.

Raven was the first to speak. 'There was another instructor on that course in France.'

'Yes,' Chee Laan agreed, waiting. She flicked her hair behind her ear and stared fixedly out through the windscreen.

'You don't recognise me,' Raven said. 'I was sure you recognised me, but none of you did.'

'It was you,' Chee Laan breathed. 'Oh, it was you! I knew there was something familiar—but back in France, you had a mask, and you always shouted, barked like a dog, quick quick, run here, run there, get down! Why didn't you say?'

Raven sighed. He pulled the car over and stopped.

'What are you doing?' she demanded in the sudden quiet.

'I'm damned well not having this conversation while I'm trying to negotiate my way over this dirt track.' He turned to her. 'I tried to keep apart from the stuff in France as far as I could, ridiculous as that may sound. I didn't want to be part of Fleischer's Barnum and Bailey. I let him talk me into it because, if you want the truth, I was bored and cheesed off with my own life, didn't know where I was going, in the doldrums. Thought a break would do me good. And then...' He paused, uncertain how to continue, turning the words over and over in his mind. 'Then I met you.'

'Yes,' Chee Laan said in a small voice, 'and I met you.'

'And I have absolutely no right...'

'No,' she agreed. 'No rights at all.' She leaned over and laid her cheek against the juncture of his neck and shoulder. She sighed. They stayed like that for a while, hardly daring to breathe so as not to disturb the fragile moment.

He moved first, gently taking her into his arms as well as he could in the cramped and crowded space. 'What the hell are we going to do?' he said. She sat up.

'We have much to think about,' she said.

He nodded. They sat in the silent darkness, reading each other's faces with their fingertips like blind people. Now that there was an understanding between them, urgency was postponed. This new relationship must be confirmed as delicately and soberly as the creation of any work of art.

Finally Chee Laan said, 'There is more to consider, besides us. Whoever was responsible for killing Fleischer and that other man, I feel one thing for sure. There will be more killing.'

Her composure took him aback. 'Why do you say that?'

'Raven, there is too much going on I do not understand. I am worried for you. For Pim—and even for Salikaa.'

'If the crash was sabotage, why do you say it and the robbery may not be connected?'

'Because,' she repeated gravely, 'there is something strange going on. That boy they caught—I have seen him before...'

'The one who tried to run the roadblock? The prisoner Sya was going to interrogate, God help him?' Raven asked, shocked.

She nodded. 'That was Tamsin, Salikaa's bodyguard, one of Vichai's men. He probably sabotaged that rally car while Fleischer and the other man were in the police post.' She gave a fluttering sigh, almost a moan. 'Two things I know for sure: if Tamsin did that, Salikaa is behind it. She ordered it, or maybe her stepfather Vichai did.'

'And the other thing?'

'Tamsin will never tell them anything. They'll have to kill him, or he'll kill himself. He will die, anyway. If he talks, Vichai will have him killed. If he does not, Sya Dam will.'

There seemed little to say to that, so Raven didn't try. After a moment he felt Chee Laan's small hand on his own. He took his hand off the wheel and gripped hers fiercely. 'I only hope I haven't dragged you into danger. Nothing had better happen to you, Chee Laan!'

'Nothing will happen to me that I don't want,' she replied lightly. 'Let's go.'

He drove on, scowling at the wet road and the dancing rain, his mind a maelstrom, yet filled with a crazy joy.

'I think,' Chee Laan said after a while, 'you will appreciate the qualities of my grandmother.'

Lee Residence, Bangkok, Thailand

Raven

It had been no mere courtesy invitation. The elegant formula concealed a peremptory summons.

At the heart of the house, I found the restrained grandeur of a widow's retreat, cool and dark, shuttered against the glare of the midday sun, fragrant with jasmine and incense from the house shrine. When the formidable Lee matriarch stepped forward, smiling, to greet me, my first thought was that she was smaller than I remembered, more fragile. She extended her hand in a practised Western gesture of welcome. Behind her, in the gloom, I caught a movement; an aged woman scuttled forward, setting tea and mooncakes before us with excessive obsequiousness, all the while darting sidelong appraisal at me. Sunii Lee clicked her fingers impatiently. Sighing like a kettle, the old servant faded into the shadows, behind a screen. Her squinting scrutiny held a mute hostility; I thought I was learning to read the Asian countenance at last.

'Doctor Raven.' Sunii Lee gave each of the four syllables equal weight. Meticulously she poured pale tea in a thin stream. I was suddenly keenly aware of the strength, as well as the delicacy, of her hands and wrists. The notion that she intended me to feel her power was unsettling. 'The Lee family has been fortunate, Dr Raven.'

'Your family is spoken of everywhere with honour and respect, Madame Lee,' I replied.

Her smile tightened in the barest acknowledgement of the conventional compliment. 'Perhaps in some quarters. It was not always so.'

I raised an enquiring eyebrow. 'The Lee Empire has many facets,' I offered courteously. 'Hotels, bowling alleys, import and export, construction, a chain of stores, a fleet of buses—all testify to the industry and skill of the Lee Family.' I allowed my voice to invite her confidence.

She nodded appreciatively. 'I began, Dr Raven, what you flatteringly call an empire with one small shop selling organdie—what the young ladies today would call a boutique. But in my case, I worked not to while away idle hours, but out of necessity. Thirty years ago, I was not a bored little rich girl, but a woman alone, with a small son to support.' She paused, staring into the middle distance, as though bygone days marched before her, marshalled for her inspection. 'Then I had a stroke of good fortune. I won a major contract—to supply army uniforms. That was the turning point.'

Thirty years ago? My mind raced, calculating. 'Uniforms? For whose army?' I tried to keep my tone respectful, despite the speculation.

She studied me for a moment. Then, with a small intake of breath, like someone submitting to the sting of a syringe, she met the challenge: 'Nippon. East-Ocean people. The Japanese.'

'So you—a woman in a small way of business, dealing with organdie, of all things—won a major contract from the enemy occupying force?'

Again that pause, a weighted silence.

The answer came in a whisper. 'I did. At—at considerable personal sacrifice.' I nodded slowly, with new understanding. Repugnance fought with respect for the strength and expediency of this woman's kind. She continued, her tone even and matter-of-fact. 'The next step was a Ministry of Defence contract for handwoven uniforms. Later, we tendered for supply of cotton sarongs. This contract also we won. I have not been idle through the years, Dr Raven. Indeed, I have found hard work to be the cure for most ills—sickness, loneliness, despair.'

I set down the eggshell teacup and watched her. She nodded her head, acknowledging my interest.

'Being a woman in such a business is not easy. Our sex is socially limited. Entertaining business contacts, most of whom are men, is difficult. Extremely so. Especially here.' She gestured toward the city, an unseen, bustling presence, polluted and clamorous, beyond the high walls that shielded this quiet oasis, with its stone lions and flowering shrubs. Her narrow lips never quite covered her strong white teeth. Though softly modulated, her diction was staccato. It was as though she tested the value of each word with those impressive incisors. Her eyelids were almost closed, as though painted on by a fine calligraphy brush above the parchment cheeks, but she held me in her covert gaze.

'The commercial acumen and practicality of Asian women are widely admired,' I offered cautiously. I had the sense that my every utterance, my every gesture, was being delicately placed in the balance. Fatuous commonplaces would discredit me.

Sunii nodded. 'We Asian women have a powerful hoarding instinct. Saving for the future. Sadly, this is a necessity. Asian men are immature. In country districts, land is still left to daughters, money to sons. Women bear the responsibility, leaving men free to seek pleasure. You see, our society, unlike yours, does not require a man and wife to go everywhere yoked together like animals. Thus we come to develop different interests, different circles of friends. But there is no resentment. We women enjoy the unseen power of manoeuvring behind the scenes, dealing in land and gems and marriageable children, while our menfolk enjoy themselves. The bargain is mutually satisfying.'

'You paint a traditional picture of Asian society. Has nothing changed in modern times?'

'Not in the essentials!' She smiled, closing her eyes tightly, nostrils flaring at some private joke. 'Marriageable children, grandchildren, precious ones and precious stones…it does not do to underestimate us, Dr Raven!'

'A wise man never underestimates any woman, Asian or otherwise, madame,' I returned.

But she refused to banter. 'In Thailand, women work harder than men because they can envisage causality and consequences. Thai men believe only in karma and coincidence. Women not only worked the rice fields; historically, they went to war. You may have seen the frieze painted by Madame Drinkwater in my Rachanee Hotel?'

I saw my opportunity to impress her.

'Indeed,' I said. 'It depicts Queen Sri Suriyothi, who risked her life on a war elephant to save her husband, in the great battle of 1563. It is splendid.'

She smiled, acknowledging my tribute. 'We Asian businesswomen are like the Chinese girl sword-fighters: we cross swords with the warriors of high finance without sacrificing our femininity. Yet once we marry, Dr

Raven, we revert to the legal position of minors. Deprived of the right to enjoy and dispose of our own property, unable to obtain a divorce on the grounds of the man's adultery.' She spoke with a kind of controlled outrage, her voice rising in pitch. 'Financial disenfranchisement would be far worse than adultery! Indeed, adultery is commonplace—fourteen per cent of college graduates are the offspring of practising polygamists, did you know that? Polygamy is not necessarily a bad thing, so long as the second wife remembers her inferior status, and the first wife is content to supervise the health and upbringing of all the children, including those her husband sires by second or third wives.' Her eyes opened wide and searched my face. 'Children are important. Grandchildren are important.'

She smiled, the ingenuous, optimistic smile of a young girl on the threshold of life. I knew that so long as I resisted the Western barbarism of the direct question, her approach would remain tangential and oblique. If I quizzed her outright, she would discount me as a savage and I would be dismissed.

'My granddaughter, Chee Laan,' she said, dropping the name syllable by syllable. 'She is a person of great value—young, hungry for life, eager to experience it all at once. She needs time. But in the end she will make wise decisions. She is first of all Chinese. Chinese, and a member of this family. She will come to realise this. It is to be hoped that life, and those who care for Chee Laan, will give her space to grow into her inheritance…'

She allowed her words to penetrate. Then she continued in a bright, social tone, the change so abrupt it took my breath away.

'You have honoured our city for some time, Dr Raven. Perhaps you are lonely for your own people? Is there someone you would like to have join you in Bangkok for a holiday? She could enjoy the shopping, the sightseeing. I should be delighted for her to stay at the Rachanee, as my guest, because you have befriended my granddaughter, have been to her as a wise uncle. I have many friends in the airlines.'

My inner eye conjured up the familiar image—once burnished by years of longing, and now curiously dulled—of Nancy's carved Sioux-squaw countenance, her splendid impatient scowl, the coltish grace of her long-limbed, well-loved body. And then I remembered our bitter parting, and all that had led up to that new coolness; I recalled Nancy's glib dismissal of her boss's invitations and his doglike devotion, and it occurred to me suddenly that complacency and self-absorption had made me blind. Gradually that once-cherished image receded; I thought now of Chee Laan Lee's secret smile, her magnolia skin, her glossy head tilting like a purple-black poppy on a too-slender stem.

'You are too kind.' I cleared my throat and met the politely enquiring eyes of Chee Laan's grandmother. 'I have no one special to me.' I wondered, *Who am I fooling—myself? Certainly not this ageless stick-insect wrapped in crimson silk!*

Sunii sighed politely. 'I am sorry. I had thought perhaps your honourable mother...'

That was certainly not what she had meant, and we both knew it. But I played along, replying innocently: 'I'm afraid my mother is no longer with us.' That part, at least, was true. My regret was genuine. No need to tug my features into the semblance of sorrow.

'Ah. By this, I think you mean she is dead.' I studied my hands without replying. 'Dr Raven, please allow me to make you an insignificant present.' She clapped her hands. The old woman servant reappeared, as if on prearranged cue. She was carrying, officiously, a small casket. She handed it over. Sunii Lee opened it carefully and took out a small book, bound in black silk with gold-edged pages, and a jewelled box. She handed the book to me.

'*The Summer Wives of Mount Lu.*' Sunii smiled. 'It is a traditional Chinese story.' She handed me the box. 'Open it, please.' Cushioned on green silk lay a piece of jade carved in the lucky bamboo shape, set in massy gold. Even to my inexpert eye, its antiquity and value were apparent.

'One day, Dr Raven, when you find a special person, you may like to give her this. You will say it was the gift of an old Chinese woman who was your friend.' She looked at me, and repeated, with slight emphasis, glancing away. 'Your friend, Dr Raven.'

At least I had learnt sufficient not to wax offensively effusive in my thanks. Excessive protestations of gratitude would reveal a niggardly desire to evade recognition of my moral obligation to reciprocate with a gift of equal value, in cash or kind.

As though reading my thoughts, Sunii said: 'Please do not think of making gifts to me in return. I am at an age where I must begin to extricate myself from worldly possessions. All I desire is the well-being of my family.

You understand me?'

She looked at me again. She was no longer smiling. Her eyes, wide open now, glistened like the nacreous flecks in her carved ebony table.

I understood all right. My acceptance of the precious bauble implied that I would henceforth desist from any pursuit of Chee Laan Lee, First Granddaughter.

But, I reflected guiltily, matters were not that simple. I was already involved in more trouble than I needed. I had been hit on the head, almost murdered, witnessed an old comrade's violent death; I had spent years in pointless pursuit of Nancy, and, having caught up with her, was no longer sure that it was Nancy I wanted; and I had allowed myself to become bewitched by a young girl from a very different culture, and, unforgivably, to indicate to her my fascination. Beneath my modest academic air I was a villain, a feckless adrenaline-junkie, with a low boredom threshold and a feeble grasp of reality. I am sure, as Madame Lee studied me, that she had reached much the same conclusion.

'I cannot accept a gift of such value, Madame Lee.'

Her eyes were steady. 'I think you would not insult me, Dr Raven? Take the trinket. Friendship is without price.'

Chee Laan and I were alone. It was the day after my meeting with Sunii Lee. My hosts were attending an official function. Apart from the servants, I had the large house to myself. The housekeeper had shown Chee Laan into my suite. A slight breeze, welcome in the roasting heat, wafted up from the garden through the open balcony doors. I was showing her the book her grandmother had pressed on me. The servant, hiding her curiosity, had brought us tea. For the first time, Chee Laan and I were at ease with one another. Speculation and uncertainty had been replaced by wonder. This time we had not just witnessed a double murder. But the situation remained far from simple.

I flicked through the pages of the book. 'Why did your grandmother give me this—*The Summer Wives of Mount Lu*?'

Chee Laan twitched her eyebrows. 'I should have thought it was obvious, Raven. The story is well known.'

'So remind me!' I lounged back in the carved teak chair, hands behind my head, watching her. I could never tire of watching her. I was like a child under the spell of a new, exotic doll—except this doll had a mind like a laser, I reflected uneasily. I told myself fiercely that I had no right to be here, that everything about this situation was wrong, but still, in spite of myself, I listened to her, and watched with fascination the movement of muscle and sinew beneath the pale skin, the innocent mockery in the dark eyes.

She recited with the sweet, slightly precious didacticism of a trained nanny humouring a wilful child. 'The retired scholar Liu Tzu-Ching enjoys the solitude, the beauty of nature and his studies in his summer residence of Mount Lu. One day, ambling about contemplating lilies and peonies, in the traditional manner of Chinese sages, he sees wonderful butterflies—red, vermilion, and soft yellow. Every day they come, and every day the scholar admires them.

'One evening, when he's waiting for the moonrise, there's a knock at the door. Outside stand beautiful young women dressed in the butterfly colours—red, vermilion, soft yellow. They tell him they are so delighted by his admiration they will take turns to spend the summer nights with him. The scholar enjoys a blissful summer. But the summer wives always evade his questions. They refuse to say who they are. After the summer Liu leaves the mountain and his butterfly brides with an aching heart.

'One day he visits the nearby temple of Kang Wang. While studying clay and painted images of goddesses, he recognizes the lovely young girls, dressed in gossamer robes of red, vermilion, and soft yellow. Liu's heart fills with dread. He is guilty of having loved goddesses, which is forbidden. He realises he is in great danger of the vengeance of the gods. Despite his longing for his summer brides, he never returns to Mount Lu.'

'So I'm being warned off.' I had not told Chee Laan about her grandmother's gift of precious jade, which I had also allowed Sunii to force upon me. I felt squeamish about letting her see the token of her grandmother's estimate of her value.

'My grandmother is merely being protective. We need to worry much more about other things, Raven.'

'For instance, how Lieutenant Fleischer ended up at the bottom of a khlong? You still believe Salikaa had a hand in it?'

She nodded.

'Salikaa has done spectacularly well for herself. Why risk losing that?'

'Because Salikaa never forgets an insult. She is extremely vengeful. That is because of her upbringing. But she was my friend, and I do not have many friends.'

'I am not surprised, if your grandmother warns them off,' I blurted impulsively.

'My grandmother is not here now.' She moved to the bed, cupped my face in both her hands, and kissed me until I thought my hammering heart would burst through my ribs.

The tea grew cold. It was not until later that we resumed our conversation. It's odd how the mind short-circuits and returns to its last preoccupation before interruption.

'Van Hooten's wife tells me Salikaa's been invited to join the royal family at the summer palace,' I said. 'Prince Premsakul has invited me to stay at his summer residence on the royal estate at Hua Hin. So I'll be there, too. At court.'

Chee Laan moved away from me and grimaced. 'Lucky you're not Chinese, then,' she said.

'Your grandmother would prefer I were.'

'Merely to be Chinese would not be enough. Not any old Chinese. You'd have to be a scion of the Five Families. A good-good person.'

I laughed. 'Not much chance of that, then!' I took her in my arms, unable to resist any longer.

Summer Palace of Klai Kangwon, Hua Hin

Salikaa leapt on life at court like a panther on its kill. She threw herself into every activity. In the small outdoor pavilion at the summer palace, she was ostensibly teaching the court ladies to dance the tango. In the blazing tropical garden around the pavilion, the crickets and the royal cockatoo seemed to shrill more raucously, as though excited by the competition with the sultry strains of the tango oozing from the amplifiers. Salikaa danced with her eyes closed, intoxicated by her own body and the rhythm of the music from the portable record player. She prowled, whipping her sinuous hips in time to the music, every fluid movement a sensual invitation. The royal ballet mistress and the princess's ladies stood around, dourly surveying this latest, most scandalously flamboyant addition to the court circle. Their faces wore the obligatory simper, but their posture, stiff with affront, expressed their profound disapproval.

'Why must we learn this vulgar dance?' one prettily plump lady whispered peevishly. Her tight silk blouse already had damp patches under the arms.

'You know we always learn a new dance for Their Highnesses' wedding anniversary,' her companion whispered back. She, too, was panting slightly from her exertions.

'Yes. Of course. But why *this* horrible, disgusting Western dance? So undignified! We are not the scum of low bars in Pat Pong red light district, where those fat GIs go—we are not red light ladies, but Princesses of the Blood!'

Behind them, the summer palace of Klai Kangwon, Sans Souci, dipped pink stone toes in a sparkling turquoise sea. On the glittering horizon the sails of the Prince Regent's dinghy and those of his companions skimmed like swallows. From the adjacent military compound rose bellowed exhortations and the thud of a football. Off-duty guards and frogmen were disporting themselves on the green between the wooden chalets that housed the summer court.

The ladies nodded, bowing and smiling, as Princess Pim silently joined them in the exotic garden. 'Your future sister-in-law is a great beauty,' one said.

'Thank you,' Pim said, watching Salikaa and frowning pensively.

'I am sure His Majesty the King will think so,' the plump lady smirked, eyeing Pim sideways as she fanned herself with a palm leaf. The proud Premsakuls were not universally beloved. Pim herself was considered to be a dangerous eccentric. Her flirtation with socialism was widely known and heartily disapproved of. Yet it was rumoured that the young king had cast his eye upon this renegade.

'The king likes pretty ladies! All princes appreciate beauty!'

Pim drew in her breath sharply. The lady looked at her in mock concern, satisfied that her barb had struck home.

'Are you unwell, Princess?' she enquired sympathetically.

'It is nothing,' Pim smiled. 'Nothing at all.' She plucked a sprig of pink oleander and went over to Salikaa. 'You have such talent! Teach us to dance like you, sister-in-law!' She tucked the sugar-pink flower in Salikaa's hair and kissed her smooth cheek. Salikaa laughed, showing her small, white, feral teeth. She tossed her head. The oleander blossom fell to the earth.

Neither woman picked it up.

The Prince Regent had returned from the freedom of the sea, and now perched with his chosen companions in full view on the stage of the great hall. He and his band played a swing number of His Multi-talented Highness's own composing, in the manner of his idol, Glenn Miller. He rose for the clarinet spot, centre stage, and saluted the Princess Regent, sitting among her card-playing ladies, wagging his clarinet; she raised a hand in acknowledgement. She was drained. Her face muscles ached, but still she smiled. In her sleep she would smile; she would smile in death. Smiling was what she did and who she was. Thailand's Smile.

She had trudged miles in the heat that day, scaled a hundred steep, shallow, knee-breaking steps to a hillside monastery; she had adorned the sacred image with a wreath of jasmine, distributed food and clothing to the poor who materialised like ghostly wraiths from dusty plain and tangled jungle to gaze and gape and grovel. Throughout she smiled, bewitchingly, valiantly, unflinchingly. Throughout she remained compassionate, bandbox spruce, photo-ready. She could go nowhere unaccompanied. Ahead of her, bellowing into his radio, loped Colonel Sya, whose armed patrolmen were deployed along the projected route. At her side trotted her panting ladies, carrying sunshades and tissues and cologne in their Hermes handbags of sequined straw. Behind her sweated and cursed representatives of the media, humping cameras and microphones. She was the queen bee; where she flew, they swarmed. It was a gigantic public relations exercise, a coordinated counterblast to the creeping erosion of insurgency, and the tarnished image of Thailand, Sex Capital of the World. The Princess Regent was the most visible asset of the monarchy. Wholesome, compassionate, so exquisitely photogenic. The most beautiful woman in all Thailand, in all Asia, perhaps—probably—in all the world.

Until the arrival of this newly crowned queen, this new betrothed. This vivid, triumphant, uncompromising beauty promised her relief, a longed-for respite. The Princess Regent's eyes rested without jealousy on Salikaa.

On stage among the musicians, her ward the young monarch was seated at the drums. As usual, he made little attempt to keep the rhythm, simply thudded and bumped away monotonously; then, as if in a paroxysm of rage, attacked his timpani with a frenzy, skittering riffs, clashing cymbals with neither rhyme nor reason. These capricious, cacophonous interludes were invariably greeted by rapturous applause from the assembled courtiers.

Young King Vajah would have been handsome but for the pettish scowl which customarily darkened his countenance. His glossy black hair fell over a high forehead; his features were well modelled, his mouth full and sensuous, red-lipped but demarcated in delicate purple, and his skin the prized pale gold of honey. He knew, because everyone told him so, that he was irresistible. Brilliant. Unequalled in charm, talent, and intelligence. To have the good karma to be born a king, he knew he must be well advanced upon the path of enlightenment. Tiresome Pim Premsakul alone failed to appreciate his splendour. Perhaps everyone was right, and she was mad. Why, otherwise, when he had proposed to her, had she not fallen at his feet? 'I could not accept such an honour,' she'd said. How dare she! His cousin—

just an ordinary little princess.

Ordinary people's lives were a closed book to Vajah. He had never held one normal conversation. At his approach, people invariably fell flat on their faces and addressed the dust at his feet. Veneration, awe, and sentimentality formed the all-enveloping cloak that concealed sharp ambition. He knew the flattery was false; he had the intelligence to penetrate the smokescreen of sycophancy and to sense the self-interest behind it. But being universally indulged by all who surrounded him had generated self-indulgence and indolence. The first lesson, the only lesson a king needed to learn, was to be the right sort of king; the king those who wielded the true power wanted. Kings who made trouble ended up as ex-kings, or dead kings. King Vajah's immediate family held numerous examples of both these outcomes. Vajah recognised that the essential heart of kingship was prudence.

However, the ungrateful Pim would have to be taught a lesson. His eye fell on the new beauty, Prince Toom the boffin's surprising fiancée. He lifted his sticks and saluted her, with an ironic and lascivious grin, making sure the gesture was not lost on the ingrate, Pim. He abandoned his drums and approached her. Pim made obeisance.

'Your brother's a lucky man,' he said, openly watching Salikaa, allowing raw desire to play across his features. 'She's red-hot. She could drive a man mad.' He observed Pim to see if his words had piqued her jealousy, but she merely looked embarrassed. 'I am sure *she* would not spurn a king's advances,' he pouted, needling.

Pim looked him straight in the eye. 'Your Majesty would not wish to waste his time.'

He laughed delightedly. 'Do you say that because she is your brother's fiancée, or perhaps, after all, are you jealous?'

'Horrible spoiled little brat!' Salikaa exclaimed. She and Pim were getting ready for the evening's entertainment, the lavish buffet, the next session of card games and jazz and gossip in the great hall. Salikaa leaned toward the bathroom mirror, outlined her lips with dark lipstick. They looked like glossy summer fruit ripe for the picking. She smacked them to spread the colour evenly. 'Do you suppose he's a virgin?'

'Heavens, Salikaa!' Pim stopped, startled, her hand holding the hairbrush halfway up to her head. 'He is the king! His head is the most sacred object in the kingdom.'

'So?' Salikaa shrugged. 'It's not his head I'm thinking about. Tonight, when I dance, every man in the audience will want me. Even the spoiled brat. Virgin or no.' Impulsively, Salikaa dropped her lipstick in the wash basin. It rattled round, smearing the blue porcelain bowl with a scarlet bruise. Salikaa threw her arms about Pim. 'Oh, Pim, I'd like to bed every man in the world. Every single one, and none of them!'

'You talk such rubbish, Salikaa!'

'No! I want my image to haunt the brain of every man who sees me, even when he lies with his own woman!'

Pim stiffened. 'Salikaa. When are you going to tell Toom the truth? That you can't marry him, you don't love him, he'll never have children by you…'

Salikaa laid a long-nailed finger across Pim's lips. She brought her face very close to Pim's. 'Shh!' she warned. Her exotically painted eyes glittered dangerously. Pim backed away, shaking her head. 'Things happen to those who get in my way, Pim,' Salikaa warned. 'Bad things. I love you, Pim, but I warn you, don't try to stand in my way. I can make the man I choose happier than he has any right to expect.'

Pim stared at her in alarm.

Salikaa picked up her little sequined purse. 'Time to go.'

They set off through the fragrant garden toward the lighted palace.

Raven sensed the tension in the air, something more than the usual anticipation of a new dance to be performed. The court ladies, twittering like an aviary of jewel-coloured hummingbirds, managed between them to locate their tango record. Giggling, they took the stage and arranged themselves in couples, a taller lady with a shorter. The young king sat between his guardians, the Prince and Princess Regent, on a red velvet sofa. All three sat bolt upright, smiling in polite anticipation. A flunky had shown Raven to a seat on the front row, to the right of the royal party. On the left of the hall he glimpsed the burly figure of Sya Dam, standing, arms folded, hooded eyes watchful. As usual, he was in uniform, but bareheaded, off duty.

The strains of the tango filled the hall, and the ladies, holding one another chastely at arms' length, began their dance. Only Salikaa danced alone, swaying, eyes shut. Some of the dancing ladies were by nature ill-suited to the tango, being short of leg and ample of bust. Sometimes the pillowed torsos bumped awkwardly, and the young king suppressed a giggle.

Nobody saw Salikaa make her move, but suddenly she occupied centre stage. Her eyes now wide open, fixed on the king, flashing a challenge, she danced, the bright chiffon gown flickering about her long slim legs like tongues of flame. The other ladies stopped dancing and fell back, staring. All eyes were on Salikaa. Prince Toom, drawn as by a magnet to the foot of the stage, gazed up at his fiancée with adoration and apprehension. Salikaa reached out a hand to him. He sprang onto the stage, and she pressed herself against him and drew him into her dance. It was her will and her desire that dominated, and the young man, acquiescent, followed blindly, in a trance, as the flame-coloured dress swirled about him and Salikaa's flying black locks whipped his face and stung tears to his eyes. When the tension in the hall had risen to fever pitch, the music abruptly ceased. Salikaa dropped Toom's hand without looking at him. She slipped gracefully down from the stage, strode across the floor, still with the hot pride of the tango in her step and her bold, shameless eyes, and dropped to her knees before the young king. Her hair, disordered from the passion of the dance, tumbled over her face like a dark curtain.

There was a stunned silence. Then King Vajah reached out a hand that shook very slightly, and lifted her chin. Seeking her eyes with his own fiery gaze, he murmured throatily, 'You are fantastic!'

Salikaa inclined her head modestly. Then she rose, her momentary humility banished by her old hauteur, and strode from the pavilion, looking neither to the right nor the left. She passed so close by Raven that her chiffon gown brushed his shin. But she acknowledged nobody. There was a rustling chorus of gasps and whispers. 'She did not request permission to withdraw!' squeaked the ladies. 'And that dancing! Shameless!'

Mrs van Hooten, sitting ramrod straight just behind the Princess on an uncompromising Louis Seize chair, uttered the one penetrating monosyllable that summed up the general astonished consternation.

'Well!'

The dancing ladies trotted to the edge of the stage and took their rehearsed bow. The royal party led polite, embarrassed applause. The king, after a moment's hesitation, joined in. A small sigh of satisfaction rose from the court. Order appeared restored. Raven looked round for Sya Dam, but he was nowhere to be seen.

Salikaa stalked unseeing through the garden, brushing aside the barked query of the guards, into the Premsakul summer villa. The house guard and servants came running. Dismissing them with a curt nod, she walked up to the first-floor suite that had been assigned to her. She went to the window and leaned on the sill, peering out through the darkness toward the distant lights and sounds of the palace. She waited, listening. She soon heard running footsteps approaching; her sharp ears caught the swish of clothing against branches, then the noise of swift, athletic footsteps, mounting the wooden stairs two at a time—a body flung against her door, fists pounding.

'Salikaa? Salikaa, let me in!' The voice, high with desperation and hurt, was that of her fiancé, Prince Toom Premsakul.

Salikaa did not reply, or even turn in the direction of the sound. She continued to lean on the sill, staring out into the night. The air, though cooler, still hoarded the heat of the day; heavy with perfume and dust, it beat softly against her temples. *It is happening*, thought Salikaa. *It is all coming together. Nothing can stop me now.* She savoured her power, lightheaded with her own cunning.

Toom burst into the room. 'How could you, Salikaa?' he demanded. His sad eyes roved over her face, desperately seeking reassurance.

'Toom, dear, you are out of breath. You have been hurrying, getting yourself excited. It will bring on your asthma. Sit down, please. Have some tea.' She made as if to ring for the servant. He dropped his hand over hers to forestall this.

'I do not want tea, Salikaa! I want to know why you made a laughingstock of me!' She raised her eyebrows in polite query. 'Dancing like that in front of everyone. You know how difficult my family has been about our engagement, the opposition we face…and this is how you behave! Playing into the hands of those who disapprove! I—I simply cannot understand you, Salikaa!'

Salikaa sat down on the pink silk divan and kicked up her long legs in the flame chiffon. She leaned sideways, selected a cigarette from an ebony box inlaid with silver, and lit it with the big silver table lighter, ignoring Toom's pout of disapproval. 'Relax, Toom, darling,' she said, blowing smoke through her nostrils. 'So we danced. Big deal. We showed up all those dumpy little dowagers with figures like sacks full of rotting durians, so they'll hate our guts—so what? They hate us already. You're a smartass little princeling, and I'm a guttersnipe, but I'm gorgeous. Nothing will ever stop them loathing us. Anyway, who gives a shit? The king liked it. His young Randiness thought our little number was just great.'

His face darkened. 'You should not talk that way about His Majesty, Salikaa! And that is another thing. I saw the effect you had on him—everyone saw, it was so blatant! I saw the way you looked at each other. How could you do that, Salikaa? He is just a boy, and you, you are my fiancée—and he is the king, Salikaa!'

Salikaa kicked her bare toes, whisking the chiffon. She blew a smoke ring.

'Precisely!' she said, closing her eyes and smiling smugly, like a contented cat. 'Little Vajah is the king!' She stretched her long limbs luxuriously, throwing her head back in a gesture that, reminding him as it did of the tango, merely increased his agitation. He struck his fist on the headrest of the divan.

'I-I won't have it, do you h-hear?' he exclaimed, rage causing his stammer to return. He stamped his foot in frustration. 'I know people don't think I'm much of a fellow, Salikaa. They think I'm weak and feeble, a pushover and a swot. But I love you, Salikaa, and I want you for my wife, and I'll face anything to make that happen, endure anything—but I can't bear it when you behave like that in public, don't you see?'

There came a discreet knock at the door.

'Yes?' Toom shouted, swinging round, irritated.

A servant entered, head bowed, hiding his curiosity, bearing an envelope and a small package on a silver salver. Salikaa extended an indolent hand, and the servant, kneeling, handed her the salver. She opened the packet first. She snapped open the small leather case and slid out the object it contained. Her features softened into an expression of deep satisfaction. Then she slipped it on and extended her hand for Toom's inspection.

The gift was a ring of white gold, its principal stone a huge pigeon-blood ruby surrounded by diamonds. Beside it, even Toom's square-cut sapphire paled into insignificance. While he contemplated the effect, scowling, with her other hand she straightened out the note. She scanned it and, wordlessly, handed it to Toom. He read: 'Salikaa: You have bewitched me. I must see you. Expect me tonight. Vajah.'

'Toom,' she purred, patting the note tenderly, 'my moment has arrived!'

He stared at her, horrified comprehension dawning. 'So that's it! You planned it all! You've been angling for a bigger fish! You used me. Exploited my love for you, tricked me, when all you wanted was to get close enough to make an impression on the king—and now that I've played my part, I can be tossed aside! For shame, Salikaa! I expected better of you.'

'Oh, Toom, darling, do get a grip on reality, you're breaking my heart!' Salikaa calmly rose from the sofa and strolled over to the mirror. She peered close to check her make-up, smoothing her eyebrows and dabbing at her lipstick. 'What time do you suppose he means, when he says "tonight"?'

Toom stared at her, aghast. Behind his thick glasses, hot tears filled his eyes; he bit his lower lip sharply to stop it trembling, and the taste of his own blood was oddly comforting. 'How the hell should I know? How can you ask me? You must be crazy, Salikaa, mad with ambition.' He was angry now, and the rage gave him courage for a moment. 'My father is right. You are just a cheap gold digger!' he said bitterly.

'And you, dear, are just a sentimental fool,' she said, turning to face him.

'Yes,' he replied, choking on the word, tears streaming unchecked down his face, 'how right you are! I have been a fool. I've had all I can take. Goodbye, Salikaa. I hope you will never feel as wretched as I do at this moment.'

'Oh, don't worry, darling,' she returned, losing interest in him and returning to the contemplation of her face. 'I don't suppose I ever shall.'

Blind with weeping, he rushed out the door, almost blundering into the young king who, attended only by one servant, was at that moment mounting the stairs.

Their eyes met for only a second. Then Toom bowed low, and the king nodded curtly.

'Cousin Toom...' he began, uncertain what words or ceremonies might be appropriate to this unprecedented situation. But Prince Toom Premsakul stumbled away, sobbing noisily, rushing headlong into the night. Behind him the mosquito screen clacked violently back and forth on its hinges. King Vajah sighed, raised his eyebrows, and continued up the stairs to the door of Salikaa's apartments. The servant who had observed this brief encounter slipped away quickly to inform his master, Colonel Sya, of the events he had witnessed.

Salikaa had extinguished her cigarette and stood waiting for him, head bowed. King Vajah marched in assertively, and then stopped, unsure how to proceed.

'I sent you a gift,' he said. Silently she extended her hand, displaying the ruby ring. He nodded peremptorily. 'Your dancing pleased me. That is all.'

She bowed to the dust. 'Your Majesty is too gracious.'

'That is all it was,' he insisted. 'A mere token of my appreciation. Nothing more, you understand.' He stepped nearer and stood looking down at her.

'Of course not,' she murmured silkily.

Some undertone of mockery in her voice stung him, and he reached out and lifted her chin, forcing her to meet his gaze. 'I am the king!' he said. He dropped his grip on her chin and saw to his surprise that his fingers had left a mark. He stared at it, fascinated. He was unaccustomed to touching the bodies of other people. The sensation was new and intoxicating. His touch had left an imprint on this woman's flesh. 'I am the king!' he repeated, with greater forcefulness, as though to convince himself.

'That is so,' she said smoothly, as one soothing a fractious infant.

'Do not use that tone with me!' he said sharply. 'I am not a child.'

She regarded him coolly, tilting her head, raising one sceptical eyebrow. But she said nothing. There were limits, it seemed, with this man.

'I am a man,' Vajah said, with emphasis. 'And I am a king. I can have whatever I please. I can have you. Right now.' He put his hands about her throat, tightened his fingers, and shook her. Feeling her tremble, he released her. Then he saw to his rage and surprise that she was quivering not with fear, but with helpless laughter.

'What's so funny?' he demanded.

'What you say may well be true,' Salikaa smiled. 'But I know one thing you can't do.'

'What is that?' he demanded truculently, staring her down, head lowered, the sensual lower lip protruding.

'You couldn't marry me. You could force yourself on me, or have me banished or imprisoned, or even killed, but you couldn't ever marry me! No king could ever marry someone like me!' She laughed triumphantly. He stared at her while the import of her assertion sank in.

'Sit down,' he commanded, seating himself on the divan and tugging her down beside him. She sat, suddenly docile. He took her hands and examined them as if he had never seen human hands before. 'Salikaa,' he said, sliding his hands up to her slender wrists and shaking them as he looked deep into her eyes, 'you are the most beautiful woman in Thailand. The most beautiful woman I've ever seen...'

'Your Majesty is very young. You are fifteen years old and have lived behind the walls of palaces all your life. How many women have you seen?'

He coloured hotly. 'They've been throwing prospective brides in my path ever since I was a child. Every headman and princeling, every politician and general, it seems, has a marriageable daughter. Even my own relations parade nubile maidens before me like prize heifers. God, but I'm weary of it! I will choose for myself.'

'You are a true king, Majesty,' Salikaa murmured, and her dark eyes mocked him.

But he was in earnest, and did not notice. 'Salikaa, if I wished, I could choose you for my bride. Thailand must have the most beautiful queen in the world.'

'Thailand already has the most beautiful Princess Regent in the world. The Princess Asra,' Salikaa said.

To her surprise, his face clouded. He dropped her hands and turned his face away from her. 'Asra, Asra. Always Asra,' he exclaimed. 'Asra is not only Miss Universe, she is an angel, a goddess. The people will never love me as they love Asra. That is why my queen must be even more beautiful than Asra.'

Suddenly he hauled her roughly against him, pressing his lips feverishly against her face, her throat, her hair.

'You are the only woman who can compete with Asra, Salikaa. One day Thailand's Smile will fade, but your beauty will still dazzle. That is why I must have you for my queen.'

He held her fiercely, burying his face in her hair, pressing his body against her. She lay in his arms, unresisting, yet unresponsive as a doll. When at last, terrified by the strength of his own feelings, he released her, she withdrew from his embrace, reordering her hair and clothing fastidiously as a cat. He watched her, unable to speak. At length, she looked at him appraisingly.

'You mean that? You would marry me, defying them all?'

He nodded. 'I have never really cared about anything in my life, Salikaa—never wanted anything this way. But I want you, Salikaa, and my mind is made up. I will marry you!' Clumsily he fell to his knees, throwing his arms about her slim hips, burying his face in the folds of her flame-coloured dress, greedily inhaling the musky scent of her, all other thoughts blotted out by his desire and his newfound resolution.

Salikaa buried her long scarlet nails in the boy-king's dark, glossy hair and pressed him closer against her. She looked down at him once, and then raised her head and gazed thoughtfully out at the dark garden. She smiled.

For a moment they remained locked together, motionless, until the sound of heavy footsteps approaching startled them apart. The door of the suite was flung open, and Sya Dam, propelling the snivelling Prince Toom before him like an arrested malefactor, burst in upon them. Behind Sya, panting from his unwonted exertions, followed Prince Premsakul himself, his customary self-satisfied smirk replaced by an expression of indignation. King Vajah leapt to his feet, scowling at the intrusion.

'What is the meaning of this outrage?' he demanded.

Sya released Toom, who slumped to the floor. Sya prostrated himself before the king. 'Your Majesty, Her Highness the Princess Regent is concerned for you. Your Majesty left the company somewhat abruptly. Perhaps Your Majesty would return to the pavilion, and reassure Their Highnesses?' Despite the deference, his tone was insistent.

Resentment flared in the young king's face, succeeded by doubt. He looked very young. Although his whims and tantrums had been indulged, he had never in his life been permitted to make a decision of any importance. With pathetic dignity, he sought to reassert his authority. 'Do you rebuke me, Colonel? You will kindly not presume to inform me of my duty. I was engaged in a private conversation with this lady.'

'Your Majesty...'

'This—this is an unpardonable intrusion, Colonel!'

'My humblest apologies, Your Majesty. Naturally, Your Majesty knows his duty best?' Even prostrate, nose close to the floorboards, the powerful body in its fatigues and polished combat boots lacked humility.

The king sighed. 'Indeed, Colonel. But in fact, your reminder is not untimely!' He threw back his shoulders. His speech had resumed its habitual formality. The momentary lapse in etiquette might never have occurred.

He turned to Salikaa.

'I shall speak with you upon some other occasion, *Khun* Salikaa. Please remember our conversation. I assure you, I meant what I said.' His defiant gaze rested upon the recumbent colonel. He looked back at Salikaa and tapped his lips with one forefinger, as a promise of business not concluded. Salikaa curtsied low. The boy-king nodded with brief courtesy and marched from the room. Two guards detached themselves like shadows from the stairwell, holstered their guns and slipped into place, one ahead of the striding king, the other following.

Sya sprang up and dusted off the knees of his fatigues. Prince Premsakul was standing over his son, shaking his head. 'Do get up off the floor and stop that tiresome grovelling, Toom, there's a good chap,' he said, prodding his son. 'Don't know what the dickens was going on here. Rum business altogether. Don't know, don't wish to know.'

Toom scrambled to his feet and stared at his father. 'Isn't it obvious?' he cried in a strangled voice, thick with emotion. 'Oh, I've been blind! I—I'm sorry, Father. You are right to despise me. I've made a mess of things, let everyone down, as usual!' He rushed from the room.

'Dear me,' Prince Premsakul grunted peevishly. 'Most disconcerting, all these young hotheads dashing about all over the shop. Better toddle along and see what the young blighter's up to. Don't know why you had to drag me along, Sya, old man. One does so deplore displays of emotion. Oh well, there we are, I suppose!' He turned and walked with unaccustomed vigour toward the stairs.

Alone, Salikaa turned to confront Sya. He moved close to her, glowering down; she could smell the hot, spicy odour of his breath and the tang of his male sweat. She shivered and stepped back.

'You are strange to the ways of court, lady.' His triangular eyes were yellow-black, but had the blood-red sheen of a rabid dog's. The drooping folds at the corners made him look age-old yet somehow innocent, like some Mongol warrior, quaffing fermented mare's milk outside his yurt as he selected a human head to play polo with.

'The court itself has strange ways, Colonel,' Salikaa retorted, meeting his gaze without flinching. They squared up to each other like boxers, gauging the challenge.

'Perhaps court life is too foreign to you. Unlike some of us, you are free, *Khun* Salikaa. You do not need to stay here. Your Princely Betrothed will release you of all obligation. He has already perceived his error, squandering his affections on a manipulative little gold digger with no family who would cuckold him before the wedding. Toom may have his head in the clouds, but he's no fool.'

Salikaa threw her head back and laughed. 'Is that a threat? I have no family, perhaps—but I have a stepfather who can command almost as much firepower as you yourself, Colonel. He fears nobody. He will not be pleased when he hears you have threatened me.'

Sya chuckled, as though in genuine amusement. 'Old Vichai, you mean? Is the old rascal still going strong? That's an oversight. We must mop up these communist-funded pockets of insurgency. Prejudicial to the stability of the realm.'

Salikaa stared at him. 'Rubbish! You know damn well Vichai isn't a communist!' She was angry now, eyes blazing, hands on her hips. A woman of the people, showing her true colours. Salikaa was no Lady Asra. She'd never be able to pass herself off as a princess.

Sya grinned. 'I might know that. But the Americans don't.'

'Since when do the Americans interfere in internal Thai matters?'

He laughed delightedly at her naïveté. 'You're so innocent, poppet. Our gallant allies help us secure our borders against the Red Threat.' He grasped her chin in an iron grip, turning her face this way and that, scrutinising. 'That Threat is wherever we see it. Wherever I see it.'

Salikaa reached out, cupped his chin, and brought her face close to his. She bit down on his mouth until she tasted his blood; Sya brought his fist up and hit her so hard that she flew across the room. Her legs struck the divan and buckled under her, and she sprawled backward onto the silk cushions. She thought her jaw might be broken. Only stubborn pride prevented her from fingering it to assess the damage.

Blood snaked down from Sya's lip. With a muttered curse he wiped it off on the back of his hand.

'If you're going to play grown-up games you'll need to grow up first, little mouse,' he said dispassionately. He turned his back on her and walked from the room.

'I'll kill you!' she hissed after his retreating back. She drove her long fingernails into her palms until they drew blood. 'Fuck you, you bastard!'

After a while, when all was silent but for the distant ocean and the cicadas in the garden, and nobody came, not the cowering servants nor the curious guards, Salikaa sat up and examined her jawbone and decided it was merely bruised, an insignificant injury indeed for a survivor of Lieutenant Fleischer's school of hard knocks. Nothing a dab of cologne, an ice pack, and a good foundation cream could not disguise. It was the insult that really stung. But there again, she might, if she wished, capitalise on it; publicly denounce Colonel Sya for his unprovoked assault. But no, this was not the right moment. She must play her cards carefully in the future. Now, more than ever, Salikaa needed Tamsin. But Tamsin had not returned from his last assignment, and this could mean only that he was in prison, or dead. If Fleischer had killed Tamsin, it would be highly inconvenient. It meant Tamsin could not do the world the inestimable favour of stifling the odious Colonel Sya Dam.

Idly, Salikaa wondered what had become of her young fiancé. Perhaps, she thought, she should go in search of him—he had looked so wild-eyed and extravagant, spouting all that rubbish. His Majesty had swallowed the bait, but Toom was still needed. A bird in the hand was worth two in the hedge. Or whatever the ridiculous *farang* proverb was.

Summer Palace of Klai Kangwon, Hua Hin

Raven

So much, I thought, *for my airy promise to Chee Laan to keep an eye on Salikaa.* I'd watched her little interplay with the young king with a growing sense of unease and foreboding. A whole Panzer division could not have looked out for Salikaa. Salikaa was a kamikaze on a self-appointed collision course.

When the king left the hall, the music died. As if the orchestra had been the last bastion of discipline, the silk-clad courtiers became a marketplace rabble, breaking up into little knots, whispering, squeaking, hands fluttering, their eyes wild with speculation.

The Prince Regent beckoned to Sya, silent as a shadow. The chatter stopped. Watched by a hundred pairs of eyes, curious, jealous, anxious, Sya inclined his shaven head with humility, then rose and saluted, leaving the hall at a purposeful lope.

Clearly, he had been despatched to find the king and present him to them once more, before face had suffered too disastrous a loss. The pillared hall seethed with speculation. Conversation flickered, sporadic now, voices muted, anxious to excuse a young and impetuous king. Prince Premsakul reappeared, smiling to everyone. He took his place beside his family. I noticed that none of them spoke to one another, and that the boy Toom had not returned to the hall.

Covertly I watched the Princess Regent. Her heartbreaking smile never wavered as she shredded the dark purple orchids with waxy tapering fingers. Hours seemed to pass before we heard again the hurried stamp of the colonel's boots. Ahead of him the young king stalked back into the hall, to an audible sigh of relief, those he passed bowing to the dust like jungle grass flattened by helicopter rotors. The boy appeared breathless and angry.

His struggle to control such a breach of manners was touching, but he had changed. Arrogance had given way to a self-contained, petulant pride. Modestly, he took his place beside his guardians. A liveried usher hastened off on some new mission, and as the Premsakul family, father, mother, and daughter, watched him go, Pim frowned. Her pale brow contracted with worry. I sensed her fear, and that it was only her disciplined upbringing that kept her sitting there like a statue when she was longing to break free and leap to her feet.

Sya Dam bowed before the Prince Regent, shaking his head regretfully in response to some unheard query. Dismissed with an anxious glance from the prince, the colonel walked determinedly over to where I was sitting. He stood looking down at me, smiling broadly.

'May I sit here, Dr Raven?'

'Delighted, Colonel.' The elderly general and his lady who had been sitting with me, courteously rehearsing the litany of politeness—have you eaten noodles, can you eat *nam pla*, how many temples have you visited, do you find the climate of Bangkok intolerable—now excused themselves and moved away, with, I fancied, considerable relief. Sya looked briefly across at the young king, sitting very straight on his velvet chaise longue.

'His Majesty was easy to find. Now they have sent another emissary to find Prince Toom. Then everything will settle down.' I doubted that very much, but Sya leaned back in his chair expansively, smiling more broadly than ever. 'Ah! The ways of the Thai court, a sacred mystery to foreigners such as ourselves, eh, Dr Raven?'

Sya carefully set his radio on the table between us. He glanced at me as if challenging me to question his foreign status, sizing me up. I allowed my eyebrows to twitch just sufficiently to indicate slight interest rather than vulgar curiosity.

'Make no mistake. I am a tribesman. To these people, I am a dangerous animal. I belong in a zoo.' Sya looked at my expression and laughed. 'Oh, yes, indeed so! The Thais are well aware of this. In that charming northern capital, Chiengmai, Rose of the North, they have established a human zoo. There, the interested visitor may view specimens from each tribe—except the Spirits of the Yellow Leaves, aboriginals, so few, so pathologically shy that no one can get close to them. They keep the tame tribespeople in an enclosure. It is convenient for photo opportunities. Tourists can shudder at the barbarity, squalor, and ignorance on display.' His bull neck seemed to thicken as anger suffused his broad golden face. He gripped the radio in a powerful, short-fingered grip like a bear's paw, and banged it gently up and down on the table, shaking the single orchid spray in its fragile vase. 'People do not realise that the tribes are a disgrace to this country, an affront to the administration and the royal family themselves, who are doing everything in their power to improve conditions, enhance the tribes' social status and self-esteem.'

I grunted. 'I don't suppose being kept in a zoo does much for the self-esteem of any species.'

'A zoo is all the tribes are fit for,' Sya snapped. 'Before real progress can be made, the opium trade must be stamped out. Our government have been very patient. They realise these people live far from civilisation, remote not only geographically, but also spiritually. They inhabit a savage world of primitive violence, peopled by ghosts, steeped in filth and ignorance. It's hard to persuade such people of the advantages of growing peaches instead of opium. They don't know what peaches are. They don't want to know. Opium they know.'

Sya shifted in his chair, tilted back and stuck his feet out straight in front of him.

'No Thai would sit like this,' he said. 'Show the soles of my feet!' He saw me looking at his boots and laughed. 'Sure. I keep my boots on. Even in drawing rooms. Know why, eh?' His eyes challenged me. 'I never saw boots until I was twelve years old. Look at my head!' He twisted his shapely naked skull. The sharp-pointed ears seemed pinned back, like an animal's, questing the wind. 'I used to pluck the hairs out of my skull one by one, and leave the back part hanging down in a pigtail. I was the first male of my tribe to have that pigtail cut off. After they did it, I lay awake sweating in terror for three days and three nights. The Thai priests, they told me it would be okay. Everything hunky-dory. But I was sure the spirits would steal my mind. I watched myself for signs I was going mad. I didn't dare go to sleep. I knew they'd come for me!' He smiled mirthlessly at the recollection. 'Some dumb fuck, huh?'

'You don't seem to have much respect for the tribes. That must make your job difficult,' I suggested quietly.

Sya looked at me. 'How, difficult?'

'I thought you were part of the government propaganda machine,' I said. 'Rallying the tribes, all that.'

'Oh, the tribes have royalty fever just like everyone else in this country. Even the Akha will trek through the mountains for days for a glimpse of the Princess Regent's petticoat.'

'So they're not terrorists.'

'Don't believe all you hear. Terrorists, dog-eaters, drinkers of blood. All big-style bullshit. Pigs and opium. That's all my people know. Hopeless people.'

He leaned forward, scraping his boots back beneath his chair, jabbing at me with a stubby forefinger.

'My father grew the poppy all his days. They would tell him to plant another crop, but somehow it never worked out. Then they sent experts. In Thailand these days, we're knee-deep in experts. The experts advised my father to abandon agriculture. They lured him, and the tribe, with the promise of a comfortable life in a state reservation. So he led his people, a hundred or more, through the jungle for days. Through those mountains where there are no tracks—they had to cut their way through. They took all they had: pregnant sows and pregnant women, old folks, babies, cooking pots, gods, sacred symbols and opium. They were never going back. They were going to start a new life in security and comfort.

'It was hard to find their way to the town, but in the end they made it, and then they were happy, for they were going to be part of things at last—in touch with the centre, the kernel strength of the nation. Know what happened?'

I shook my head, reluctant to interrupt his flow.

'They were turned away. Too many tribespeople wanted places in the reservation. The land allocation was inadequate. In short, somebody had goofed. Or it had been intended like that all along.'

'So what did they do?'

Sya regarded me without expression. 'What should they have done? For a day or two they sat around on the ground. Some of the foreign experts and Thai officials took their pictures.'

I'd seen some of those award-winning anthropological studies, giant blow-ups mounted on chipboard screens. Zeiss and Leica had lingered lovingly on those handsome, sullen people, picking out every detail of the richly ornamented costume, every lineament of the proud, hard-bitten countenances.

'My tribe still wears the scarlet, black, and silver,' Sya said. 'It shows up well. The women's headdresses are especially photogenic. They decorate them with old silver coins and scarlet feathers. They wear them from puberty to death, never take them off.'

'Awkward in the shower,' I quipped, and immediately regretted it.

Sya snorted with laughter. 'You kidding? Akha don't shower! What do you think we are—you imagine we go in for ritual bathing before entertaining customers, like some Thai tart? Three times is enough for any body to be washed. At birth, marriage, and after death. Washing is dangerous. Water spirits. Worst of the lot.' He looked at me a little longer than necessary. 'Tribesmen fear spirits and devils, it's true. But the most powerful devil of all is the secret devil that lives inside every tribesman. The devil that never dies.'

I felt a prickling sensation along my spine, the fine hairs stirred on my neck. The warning was clear. Sya smiled, his eyes almost disappearing behind the bulging cheekbones, like a Japanese garden Buddha, both genial and malign.

'I do not think my brother officers will find Prince Toom,' he said. 'I guess I'll go help. Excuse me.' The smile disappeared; only the warning remained. While I sat thinking about this, I heard a low voice close to my ear.

'Dr Raven.' Suddenly the Princess Pim was beside me, her narrow face darkened with anxiety. I looked at her trembling lips and half rose, pulling out the chair for her. 'Forgive the intrusion. I have a feeling that something really bad has happened to my brother. He—he was so distressed.'

Then I knew. If something bad hadn't happened to Toom, it was about to. 'Excuse me, Princess!' I said, setting off as fast as I could after Sya's retreating figure.

My exit was blocked by the sturdy figure of van Hooten, who had been listening unashamedly from the next table. He too swung into decisive action. 'You go on over and visit some with your momma, young lady,' he said to Pim, 'and the doc here and I will offer our services. We'll stroll around, do a recce, and report back in due course. But there's surely no need to upset yourself. Boys will be boys, eh, Raven?'

Pim's eyes stayed on my face, unwavering. 'We're very close. I have this really bad premonition...' she entreated.

Van Hooten dropped an avuncular paw on her slender shoulder. I saw her wince at the liberty, and just as quickly control herself, standing meekly with the large freckled hand creasing her dark blue silk dress.

'Now, never you fret, Princess! We'll bring your brother back, dead or alive!' He guffawed at his own wit. The girl rose, and looked from one to the other of us, the blood draining from her face.

I followed van Hooten at forced-march pace along the sea, a dark, breathing presence that was visible only as the small waves broke, showing their white teeth. Further down the quiet beach other searchers ran, torches bobbing. The torches converged; voices were raised. I broke into a run. Beside me, running easily for such a big man, the American kept pace. The torch beams flickered over the blue, green, and scarlet hulls of the beached sailing dinghies.

'One of the boats is missing!' Van Hooten pulled up to a walk. 'The damned young fool!'

Even in the darkness, it struck me that my companion's expression was one of satisfaction rather than regret.

The body washed up the next morning. The guards, running along the golden sands in their dawn training session, discovered it, lying dark and still as a beached log. They stopped their cheerful yelling and quickened their pace. The young prince lay face down on the sand, one arm draped across his head as though resting. Deprived of his hallmark spectacles and permanently worried expression, when they rolled him over gently, his eyes gazed at the sky without reproach. For once, Toom the scientist seemed not to be searching for answers.

He had been killed, it was ascertained, by a severe blow to the back of the head—doubtless from the boom, which had swept him into that blood-warm water, which in turn had cradled him until he slipped from unconsciousness into lifelessness. An easy death, or so Sya assured the distraught mother and sister. His princely father received the news with admirable stoicism, his famous aplomb unruffled.

The missing sailing dinghy was not found until sometime later. There was not a mark on it, but then, no one seriously expected there to be.

'So very sad. That fine young man.' General van Hooten murmured the conventional regrets to Colonel Sya as the pair of them walked purposefully toward the Premsakul villa. 'Clever boy, I hear. Untimely death.'

'What is to one man untimely is to another timely,' Sya replied evenly, without looking at him. 'Events have their seasons. Their inner logic.' With the small cane he carried, he slashed at the bright faces of blooms in the flowerbed as they passed.

'Now you've lost me, Colonel. I'm a babe in arms when it comes to Eastern mysticism.' The American's Southern drawl purred like molasses. Sya snorted and shot a sideling glance at his companion.

'We are not all mystics, General. We too have our notions of expediency.'

Now for the first time, the American swung his heavy jaw round and looked at the shorter man who walked very straight beside him. 'Why, Colonel Sya, I surely do not comprehend your use of an expression such as "expediency" in the present terrible circumstances! Now, for land's sakes, what expediency could there ever be in the heart-rending tragedy of that fine boy's death?'

Sya stopped and looked at him. 'I wonder,' he said softly. He walked on through the blazing garden into the house of sorrow, where the wails of Princess Premsakul floated from an open window.

Salikaa had remained at the villa. Nobody seemed to know what to do with her. She had become an embarrassment. Now Sya himself would speak to her, and, for reasons he did not choose to divulge, had insisted the American must accompany him.

'Let's go pay our respects to the grieving fiancée,' he suggested. Again van Hooten fell into step beside him.

A frightened servant showed them into the sitting room. They hardly had time to take in the view of hills and sea, the delicate shell-pink furnishings, when the troublesome creature burst into the elegant room like a fury.

'I want to see the king! Take me to Vajah!' She flew at Sya and shouted into his face. 'I won't be treated like this! I have an understanding. You can't treat me like nothing.'

He looked at her, considering. 'You are nothing. You have nothing.' He tilted his head. 'But you may, perhaps, have something. A husband. Yes, that's what you need. A husband with a firm hand.'

'Don't think you can bully me,' she shrieked, beside herself. 'You can't sweep me under the carpet. My stepfather Vichai is the most powerful man in his province. He will protect me!'

'Would that Vichai be….?' the American queried, suddenly alert, leaving half his question dangling in the air.

'Vichai the Bandit!' exulted Salikaa. 'My stepfather is Vichai the Bandit!' She advanced the information with the air of one producing the ace of trumps. 'A king among bandits!'

General van Hooten looked thoughtful. 'I believe my presence here is somewhat *de trop*,' he said, 'so, if you will excuse me—Colonel, ma'am.'

Sya nodded. The American had swallowed the bait. Sya had what he wanted. Salikaa, glaring at Sya, ignored van Hooten. After he had left, Sya continued, as though without interruption:

'I have just the husband for you. My cousin Vasit.'

She stared at him. Her lip curled like a snarling cur's. 'Your cousin. A tribesman?'

He grinned wickedly. 'A black Akha. He will teach you manners. If I were not so busy I would marry you myself.'

Her mouth was dry, but she screwed up her jaw and spat. The spittle glistened on his chin. He caught her by her snake of black hair, spun her around, and pulled her back against him, twisting her head back so far that he could look down into her furious eyes, up her flaring nostrils. Holding her with one hand, he wiped his face clean with the switch of hair. 'Too far, young woman—you have gone too far!'

'I'll kill you,' Salikaa hissed.

Laughing, he released her. 'Someone, somewhere, surely will,' he said. 'Why not you?' Contemptuously, he added, 'Except I don't think you have the necessary talent.'

Van Hooten had returned to his office. Feeling well pleased with his own endeavours and deviousness, he extracted a cigar from his desk drawer and sat chuckling at the beautiful symmetry of it all. Miss Amphorn, his secretary, had composed two letters in Siamese, wondering greatly but too well trained to enquire. The first she addressed, with a disapproving sniff, to a figure of myth and legend, Vichai the Bandit. She signed it as instructed 'a friend of your stepdaughter.' Honourable stepfather was urged to come across from his riverside stronghold to meet his stepdaughter on the outskirts of a neighbouring village. Only his intervention could save her from a terrible fate. If he came, all would be well, there would be celebrations, and Miss Thailand would achieve all her dreams.

The second was addressed to Colonel Sya of the Border Patrol Police, purporting to come from Vichai Kiengsri, whose rat's nest of escaped villains had long been a thorn in the flesh of the local administration and hence of Sya himself. It was to be businesslike, but not too educated, this quality to be demonstrated in a certain illogical emotionalism. It was to offer unconditional surrender. 'Weary of a life of crime, a social outcast, hunted like an animal, I wish to change. Now my adopted child has been accepted in high circles, I would not wish to embarrass her. In a token of good faith, I will hand myself over, on with my armaments and a substantial sum of money, so long as Colonel Sya is personally involved in the event. He is the only policeman I ever respected.' Miss Amphorn read back her composition in translation with a certain satisfaction.

'That's great, Miss Amphorn. Go buy some cheap Chinese stationery to type it on. And get a couple Cokes from the canteen while you're at it, heh?' Her smile disguised her exasperation with the peculiar ways of foreigners.

While she was gone, with one finger the general typed out a press release for future deployment:

Gallant Officer Falls in Gun Battle with Bandits

Colonel Sya of the Border Patrol Police, a gallant officer famous for his zealous eradication of corruption in the armed forces and in local administration, as well as for his unflinching devotion to the Chakri dynasty and the Thai people despite his tribal origins, fell yesterday in the course of duty. The colonel was shot while attempting to destroy a nest of communist terrorists under leadership of notorious bandit chieftain Vichai Kiengsri, whose depredations have long terrorised border regions. Colonel Sya's indomitable courage and devotion to duty will long be remembered.

He put it in an envelope, addressed it to the Editor-in-Chief, *Bangkok Herald* English Language newspaper, and tucked it in the picture frame behind his wife and daughter's smiling faces. Catching their eyes, he sighed. He wondered how soon he would have to cut his losses and run if things didn't work out.

Miss Amphorn was a conscientious girl. Even if it pleased her strange foreign boss to write letters in the name of a bandit terrorist, certain formalities should be observed. There was an oversight, but Miss Amphorn was blindingly efficient and would soon put it right. Smiling at the thought of how pleased the general would be, Miss Amphorn completed her task. In the top right-hand corner of the cheap white envelope, the stamped legend was clean and clear: US MAIL.

Miss Amphorn prided herself upon her meticulous attention to detail.

Now the recipients would be sure to know the official provenance of the letters, and would accord them due respect. She would not point out his little mistake to the general. She would wait until he discovered her cleverness, and rewarded her, perhaps with a bag of apples from the PX. Apples were so expensive in the Bangkok market, but admirable for one's complexion.

Summer Palace of Klai Kangwon, Hua Hin

Raven
I was strolling in the gardens of the summer palace, feigning an interest in the royal herbaceous border (a magnificent testament to the fifty gardeners' industry) and reflecting that I had been mercifully free of any communication from Smith for a considerable time. Our sole means of contact was through Drinkwater's diplomatic bag. He had sent me a couple of chivvying notes, which I had disregarded, and likewise his fussy instructions to 'keep him posted'. Now I was in Hua Hin, and not Bangkok, which eliminated that possibility. International telephone calls in Southeast Asia were a nightmare. Nothing was secure, anywhere, ever. Heaven only knows how the Americans managed to conduct a war with such a primitive and ineffectual system. As I strolled I was also keeping a close watch on Sya; he was sitting on the stone steps beside a large ornamental lion and yelling into his radio, when suddenly a motorcycle courier roared up with a post for him. He glanced at the letter and the envelope and grinned broadly. He yelled across the garden: 'Hey, Professor! I gotta go check something out. Fancy a joyride?'

I wanted to keep Sya in my sights, so I accepted. I reflected later that the last thing I fancied was a helicopter jaunt to witness battles—first the degrading spectacle of a cockfight, which seemed symbolic of the second battle, with human rather than avian casualties. Sya bawled over the noise of the rotor blades: 'We will see traditional Thai entertainment, Raven. More exciting than the *ramwong* dance! Better than the tango, even!' He grinned malevolently.

After we landed in the usual upcountry clearing, I followed him and the men who had come to meet him down a dusty path to what passed for a marketplace. He had not introduced me, and I was happy about that. I was less happy when I realised the nature of the spectacle we were about to witness.

The contestants held the two fighting cocks face to face. Bred for fury and bloodlust, these two, one black and one gold, had been handpicked for their savagery. Already their beaks were slashing the air. The market square was cleared, and the betting had already begun, men waving fistfuls of banknotes as the proud owners bound steel blades to the birds' spurs. The judge inspected the bindings. The betting boiled up suddenly like a pan of oil and then died away into an ominous silence. The two cocks were set facing each other, mad yellow irises glaring. Shaking free of the hands that restrained them, they hurled themselves at each other, squawking, and exploded in a shower of feathers. The blades opened a vein of deep purple somewhere deep in the gaudy plumage. There was no shriek of pain. Blood puddled the earth in thick gobs. Blood-maddened, the black cock drew back and in a frenzied attack drove its blade home. The golden bird staggered and fell, its neck gaping open.

The victor strutted over its paralysed victim, dragging its blade. Its owner, sweating with excitement, handed Sya a broad knife. Without expression he hacked off the golden cock's legs and tossed the mutilated rag of its body back into the ring. Even then it would not die, but struggled to its bloodied stumps, its mad eye blazing defiantly at its tormentors and the sun. The onlookers tossed it from hand to hand, tearing out its feathers. Finally, it was thrown into a basket, where, much later, in a shudder of blood-speckled feathers, it died.

As we left the place, Sya was still breathing hard like a blown horse, his eyes fiercely slitted. I was doing a fair job of controlling my nausea. Sya looked at me and laughed. 'Sentiment, my friend! Losing always has its price. These birds enjoy the battle. A bit like you and me, huh?' He looked down at his blood-stained hands and laughed again, twisting his wrists like a *ramwong* dancer. 'But there's only one winner. Blood!' he observed wryly. 'If you want to see blood, you should come to my village when we slaughter buffalo. We drink the warm blood and tear the raw flesh with our bare hands!' He paused, and then added, with sinister mischievousness, 'I wonder how Miss Thailand will adjust to the life!'

We entered a café; Sya called for two large Singha beers.

'You think I'm a barbarian? You should meet the rest of my family!' As he spoke he scanned my face intently, searching for a reaction. Something about his hyperbolic rant seemed false. I could not put my finger on it. I wondered how much he knew, then cursed myself for a fool. He knew everything. Of course he did.

'Raven, Black Bird.' He dropped his tone to a purr of feigned intimacy. 'Forget the damned tribes! The root cause of unrest in this country is not the tribes—it's the Chinese. Ruthless, clannish, ineradicable, like some creeping, poisonous weed. They spread their suckers everywhere. Can't rip 'em out, can't burn 'em out. Don't talk to me about the traditional Thai policy of assimilation—it's broken-backed. Until the Chinese stranglehold on the economy is broken, stability in Thailand will remain a pipe dream. Once it was the *farang* who owned the corporate conglomerates. Who do you think owns them today?'

He thumped his fist on the table.

'Even the civil service is now crawling with second-generation ethnic Chinese. Status for them is defined in terms of wealth. The Thais are individuals; their status is birth, landed wealth, government employment, religious merit.' The waiter, hearing the raised voice, approached tentatively, and set the large glasses before us on the rickety tin table. He retreated, smiling nervously.

'So what would be your solution?' I asked evenly. I was now sure he was deliberately needling me. I adopted an unconcerned, rather quizzical expression, which, I was pleased to see, irritated him. But he was off again.

'Stop them marrying Thai women. A Thai girl who marries a Jek—a Chink—vanishes, swallowed up by the family. A breeding machine for another generation of Jeks to suck our blood. We should marry their women ourselves, and get Thai sons on them. Trouble is, they're so damn ugly—Cantonese girls look like pugs, Taechew girls have rat's teeth. A man'd need more that this cat's pee to fire himself up to do his duty!' He tapped the tall golden glass mockingly, threw his head back, and drained it, wiping his mouth with the back of his hand. I'd never seen him so relaxed, so expansive. It made me uneasy. I was heartily sick of these warnings.

'Yet you told me you were no Thai, but a foreigner, like me,' I said slyly.

But Sya only laughed, even more uproariously. Sobering, he looked at his watch. 'Nearly showtime,' he said. 'Let's go.'

Bandit Country, Northeast of Bangkok

Sergeant Seamus McCluskey was trained to do and die, or at least see that other men did and died, without question.

'Now hear this, men,' he bawled hoarsely in a *sotto voce* roar, his best approximation of a whisper. 'We gotta boatload of Gooks gonna be coming up this stream all bright and sexy and unsuspecting, in a matter of...' He consulted his timepiece, scowling. '...five minutes flat. We're going to give them a welcome. We may get support from the locals, and then again, maybe not. No matter. If local support is a no-show, we start the party without 'em.'

The youngest man, an overgrown hobbledehoy farm boy, large-lobed ears pinned back to hear the winds of the great plains, peered through field glasses and turned puzzled blue eyes on the sergeant. 'But, Sarge, those guys in the boats, right—they're not real Gooks, not terrorists, not Cong. For Chrissakes, Sarge, they're just Thais! Friendlies!' His hand was sticky with nerves. The sergeant gave him the old nose-to-nose glare.

'You aiming to give me an argument, soldier? Now get your ass the fuck behind that bush, and when I say the word, you give them Gooks hell, or you're going to be worth less than an ol' rubber boot fulla pig shit. Boy, I'm gonna make you feel like your nuts was cotton candy chomped by a kid wearing braces!'

Right on cue, to the sergeant's satisfaction, he saw movement through his field glasses. Across the stream, Vichai's convoy of small rivercraft hove into view. The men aboard them were in evident holiday mood. The small vessels were laden with the ingredients necessary for a real old-style feast, meat and drink, gifts and fireworks. One boat was crammed to the gunwales with sumptuous presents for Salikaa, the leader's adopted daughter—bolts of silk, garnets, and sapphires exacted in tribute from local merchants and mine owners for the pirate princess.

'Miss,' they called her now, with pride, for they had known her before she was a Miss, known her before the world did. She was Miss Thailand, now—she was Somebody! The reports of her engagement to a royal prince impressed them less. 'Going respectable' was hardly admirable, but females liked security; it was another of their incomprehensible instincts, like nesting and suckling, gossiping, and laying out the dead.

The women were left behind, of course, but they had prepared a roast pig. It reposed on a bed of palm leaves in the third boat. Vichai's own boat carried a whole crate of whisky—the good stuff, not Mekhong rotgut. The men had watched, wide-eyed, at its loading.

Vichai, flushed and eager as a schoolboy, stood in the prow of his own boat. 'Can't you get more than two knots out of this old can, Grandpa?' he chaffed the boatman. He was in chortling good humour.

'All right, men! There's your Gooks!' bawled Sergeant McCluskey with a war whoop. 'Now, blow 'em to hell!'

Vichai was still laughing when the hail of bullets struck.

'Ambush! Turn back!' His second-in-command leapt boldly to the thwart beside the chieftain to cover him with his own fire.

'Yellow dogs!' grunted Vichai, tugging his weapon free from the waistband of his pants, cursing his plump belly. The next volley took Vichai's lieutenant in the throat. He lay at Vichai's feet on the bottom boards where the impact had thrown him, his eyes clouded with surprise as he died. This sight so inflamed Vichai that he began cursing, striking savagely at the elderly boatman, a man as old as himself, who attempted to steer the boat around and head back down river. His nostrils distended by the stench of cordite, Vichai fought like a man possessed, blazing in all directions. When every bullet was expended, he seized the firearms from the hands of those who fell around him—choking, groaning, coughing blood, gripping their exploded bellies. Vichai fought with the desperation of an old wounded tiger, his eyes wild, his face greased with grime and sweat.

'Doesn't he know when he's beat?' grunted the sergeant in grudging admiration.

'Whassee keep hollerin'?' the youngest soldier muttered to his companion, a wild black boy who liked Thai grass and Thai ass, even though only the oldest and ugliest of the Bangkok ladies of the night would go with black men, and even then it cost him plenty.

'Why, man, thass some heathen charm, maybe,' the black soldier drawled, taking aim. He had a whole load of grief to dump. He rose incautiously from his cover, spraying bullets in a wasteful arc, at whose centre was the baleful, maddened figure of Vichai.

'Salikaa!' Vichai yelled, struggling single-handed to push out of range the sole vessel left intact, his own cherished speedboat. Caught in the storm of bullets, he spun around, stumbling blindly over the dead and the dying as he fell. He choked on her name in the spreading pool of his own blood. His last thought was that the girl had betrayed him. She was a cop's get, after all. She'd sold him out. The bitterness of that thought was worse than dying—the worst pain of all.

The Americans gathered around their own casualties with urgent instructions, followed by muttered groans and imprecations. The operation had been unexpectedly costly. Some men turned away into the bushes. There was the sound of retching, and elsewhere the words of prayer.

Down at the riverside, after the explosion of violence and noise, everything was calm. The river lapped the bank. A snowy egret stalked the brown water. The sunlight gilded the ripples.

The Americans, with heavy hearts, now waded into the water at the sergeant's command and dragged the boats to the shore.

McCluskey went down to the speedboat, holed below the water line and rapidly sinking. It had been beached just in time. The water stirred Vichai's hair and gave the illusion of life. The red stain spread like a cloud in the water. McCluskey turned Vichai's body over—not gently, but not disrespectfully either. His mouth was full of phlegm. He turned his head to one side and spat.

'More blood 'n a fucking plasma bank, and for what?' He was upset. A poxy routine mop-up operation, and now two of his boys were going home in boxes.

The black soldier dragged another of the crippled boats to the bank. Blood was pouring from his arm, but he appeared unaware of it.

'Will you look at this stuff?' he cried, discovering the crate of whisky, then ripped open a bolt of rose brocade and draped it about his athletic frame, strutting. 'Reminds me of a suit I bought me back in Tallahassee!' He grinned, posturing outrageously.

'And next time you break cover without orders, I'll nail your sorry ass!' McCluskey glared at him with a sudden fierce rage. He growled. 'Now, load that junk in the vehicles and hustle your ass, no shit. God knows what today was all about. It has to be more than just a crate of whisky...'

'Jeez, Sarge, ain't that enough? A whole crate of whisky?'

'No,' McCluskey grunted softly, looking at his two canvas-wrapped casualties. 'I guess it ain't enough, at that. *Way* not enough.'

Sya tapped the helicopter pilot on the shoulder, indicating to him to put down on a treeless plain just below the forestation line, and then to wait. The pilot obeyed, and watched as the tall *farang* and the colonel climbed out of his craft. The pilot was an expert at killing time. He would snooze, smoke, squash a few bugs, thread a few field flowers on a straw to garland some part of the helicopter. He had already painted an eye for it, as the fishermen did on junks, so it could see where it was going. Somewhere, in some obscure paragraph, it was forbidden to ornament or otherwise deface military material. Exceptionally, Colonel Sya did not appear to attach undue importance to this regulation. He had noted the eye and the garlands without comment.

'You may find this interesting,' Sya said to Dr Raven. 'We shall make a brief reconnaissance. Then we fly back to Hua Hin. Okay?'

Raven nodded. Clutching his field glasses, Sya scrambled up the scree in his heavy boots. It was a tough climb to the top of the rocky outcrop just above the famous caves, but the vantage point commanded a view of the whole valley and the river that ran through it, its steely surface flecked by a series of small splashes. Sya crouched over the field glasses, his eyes and hands steady as stones. The riverbank scrub sweltered, still as death beneath the baking sun. Raven, too, remained silent in the makeshift observation post. The first boat approached the beach. On the boats men looking like dark ants moved about, preparing for the landing. Without warning, puffs of smoke arose from a bush. Then another. Then a series of dull thuds reached his ears. They were too far away to catch the deadly rattle of the submachine guns, but he recognized their presence. From this distance, the reaction of the ants was almost comical. Some jerked in the air and fell; others scattered and scrambled for the boats. Some ducked between the hulls. Raven and Sya saw the flashes as they returned fire. A tubby figure in black pangolin pants attempted to relaunch a boat with one hand while firing with the other. Eventually he too lay still. Sya handed his field glasses to Raven without speaking. Raven saw other figures, in the dung-coloured uniforms of the Special Detail, tropical duty camouflage colour No. 317, stepping out of the bushes. Raven supposed that somewhere children still played games like that—one side shouted 'Pax!' and those who had been playing dead all got up again. But the toppled figures stayed still. The dung soldiers clustered together. Later, they broke up and went down to the water, at first with caution, then boldly. They waded out and pulled the boats to the bank and began rummaging around in them. A Willys jeep detached itself from its place of concealment in a cloud of red dust. The uniforms loaded bodies into it, first those that had fallen out of the bushes, and then, less tenderly, the others from the boats. As a final gesture, one man ran back to the boats and stove in their bottom boards with a vicious thrust of his weapon stock. Raven had seen enough. He handed the glasses back. The jeep bucketed off up the track. The boats quickly filled with water, and the river closed over them.

Sya watched to the end, then dropped his field glasses with a sigh of satisfaction. He turned to Raven, grinning.

Sergeant McCluskey twiddled the dial on his radio and listened, pausing to curse the static on the CB. A voice crackled:

'Sea-breeze to Zorro, Sea-breeze to Zorro, do you copy?'

'Zorro to Sea-breeze.' As he made his report, McCluskey tried hard to hide the elation in his voice, deeply conscious of the heavy presence of those two silent, blanketed figures.

'Local supporting force?'

'Negative. Bastards never showed,' McCluskey growled.

The weird disembodied voice became suddenly human. 'Never showed! What the fuck is that supposed to mean, McCluskey?' it rapped.

'What it sounds like it means, sir. The mothers never showed.'

There was a pause, broken only by static. Then the voice demanded sharply, 'I will be a monkey's flunkey! The Thai forces suffered no casualties—no fatalities?'

McCluskey had had a long day, and it was only noon. He said, very distinctly: 'Like I just told you, sir. They didn't take casualties because they weren't there. To win it you gotta be in it. We never saw the Thais. Only the hostiles.'

Another silence. Then the voice said, ponderously, deeply shocked: 'I'll be damned.'

The communication ended. McCluskey attacked his dials again. Finally he socked the radio with his fist. It remained stubbornly silent.

'Fucking brass!' rumbled McCluskey, without malice. He loosened his belt, fumbled for a Camel pack and lit up. Off Sukhumvit Road in Bangkok's high-rent quarter, they sold smokes in original Camel packs for the same price as regular tobacco. The characteristic scent of new-mown hay made his head spin a little. He sighed. He shoved the half-smoked weed between the purple bee-stung lips of the black soldier, who had shot the bandit chieftain and had taken a slug in the left arm. The man inhaled deeply, his dark eyes signalling their thanks.

'Fucking Thais!' McCluskey shut his eyes. 'Who needs 'em? Who cares if they don't show?' He braced himself against the jolting. He was ticked off to have lost a couple of good men in such a pissant, piddling mop-up operation. He retrieved his joint from the wounded man and gratefully drew fragrant happiness into his lungs.

'When Irish eyes are smilin',' he warbled in a passable tenor—muted, out of respect for the dead.

Van Hooten's adjutant sat staring unhappily at the silent CB. He wondered how he was going to tell the general that the operation had been successful, but that, unfortunately, the patient had not died. The little fish were netted, the big one got away. *How the hell did that happen*, he demanded helplessly of the silent radio. 'Now it's all going to hit the turbo.'

Sya and Raven scrambled back down the scree. As they walked back to the helicopter, Sya said casually, 'This Vichai. Once he was an honest bandit. Extortion, occasional murder, blackmail. But he became the running dog of hostile external powers. So...' He made a chopping movement in the air with the edge of his hand. 'He has to be stopped. Dead. In his tracks.' He chuckled conspiratorially.

'How do you know he was a—what did you call him? A running dog?'

'Obvious. No bandit makes a daylight raid across river unless he feels secure, feels he has unseen backup.'

'But he didn't. They wiped him out.'

'True.' Sya pulled a face of mock regret. 'On this occasion, his terrorist allies let him down. Too bad.' He waved a hand. 'Look! Sleeping beauty!'

The helicopter pilot was asleep in his seat. He held his cap in his hands. Behind one ear he had tucked a small wild orchid. In his innocent slumber he smiled, puckering his lips like a dozing infant.

Sya kicked the pilot's seat viciously. '*Bai Hua Hin diawnee, krup!*' He barked. 'Hua Hin, let's go, please.' Even as he kicked the seat, he added '*krup*', a word men used to show civility. He was more than tough. He was a barbarian. By displaying aggressive good manners he made sure nobody dared remind him of the fact.

It had been a satisfactory outing.

Raven knew he had been taken along as both witness and alibi, and it irked him. Though he was no stranger to violence, he'd had no forewarning. He was still shocked by the suddenness, and at the same time he wondered about the meaning of the brief military engagement he and Sya had been spying on. Over the chopper's roar he shouted,

'What will happen to Salikaa, Colonel?'

'If she is wise, she will accept my cousin and retire from court for a while, if not forever. She has made many enemies in the short time she has been there. Enemies are bad for the health.' He smiled. 'I think you did not enjoy your day, Doctor Raven. A little roughhouse, as you say.'

'It was interesting, Colonel, I assure you.'

'I am so glad.' Sya smiled smoothly, and Raven realised that this had been a display of Sya's power to orchestrate events, and of the quality of his intelligence network. Most of all, it was another subtle warning, and Raven again found himself breathing fast and shallow. His spine tingled, and the hairs on his neck rose.

Salikaa, once fortune's darling, went without protest to be married to a beetle-browed Neanderthal with a greasy pigtail and green teeth. She went without a friend to fasten up the back of her dress, only the personal maid Sya had appointed to attend her. Salikaa could not yet make up her mind whether the girl Pawn was a spy or whether she was just simple-minded, but either way, she loathed her immediately, as a servant of the unspeakable Sya, and called her the ex-tart.

Pim, still drowning in grief for her brother, felt Salikaa bore the responsibility for Toom's death. Chee Laan was preoccupied with the affairs of her family, and absorbed in the fascination of her newfound acquaintance with Raven. Salikaa felt herself alone, and closer to despair than she would have thought possible.

She had raved and stormed, begging for an interview—five minutes even—with the young king. She had encountered a slippery-smooth wall of implacable courtesy, with no handholds. Prince Toom's mother and the Princess Regent had allied themselves with Sya, accepting his suggestion of an alternative bridegroom with gratitude and sighs of relief. Embarrassment and tragedy were bad enough; scandal must be avoided at all costs. Salikaa must be spirited away from court with all haste before she could do any more damage.

And Vichai, Salikaa's doting stepfather, her last resort, her bastion, was gone—his empire dispersed, his troops, for the most part, dead, dispossessed as pariah dogs. He had received an obituary of sorts in the columns of the *Bangkok Herald*. Salikaa had read it, weeping and snorting with rage.

Successful Anti-Terrorist Action

Gallant officers and men of the Border Patrol Police counter-insurgency forces yesterday achieved a major breakthrough in the campaign against communist terrorists when they successfully put down an armed rising by communist-influenced bandits who have long terrorised the northeast. Brigand chief Vichai Kiengsri, notorious for extortion and violence, was shot to death in the encounter. The BPP received support from U.S. special detail troops who happened to be on manoeuvres in the area from nearby Korat Airbase.

The BPP had no casualties to report...

Salikaa's last rational act was to cut out the piece, fold it carefully, and slip it inside her bra. The royal physicians then administered tranquilizers to subdue her. As the sedative took effect, Salikaa struggled to marshal her thoughts. Her head felt as heavy as lead. Her limbs seemed to belong to someone else. Nothing made sense anymore. Why had Vichai, always so suspicious, and cunning as a rat, allowed himself to be lured from his lair, to be cornered and shot to pieces in broad daylight? Had he lost his touch, or had he been betrayed? Had she herself been used to bait the trap? Did she have his death on her conscience, as well as the disappearance of her bodyguard Tamsin, dispatched on a mission of vengeance and never to return? It had all been going so well. Now her universe was disintegrating. Everything was evaporating, falling apart, breaking up. The reek of death and betrayal was thick in her nostrils as she succumbed to oblivion.

Drinkwater Residence, Bangkok

Raven
It was two days after the gun battle I'd witnessed with Sya Dam. The Drinkwaters and their household, under the spell of Laila, personification of the artistic, zany, laid-back sixties, now showed Chee Laan up to my suite as a matter of course, brought us refreshment, and then stayed discreetly in the background. What they thought privately I never knew.

Chee Laan and I sat on my veranda, scanning the paper. I read the English and sometimes, slowly, the Thai; Chee Laan compared the versions published in the English, Thai, and Chinese papers, absorbing the gist in as short a time as it took me to struggle with a paragraph of Thai curlicues. It took me a moment to connect the *Herald* article with the violent exchange of fire I'd witnessed with Sya.

'Border Patrol Police!' I thumped the page incredulously. 'The gunman who shot the leader of the boatmen was a huge black soldier!'

She shrugged. 'What do you expect? BPP is Sya's show. The glory boys. Let's see what that drooling social columnist has to say about the wedding of the year. *Sanita's Social Roundabout, Bangkok Herald.*'

With barely concealed scorn, she read:

> 'Their Royal Highnesses the Prince and Princess Regent today graciously sponsored the nuptial celebrations of Salikaa Kiengsri (Miss Thailand) to Khun Vasit, cousin of Colonel Sya Dam, of the Border Patrol Police. After being granted audiences with their Royal Highnesses, the happy couple received guests at a sumptuous reception held in a pavilion on the grounds of Chitr Lada Palace. The banquet was attended by the crème de la crème of city society,

the great and the good, all the beautiful people of the City of Angels, Thai and farang Thet, members of the court, and foreign diplomats. (For a description of the fashions, the bridal gown, etc., see photo spread feature, p. 9-10).'

Chee Laan read it aloud mockingly. 'Not quite what Salikaa planned,' she said in her normal light ironic tone.

The story kick-started my memory of that extraordinary day. We had both been invited to the ceremony. As we approached the palace, I'd asked her if the breathless haste of the marriage didn't shock people. She said, 'Why should it? The royal astronomers have calculated the auspicious moment. At dawn today the happy couple offered food to the monks to ensure abundant merit. The religious ceremony itself takes place at 15.02 precisely, as calculated by the Brahmins. Everything is perfectly arranged. But, Raven, look at Salikaa! What have they done to her—she's like a zombie!'

Salikaa moved like a sleepwalker. Out of her artfully tinted face, surmounted by the lacquered coils of her coiffure, her hollow eyes stared, unseeing. At her side, her bridegroom ignored her, picking his green teeth with a long black fingernail, sucking with a small hiss any stray scraps of food. Under a gaudily striped marquee the Royal Thai Navy Orchestra sawed and puffed its way through its 'B' repertoire—'Songs from the Shows.' Screening the bridal party, jasmine buds threaded on palm fronds created a Brussels lace effect. The wedding guests congregated excitedly, clothed in their best apparel. Uniforms clanked with medals, the ladies dazzled like starbursts in their jewelled and beaded silks. Members of the media, officially invited to cover the wedding of Miss Thailand, and unofficially in order to avert any outpouring of speculation, scribbled feverishly on their notepads, their natural cynicism for once overawed by the flood of titled glitterati.

Khamthorn, the photographer, oblivious to everything but the angle of his next shot, backed into Chee Laan, jumped as if burnt, and, upon recognizing her, bowed low, mumbling a horrified apology. Chee Laan smiled.

'Candid camera shots, *Khun* Khamthorn?' He grinned sheepishly, baring his betel-dark gums. Chee Laan whispered to me: 'He's a closet Chinese chauvinist and repressed anarchist. He photographs every riot and demonstration, whatever his assignments. If the *Herald* daren't print the controversial ones, he markets them to foreign wire services!'

Now Pim approached, smiling. Khamthorn disappeared into the throng. Pim slipped her arm though Chee Laan's and kissed her cheek. The man who had followed Pim cleared his throat, and the girls drew apart. Prince Premsakul stood there, beaming like a beacon, solid and imperturbable as a polished brass Buddha. He greeted me genially, but his smile concealed irritation as he looked at Chee Laan.

Prince Premsakul addressed me. 'Simply 'straordinary! Even m'daughter's pinko chums couldn't have dreamt this one up, what? Coupla Johnny nobodies, and all this laid on for 'em!' He spread his hands, indicating the scene. 'Royal-sponsored wedding, I ask you! We all know the illustrious Colonel Sya, who does not? But this chap? This cousin, or whatever...and the girl? Oh, a pretty enough little thing, in her way, I grant you, but who is she? Nobody knows—or at least, not to one's satisfaction...'

'Yet you were willing to let Salikaa join our family.' Pim's eyes were accusative.

Her father sighed. 'What does one not do for one's beloved son?' He spoke to me over her head, with sanctimonious self-congratulation and sublime operatic pathos. Pim clenched her fist and chewed her lip. Prince Premsakul, smiling still, said, 'We must present our gifts.' He led the way toward the pavilion, Pim following moodily in his wake.

At the door of the inner pavilion the greeter and gift-assessor received us, offering a golden coronet-shaped salver upon which to place our offerings. Courtiers alternated with Sya Dam, the only apparent relative, to perform this function.

Chee Laan moved close, whispering, 'The bigger the packet, the gaudier the wrapper, the greater the face gained. It will be noted. But don't expect it to be acknowledged, or even referred to ever again.'

Down the long table towered a mountain range of costly packages. After placing our gifts on the salvers, we were ushered into a two-tiered galleried hall. The Asian guests huddled close to the walls in respectful anticipation. A few *farangs* surged into the vacant centre, filling it with their big, awkward bodies and their barking voices. Palace staff had to restrain some from throwing themselves prematurely upon the buffet.

The orchestra abandoned the Blue Danube for the national anthem.

The Princess Regent swept in, swathed in a cloud of apricot chiffon. Now the bridal couple, wreathed with jasmine, moved among the guests, distributing wedding favours, miniature glasses filled with sandalwood chips and engraved with an intertwined V and S in Thai script. When at last they resumed their seats at the top table, a foreign correspondent thrust a microphone into Salikaa's face.

'Is this a love match, Miss Thailand?' He did not trouble to keep the incredulous sneer out of his voice.

The scowling bridegroom lunged, grabbing the reporter by the collar. He seized the microphone and thrust it into the man's mouth. The reporter broke free, gagging, clutching at his bleeding lip. Servants quickly escorted him away. Salikaa's bridegroom bared his teeth, then relapsed into his former torpor. His mouth fell slackly open. The membranes of his broad nose vibrated, and he snored. His greasy pigtail tumbled over his shoulder into his plate.

Sya approached us. 'So, Raven, what d'you think, eh?'

'Your cousin is a remarkable-looking man,' I said.

Sya flashed his white teeth. 'Believe me, he has a personality to match.'

We surveyed each other in silence. Sya's triple row of medals dangled almost to his waist. Temporarily awake, the bridegroom too was staring at Sya, revealing his unhealthy teeth and betel-red gums in a jovial grimace. He pulled out a lump of semi-masticated food and threw it on the floor. Impassive, swooping like a Wimbledon ball-boy, a butler swept up the offending mass in his white-gloved hands and removed it.

Sya sighed. 'He could have had his place at court, you know.' He jerked his head toward the bridegroom. 'Tame tribesmen, like tame cheetahs, are at a premium. Every privilege I enjoy could have been his for the asking.'

He moved to a small alcove overlooking a flowerbed. He leaned upon the stone balustrade, turning his gaze from the interior, where the brilliant guests strutted and preened, to the green lawns where the peacocks paraded and shrieked under the shade trees. I followed him, taking up a position leaning on the balustrade at his side.

Presently Sya said, 'I guess you know the old story about Dog and Wolf. Stock in trade of every English teacher I ever met. First reading book. They imagine Orientals adore parables and epigrams. Anyway, Dog tries to recruit Wolf to serve Man. Wolf is attracted by the description of the creature comforts the Dog enjoys—the fireside, the food, and so on. He agrees to join Dog. But on the way to the village, the moonlight glints on Dog's chain. "What's that?" Wolf asks. "That? Oh, that's just where they chain me up," says Dog. "Goodbye, Dog," Wolf calls, running back to the forest.'

'Ah!' I murmured. 'Freedom; the last glorious deception.' I wondered if Sya were one of those who seek power, dazzled by the illusion that power and freedom are the same. 'I didn't know there were wolves in Thailand,' I prompted.

Sya grinned. 'You're right. That particular allegory was of European origin. We have something not dissimilar in the Thai. "Sooner will the hungry tiger starve than beg." That wasn't translated by Prince Premsakul— just by me. You must excuse a rough man's rough translation.'

'I imagine it's very difficult to reproduce Thai poetry in a non-tonal language. I think I know that poem.' I felt rather pleased with myself. 'A *loganit*, isn't it? Taken from the Laws of Life. Based on Buddhist principles. "Truly, there's a dearth of the wise among men…" It's inscribed on the cloister walls at Wat Po.'

Sya regarded me coolly. 'You want to watch that erudition of yours, Raven. Many folks sorely despise a smartass.' He grinned again. 'But you're right. His Majesty King Rama III had all those poems collected and inscribed there in 1831.'

'So, if we return to your allegory, you would compare yourself to a chained dog, Colonel? I had you cast as the wolf.'

Sya spat expertly into the flowerbed. 'I am yet to metamorphose into either dog or wolf. I am in a state of transition between forms, merely a pet fox. A bagged fox. Trapped, caged, taken to some place to be released, to be hunted by gentlemen with dogs. For their sport.' He looked at me. 'We are all of us bagged foxes.'

'In what respect?'

'From the moment the cage is sprung to the moment the pack catches up, we live our lives on the run. How long we last is just a question of luck.' He raised a hand as if to forestall possible objections, though I would have made none, reluctant to interrupt the flow of Sya's thoughts.

Still, I found myself saying, 'What about the Buddhist concept of rebirth?'

Sya looked scornful. 'Do not talk to me about rebirth and the cycle of lives. I believe only in my life, this life, and only in myself.' He thumped his chest brutally enough to stop a weaker heart. 'You get one chance at it, that's all.'

'One chance at what?'

'One chance to make your run for it. Try to escape—by cunning, by speed, by sheer guts, but there's only one end, and only one hope: that the end will be quick. That the lead hound will snap your backbone before the pack start ripping off your balls.'

'Hardly a cheering prospect.' I shrugged.

'Realistic. In this world of ours, Raven, nobody ever makes it back to base.'

Despite myself, I had felt intrigued, not by the mundane nihilistic sentiments, which resembled the run-of-the-mill amateur cynicism spouted by students in drinking places late at night, but by the force of the conviction behind them, the disillusioned power of the man himself.

'Supposing we accept this allegory of yours,' I said, 'who are these hounds you speak of?'

Sya glowered. 'You think the hunted fox demands ID? Some have names, others are nameless. Cancer, TB, syph. Some get caught by these. The lucky ones meet another fate—a bullet, a bludgeon, a blade.' He looked piercingly at me. 'Perhaps we're the hounds in each other's stories, you and I,' he said. 'We might even hound each other to death.' He grinned again.

He shifted in place. We were spruced up for the occasion, groomed, shaven, showered and perfumed, yet I caught the strong scent of musky sweat and starched cloth, a burnt, sharp smell that plucked at my nostrils. Sya gulped down the contents of the glass he had been neglecting and tugged his tunic straight. His eyes moved to the high table and grew speculative. 'Perhaps my cousin was wise to refuse to remain in Bangkok. And he is more use to me this way.' He was throwing out a challenge, toying with me, because he knew I still didn't know what his game was. But I was more determined than ever to find out—and stop it, if I could.

I remember noting that the uncouth bridegroom was now pulling the floral decorations apart and bombarding the court ladies with petals.

'Nobody likes a smartass, Raven,' Sya repeated softly. 'Take a friendly warning.'

Nodding chummily, he strolled away to rejoin the wedding party.

My recollection of the celebration retreating, I returned to my perusal of the *Bangkok Herald*. According to the report, immediately after the wedding, Salikaa and Vasit had left town to take up residence in the far north, in the bridegroom's home village. The gossip columnist noted with regret that His Majesty the young king had been unable to attend the glittering occasion. He had recently become an army cadet, as part of the royal initiative to sample many facets of the people's lives, the better to lead and guide them. At the very time of Miss Thailand's nuptials, His Majesty was upcountry with his unit on manoeuvres.

He had, however, been gracious enough to send his good wishes, which were received by the young couple with respectful rapture, as was the magnificent bride gift of one million baht, presented by the Princess Regent on her royal ward's behalf.

'So they paid Salikaa off.' I pointed to the newspaper.

'No.' Chee Laan shook her head. 'They paid *him*. They could never have bought off Salikaa.'

'So why did she go through with this whole charade? You're not going to tell me she was in love with that man?'

She looked at me scornfully. 'You saw her face, Raven. She was drugged out of her skull.' Scorn gave way to anxiety. 'I don't know what's going to happen when she comes to her senses and realises what Sya's done,' she said, frowning.

I reached for her hand. 'Chee Laan, we have so little time, you and I. Must we always waste it discussing Salikaa and Sya?'

She looked at me quizzically, tilting her head to one side in the way I loved. 'You had something more important in mind?' she asked.

'Perhaps.'

She looked up at me, laughing. I took her hands and pulled her close, more roughly than I intended. Sometimes a beautiful thing creates suspense that's unendurable; you're poised on a knife edge between the longing to preserve it, frozen in time forever, and the urge to destroy it because perfection is a kind of agony. No pain I've ever known ambushes you like love.

Drinkwater Residence, Bangkok

'So the good pastor neglects his flock, and comes to frolic in the fleshpots!' Siegfried announced with malicious glee, waving Waddle's letter around Laila Drinkwater's terrace.

Chee Laan had left. He and I were seated at a glass-and-rattan table, drinking iced coffee. Laila, wearing a tentlike brown caftan, her hair skewered on top of her head with a pair of chopsticks, was kneeling at Siegfried's feet, tracing intricate designs on his bare brown legs with phosphorescent paint. This was the initial, experimental stage of a happening they were planning to celebrate the opening of a new nightclub.

Siegfried sighed dramatically. 'I suppose I shall be obliged to escort him hither and thither until he meets somebody who can put up with him. *Dieu! Que c'est ennuyeux!*'

'Why do it, then?' I asked innocently.

'Oh, *noblesse*, you know, *oblige!*' Siegfried lay back and closed his eyes. 'The touch of that paintbrush is *delicieux*, Laila! Immensely relaxing!'

'Siegfried does it,' Laila murmured, intent on her work, 'because he is a vain, wicked little thing who loves pretty rubies. Keep still, *mon chéri*, my line's going all over the place!'

Siegfried sighed. 'Alas! It is true!' He pouted in mock penitence. 'I am a sadly venal individual. I will take Waddle to the Smart Cat Key Club. He will make some lovely new friends.'

'A gay dive on the edge of Chinatown,' Laila explained over her shoulder. 'Siegfried, you astonish me! The Smart Cat is extremely *declassé!*'

'*Tant pis!*' Siegfried replied coquettishly. 'It is my *nostalgie de la boue*. You would not care to join us, Raven, I suppose?'

'Maybe another time, thanks all the same.'

Nevertheless, I thought it might be interesting to see just what Pastor Waddle was up to, so I subsequently extracted directions to the Key Club from Laila Drinkwater. She betrayed no surprise at the enquiry. I guessed her mind was on higher things.

'I'm not sure gold phosphorescence will strike the right note, you know,' she mused. 'Perhaps silver? What do you think, Raven?' She scratched her head with the end of her paintbrush.

I dined with the Drinkwaters and excused myself later that evening, saying I might meet up with friends for a nightcap at the Oriental Hotel. I hailed a passing samlor and went through the motions of bargaining before a price was reached that left both parties feeling pleased. I found the Smart Cat Key Club's flashing blue sign, featuring a louche-looking cat clutching a key in its paw, without difficulty in Chinatown's colourful neon jungle. Although it was a Western-style club, I assumed it would be Chinese-owned. The government had been trying to clamp down on the entertainment industry, but financial interests usually triumphed in the end. After I finally persuaded the doorman to admit me, and my eyes grew accustomed to the gloom, I saw Siegfried at once, centre stage, entrancing the audience with a virtuoso performance. I glanced around, but there was no sign of Pastor Waddle. With a premonition of disaster, I pushed my way back to the door, deciding to check the outside of the premises.

Smart Cat Key Club, Bangkok

Pastor Waddle had enjoyed a convivial evening. Siegfried drew on his joint thoughtfully and contemplated his companion's excited face. Waddle had tugged from his pocket a crumpled white canvas hat, which he now donned. The action made Siegfried frown.

Siegfried had introduced him here, at the seedily plush Smart Cat Key Club, past the vigilant bouncers, and had also introduced him to the exquisite Prachin, with whom Siegfried had once whiled away an evening. At first Prachin, sought-after and selective, flounced away. Later, however, he returned, docile, bearing the special under-the-counter whisky usually reserved for members of the police force, who were responsible for ensuring its supply. Prachin was now clearly disposed to be adorable to Waddle, at the same time flirting outrageously with Siegfried. But Siegfried continued to sip his iced tea, his eyes half-closed. Never repeat a success, Siegfried often said.

The national ban on foreign musicians did not apply to the Smart Cat. After a while, the Filipino band's insistent rhythm became too much for Siegfried. He rose, sauntered over to a flamboyant group by the bar, handed his cane to one, his jacket to another, and took the floor. Other patrons stepped back to watch as Siegfried, a frown of rapt concentration on his magnificent face, danced in controlled frenzy.

Prachin handed Waddle a glass. 'You drink,' he encouraged. 'Nice. You like.'

The pastor had drunk a considerable amount of whisky already, to which he was unaccustomed. He glanced up from his glass, struggling to focus his gaze. Prachin's skin was as fine as a dark apricot, and his false eyelashes were real mink. His dress of beaded pink chiffon came from the best tailor in Chinatown.

Prachin was able to afford nice things because he did favours. Most of the people he obliged paid him well—but this favour was for Sya Dam, who not only wouldn't pay one cent, but who would, moreover, ensure that, should Prachin fail to oblige, unpleasant things would happen to him. Acid, razors, ground glass; Prachin knew of people who had experienced such episodes, and, although it was never proven, everyone suspected who was behind it all. So Prachin was resentful, but he did not dare refuse. Prachin was no hero. He was also too young and gorgeous to die.

This *farang* was disgustingly ugly, with his big nose, and perhaps he was mad, too, for when Prachin leaned toward him and laid his hand softly on the cotton, the colour of chickenshit, that clothed his bony knee, the Westerner jumped as if burnt, and shouted out strange, wild words.

'Comest thou to tempt me, demon? Begone! I spew thee forth!'

Prachin sighed. The deformed and demented were beloved of the Buddha. Prachin was devout. Before every sexual encounter, he insisted not only upon the ritual bath, but also upon a floral offering and hasty prayer to the Lord Buddha. Most of his friends found this piety rather endearing, and indulged him.

'Come on, darlin', nice dwink,' Prachin cajoled. He rubbed his smooth cheek against Waddle's own. 'Then we go, you like? I think you like very much!'

Taking courage, Waddle tossed down the drink in one gulp. The dimly lit room blurred; objects detached themselves ponderously and appeared to float in the air. Waddle was vaguely conscious that Prachin was fumbling with his clothing, but he was paralysed, unable to protest. As Prachin's tinkling laughter rang in his ears, the wooden floor rushed up at him and clubbed him hard on the skull.

He remained unconscious when Prachin's hulking associate threw him over his shoulder like a sack of rice and disappeared through the private back door of the Key Club. Prachin peered round the door and regarded with distaste the figure in the dun-coloured suit sprawled in the alley's filth. The alley was unlit, but the garish neon signs from the street lent it a nightmarish lividity. The big man who had carried the pastor out wiped his knife carefully on a bit of rag, which he then stuffed in his pocket. He grinned at Prachin—an unpleasant sight. Prachin shuddered.

The twenty years that had passed since Archin had been sentenced to life imprisonment for the murder of Salikaa's parents had not been kind to him. He had lost several teeth and half his left ear, and his face was seamed and pockmarked like earth ravaged by the elements. The pits and deeply etched wrinkles stood out boldly under years of dirt that had engrained deep into his skin.

But he had found his niche. Happy fortune had brought him to the attention of Colonel Sya Dam, whose habit it was to scan the prison records for information on incarcerated lifers in case any of them appeared potentially useful. After an interview with Archin, Sya had persuaded old King Rama to include Archin in the fifty prisoners released to mark the king's birthday—the last birthday the old king lived to see. Sya made sure Archin knew who was responsible for his release. Now, Archin was Sya's man, body and soul. He was employed to do the work he liked best—killing—and there was, mysteriously, never the shadow of a policeman when he was sent on a job.

Prachin grumbled. 'Don't leave the thing there, stupid! Go and chuck it in a khlong!'

He scuttled back into the club. Archin shrugged off the suggestion and lumbered toward the street. He had almost reached it when he heard the sound of running footsteps and froze, growling.

Raven pushed past the doorman, hurried through the front door, and broke into a run as he rounded the corner into the back alley. It was darker there, and in his haste he did not see Waddle until he tripped over him. The impact brought him to his knees on the filthy concrete. He recognised Waddle at once. His body was warm, but he did not appear to be breathing. Raven found his own hands were already covered with blood, sticky and tepid. He felt around under Waddle's collar for any sign of a pulse. He shouted the man's name into his face, his urgency increasing as Waddle failed to respond. He did not hear Archin return.

Archin had been trained not to cut without orders. He did not need his blade for this simple clean-up operation. His left hand hooked under Raven's jaw and lifted his head into the path of his right fist, which descended, bulky as a jackfruit. The blow almost snapped Raven's neck.

Archin did not wait to find out whether it had or not. He let Raven's limp body drop on top of the other foreigner and left the scene at a shambling run.

Siegfried stopped dancing abruptly, slipped modestly through his applauding audience, and followed Prachin into what passed for a toilet at the Smart Cat Key Club. He kicked the cubicle door shut and bolted it behind them.

'Where is he? What have you done with him?'

Prachin rolled his eyes and coughed nervously. 'I don't know what you're talking about.'

Siegfried raised his walking stick horizontally like a bar and pressed it up under Prachin's chin and across his windpipe, jamming the boy's head roughly against the wooden partition. Prachin gasped for air and tried to kick out, but Siegfried was too quick for him. He kept the pressure on.

'Enough? Lift your hand when it is enough!' Siegfried hissed, tightening his grip. Prachin raised a feeble hand. He had tears in his eyes. Siegfried removed the stick and the boy sank to a squatting position well away from the noxious hole in the floor, and as far as he could get from Siegfried. He rubbed his throat delicately. An ugly red mark was spreading.

'Damn you, Siegfried!'

'Where is the foreigner, you sow sucker?' He lifted his cane warningly and the boy raised his hands to protect himself.

'In the alley, Siegfried—he went to pee in the alley!'

Siegfried moved fast. What he saw in the alley caused him to leave the establishment without waiting. He hailed a taxi on the main street and removed himself from the neighbourhood as fast as the old Datsun could go. He strolled casually onto the terrace of the Erawan Hotel, sat at a poolside table, and asked for a telephone to be brought to him. He phoned van Hooten's secure line, spoke briefly, and then ordered tea. His hands were shaking as he lit his joint, and he saw to his annoyance that he had broken one of his long, polished fingernails. He leaned back against the chaise longue and watched the late-night revellers splashing in the blue-tinted pool.

The Erawan Hotel never slept. The night was fragrant with the scent of flowers, and the aroma of Siegfried's first-quality grass blended agreeably with the soft air.

Lee Residence, Bangkok

Chee Laan Lee
It had been two days since Salikaa's wedding. Thinking of Salikaa, and Toom, and then of Raven, I went to bed enervated and oddly depressed. I tried to read but the ideograms swam in front of my eyes. Then I tried to sleep, but I was restless and wakeful. Toward dawn I fell into a troubled slumber. It was from this uneasy sleep that Ah Lee roused me, knocking gently as she always did, trying not to startle me awake before my spirit had time to return to my body.

'American, he telephone you.' The hour was mercilessly early, the caller unexpected, but Ah Lee's wise old monkey face betrayed no emotion.

I took the call. 'Chee Laan Lee.'

'My apologies for ringing you at such an hour, ma'am,' General van Hooten said earnestly. 'Fact is, there's been a little trouble. Dr Raven…'

'What has happened? Is he hurt?' I only wondered much later why the American was contacting me instead of helping Raven himself. 'He's not dead, is he?' I whispered, horrified to imagine what I would do if he replied in the affirmative.

'No, no, no, Dr Raven's going to be just fine, ma'am. He just fell afoul of some thugs. They were after his wallet, probably. The truth is, this is kind of delicate, but the fact is, it might be best if a local friend were to collect Dr Raven before the police arrive on the scene. Matters tend to get a mite complicated once there's official involvement. Simple is best in my experience, ma'am.'

'Where is he?'

'He's in an alleyway at the back of an establishment called the Smart Cat Key Club. Chinatown.'

'I can find it,' I said. Then another thought struck me. 'Why are you ringing me? Why didn't Raven ring himself?'

'Well, my information is that he's not really in a condition to do that at the present time, ma'am. You see, he's still unconscious.'

Van Hooten rang off, leaving me staring at the wall, momentarily dazed. Then I leapt to my feet and ran. I dressed quickly and in a few minutes I was driving grandmother's Mercedes toward the gates. The old gatekeeper stared at me in amazement, and I wished I could have taken him and the garden boy along to help—but I couldn't afford to, for I knew they would report everything to *Tsu mu* before the day was out.

Even at this hour the traffic was building up, but at last I swung the big car up over the broken kerb and into the narrow lane at the back of the Key Club. A small group of men was standing around looking at Raven, who lay motionless in the dust amid the garbage. I fought down my fear, turned off the engine, and rolled down the window. I spoke loudly but calmly, without looking at anyone in particular.

'Whoever has his wallet, please give it here. And his watch, too.'

I could sense them staring. They stood in shocked silence. I rapped my fingers on the side of the car and held a large denomination note out for all to see.

'Now, please!' I said sharply. I did not let my voice tremble.

They stared, sullen and unmoving. Then someone said: 'It is the First Granddaughter of the Honourable Old Lady!'

'Lee, the Lee family,' I heard the murmurs, and now they stirred, and suddenly Raven's wallet and watch were passed through the crowd by willing hands until the nearest man handed them to me.

I took them, locked them in the glove compartment, and stepped out of the car. Now I looked around at the faces and smiled. 'Thank you all,' I said in Taechew, giving a Chinese gesture of greeting. 'Thank you all, good people, for taking care of the foreigner's possessions for him while he was ill, for saving his valuables from others less honest than yourselves.' I thanked all the gods that whoever had mugged Raven had had the grace to do it in Chinatown.

I handed the note to a dignified old man with an honest face. 'Uncle, see these good people are compensated for their trouble,' I said. 'Now, complete your good deeds! Help me lift this foreigner into the car!'

There was quite a lot of blood on his face and his clothes, and his thick, dark hair was matted with it. I went close and stood looking at him. I did not allow myself to touch him, and he did not open his eyes. I don't think he knew I was there. Some men began to lift him, and I heard him swear and groan, and then he said in a surprisingly strong, irritated voice, 'For God's sake, let me sleep!' and I felt less anxious. I opened the back door and three men lifted him carefully in and laid him on the seat, half sitting, half lying flat. I propped an embroidered cushion under his head and he opened one eye and tried to smile. My heart leapt. I thanked my helpers. Some of them ran to the end of the *soi* to see me out as I gingerly backed the car into the crowded street.

When I arrived at Dr Pien's clinic, half-naked street urchins gathered around the car immediately. 'You,' I said to the most alert, 'you're in charge. You can sit on the bonnet and take care of this car, and if you do it well, I'll give you twenty baht when I come back!'

Dr Pien left her work at once and came bustling down to the car with me. She inspected Raven, who was unconscious once more. She pulled down his eyelids and tested his pulse and listened to his breathing. Then she straightened up. 'He'll live,' she declared brusquely. 'Just a little tap on the head. Take him to the *farangs'* nursing home—Laila Drinkwater will fuss over him like a wet hen if you take him to her. More discreet, the nursing home. You'll need a doctor's signature. This'll do.' She scribbled on one of her prescription pads and tucked it into my hand. She looked at me oddly. 'You're a good girl. Even if you haven't inherited your grandmother's looks, at least you've got some of her brains!'

Bangkok Nursing Home is like a luxurious health spa. Each room has a private bath and a balcony overlooking gardens where squirrels play in the rain trees and huge butterflies flit through the hibiscus bushes. It caters to foreigners suffering from hepatitis and malaria, amoebic dysentery and heat exhaustion, and every so often a patient comes to die of rabies. They looked at Dr Pien's note and called a *farang* doctor, who told me to wait while they made some phone calls. In the meantime, orderlies carried Raven into an examination room.

The matron was a large English lady. Her starched and pillowy bosom gave her a strangely authoritative manner. I knew at once Dr Pien was right. Raven would be better understood among foreigners, his own kind.

'Now, my dear, we've got your details and you've spoken to the doctor, so there's nothing more you can do here for the present. I should run off home now, get some rest. Pop in and see your friend tomorrow if you like—just ring first to make sure he's well enough for visitors.'

'What are the visiting hours?' I asked.

'Oh, nothing like that here! People come any time!' She chortled cosily. 'That's why our patients leave here exhausted. Like a ruddy social club at times, this!'

Pim accompanied me, for the sake of propriety. The matron herself escorted us, which surprised me, until I saw the way she looked at Raven and I realised he had already established himself as a favoured patient. He was sitting in a cane chair on his veranda, in a dressing gown, looking pale but rather handsome, with an impressive bandage around his head.

'Here's your good Samaritan, Doctor,' the matron announced loudly, addressing him as if he were a medical doctor, and rather hard of hearing. I felt sure she bullied the doctors of the nursing home as well as the patients, and later found out I was right. But her nurses adored her. 'This young lady picked you up in the street and brought you to us!' she said.

'Chee Laan!' Raven exclaimed, staring at me with wide eyes. 'How did you find me? How did you know?'

'Tell you later,' I said. I sat on one of the chairs with its sun-faded cushion, and Pim took the other. The matron walked around Raven, studying him.

'Hm. Lost a lot of blood, you did. Pity. Could have used some of that. Got a patient in right now needing your type. Had to put an emergency call out over the radio. B Rhesus negative. Did have a girl in earlier offering B Neg, squeezed half a pint out of her in the end—but nothing like enough. Have another crack at her later.' She peered at Raven. 'Look a bit peaky still. Fancy a cup of tea? Oh, I brought you a paper, too.' She folded it and jabbed at it with her finger, thrusting it before Raven. 'Think yourself lucky, young man! This is the sort of thing that happens! Could have been you! Well, now, don't go tiring him out, you girls.' She left the room on that note of remonstrance.

Raven read the article and passed it over so we could read it too.

Unknown Foreigner Slain

A foreign visitor was found dead this morning in Soi Samarn, Petchaburi. He had been stabbed. Police believe the tragedy occurred after hours. The ill-fated visitor may have been unaware of the new closing times enforced on clubs and bars by the forces of law and order in an initiative to minimise illicit activity and crimes of violence. The unfortunate man was clearly the victim of thugs or terrorists. No wallet or personal papers were found. All attempts at identification have failed. This will remain yet another unsolved mystery of the Bangkok night.

'That's crazy,' Raven said. 'It was a man called Waddle. Any number of people could identify him. Siegfried could. Van Hooten could. Even I! To say nothing of the U.S. Embassy; they must have records. Why do they say he can't be identified?'

'Because it is not convenient,' I said. It seemed to me so obvious. 'But you were in Chinatown, Raven. You were nowhere near Petchaburi. Why does the paper say this dead man was in Petchaburi?'

'Different dead man?' Pim suggested.

'That's possible,' Raven reflected. 'If so, it's quite a coincidence. I'm amazed that you found me, Chee Laan.'

'Van Hooten phoned me,' I said. 'He told me where you were, and that you were hurt.' Raven stared at me. 'I am puzzled why he didn't send someone to help you, or go himself, instead of ringing me. He hardly knows me. How does he even know we are friends?'

'I think General van Hooten knows a great deal,' Raven said slowly. 'And you're right. I'm sure it is not convenient for Waddle's identity to be broadcast.'

'They don't call for witnesses,' Pim said, rereading the article.

'What are you going to do? Are you going to offer to identify this dead man?' I wanted to know.

'No. Not for the present, anyway.'

'I think that's sensible.'

And, I thought, *in this country, they cremate bodies quickly.*

'The earth rises higher,' I said, with an air of finality. Then I remembered. 'There was no body in that alley when I picked you up. So where was it?'

'Someone must have got to that other man. If it was the Thai police, why did they leave you there?' Pim looked thoughtful.

'Maybe it wasn't the Thai police who found Waddle, but someone else, and they only informed the police later,' Raven suggested.

'Or maybe the Thai police were told to keep their noses out of things where you were concerned. You must have a lot of influence!' I said, more cheerfully than I felt. I was uneasy. Not many foreigners have that kind of influence in Bangkok, and Raven had not been there very long. I knew he was not just a visiting lecturer, but I thought perhaps he was an undercover journalist doing some freelance investigating. There were secrets between us, but I felt his heart was good. Whatever he was doing, I did not think it could be unworthy. Now it was his turn to look pensive. I guessed he too was mystified. I wanted very much to touch his hand.

Tactfully, Pim went to the edge of the veranda to watch the squirrels. I said to Raven, in a casual tone that did not show how earnest I felt:

'Now you must be more careful. You see, I am responsible for you from now on.'

'How so?' He looked at me steadily. His eyes were very gentle. He gazed into my face as though he had never seen me before, as though he were imprinting each of my features on his mind.

'The Chinese say, if you save a person's life, that person is your responsibility forever.' We smiled into each other's eyes.

Pim's voice sounded sharp with surprise. 'You'll never believe who's coming!' I jumped to my feet and ran to her side. We watched Colonel Sya Dam striding along the path toward Raven's room. He spotted us and saluted us gravely, then strode up to the veranda, stepped into the flowerbed, and leaned on the railing. He removed his uniform cap and looked at Raven, who had started to get up from his wicker chair. 'Princess. Miss Lee.' He nodded at us, without any Thai salutation. 'Hello, Raven. How's the head?' he asked genially.

'I've had worse hangovers,' Raven grimaced cheerily.

'Should have more sense that to prowl about Chinatown after hours on your own,' Sya reproved.

'I wasn't on my own when I was mugged,' Raven returned evenly. 'I was with a man called Waddle.'

Sya's eyebrows shot up. 'Indeed?'

'Yes. Unfortunately, he was dead at the time.'

'You are confused, I think. The only other *farang* attacked last night—fatally, poor chap, in his case—was found in Petchaburi. You were in Chinatown, Raven. Other side of town. You are mistaken!'

'Of course I'm not mistaken!' Raven protested hotly. 'I was examining the poor devil when someone hit me over the head!'

Sya reflected for a moment, looking down at the brown earth in which he was standing. He scuffed at it with his boot. When he looked up again, it was straight at me.

'In that case, this other man would still have been there when Miss Lee got there. Perhaps he was there all along. Perhaps, in her concern for you, her friend, Miss Lee left that poor man to die.' His eyes gleamed calculatingly. He was sizing me up, trying to anticipate my response.

'Of course he was not there,' I retorted, walking up to him, refusing to show fear. 'You said the dead man was found in Petchaburi. The paper says that, too.'

'I don't know what all this is about,' Raven was angry, 'but I fell over Waddle's body! In Chinatown, in that back alley.'

'Oh, dear me,' Sya murmured regretfully. 'I am sorry to hear that, because, you see, that would mean Miss Lee here would need to come and have a little chat with the police. Are you sure you are not mistaken, Raven? A blow to the head can be very confusing.'

I felt cold. I hoped Raven would not persist. Pim moved close and took my hand. I had done nothing wrong, but in Bangkok that is academic. Guilt and innocence are arbitrary—what is important is in whose interests it is for someone to be guilty or innocent. Facts are governed by expediency. I remembered my old nightmare of the kite girl. I looked at Raven earnestly. To my relief, he dropped his gaze.

'Perhaps you're right, Colonel,' he admitted with assumed humility. 'I may have tripped over a boulder or a dead dog.'

'Indeed, Raven,' Sya smiled. 'A sack of rice, a rotten durian…'

'But,' Raven went on, and I wished he would simply let matters rest there, 'there's still something I don't understand.'

Sya stood up straight and replaced his uniform cap. 'I don't doubt there are many things neither of us understands. The world's complexity is ever increasing. I'm glad we've cleared up that particular little misunderstanding, though. Only one dead foreigner was reported last night. In Petchaburi. Then, of course, one dead *farang* is very like another!' He grinned, saluted us all, and strode off, whistling.

We all stared after him. The brief interlude had shattered our mood.

'I'm glad you didn't insist,' I said. 'Sya could make things very unpleasant. Best to let it go.'

'I expect so,' Raven said. 'Though it all seems highly irregular.'

'Not for Thailand,' Pim said. 'For Thailand, it's normal. That's just the trouble.'

We chatted some more, about Pim's political plans, a demonstration the students were organising. It was Bangkok normality. When we left Raven stood up and came to lean on the railing of the veranda, watching us. We turned many times to wave, and he lifted his hand each time. I thought his eyes looked worried, but perhaps it was only that his head hurt.

Kao Yai National Park, Isaan, Thailand

The two gunmen picked their way carefully through the leech-infested swamp paths, carrying their newly acquired sniper rifles with great care. The path took a twist to the right, but the vegetation was just as thick here—although there was not so much mud, which was less wearying.

'Now what?' muttered the younger and less experienced man.

'Now we wait,' his companion replied, seating himself on a gnarled tree trunk.

Waiting was no hardship while their spirits ran high. The soldiers' secondment as game wardens in Kao Yai National Park was new and exciting, like the bright, shiny tin badges they had been issued. The younger man rubbed his badge experimentally on his sleeve.

'Why can't we climb up to that lookout hut?' He jerked his thumb toward a reed-thatched observation post on high stilt legs, clearly visible through the leaves. 'If there's going to be shooting, we'd be better off up there.'

'No. Here.'

'Give me one good reason why we shouldn't go up there.'

'Colonel said.'

There was silence.

'Oh, right,' the younger man said resignedly, and asked no more questions. When the silence became too oppressive for him again, he patted his weapon admiringly. 'Sure is a handsome piece of hardware.'

'*Chai*...yep...very,' the older man grunted.

'And that sharpshooter course. Wasn't that something? I really enjoyed that!' The younger man, animated, began to fiddle with his gun.

'Quit that!' his companion commanded harshly. 'Quit messing about. We need to be ready.'

The roar of the helicopter battered their eardrums and the beating of the rotor blades flattened the foliage like a hurricane. The older gunman dropped to his knee, raising his weapon. 'This is it!' he cried. The young sniper, dizzy with excitement, followed suit.

Inside the helicopter, too, spirits were high. Rowdy toasts were made, drinking songs were bawled, and passengers drained their bottles and threw them merrily out, whooping as they watched them spiral down into the green heart of the jungle. In spite of the racket going on behind him, the Thai pilot made a textbook landing in the clearing. The game wardens watched four plump, happily inebriated men descend from the helicopter, followed by three servants. The pilot got out last and walked away from the group. The cheery comrades were busy directing the servants to drag heavy animal carcasses from the nearby jungle and stack them in mounds. Then the four hunters, with much back-slapping joviality, sent the servants to bring their guns from the helicopter, and were photographed, arms about each other, their feet reposing proudly upon their 'bag'.

'Now!' murmured the older game warden, aiming for the central figure, a fat, grinning Chinese. They fired in unison, and the four hunters dropped one after the other on top of the dead deer. The pilot leapt into the helicopter, and the servants bolted, screeching, into the jungle. The younger game warden rose from his cover and fired like a madman at the helicopter's rotor blades, shouting at each report. As the pilot realised what was happening, he leapt out again and made a dash for the cover of the trees in the wake of the fleeing servants.

'Enough!' the older gunman shouted. 'Let's go!'

'What now?'

'Now, we go back and report.'

'Report what?'

'Poachers in the National Game Reserve were killed when their helicopter, laden with game, failed to take off.'

'Oh...'

Lee Residence, Bangkok

Chee Laan Lee
It is a terrible thing to lose your father and rejoice. I had known only my father's weaknesses and not their causes. Understanding might have bred in me tolerance, I suppose. Now he was dead, I wondered if there had ever been, could ever have been, anything between us but mutual wariness, tinged—on my part, anyway—with loathing.

My mother, of course, threw herself wholeheartedly into the theatricality of mourning. My brother Pao was more upset than anyone expected. He took to his bed, refusing to speak to anyone. The younger sons, by Father's second and third wives, were heartless children. Their grief stemmed mainly from a fear that they would be banished from the Lee family home, and that their pocket money and sweets would stop.

The *Bangkok Herald* and all the other newspapers carried pictures of the dead, and a sober little story:

Copter Tragedy: VIPs Killed
Three leading government officials—Mr Sarit Samarn, Mr Derm Sarasin, and Mr Thep Wittiyakara—together with well-known local business tycoon Mr Ching Lee, director of the Lee Bangkok Bank, died tragically yesterday when their helicopter crashed near the Khao Yai National Park nature reserve.

I was reading all these meaningless and perverted accounts when Ah Lee appeared. She announced impassively, with the air of one refusing to be impressed: 'Thai Princess girl come.'

I rose to greet Pim, took her hands, and drew her to the tea table. We sat in our straight-backed chairs beside it in silence while Ah Lee served us. When she had gone, Pim said, 'I am sorry, Chee Laan. He was your father, after all.'

'Yes,' I said quietly.

We were silent again, then Pim said, 'Shall I tell you what I heard? About why it happened?'

'My father was infatuated with helicopters.'

'Your father enjoyed shooting deer, Chee Laan. He liked shooting deer from helicopters. Especially in game reserves. They all did.'

'How do you know?'

'The others were government officials. It was a government-sponsored trip. The helicopter was laden with illegally shot deer carcasses. It couldn't take off properly.'

'I asked how you knew, Pim.'

She shrugged. 'They were members of the government. Servants talk. Pilots talk.' She sipped her tea delicately, but set it down harder than she intended, a little of the liquid slapping its porcelain rim. 'It's typical, I'm afraid, Chee Laan. This government is rotten to the core,' she said bitterly. 'We are planning the biggest peaceful demonstration ever. There are thousands of us. All inter-university feuds are forgotten.'

'When is all this happening?'

'One week from today, we march. We'll besiege them, we'll take turns addressing them through megaphones—we'll make them listen!' She shut her eyes, looking suddenly very sad. 'If only Toom were here,' she said. 'I have to do it for both of us now. I say to myself, even if my father beats me, even if he chains me up, I must do it for Toom, for both of us. There's only me now.'

'You do exaggerate, Pim. I cannot imagine Prince Prem would beat you, much less chain you up.'

She shook her head. 'My father is a very bad man to cross. After the last demonstration, I was made to crawl around the room for hours until my knees were raw.' She laughed at my expression of disgust and anger. 'I think the authorities are nervous, too. So far there have been only reprimands and expulsions, very few casualties. I think this time it will be very different.'

'I'm sure you're exaggerating, Pim,' I attempted to reassure her.

'You'll see,' she said. 'But if the police or the soldiers recognise me, they will take care not to harm me. I shall be in a privileged position, less in danger than my comrades.' She sounded regretful. Then she smiled gently. 'Remember the Buddha's teaching: unity in a group is a cause for happiness.'

I capped the quotation: 'Concerted effort by a group is a cause for happiness!'

She got up to leave, and we embraced at the door, holding together a moment longer than usual. I said, 'Thanks for coming. Take care of yourself, Pim'

Of course she didn't. Neither did she exaggerate.

I never spoke to Pim again, though I thought of her often, remembering with a stab of pain the contrast between her commitment and resolve and the sweet expression on her earnest face.

Her father, Prince Premsakul, HRH, once Ambassador Extraordinary and Plenipotentiary to the Court of St James, did not beat his only daughter. He had her servants strip her naked and tie her to the bedpost with padlocked cycle locks, chains in lengths of hosepipe. The servants were told that the princess was suffering from hysteria, a well-known complaint among unmarried young women.

Pim managed to extricate herself from her bonds. She tore up a bed sheet and fashioned a rough toga-like garment. When it was dark, Pim slipped out and climbed over the compound wall. The watchman, as usual, was sound asleep. Watchmen always sleep more soundly than anyone else in the household, as being a watchman is not a job for those of a nervous disposition. She made her way to the home of friends, in readiness for the great march of freedom.

It is from them that I learned all this. But that was later, when it was too late to ask Pim herself.

State Railway, Northbound from Bangkok

Pawn hunched in a corner of the railway compartment, moaning, lost in the contemplation of her misery. Without warning, Salikaa's hand cracked her hard across the face. The girl shrieked and cowered, staring in terror and pain at her mistress.

'Stop that bloody snivelling!' Salikaa cried. Salikaa's bridegroom, slumped in a corner seat, his clothing undone, giggled. He belched and tilted his head back, pursing his lips to receive the bottle. The train shuddered violently and whisky spilled down his neck.

Pawn glanced at her new master and mistress and continued to sob, but more discreetly. She was worried for the baby she'd had to leave behind, and sick with fear for herself, summarily dispatched with these terrifying people to the wild lands—inhabited by ghosts, terrorists, and the notorious tribes—by the man she feared with an almost superstitious dread, Colonel Sya Dam.

Pawn was fifteen years old. Her story was banal, typical of many Bangkok's teenage prostitutes. At thirteen, employed as a servant in a wealthy Thai household, she was seduced by the teenage son of the family. The boy was mildly admonished. Pawn was thrown out on the street. In her new line of work, fate occasionally rewarded her with a GI, his pockets stuffed with green. She could wheedle as much out of a GI in a few hours as a maidservant earned in a month. If she got lucky, she could encourage the man to drink so much that he was incapable of exacting value for money. The next day, Pawn would roll her eyes in exaggerated admiration of his virility. All men believed that sort of lie, Pawn learned, even if the last thing they could remember was falling upstairs. Pawn liked Americans. They bought her trinkets and took her to the movies. Her baby was an Amerasian redhead, sired by a GI whose hired wife she had been for a few weeks. She'd had six rough-and-ready backstreet abortions already, and the abortionist warned her she was unlikely to survive another, so she'd let the baby happen, secretly hoping the Yank would marry her and take her to the States, which she imagined as one huge PX, crammed with desirable consumer goods and large, smiling people.

But Pawn's luck never lasted. The spirits were against her. She'd tried, had a steel bridge hammered into her flat Asian nose, and her eyes slit, to open them out and create eyelids. These agonizing operations had cost a lot of money. Her American took her to Thai Daimaru, the glittering Japanese department store in Rajprasong Shopping Centre, to buy things for the baby. He kissed Pawn, told her to take care now, you hear, and then left.

When the little girl was born, Pawn boarded her out with an old woman who minded five other Amerasian redheads in a khlongside slum. The toothless hag was a slutty semi-retired old-timer from the Khlong Tooey circuit, who occasionally, for favoured customers, still performed fellatio. The rest of the time she reclined in a deck chair, fanning herself and chewing betel. Meanwhile, her infant charges crawled about on the slimy duckboards among the refuse and the flies. Their noses ran constantly, and their arms and legs were encrusted with sores, which never seemed to heal. But not everyone welcomed a red-haired, half-caste brat, and the woman only charged five dollars.

Now that Pawn was properly organised with a Mama-san, she could manage that. Nobody bothered the organised girls, or bullied them into giving it away for free to anyone wearing a uniform. The local police often came in for a drink with the Mama-san. When they left, they were mellow, and the back pocket under their gun holsters bulged. Every so often, the Mama-san would say it was Pawn's turn to do her a favour and show the officers a good time.

But not on Sunday, as Sunday was Pawn's day off. She rose late, and dressed herself in her Sunday best, and played her favourite game of respectable housewife. She collected her baby and covered its weeping sores under pink lace tights and frilly frocks and a sun bonnet, and paraded it in a push-chair, window-shopping and dreaming. And then, one Sunday, Pawn went to collect her baby, and there, instead of the old woman, sitting in the chair and fanning himself, sat Sya Dam.

She thought he'd come for some other purpose, and was about to protest that it was her day off, but he pointed to where the infants normally crept in the dirt. She saw then that there was no sign of the children, and she screamed.

Sya Dam said loudly and accusingly, 'These children were not being cared for adequately. They are unkempt and riddled with disease.'

'What have you done with my baby?' She stared around, wild-eyed, as if to conjure up the vanished infants. She shouted again, with mounting hysteria, 'Where is the old woman?'

He stood up then, towering over her. Before his natural authority, Pawn cringed, as though she were guilty of some crime.

'She has been charged with selling babies. The children found here will be sent to a state orphanage,' he said severely.

'No!' she shrieked. 'They'll die there. I've seen those places!'

'So sorry!' He spread his hands, staring her down impassively. 'The law is the law.'

'I want my baby!' Emboldened by grief and rage, she flew at him. He caught her wrists and laughed mockingly down into her stricken face.

'Now,' he said, 'if you ever want to see your child again, you must listen very carefully to what I have to say. And then you must follow instructions. Someday it may be possible to trace your child and have her returned to you. Or not...' He allowed his voice to trail off menacingly. He let go of her wrists, and she stumbled backward, rubbing at the red finger marks left by his grip.

'I'll do anything you say,' she whispered abjectly. 'Anything.'

'You are a sensible girl, Pawn,' he said. 'My officers have given me good reports of you. Many women of your kind are too stupefied by drugs or drink, or too selfish, to care about their children.'

'My baby is all I have in the world.' Pawn was weeping noisily. 'What must I do?'

She was to don the black-and-white uniform of a maidservant again, and to attend Miss Thailand, the lady Salikaa, more beautiful and more vindictive than anyone Pawn had ever met. Already her arms were black and blue with Salikaa's pinches; her dented shins ached with the impact of Salikaa's sharp-pointed Italian shoes. As for the bridegroom, he was, if possible, even more terrifying. Learning she was to live among the Akha, Pawn's world collapsed; she felt she had been handed her death sentence.

Now, her face still stinging from Salikaa's slap, she huddled wretchedly on the hard wooden seat, peered out at the dramatic landscape, and wished she were brave enough to hurl herself out as the train steamed over a deep gorge and end it all. Only the thought of one day being reunited with her baby stopped her. The slow tears trickled down from her Westernised eyes. She dared not rub them again.

Drinkwater Residence, Bangkok, Thailand

Raven

Why did Chee Laan decide on our excursion to Chinatown? Was she making some obscure ethnic point, or did she know what was going to happen in the city, and wanted me out of the way?

I didn't know then, and I still don't, though I've since turned it over in my mind innumerable times.

Laila Drinkwater handed me a note. I recognised Siegfried's elegant hand. He was 'charged by the Prince and Princess Premsakul to invite Dr Nathaniel Raven to an impromptu twenty-four-hour riverboat party to celebrate the princess's fifth cycle birthday.'

'That means she's sixty,' Laila said. 'Premsakul never normally marks her birthday; he must have a hidden agenda, this sly old fox. Siegfried is Master of the Revels—he devises the entertainment and décor. All the diplomatic corps and the media will attend. One does not refuse Prince Premsakul.'

'I have a prior engagement.' I said it as casually as I could, but Laila, sharp and world-wise, knew instinctively that I planned to meet Chee Laan.

'I'll make your excuses to Siegfried. He will be devastated, but he will recover immediately. As will the prince. You have recently been the victim of a savage mugging. Everyone will understand. Your poor head still hurts!'

There was to be no Mercedes today. Chee Laan haggled with a passing samlor and we embarked on a noisy, smelly ride to the heart of Chinatown. We crouched, cramped together on the torn blue plastic seat. The violence of the driver's death-defying swerves meant that our bodies were often flung against one another, and we clung, exhilarated, laughing and breathless as children on a carnival ride, with the same spice of apprehension, of pulse-quickening risk. Plunged into the bewildering hurly-burly of a country fairground, with its bustle, lights, noise, and colours, we clung to each other, daunted and impressed.

Gradually I regained focus and the hive of industry and commerce that was Chinatown began to take shape. Stalls offering books, clothing, pirated records, cosmetics, bolts of cloth, spilled over onto the narrow, crowded sidewalk. Jewellers' shops with scarlet boards emblazoned with golden ideograms jostled with antique shops full of porcelain vases and dark furniture inlaid with mother-of-pearl. Already the Chinese movie theatres were ablaze and blaring. Everywhere, in baggy pants and shapeless *blouson*, in miniskirts, in elegant *cheong sam*, the Chinese went about their business. Some squatted before their shops, chewing, fanning themselves with plaited rattan fans, yet it was a scene febrile with violence: above every shop, one glimpsed the metal blind, which the shopkeeper bolted to the pavement each night before retiring to his quarters over the store.

The herbalist advanced to meet us. His own medicine did not appear to have done much for him. He was sere and wizened as a gnome. He bared several yellowish, horsy teeth. Behind him, in glass cases, the coral branches of the ginseng root, pigs' bladders, dead snakes and lizards were displayed. He handed Chee Laan a parcel, and she handed over a bundle of twenty-baht notes. He bowed and accepted them without counting them. I appreciated this courteous token of respect for Chee Laan.

He said something to her in Taechew, and she frowned. 'He wants my grandmother to come in person,' she said. 'For a competent diagnosis.'

The herbalist turned to me then, and, smiling, led me to a corner. Here he produced a shiny pyramid-shaped horn. With a series of suggestive grunts and a veiled pornographic pantomime, he intimated that this was rhinoceros horn, the remedy for failing potency.

'I'll certainly bear your advice in mind. Should the need arise.' I backed off smartly.

Chee Laan burst into peals of laughter. 'He is telling you that, in less advanced cases, snake is also very effective, but the gentleman should take care to patronise only a reputable dealer, meaning himself! Unwary customers have been known to have eel palmed off on them instead.'

We left the herbalist's, to my relief.

'Pim claims the demand for rhino horn in love potions caused the rhino to become extinct in Thailand,' Chee Laan said, shaking her head, though her eyes still retained the merriment she had expressed at my momentary discomfiture.

'Doubtless because of the unreasonable demands of polygamy,' I grinned, privately reflecting it was no wonder the countryside was so denuded of fauna and well-intentioned conservation lectures were received with blank stares.

We entered a pavement-side noodle shop, and she ordered chickens' feet. When the legs arrived, descaled and gelatinous, with yellow claws, she showed me how to snap them neatly at the ankle joint and bite off the fleshy nub of the sole. I sucked the flesh from those chicken feet like an old China hand. I would have swallowed hemlock, I think, gazing into her dancing black eyes. I felt quite unreasonably happy and relaxed. Nancy was pushed somewhere out of sight, into some sealed compartment in the back of my mind; Sya and all his apocalyptic works, war, death, and pestilence, had temporarily ceased to gallop through the wastelands of my brain. I chewed my chickens' feet and looked at Chee Laan Lee, and all at once, I was mellow.

I had to blow it, of course. 'What did you buy for your grandmother?'

'Liver medicine.'

'What's that made of, Malay bear spleen?' She slanted her eyes up at me, but forbore to reply. She toyed with the gnawed chicken foot beside her bowl. 'Chee Laan, you can't really believe all this disgusting mumbo-jumbo?' I burst out before I could stop myself.

'You mean,' she said coolly, 'I who have enjoyed the benefits of a Western education, I should know better?' She sighed. 'Did you know smuggling rare animals out of Thailand to Singapore and Malaysia is as profitable as smuggling opium?' She looked at me hard. 'If Chinese medicine were not effective, do you suppose for one moment that my grandmother would bother with it?'

Before I could reply, a waiter placed bowls before us crispy *mae krob* and succulent white boiled noodles lustrous as silk ribbons. A group of samlor drivers sat down at the next table and called for coffee made with condensed milk and chips of ice, which was served in tall, greasy glasses. Their voices grew animated.

'Grassroots politics.' Chee Laan listened to the men's talk, her head lowered. I listened, too, though they spoke so fast, and with different accents, that I had to concentrate to follow.

'Price of rice up again,' a villainous scarecrow in a yachting cap grunted. 'Poor devils upcountry are starving. Here in town, at least we can make a bit extra, delivering customers to the big bosses' whorehouses at so much a head.'

'All right down south, though. Ant army, smuggling Thai rice into Malaysia!' another man said, through a mouthful of noodles.

'Ant army, my arse!' The scarecrow spat contemptuously beneath the table, to the disgust of a skeletal striped cat that was clawing at the chair legs, purring raspingly.

'Big deal operation. Five-truck convoys, every night since the government brought in the rice price control bill.'

'Five trucks! How you going to get five truckloads of rice past the checkpoints?' a fat man asked scathingly.

A huge, very dark-skinned man with the look of a Malay Straits pirate pulled the excited man down to a chair in a rough, comradely way. 'Keep calm! We all know any official is immediately struck dumb by the sight of a hundred-baht note!' There were shouts of laughter. When it subsided, the big man said, soberly, 'Except, of course, for the Incorruptible. The Black Tiger.'

The others glanced about apprehensively, and one hissed, 'Keep your voice down, Yen! Gestapo are everywhere.'

I frowned at Chee Laan, puzzled.

'Nickname for the Gaw Taw Paw, Field Marshal Praphan's spies!' she whispered.

The big man guffawed scornfully. 'Gestapo! What can they hear, inside their air-conditioned limousines?'

'Inflation's driving me nuts!' complained a rangy youth with legs already gnarled and old, as if he had graduated to samlor driving from pedalling an upcountry pedicab. 'I tell you, it's driven me to the Planned Parenthood centre!'

'How come?' the Southern Thai chuckled, astonished.

'Well, see, the girls are charging two hundred baht a trick, instead of sixty, like the good old days. These days, the only lay I can afford is my own wife!'

A gale of laughter swept the table. Then someone, in a new, more serious tone, asked: 'Anyone see the demo today?'

'Students!' The scarecrow spat again. 'Idle layabouts!'

'Not this time. Demonstrating for the working man. Price of rice, not just politics!'

'I heard there was some deaths. Up Rajdamnern Avenue. Young girls, too. Doesn't seem right.'

Chee Laan had been listening with interest and amusement. Now her expression changed. She signalled to the waiter urgently. He appeared, wielding his small black abacus, ducking under the table to check for empty bottles.

'The evening papers will be out,' Chee Laan said. She spoke quickly and urgently to the waiter, who immediately ran into the street and soon returned with a sheaf of newspapers. All carried stories about Prince Premsakul's riverboat party. Revelling socialites were depicted in attitudes of refined debauchery. Only one small Chinese newspaper carried a report of the demonstration, with a few pictures.

'Bless Khamthorn!' Chee Laan exclaimed. 'The *Bangkok Herald* probably refused to print his pictures, so he sold them to this Chinese newspaper.' She translated quickly: 'The streets of Bangkok ran with blood again last night. After a citywide student action, which left several demonstrators dead, six universities and a college of education have been closed down in the Greater Bangkok Area for an unlimited term. The student protest centred on the expulsion of six Chulalongkhorn University students, who had produced a news sheet accusing the government of corruption, injustice, and ineffectual administration.

'The students held an all-night candlelight vigil on Rajdamnern Avenue, around the Monument to Democracy. They demanded interviews with the Director of State Universities, the President of the Universities Council, and Colonel Sya Dam.

'Futile!' she said, looking up. 'They'd never agree. They couldn't; they'd lose so much face if they showed up just because a student rabble summoned them!' She held up the paper, trying to make out images from the blurred photograph. Together we looked at the sprawled bodies of the dead. We didn't recognise any of them. In the centre lay the body of a young woman in a curious white shift, like that of a Buddhist nun. Her face was covered. The slender limbs were folded over themselves like a drooping marionette.

'Pim was there.' Chee Laan folded the paper and stood up abruptly. 'I don't believe they would arrest Pim. They wouldn't dare—she's too well known! Her family are too well connected. We must go to her at once. She can tell us what happened.'

In innocent anticipation, we left Chinatown and set off for the Premsakul mansion. Chee Laan was quiet, but composed. I was still dazed with a sense of unaccustomed euphoria, delighting in our intimacy. It's strange to recall that now. Strange, and uncomfortable.

Rajdamnern Avenue, Bangkok, Thailand

The demonstration had seemed at first a momentous success. Rajdamnern Avenue, Bangkok's most majestic carriageway, swept as wide as the River Chao Phraya around the Monument to Democracy. From one blood-red wall to the other, it brimmed with a tide of humanity. Eight thousand students had gathered to protest against the sacking of the six student editors and the price of rice, demanding greater political freedom. Steel-helmeted riot police, armed with truncheons and tear gas, formed a cordon four deep across the avenue in front of the Thai Military Bank. Five hundred riot police from all the Northern Bangkok stations and the notorious Crime Suppression Division of the Special Branch reinforced them. A memorandum was formally read out: the Prince Regent exhorted the police to avoid bloodshed at all costs. This was greeted with ironic cheers. Pim, helped up onto a small pillar by willing hands, had called upon the students to sing 'Thailand, Awake!' and they responded enthusiastically, despite the tension and their exhaustion.

A small delegation of students was permitted to leave the cordoned-off area to seek provisions for their comrades. On their return, police refused to allow them to re-enter the area. A male student was struck in the face, smashing his nose. A student leader, seeing the blood, seized the microphone and shouted a denunciation of police brutality; a breakaway group of students charged the barricade and rushed the police cordon.

Police retaliation was immediate and savage. Several students were beaten down with truncheons. Members of the Arrowhead, the student leadership group, sought to control the angry demonstrators by holding hands and placing themselves between the police and their fellow students. Over the loudspeaker, again and again, the Arrowhead spokesmen urged,

'Non-violence! Remember, comrades, non-violence!'

Stones were thrown. The demonstrators vented their rage on a police minibus, denting it and breaking a window. Tear gas canisters were tossed into the heaving mob, and shots rang out. When the gas cleared, the bodies of six demonstrators lay on the pavement. Ironically, all six were members of the Arrowhead—pacifists who had struggled to prevent the demonstration from getting out of hand. All the newspapers in Bangkok ran a story covering the riots.

> *Riot police today opened fire on demonstrators at the Monument for Democracy. Six students were killed.*
> *Bangkok Lucky Sun*, Chinese-language daily

> *Among the students who tragically lost their lives in the assault on a peaceful demonstration on Rajdamnern Avenue was Princess Pim Premsakul, only surviving child of Their Highnesses the Prince and Princess Premsakul. Speculation is rife that the attack was funded by certain powerful elements in the business community to discourage the students from pursuing their anti-protectionist campaign.*
> *Bangkok Herald*, English-language daily

> *The Bangkok Riot Squad was called into action again today when a rebellion was rumoured to be imminent among samlor drivers in Lopburi Province. When police arrived on the scene, order was restored.*
> All Bangkok Thai-language newspapers

> *Stop press: Bangkok's Chinatown ravaged by arson and assassination. Widespread damage to property. Number dead not yet known.*
> UPI wire service

The samlor drivers of rural Lopburi, far from being rioters, proved to be model law-abiding citizens who were mystified and flattered by the unexpected attention of the Bangkok Riot Suppression Force. The mayor hastily delivered an impromptu speech welcoming the police. The riot squad removed their helmets and boots and sat around under the giant sacred monkey tree, smoking, scratching, and enjoying a well-earned rest from their uncomfortable jeep ride up the northern highway. Some enjoyed a nap. Others sampled the local noodle stalls and threw gobbets of food at the sacred monkeys, who returned fire with nuts and dirt.

It was as good as a holiday outing to the zoo. There was general regret when the sergeants started prodding the drivers of the jeeps and minibuses into action.

However, when they reached Bangkok headquarters, they were blasted out of their idyll, encountering a thunder-faced captain who demanded where the hell they had been.

'Lopburi, sir!' the sergeants shouted.

'I suppose you know what's been going on here?'

'How could we, sir? Please, sir, we've been in Lopburi!' one young sergeant asked innocently. He'd not long worn his sergeant's stripes. Judging by the look his superior officer bent upon him, he would not retain them.

'All hell's loose in this city!' the captain accused. 'And meantime, the Riot Squad goes joyriding!'

'I bet it's those wastrel students again!' someone muttered.

The captain spun on his heel and confronted him. 'Quite right! Reprisals! There's a hysterical mob running amok through Chinatown, burning, looting, murdering!'

'Murdering the Jeks?' someone asked, amazed.

'Naturally! Haven't you read the papers? The people who gunned down those students were in the pay of the Chinese!'

Now they all stared. Every man knew who among his comrades had fired on the students. Impossible to say who had hit what, but they all knew who had fired into that crowd of girls and boys armed only with stones and loudspeakers and sheets of paper.

'But, sir...' The young sergeant broke off, biting his lip.

The captain's fierce eye quelled him. 'Those who killed the students were bribed by the Chinese. It was a cunning plot by the Triad societies to discredit the Thai Riot Squad and reduce the confidence of the public in its constituted defenders. I want every man here to remember that.' He swept his compelling gaze from one face to the other. 'This episode was intended to turn public opinion against you, you dunderheads, brains of water buffalo—and against the state, whose honourable servants you, with luck, may remain. Now, back aboard those vehicles, men, and proceed to Chinatown, where your orders are to take control of the situation.'

'You said there'd been more killing, sir?' one sergeant asked.

'Some,' the captain nodded curtly. 'In Chinatown. But now they're setting buildings on fire and damaging property, and that's more than the city can afford. So you get in there. But remember: the Jeks asked for it. In the eyes of every right-thinking Thai, the Jeks are getting a gobful of the rotten fish they serve up to everyone else.'

'Very good, sir!' they shouted. They rushed to their vehicles, eyes alight with excitement and rapacity. There was booty aplenty in Chinatown—the looter's El Dorado. With the Jeks on the run, anything might happen. As the jeeps reversed showily and screamed off, there were war whoops and horseplay among the younger men.

The captain watched them go, then turned to make his report to Colonel Sya Dam. He had, he reflected with satisfaction, followed Colonel Sya's instructions to the letter.

Drinkwater Residence, Bangkok

Chee Laan Lee

'That beastly riot,' pouted Siegfried, 'quite spoiled my party!'

Raven and I had been refused admission at the Premsakul home. A weeping servant informed us Pim was dead. In numbed silence, we made our way back to the Drinkwater residence, where we found Siegfried and Laila on the terrace, as usual, reclining in the limp, self-pitying attitudes of those nursing hangovers. Neither Raven nor I offered our sympathy. We exchanged glances that spoke volumes. When I heard Siegfried's reaction to the night's events, I glared at him, outraged by this exhibition of egocentricity.

'It was the most marvellous party, Raven, darling!' he declared defensively, alert to my unspoken censure. 'Truly, you should have stayed with us! Three huge pleasure craft and the temple guesthouse all to ourselves, lavish feasting, exquisite dancers, fantastic musicians. Wonderful fun, especially after our host and hostess, the Prince and Princess, retired to the temple.' He sighed, remembering. Then his face became solemn. 'They sent a motorcycle policeman there, to tell them about the princess. Poor young girl! Ah, *quelle dommage, si élégante, si gentille!*' Siegfried's affectation of sorrow came too late to appease my fury.

'Why this sudden attempt to blame the Chinese?' Raven demanded. 'The Chinese had nothing to do with it. The demonstrators were gunned down by the Thai riot suppression forces, surely?'

'Look, Raven,' I said, conscious all three foreigners were watching me: Raven protectively, Laila anxiously, Siegfried with a hint of malice. 'It is clear! The forces of law and order'—I did not attempt to curb the bitterness which crept into my voice—'cannot be blamed. The gallant police force will be exonerated. Otherwise, Pim would be condemned as a violent demonstrator.

It would reflect badly on her family, who are very powerful. The left-wing students, in turn, would proclaim her a socialist martyr. This would not please her family either. Therefore, a third agent has to be identified. What more convenient villain than the Chinese?' I added. 'Not that Premsakul himself has the brains to devise such a solution. I am convinced there is someone cleverer pulling the strings.'

'Such as?' Raven's eyes bored into mine. His expression was tense. I knew he was remembering our day in Chinatown, who I was, where my loyalties must lie.

'Who else but Sya Dam!' Even the air seemed to quiver apprehensively around the syllables of his name.

'When he got the news about the demonstration and his daughter,' Siegfried said thoughtfully, as though considering my suggestion, 'Prince Premsakul requested that the patriarch of the local temple address the assembled members of his influential riverboat party, presenting what he called the "true facts."' He snorted contemptuously. 'The patriarch is a saintly geriatric whose view of events faithfully mirrored Prince Premsakul's own. He claimed the bloodshed was Chinese instigated, because so much of the country's capital is in Chinese hands.'

'So left-wing agitators could be regarded as a threat to the Chinese business community,' Raven interjected, nodding.

'Exactly. And,' I added, 'if the government wants to hand a scapegoat to the left wing, they can easily sacrifice the Chinese! Eighty per cent of the Thai population will not move a muscle to defend us, and the other twenty per cent will delight in our discomfiture.'

'It is true.' Siegfried nodded sagaciously. 'Of course, all the journalists became extremely agitated at missing the big story and rushed off to Bangkok in fleets of taxis. The riverboats were much more comfortable after that. Room to stretch your legs, and nobody being sick over the side.'

'I bet the prince planned that whole party as a diversion!' Raven said.

I felt sick. I wanted to beat my fists against something, preferably Sya Dam's face, and I wanted to scream until I was hoarse. Surely now *Tsu mu* would see Sya for what he was and break off her association with him. 'Of course Premsakul planned it!' I snapped. 'He lured the media and the high-ups away from the city. It was very cunning!'

'And now, all this ethnic hysteria!' lamented Laila. 'This witch-hunt! It will tear the city apart, and it is all quite ridiculous, when the Chinese are innocent.'

'Oh, pooh, who cares whether the Chinese are innocent?' Siegfried snarled. 'The point is, they'll have to point the finger at someone. Why not the Chinese? Why not the Cambodian refugees, or the boat people, or the Indian shopkeepers, or the *farangs*? Why not the Malays? Why not the monks, for God's sake?' He snapped his fingers and rose, still dressed for the party in his white on the Cossack smock, with a sumptuous, bejewelled leather belt low about his narrow hips. He stalked toward the stairs, yawning. 'Just so long as nobody fingers the Brothers!' he said. 'I'm off to get my beauty sleep.'

Perhaps this affectation of callousness was Siegfried's way of dealing with unpleasantness. Buddhists believe one should not display sorrow at the death of a fine person, for their good karma will certainly ensure a superior reincarnation. Or else they will join their ancestors. I do not know what happens. Some say religion is childish nonsense. It depends, I think, on how near one is to death.

In the year 300 BC, the master wrote, 'How do I know that the wish to live is not a mistake? How do I know that hating to die is not to think one has lost one's way, when all the time one is on the path that leads to home? While a man is dreaming, he knows not that he dreams. But when he wakes then he knows it was a dream. Not until the Great Awakening can he know that this was all One Great Dream.'

I couldn't help but think of Pim, my brave and gentle friend, and her great dreams. I hoped she was on the path leading home.

'I must go,' I told them. 'My grandmother will be concerned, especially just now.' Raven walked me to the door. Mrs Drinkwater had ordered her car to take me home, and the chauffeur stood waiting.

'Chee Laan,' Raven said, his eyes holding me, reluctant to let me go, 'please take care. Why do you need to go so urgently?'

'Because,' I said, 'my grandmother may need to visit Chinatown. I can't let her go alone.'

'For God's sake, Chee Laan, Chinatown at this moment must be like a lit fuse. You are not going to Chinatown!'

I laid my finger gently against his lips. 'I am not the person who got attacked in Chinatown,' I said gently. 'Remember? I will see you tomorrow.'

He kissed the tips of my fingers and I snatched my hand back, conscious of the waiting chauffeur, and ran briskly down the steps.

In the old days of diagnostic dolls, *Tsu mu* would not have needed to visit the herbalist in person, our ill-fated foray into Chinatown that day would not have been necessary, and Ah Lee would still be alive.

In the olden days, no Chinese female could be examined by a doctor, who would always be male, since girls were not worth educating. Thus, a lady would indicate her symptoms on a small ivory doll, and the physician would prescribe accordingly. But *Tsu mu*'s herbalist claimed a personal interview was necessary if a proper diagnosis was to be effected. In reality, I felt sure he had identified some area of his life where he hoped *Tsu mu* could be of assistance. That is something one negotiates, not through third parties, but eye to eye. Of course, even in our enlightened times, she could not consult a doctor unattended, so Ah Lee and I accompanied her, as her status demanded.

We did not even take the driver. Despite my heavy heart and sense of foreboding, I enjoyed the sensation of piloting the big car through the narrow streets, while *Tsu mu* and Ah Lee argued about food prices like two old market women.

I was anxious about my grandmother's health. Since Father's death she had a new fragility; her eyes were like cigarette burns in ancient parchment. She had grown sombre, full of reserved glances and silences. Sometimes she sighed, murmuring to herself, 'I did not mean it to go so far, to be like that,' but then she would fall silent, say no more. I knew that she disapproved deeply of my relationship with Raven. But I had never in my life felt anything so powerful as the attraction he held for me, and, though one day I knew I must give him up, I could not do so yet. I hugged my secret love close to my heart, dreading the time when I should have to relinquish it.

I felt my grandmother had begun to question whether my father's death was an accident, and the suspicion was sapping her confidence in life. It was almost as though she felt that in losing her only child, her own sun had drawn nearer its setting. She had begun years earlier to train me up in earnest to inherit her mantle. All my waking hours, apart from the few precious moments I stole to meet Raven, she pounded away at me, remorselessly cramming me with every detail of the family business. She also expounded her philosophies of business and life. It troubled me to have been singled out already as her heir, appointed above my brother and half-brothers. They would receive cash and some shares in the business. But most of the family's assets were in real estate and banking, and everyone knew it. Whoever held the property held the keys to the Lee kingdom. The property and the power that went with it were to be mine.

I knew there would be difficulties. I was not sure I was ready for it. Power is seductive, but it curtails your freedom. The day I stepped into *Tsu mu*'s shoes, I would have to abandon my free and easy *farang* ways.

But for now, as I piloted the big car and listened to the two old women's pleasurable wrangling, I tried to convince myself that grandmother would not slacken her grip on the reins for many years. She was stronger than all of us. My happiness depended upon her living.

She occupied the back seat of the Mercedes in solitary state. She had shrunk recently, so that her clothes enveloped her delicate frame. Beside me, Ah Lee sat clutching her woven basket, turning her head now and then on her yellow tortoise's neck to argue with *Tsu mu* or exchange glares with her.

'Begging your pardon, Honourable Lady. The best fish sauce is not bought at Pratumwan. Never has been, never will be.'

'Deaf as a doorpost, or wilfully stupid,' *Tsu mu* snapped. 'Sheep meat, I said, not fish sauce, old woman. Muslim market's the place for sheep meat. Any fool knows that!' She sounded, I realised suddenly, as old and querulous as Ah Lee. I could not help chuckling at the thought.

Ah Lee snorted.

'Are you afflicted with a head cold, Ah Lee?' *Tsu mu* enquired sweetly.

'Not in the least, Honourable Lady. I have received your gracious enquiry,' Ah Lee replied with great dignity, glowering covertly at me. 'I merely suffer from an old woman's anxiety about being driven about in motor cars by young persons grinning all over their faces like demons.'

We were already in the medicine store when the ugly sounds reached our ears. Thuds, whoops, and screams, the noise of running feet, rushing through the network of narrow streets like a tide. At once there was a new sound, the rattle and crash of the armoured shutters as panic-stricken shopkeepers dropped iron lattices over doors and windows.

'I am sure it is nothing. I will go and check,' the herbalist muttered courteously. 'Excuse me.'

'Honourable Lady's motor!' Ah Lee shrieked, peering out through the shutter. A group of dark-skinned Thai toughs were hammering on the coachwork of the Mercedes. As we watched, powerless to intervene, they began to rock the heavy car, chanting. By sheer weight of numbers, they managed to overturn it. They struck out its windows with improvised clubs. The glass tinkled on the pavement.

Ah Lee left my side and darted forward. 'Stop that!' she howled, scuttling out of the shop door, waving her thin old arms. Just as she reached the car, one of the men threw some liquid from a bottle and, with a single shout, tossed a lighted match after it. It seemed to move in slow motion, and everyone had time to take cover. Even the match-thrower sustained only minor burns. Everyone, that is, except Ah Lee—old, deaf, and determined to do battle for *Tsu mu*'s car. As the petrol tank exploded, Ah Lee's slight figure was silhouetted against black-edged billows of orange fire. She tottered for a second, then toppled forward into the heart of the fire and vanished from view in a plume of flame.

I leaned against the shop window, shaking with shock and horror.

'Chee Laan! What is going on?' *Tsu mu* spoke in the voice of an old woman, dazed and frightened. She stumbled toward me, one hand clutching her throat. The shopkeeper ran back, bundling us together and herding us outside, with a respectful tenderness despite his urgency.

'This way, honoured ladies!' He glanced back at the street and then quickly looked away. 'The poor old lady!' he groaned.

'Come, *Tsu mu*!' I urged.

'Chee Laan!' she shouted in a surprisingly powerful voice. 'Have you gone mad? Where is the old woman? Where is Ah Lee? How can we leave without Ah Lee?'

'Hurry, ladies, please!' the herbalist wailed. 'Mind the step!'

'I refuse to be smuggled out through back alleys like a criminal!' my grandmother retorted, resisting strongly. 'My car is parked out the front. Take me to my car! And where is my servant?'

I dropped to my knees before her, desperate, knowing her iron will. If she refused to leave the shop and take refuge, we were all as good as dead.

'Please, *Tsu mu*, just come away now, at once. This man is afraid for his shop. He is showing us a back way out so we can get away without becoming involved.'

'Involved with what, pray?' she demanded haughtily.

My self-control was about to snap. I felt like screaming. The shopkeeper plainly felt the same, because he began to rant and rave uncontrollably, 'Involved with the Thais, Honourable Lady! The murdering, ransacking, racist pigs of Thais! Oh, I've seen this coming for years, the gradual unleashing of violence. Now they see a chance to blame the savagery of their own brutish police on our law-abiding community!' He broke away and ran back toward the shopfront.

'Don't be a fool, man!' *Tsu mu* shouted in tones accustomed to instant obedience.

'My premises—my property! Must protect them!' Frenziedly he gripped the steel pole that connected with a bolt in the steel curtain. He was hauling desperately on it as the first bricks came flying in, crashing on floor and furniture, smashing the glass cases and bottles.

It was a cheap grill, with wide-meshed interlocking steel grid plates. As the man stooped to bolt the curtain to the sill, a brick bounced through the grid and laid open the back of his head. He mopped his skull with the cloth that dangled always at his waist, gazing, bewildered, at the scarlet dampness spreading over his hands.

A brown face leered through the grill, observing the effects of its owner's marksmanship. 'Go swallow a black beetle and a snake's pizzle and see if that'll cure you, Jek quack!' The rioter was feeling confident and inventive.

'You're hurt, man!' *Tsu mu* said, sounding almost like herself again.

'Ladies, hurry, please! Go out the back way, escape while you can! They mean to murder us all! I tell you, I've seen this coming!' His earnest brown eyes popped out in his face. He swung back toward the street, glaring through the grill like a baited beast. 'Rabble! Murderers!'

'Calm yourself,' *Tsu mu* entreated. 'Kindly open that door. I must see Ah Lee.'

I took both her hands, planting myself squarely before her.

'*Tsu mu*,' I said gently, 'they have killed Ah Lee. I am so sorry.'

She sighed, once, a deep, fluttery sound. Then she recovered herself and my grandmother stood there once more, a strong spirit in a tiny, erect body.

'You should have said so at once and saved time,' she rebuked me. 'Let us go.'

We ran up the steep back stairs and emerged into the street, blinking in the sun's vengeful white glare. The alley was deserted but the sounds of the mob were closing in. I stared around, bewildered, wondering which way would be the best escape route. Chinatown is a warren of alleys. If you are only accustomed to driving about in a Mercedes and parking it on the pavement, you are lost and disoriented when you step into the back lanes.

'Go right. That is our only chance,' *Tsu mu* said. She set off, her pace rapid and unfaltering. 'This riot has been provoked. But why? And by whom? We are natural scapegoats, of course.' A few steps further, she continued: 'It wouldn't take much manpower. It could be engineered by a small group, or even one man.'

'Like Sya Dam?' I suggested. It seemed so obvious.

She nodded. 'Exactly. As a distraction from something else, or to divert blame. Or for some ludicrous test of loyalty; or to demonstrate the efficiency of the riot suppression squad, who will doubtless be permitted a brief appearance to quell the disturbance.' She looked at me, her eyes narrow with warning. 'This farce will not end until sufficient numbers of Chinese have been murdered. To teach Chinatown a lesson.'

I was surprised at the bitterness in her voice. She laughed.

'Wait till you've lived with it as long as I have, child! Now: our alternatives. One, the temple. These Thais are notoriously superstitious; they disdain our gods and spit upon ancestors, but they fear the spirits who linger in temple courtyards.'

'Is there a temple near here?'

'There is a small, ill-frequented shrine to Kwan Yin, Goddess of Mercy. There is also a small crèche there, run by charitable ladies for Chinese orphans. Supported by donations from the Chinese community…'

'Even Thais wouldn't attack an orphanage!' I cried. The sounds of the disturbance were growing louder. 'We shall be safe at the crèche!'

The next moment the mob swept into the alleyway, surging toward us. I seized *Tsu mu*'s hand and we began to run like two frightened children, staring wildly around for somewhere to hide.

A huge spirit house stood on a pink pedestal in the centre of the courtyard. It was wreathed in garlands, littered with food offerings and half-full bottles of 7-Up, the fragrant incense sticks still smoking. *Tsu mu* and I clung together behind the spirit house platform, cowering, as the mob surged past us down the lane. In the distance we heard the crash and tinkle of breaking glass, yells of pain and anger, a percussion staccato of sticks and stones on wood and metal. Then the piercing screams began. Beneath the screams, somewhere at the dark, confused centre of the racket, there emerged a constantly repeated cry, a groundswell of contrapuntal rhythm: 'Kill, kill, kill the Jeks! Kill the Jeks!'

The image of Ah Lee, her hair and clothing ablaze, assaulted my consciousness like a physical blow. Suddenly nauseous, I retched with terror. My mouth was dry, and I gulped greedily for air like a diver too long submerged. I glanced at my grandmother. Ah Lee had boasted often that the Honourable Old Lady's slender eyes were the ideal of Chinese beauty. Now they were as wide as a feverish child's. There was a reddening blaze on her parchment cheek.

With relief, I became aware that the cries of the rioters were growing distant again. Mercifully, they had passed, surging on in their murderous quest. Silently, we eased ourselves from our hiding place and made our cautious way along the deserted street. We reached the crèche without incident. Nobody came into the street. The houses stood silent, their windows covered. *Tsu mu* rattled the door of the crèche, then rapped briskly on a windowpane, sharply and persistently. Minutes passed as we stood in silence, our hearts in our mouths. We were both trembling. I felt hollow and slightly sick. Finally the bamboo curtain was twitched aside. The lemon-pale face of a young girl peeked out at us without recognition, eyes rolling, blank with fear. *Tsu mu* pushed her face close to the window. She announced clearly, in a voice that brooked no demur: 'It is I, Sunii Lee. Collect your wits, girl. Do not leave me standing in the street.'

The curtain fell. We stood in the empty street, horribly vulnerable. At last the bolts crashed back and the door opened. The supervisor of the crèche, a neatly dressed, middle-aged Chinese woman, stood aside politely to let us pass. As soon as we were inside she reached past us with a muttered apology. The bolts slammed back into place behind us.

'Honourable Sunii—too much honour!' the supervisor murmured. 'Come in, come in. Are you in good health?'

'I have received your enquiry,' my grandmother acknowledged the courtesy.

'Have you eaten?'

'Yes, I am ashamed to say.' There was reassurance in the formula. I felt torn between impatience and familiar relief.

'Here you will be safe,' the supervisor said.

'We are blessed in our friends. The blind cat stumbles on the dead rat,' *Tsu mu* said.

'The honour is ours.' The supervisor turned on her heel and led the way into a simply furnished inner room. A bare light bulb glared from the ceiling. I wondered, irrelevantly, how we Chinese, so exquisite in matters of form and colour, remain impervious to the barbarity of unshaded light bulbs. Returning from the West, I found myself constantly shielding my eyes against that glare in rooms full of priceless inlaid furniture, porcelain, and silk. I dropped my head, allowing my hair to block out the brightness.

'Please sit!' the supervisor cried, in a display of frenzied hospitality. The maid who had first looked out at us stood by, shifting her feet; the supervisor clapped her hands almost in the maid's face. 'Drink tea!'

'With thanks.' *Tsu mu* seated herself neatly, folding her hands on her lap with doll-like dignity, as if this were a social call, mob rule and mayhem a thousand worlds away.

The maid scampered off. The supervisor sighed. 'People have lost their minds, lady! Lies, slanders…such hatred, such violence!'

'Evil will be rewarded with evil, lady,' *Tsu mu* said. 'Perhaps not immediately, but eventually. *Ji suo bu yu, wu shi yu ren*! As you treat others, so will they treat you!'

The supervisor nodded. For a while we all sat in silence, considering the Confucian principle of reciprocity, while the rioters, murder in their hearts, ravaged Bangkok's Chinatown. I knew my companions were remembering other days, other Chinatowns.

The supervisor raised her eyes to the wooden ceiling, as if in prayer. 'Poor Mr Chang—tailor, next street—murdered. Last time the madness took them. Stabbed with his own scissors! Terrible!' She shuddered.

'Indeed. Alas, that we should see such times come again. I myself have today lost a worthy soul who grew old in the service of the Lee family. I must speak to Wong Kao, and arrange for the collection of the corpse.'

The supervisor exclaimed, with a burst of animation, 'Nothing easier! Why, Mr Wong Kao is already seeking refuge in our humble home. It is fortuitous.'

'Indeed, I am blessed in my friends!'

The maid, her eyes rolling with terror, bore in the tea. Her mistress slapped her cheek, lightly but firmly. 'Ask Mr Wong Kao to join us, girl!'

Mr Wong Kao bustled in, sweating with excitement and fear, mopping his brow with a grubby bandana. Immediately embarrassed by this article of coolie's clothing in the presence of distinguished ladies, he sought a place of concealment for it about his person. His options were limited, dressed as he was, for business rather than socialising, in a vest and white trousers. He compromised by binding the bandana about his ankle and dropping his trouser leg over it, hoping thus to escape attention.

'Ah! Ladies!' he exclaimed.

I had heard of, but never previously encountered, the famous funeral director, that excellent servant of the dead. I think I had expected someone more prosperous-looking, fatter, with greater gravitas, befitting his noble calling. But I could not fault the solemnity with which he listened to Grandmother's account, pursing his lips, nodding gravely. The sweat rolled unheeded into his eyes.

Tsu mu explained that her servant Ah Lee, sharer of the family name, had died valiantly, in the evening of her life, defending her employer's property. She should be treated with all honour. Wong closed his eyes in respect. Only when the narration reached the account of the destruction of the Mercedes was his professional impassivity shocked into animation. His whole skinny frame shook with outrage.

'I shall personally arrange for a paper Mercedes to be burned with the One Who Has Left the World,' he assured. 'Then she can drive it around heaven!' He looked from one face to the other, spreading his hands, as if to say, *Well, I can't say fairer than that, can I?*

Tsu mu smiled faintly at the absurdity of the notion—Ah Lee behind the wheel, racketing about heaven. I had a sudden uncontrollable urge to giggle. *I am growing hysterical*, I thought weakly. *My mind is breaking down.*

'Let it be pink,' *Tsu mu* said. 'Ah Lee never wore pink, but she was nevertheless very partial to that colour. And there must be a paper ship, to sail her soul back home. And a hill of silver, of course, from which she can draw funds, during her sojourn in the Other World.' I recognised, in my grandmother's attention to detail, her need to make these arrangements, as if drawing comfort from her own meticulousness. *Tsu mu* and my *amah* had seen each other's faces for many years, had been young and then old together.

Wong bowed low. 'How else may this unworthy person serve? Servants in effigy, perhaps?'

'Servants in effigy will not be required. Ah Lee was a woman of the people. But let her have a house, and a safe for the money she draws from the hill of silver. That is very important. Ah Lee was always careful about money.'

Wong bowed again. 'All will be ready for burning twenty-one days from today, the death-day, when the priests jump. Although, with all this terrible violence…' A gleam of avarice lighted the little man's beady eyes briefly. 'Things are not easy!'

'People suffer; fortunately, business does not always suffer,' *Tsu mu* suggested flatly.

'The craftsmanship will be of the highest level,' Wong assured her hastily, with a sharp look. 'Everything exquisite! As befits the worthy servant of an honourable house!'

'Seems a waste, when it's all just going to go up in flames,' I blurted out ungraciously. These complicated arrangements, this lavish expense, seemed to have little to do with the real Ah Lee. They seemed almost a betrayal of her lifelong frugality—she who would beat down the price of a pineapple in Pratumwan market, for the gain of two satang and the satisfaction. Ah Lee, a woman as scathing of vanity and waste as any nun, as starkly courageous as any martyr, dying for her own notions of righteousness, a lone protest against a world gone mad. 'Waste!' I repeated, twitching my feet irritably. 'Ah Lee would think it a waste!'

Tsu mu flashed me a look of mild outrage. 'My granddaughter enjoys the benefits of a Western education,' she observed dryly. The harsh rebuke delivered before other people stung, as it was intended to. The supervisor jumped up and rushed about replenishing teacups in embarrassment. Wong busied himself with his notes, clearing his throat.

'I take pride in carrying on the craft of my ancestors. For how long, who can tell? Demand is slackening, especially here. Irreligious land, irreligious times, lady! All pop and plastic nowadays! But I still take pride in it. It's a useful occupation for a worthless man. Reminds him that death has an appointment with each of us. We should never forget that!'

'Indeed,' *Tsu mu* quoted smoothly. 'The wary avoid death. The reckless are as good as dead.' The sound of rolling thunder invaded the street, reverberating off the house walls.

'The riot squad! So it's over!' The supervisor tweaked the slats of the bamboo curtain and squinted at the scene outside.

'Over for now, perhaps!' Grandmother did not sound convinced. I joined my grandmother at the window. Lifting a corner of the curtain, I peered out at the tanks lurching through the street like gigantic reptiles, crushing their tiny prey. The street was narrow; there was a mere eighteen inches between the vehicles and the wall. Tanks, guns, helmets, even the soldiers' faces: all seemed composed from the same dirty grey-green putty—featureless, alien, a menace out of proportion to the narrow alleyways, crashing like a trapped electric storm.

When the column had rolled by, my grandmother rose. 'It is time for us to leave. Thank you for your hospitality.' She extracted her wallet from her purse. 'Allow me to contribute a trifling donation toward your excellent work.'

'Honourable Lady,' Wong Kao burst out excitedly, 'how will you get home? Your car! Your fine Mercedes car! A tragedy! I only have my poor hearse, but it is at the ladies' disposal. Most gladly, if unworthy!'

Wong Kao possessed a hearse of the latest model. He now reversed this precious example of modernity gingerly from its place of concealment behind his shop. *Tsu mu*, smiling archly to indicate that this was certainly not loss of face but rather an absurd whimsical fancy, took the front seat beside Wong Kao. So, although Wong apologised profusely and fussed with rugs and an embroidered pillow, there was nothing for me to do but to scramble in and lie on the space normally occupied by the coffin. As the hearse trundled through the streets, I lay on my back studying its polished wooden ceiling. The inside of the hearse smelled faintly of polish, flowers, and an unidentifiable, pungent chemical. It was not unpleasant, not unlike the smell of the refectory at the convent. But the reality of death, the image of leaping flames, and of Ah Lee, silhouetted against them, dominated my thoughts.

Royal Hua Hin Golf Course, Hua Hin

An impatient Colonel Sya Dam scowled about at the eighth hole of the Hua Hin golf course. He checked his watch and set off toward his rendezvous, stomping purposefully over the artificially watered green, oblivious to the divots thrown up by his heavy military boots. He walked where he pleased.

In the distance, nestling soft and palest rose-pink amid its bright flower gardens beside a gleaming blue and silver sea, lay the Royal Summer Palace of Klai Kangwon, Sans Souci. The two men meeting him had already dispatched their caddies in search of refreshment. They were comfort-loving men whose chauffeurs had been instructed to bring up the cars so it was a shorter walk from the final tee. Sya took up a position atop a bunker, so that they were forced to blink into the sun, and, when they reached him, they were obliged by his elevation to look up at him, despite their superior birth. He noted their ill-concealed resentment at this gross breach of etiquette, and his smile broadened.

'Well, gentlemen?' he said. The other men recognised the invitation to report the state of play.

'I think we can credit ourselves with a great success in pinning it on the Chinese,' Prince Premsakul said, wringing his plump paws in satisfaction. He did not need to spell it out, to state, damningly, where the blame for the massacre of the students at the Monument to Democracy lay. Neither of his companions would have expected him to. To lose a daughter like that…a charming girl, though headstrong, a Princess of the Blood, and alas, the fat princeling's only remaining child—making such a tragic spectacle of herself, hobnobbing with Reds, rebels, enemies of the state for all to see. Field Marshal Praphan, an emotional and sentimental man, harrumphed in sympathy and covered the sound with a cough.

'Naturally, the Chinese business community were aiming to establish a branch of the Hong Kong Triads, whose functions would include undermining confidence in the government,' Praphan contributed helpfully.

'We need to tighten security,' Premsakul pronounced. Praphan bristled, blowing out his field marshal's moustache. 'But it must be done with subtlety.' Premsakul raised a hand and described minute circles in the heavy air to indicate the nature of this quality.

'If we do reintroduce martial law, it cannot appear to be a retrograde step,' Praphan said. 'That will provoke more determined resistance from…' He had almost said 'criminal and antisocial elements,' but stopped himself just in time out of respect for Premsakul's daughter's memory. 'Disaffected factions,' he finished.

'We cannot be seen to initiate a return to martial law.' Prince Premsakul was alarmed, his smooth, round features glistening with moisture like a damp wall. 'We are committed to the status quo.'

'We,' corrected Sya, with deadly emphasis, '*are* the status quo!'

'Also, the CIA, who have so generously contributed to our favourite charities…' Premsakul and Praphan looked at each other and sniggered like schoolboys. '…will want to be given credible reasons for any sudden *volte-face*.'

Praphan looked from one to the other, his shoulders hunched, his piggish eyes glinting. 'No, the initiative cannot be perceived to originate from the Establishment. In public life, consistency is all.' The bland phrases gave him confidence.

Sya's tone was cold and impatient. 'The identity of the paper men is immaterial. We know where the real power lies.' As they stared at him, he spread his hands wide. 'I agree. The time is ripe for a return to martial law. The most economical way of achieving this is through another bloodless coup. I've drawn up a list of useful dopes—members of the present cabinet who can be conveniently exchanged for other ciphers.'

'We shall need an overall figurehead,' Praphan said. 'We can't do it without a proper leader.'

Sya nodded. 'We shall choose some muddle-headed liberal for that role—there are plenty of woolly thinkers—or somebody who recognises his personal interest. What we want is an agreeable lightweight, malleable and accommodating, someone with a following and a pleasant reputation. Any suggestions, old boy?'

'A *bien-pensant*, a jolly good chap! That applies to all liberals!' Prince Premsakul smiled. 'Perhaps some lefty professor from one of our more militant universities…to flatter the radicals.' These bleeding-heart lefties had alienated the natural affections and aspirations of his children through their cynical manipulation of those innocent young minds. Premsakul wanted to see every filthy pinko on a funeral pyre, along with the insufferably successful, treacherous Jeks. But, he assured himself, it didn't matter who was chosen as their straw man. Who, more importantly, was to assume responsibility for the new line? Who was to be the sacrifice?

Sya turned and stared at Praphan without blinking. Portly Praphan, already sweating, mopped his brow under that unwavering yellow gaze.

'It is time for you to take a more prominent part, Field Marshal. You are the iron man. A show of strength is expected.'

Praphan considered. His reflections did not appear to afford him pleasure. Outranking Sya, he could simply have refused. But he knew better.

'Then—when the time comes—I'm to be scapegoated.' Praphan's porcine features contorted, a study in animal cunning. 'What do I get out of it?'

Sya smiled appreciatively, as if applauding a bright child. 'In anticipation of your services there must be adequate provision. This debt will be recognised. Any objectives you may wish to pursue will be arranged. Swiss bank accounts, anything needing the selective blindness of the official eye. A man of your eminence, Field Marshal, has many temptations, but also many opportunities.' He paused, to make sure they had understood. 'I shall inform Their Highnesses tonight. Prince Premsakul, perhaps you could organise your tame journalists. Inform your friend van Hooten, too. Field Marshal, you will prepare the army. On a need-to-know basis only, of course.'

Praphan considered. Then he nodded. He looked up at Sya, squinting in the dazzle of sun that blazed off the colonel's cap badge. 'Very well.'

'Good man.'

'Capital ruse! Think Their Highnesses will buy it?' Premsakul mused, moving on quickly, as if the outcome had never been in doubt.

Sya smiled. 'Their Highnesses will do as Their Highnesses are told.' His arrogance both astounded and infuriated his companions, but he only grinned. 'After all, we're a constitutional monarchy now!'

He leapt lightly down from the bunker and slapped both men on the back at once, laughing as he felt them recoil.

SEATO Headquarters, Bangkok

Blaze van Hooten held the telephone a foot away from his ear and grimaced at it, rolling his eyes. He was profoundly weary of attempting to explain the intricacies of Thai politics, insofar as he himself grasped them, to his superiors. He had the American newspaper article under discussion before him, and as he listened to the stream of questions pouring down the line into his ear he scanned the print. He sighed, cupping his other palm over the receiver to muffle the sound of his impatience. Van Hooten had natural American courtesy.

> **Military Coup in Thailand: From Our Correspondent in Bangkok**
> *Field Marshal Praphan and his military cohorts have consolidated their position as the major players in the Thai political scene by means of the traditional Thai method, the bloodless coup. Martial law has been reintroduced in the country, and hardline policies are to be implemented against economic imbalance and minor (if not major) corruption. Communist infiltrators will be pursued with renewed vigor. At the same time, it would appear that the irksome impedimenta of constitutional democracy are to be abandoned—free democratic elections, a vocal and critical opposition, and an unfettered press have been pronounced benefits for which the great Thai nation is not yet ready. The decisions echo the decision taken by His Majesty King Chulalongkhorn back in the 1890s that the people were not yet ready for democracy. Oh, and the position of the Royal Family, as figureheads and national icons, remains unaffected. Plus ça change...*

'Oh yes,' van Hooten said into the receiver. 'The reporter is correct. I can assure you that nothing here has changed. Nothing substantive. The status quo prevails. There is no immediate cause for concern. No, indeed! You have my personal guarantee on that.' He listened respectfully. 'Oh, that! These are isolated incidents. When taken in context, they are much less dramatic than they appear. There is no sense of coordination. A chain of purely fortuitous occurrences, no political significance whatsoever.' He laughed. 'Truth to tell, I doubt they're capable of that kind of lateral thinking. Thank *you*, sir! I certainly shall...'

He looked at the receiver before replacing it softly in its cradle, and sat for a moment lost in thought. Then, as if making up his mind, he took up the telephone again and dialled his house phone.

'Honey, it's me. I think things are moving.'

'Not before time,' she said icily. 'I may need to make another journey myself soon. There is anxiety.'

'Rich folks are always anxious. Just so long as you don't allow them to exploit your good nature. Never forget: for all their graciousness, in their eyes, we're all expendable. We're peons, honey. Not worth jack squat.'

He rang off. His eyes wandered to the signed photograph of the First Family posed in front of the White House; his eyes were drawn to another signed photograph beside it, of a lizard-faced man with big ears, ostrich-leather skin, and clever, calculating eyes. The elder statesman and potential peacebroker whom it was his duty to protect.

He sat studying his wall of photographs, as if the answer were to be found there, in the First Family's smiles—the white pumps and stiffly lacquered hairdos of the women, the hail-fellow politician's grin of the president. He considered the other photograph once more, and studied thoughtfully the big, powerful-looking man with a strong Jewish cast of his features, perfectly matching the strongly formed signature scrawled across it. On an impulse he bent and pulled open the bottom drawer of his desk and took out the bottle of bourbon. He unscrewed the top and took a meditative swig, raising his bottle in salutation.

'Happy landings, Henry!' Henry K seemed to smile back, his eyes wise with ancient sorrows, his grin wider than a crocodile's. 'We'll see you right, old boy!' Van Hooten raised his bottle again. 'We won't let you down. Don't you go getting your ass shot off on my turf, y'hear?'

He wiped his lips with the back of his hand, put the bottle back in the drawer, and popped a strong mint into his mouth.

Akha Village, Near Mae Chan, Northern Thailand

Salikaa

Sya had told me I had no aptitude for killing. Sya could go hang. I had not expected it to be so simple.

'Pawn,' I commanded my maid, that stupid creature, 'I am weary. Go lie in my sleeping-place. If Vasit comes to you, make him welcome.'

'But...' she started, stammering. Her face went slack. I gave her a threatening look. She stopped arguing.

Later, Vasit tumbled in, grunting like a beast. I peered through the bamboo curtain and saw him fall upon the skin couch and the servant girl's warm, accommodating flesh. She squeaked and squirmed, but then she resigned herself, recognising her fate. She went catatonic. I had the bone needle hidden and ready. When he was sated and snoring, I made my move. As he slept, still sprawled upon the limp body of the girl, I stabbed it through his ear, finding the soft tissue of his brain. The girl, breathing heavily beneath Vasit's dead weight, her mouth half open, never stirred. I dropped the needle and I ran, hitching up my skirt, twisting my hair into a plait to prevent it catching on the branches running, breathless, straining to hear if they came after me. I fled, stumbling through the undergrowth. I did not know this hill country. A stranger cannot hide for long in such an environment. As I fled from the Akha, my breath bursting painfully from my chest, my heart pounding, memories flashed before my inner eye, filling me with terror and increasing determination. Tripping over rocks and tree roots, the vegetation tearing at my clothing, I ran from the memory of my wedding night.

Vasit had deserved to die.

Alone at last, we ill-matched newlyweds had stared at each other with growing revulsion. My lip throbbed where he'd hit me; I could feel it starting to swell, but I was damned if I was going to touch it, or show my fear. I turned my back on him and started to remove my wedding jewellery. My hands were trembling. I tried not to dwell on how different this wedding night should have been, tried not to wish myself a million miles away from this horrible primitive hut and this loathsome creature. I had to think fast, find some strategy to deal with my dread. There was no time for self-pity. I'd gambled for high stakes and lost. For the moment, my enemy, Sya, that devil, had outwitted me—but only for the moment.

There was nothing resembling a closet in that dump, so finally I just collected all my expensive baubles and dropped them in a heap in the middle of the floor. I began to uncoil my hair as slowly as I could, my mind still racing down different alleyways, each one blind. I pulled out pin after pin, allowing each heavy lock, rigid with lacquer, to bounce about my neck like fat springs. Naturally, there was no mirror. My nuptial bed was a pile of malodorous hides. God knew what creepy-crawlies lurked there! When I was Miss Thailand, almost a princess, I'd have struck an attitude. I'd have snapped my fingers and six maids would have scurried about, assisting me with my toilette for this night of nights.

Now all I had was that simpleton, Pawn. I was damned if I'd lower myself to complain. Besides, I didn't want that filthy brute Vasit, my lord and master, to clout me in the chops again. So I said nothing. I even hummed a little tune to indicate my mastery of the situation.

Vasit was leaning in the doorway, watching me with a nasty look in his eye. Without warning, he launched himself at me like a rat off the wall, tearing at me with teeth and claws. He seemed to have a dozen limbs. For such a scrawny fellow, he was wiry and had a horrible strength. I kicked out wildly. He grabbed the waistband of my long silk skirt and pulled. The cloth unwound and tumbled round my ankles. Now he was tugging at my pants. I fought back with the strength of desperation, but he was too strong.

'All right!' I panted at last. 'All right. Just—just let go of me, will you?'

He went quiet. 'No tricks?' he grunted. He had the suspicious nature of all truly stupid people.

'No tricks.' I pulled myself free and stood up. There was, after all, nothing else to be done. I removed the rest of my clothing and turned to face him. *At least*, I thought, *I have a beautiful body.* My face, however, must have looked like a massacre. My lipstick was smudged, my cheeks were streaked with mascara, my false eyelashes were hanging off like dead spiders, and I could sense the unsightly bulge in my lower lip where he had struck me. He took his time, the bastard. Looked me over, lingering insultingly, from crown to fork and back again, and then he threw back his head and laughed till he cried. Sinking down against the wall in a paroxysm of mirth, shaking his head this way and that, the greasy ponytail flicking like a whip about his shoulders, he studied me more closely. I was not sure what reaction I had expected, but this was certainly not it.

'The king, and Prince Toom, and my own cousin Black Tiger—you fooled them all! You little beauty!' Vasit finally gasped in his rough accent. He scrambled to his feet and lunged for me. 'I can't believe it!' he chuckled coarsely. He clutched me round the waist, pulling me against him, thudding against my thighs, bone grating on bone. 'Oh, they will pay for this!'

'So now you know—so let me go.' I struggled in his grasp. But he was strong, and determined.

'Likely!' he barked. 'I've got you, and I'm not letting you go! Nobody makes a laughingstock out of Vasit! I'm going to have my money's worth out of you, my pretty dear!' He thrust one hand into my mouth. I bit him as hard as I could, but he just laughed. Then he threw me forward, plunging my face into the heap of stinking skins, and closed with me.

I thought I would die.

But I lived. I lived to take up my new life as a bride among my husband's people, the Akha.

Nothing had prepared me for the Akha. I doubt if anything could have done. The men smoked opium all day. I was expected to join the women, tending pigs, grinding rice—despised, beaten, and abused. Sometimes my dear husband Vasit came to me at night, stinking, unpredictable as a mad boar, quick to flare into violence—at best lice-covered and slobbering, dazed with opium and mercifully incapacitated, at worst, vigorous and vengeful.

Somehow I endured it, struggling to keep my looks and my pride, because without them I had nothing.

I discovered there was another aspect to Akha life besides opium. There were three government-subsidised transistor radios in the village. Whenever

Sya Dam was due to speak from Bangkok, groups of men gathered, grunting approval, thumping staves and bare feet on the ground, occasionally shouting. I was amazed to see those grim zombies aroused to such animation, as most of the time they drifted through their aimless days in drug-riddled apathy, apart from spasmodic outbreaks of violence, generally directed against a weaker creature, dog or woman.

I began to wonder what Sya was preaching that got them so excited—surely not the official doctrine of centralisation, loyalty, and stability. I began to suspect he was denouncing political corruption at the centre, discrimination against ethnic minorities, and calling for independence for ethnic groups. I hadn't forgotten his fabled loyalty, his professed hatred of the Chinese, but I started to speculate about just where his true allegiance lay. I stored every scrap of information I could glean for future use.

Meanwhile, I had to endure my odious husband. As my fear and hatred of him grew, I became more deeply resolved to make a bid for freedom. I would shake him off like some loathsome insect. I steeled myself to his taunts and blows, his disgusting physical presence. Planning escape and revenge kept my spirit alive.

One thing was clear: only Vasit's death could set me free. I would have to kill him. The thought held no terror for me, no moral dilemma. Living with Vichai had schooled me well in the ways of dealing death, both secret and overt. Daggers, guns, poisons, ropes, concrete boots. Death by water, death by fire. He taught me that anything at hand could be utilised. There were a thousand methods, a thousand weapons, many of them surprisingly simple. Fleischer had perfected my techniques in boot camp. When the moment came, I always knew I would be unafraid. My hand would be steady to strike, my heart strong.

I hoped they would suspect the idiot maidservant, Pawn, at first. This would buy me time. But unless I could make it to civilisation, I could not escape the Akha for long. Panic surged through me, filling me with a desperate energy as I ran.

Akha Village, Near Mae Chan, Northern Thailand

Salikaa's assumption was right: at first, the tribesmen had, indeed, accused Pawn. However, the absence of Salikaa was suspicious, and they set out to pursue her. They tracked her headlong flight without difficulty, spread out in a circle among the young trees, and closed in on her. She made a couple of breaks for freedom but knew she was cornered. She pressed her back against a tree trunk, panting, and then they were on her. Though she fought like a tigress, biting, clawing, and kicking, they dragged her back, half-fainting with fear and exhaustion. They tossed her into a hut under guard to await judgement.

As the nearest and most distinguished kinsman of the victim, they sent an urgent message for Colonel Sya to officiate at her trial. Two days later, during which time Salikaa had been given neither food nor water nor toilet facilities, during which she reeked and raved and bit her own arm and sucked the blood to wet her parched lips, a helicopter clattered over the hillside. The pilot dropped Sya Dam at the clearing and swooped away as fast as he could. He had seen the Akha from a distance, and had no wish to renew the acquaintance. Shortly thereafter, Sya Dam, the sun glinting off his cap badge, strode into the village wearing a pristine uniform and an impatient scowl. He met and talked gravely with the elders. Robed in their filth-encrusted black and silver, these were men of stout heart in their own territory. They did not flee in terror but stood their ground, even when the great metal bird alighted noisily out of the skies. Sya smoked the greeting pipes of opium they brought and accompanied the elders through the jungle to the village.

He took with him only one attendant: Archin, huge, mad Archin, with his loose, twitching face and rolling eyes. Archin who in his cups had prostrated himself before Sya, and had lifted Sya's boot and placed it upon his own sturdy neck—Archin who feared every kind of ghost and spirit, but worshipped no god but Sya.

In Archin the Akha people found a kindred spirit. He proved himself a cut above other Thais, those city types and milk-sops. For example, he not only enjoyed beating up women, but he had a craftsman's appreciation for the arts of torture and killing. He displayed an admirable indifference to creature comforts and cared not what he ate; he slept curled up upon the ground, snoring like a happy hog. He picked maggots out of the rotten fish and devoured them appreciatively, with a rumbling chuckle. He made a good tribesman. When the finer points of the execution procedure were explained to him, he savoured these with the relish of an Akha. Throughout Salikaa's brief trial, he observed his colonel's every gesture, squatting untidily like a large, faithful dog among the tribesmen.

Salikaa, steeped in filth and faint with hunger, sat ramrod straight and unflinching. She faced Sya stoically. Solemnly she listened as the evidence was presented. Gravely Sya studied her face for any sign of remorse, for any hint of fear. Her gallantry mocked him until the moment when he said, '*Khun* Salikaa, are you aware of the tribal punishment for a wife who murders her husband? They will bury you alive, with the corpse of your victim on top of you. You understand? You will not die by suffocation, but slowly, gradually, by the contagion of putrefaction.'

She stared at him, horror dawning as he described the penalty for her offence. The effect of his words was gratifying.

The sentence was to be carried out immediately, as his presence was required in Bangkok. There would be no delay.

The women of the tribe came to wash her. Their hands were rough. In their eyes there was revulsion and horror, whether for Salikaa or for the water spirits she could not tell. They refused to meet her gaze. When they had finished, they led her out under the judgemental gaze of the elders. Sya, in his spotless uniform, stood at ease, legs slightly apart, and his hands behind his back. Salikaa made no attempt to resist. Later, she would be drugged, as she had been for the wedding—injected with poppy juice, swaying mindless through the shifting clouds of opium, every capillary tingling like fire. Now, her eyes raked their expressionless faces. There was no mercy there.

She walked obediently, occasionally stumbling on the rough ground, to the grave site. If she were put to death too near the village, the tribe dreaded the vengeance of her ghost. The group slowed as they reached the appointed spot. Somehow, Sya had gotten there before them. He stood waiting, arms folded. Beside him an open pit gaped in the red earth. Close to the grave was a vile object to which her eyes were inexorably drawn. She glanced once, shuddered, and plunged her face in her hands. Decomposition had begun. The maggots were already about their work in the dead flesh. The features of the corpse appeared to have melted and had acquired an oily green viscosity.

'Into the grave!' Sya commanded with quiet authority. The women, squeaking with hysteria, seized Salikaa roughly. She tried to fight them off, but they were too many. Then the men impatiently cuffed the women aside and they tumbled and scattered, screaming like monkeys. They pushed Salikaa down on her back into the pit, laughing as she clawed at them, breaking her nails. They plucked her fingers away when she tried to grasp their hands and arms. They spat on her, and dribbled in their excitement. Salikaa tensed her limbs and braced her body. She shut her eyes, half-fainting. Then she felt the dead weight drop onto her chest, felt the clammy touch of dead flesh. Close to her face, the grave-smell clogged her nostrils. She was suffocating. She could not bear to draw a breath through that stinking pall. The dead limbs pressed down. From above, the faces peered gloatingly into the grave. Through swollen, half-closed lids, her last sight was their eyes, gleaming in the half-light like wolves around a kill.

She heard Sya bark a command. Clods of red earth fell heavily, blocking out sun and air as they filled in the grave. They did not stamp the earth down firmly. As Sya had explained, the sentence was not death by suffocation. The rotting corpse of her victim must have its revenge. The husband killer should not have a swift or easy death.

As Salikaa sank into unconsciousness, the last sound she heard was the heavy red earth falling endlessly over her head.

Sya Dam took the first watch at the graveside. When his fellow tribesmen were deep in their opium dreams, halfway through his watch, he ordered Archin to bring the servant girl. Archin returned with Pawn slumped on his shoulder. Her neck was broken and she was slung behind his head like a dead deer.

'Sorry,' Archin mumbled, shamefaced. He put his hands over his ears. 'Archin hates them yelling,' he explained. 'Have to keep them quiet, see. Yelling, women's yelling, hurt Archin's head.'

'No matter. It is well. Set her down here.' Sya pointed to the turned earth beside the grave. 'Now, Archin, dig away this earth.'

Archin complied. He did not need tools. His big hands were strong as spades.

'Good,' Sya said. 'Now down into the pit.'

Archin's eyes rolled in terror. He forced himself to obey, braving the evil spirits of the dead and dying, because he was even more afraid of Colonel Sya Dam. Sya stood on the edge of the pit and scrutinised Archin sternly. Archin was as superstitious as any Akha when it came to demons. Archin, still struggling to avoid unnecessary contact with the loathsome decomposing flesh, which was at the point of liquefaction, managed to drag Salikaa out from under the corpse. She was still unconscious. Her limbs were entangled with those of her former husband. He had to raise the dead man, roll him aside, and pull. Archin was not easily nauseated, but the odour of putrefaction, combined with his superstitious terror, made him vomit.

'Is she still alive?' Sya barked.

Archin shook his head. He wasn't sure. She looked dead, or perhaps in a fit: her eyes were turned up, blind and marble white, like the unseeing eyes of a stone temple gargoyle. Her mouth hung open. As Archin pushed her clear of the grave, Sya bent, wiped her mouth, and pressed his own against it. He felt the breath. She was still alive.

Sya took a syringe from his pocket, filled it, and plunged it into her arm. She neither stirred nor moaned. Sya wrapped her limp form in the thick army blanket that lay at his feet.

'Put the other one in her place, and hurry up!' he commanded. Archin pushed Pawn's body into the grave and kicked Vasit's corpse in after it. Finally he picked up handfuls of red earth and threw them in. When he had filled in the grave, Sya gestured at Salikaa, wrapped in the blanket. Archin carried her shrouded form to the Land Rover concealed in the margins of the forest, which Sya had commandeered days ago.

It was a rough ride over the unmade tracks, and at a breakneck speed, though Sya was used to worse. He had no time to waste. This Salikaa business had been an unwelcome interruption to his plans. He was involved in a high-risk venture in the corridors of power. He could not afford diversion; he needed to be on the spot. It was imperative that he return to Bangkok as quickly as possible. As he raced against time, preoccupied, driving like an automaton, he considered his position.

    Happily for them, his passengers gave him no trouble. The drugged girl lay as one dead; the big man had fumbled in his shabby pants for the pipe presented to him by his new Akha friends, and now slumped in his seat, slack-faced. Occasionally he belched and chuckled softly in his dreams. The hazy sweetness of opium permeated the air until Sya, too, felt lightheaded.

Rachanee Hotel, Bangkok

Chee Laan had spent two days since the Chinatown riots moving her desk and files into the new office she had been given in the cosseted luxury of the Rachanee Hotel, on the very top floor of the building. She still felt a sense of unreality, as though she had stepped into a parallel universe. The violence and tragedy she had witnessed only forty-eight hours previously seemed a bad dream. But Chee Laan's nerves were ragged. A series of dreadful images and sensations—the death of Ah Lee, the terror she had felt in the riot, the roar of the fire, the shouts and screams of the mob—flickered through her mind like a horror film playing on a loop she could not stop, even in the seclusion of her new executive suite.

Only the penthouse suite, on the same floor but on the opposite side of the building, offered such privacy and such a breathtaking panorama over the city. Chee Laan's new office had two floor-to-ceiling glass walls swathed in purple Thai silk drapes. Outside the glass walls lay the roof garden, which commanded a view of the intricate mosaic of houses, crowded streets, and khlongs. At the garden's centre, ringed by flowers in tubs and small palm trees, was a smooth, bare plateau, which Chee Laan had often considered would make a splendid helicopter pad. The windows of her office suite could be covered and the view blocked out at the touch of a switch, which released huge blackout blinds. But Chee Laan needed light about her just now.

Without realising what she was doing, she rose and began to pace about the room, picking things up and putting them down again, rearranging. She aimed a kick at a carved wastebin. She rolled down the blackout blinds and snapped them up back up again with a satisfying noise, and would have done it over and over but she pulled up, telling herself that it was not a toy and she would break the mechanism and the system had cost a lot of money to install. She could just imagine her grandmother's disapproval, and Ah Lee's growl of remonstrance. At the thought of Ah Lee, she gave a dry sob.

She closed the blinds again to shut out distractions and turned her new music centre on full blast. Joni Mitchell's mesmerising lilt filled the room. 'Bows and flows of angel hair…' She felt the room sway. Delayed shock, she told herself severely. She must not allow herself to descend into hysteria. She must move on.

She shook herself and sat down at her desk again. With a sigh she turned to the sheaf of documents already piled in her In tray.

Without warning, the heavy teak door was brutally flung open and her brother Pao rushed in. Chee Laan regarded him with a chilly stare. He pounded up to the desk in fervid agitation, slammed both his hands on it and shouted into his sister's face, 'So here you are lurking!' He glanced round the room. 'You have made yourself a cosy little nest, sis! Well, here's some news to wake you up! No good lolling here playing the big shot! This a crisis! We have to do something!'

Chee Laan studied him, wondering what he was up to now. His bullying stemmed from insecurity, and his aggression from jealousy and feelings of inadequacy; she could pity him, and when he went too far, she allowed her pity to show, as the most calculated revenge. But the thought of his duplicity, his acting as go-between between *Tsu mu* and the Black Tiger, turned her stomach. It tested her loyalty to her grandmother to the maximum. Looking at him now she thought how like their father he was, his youthful good looks already dissolving in fat, the expression of peevish cunning settled more permanently upon his face.

'What is it, Pao?' she demanded with ill-concealed irritation. 'Why are you yelling at me like this? I don't need this right now. *Tsu mu* and I have had a very difficult experience. Poor Ah Lee has been murdered, and we were nearly killed ourselves.'

He snorted dismissively. 'I heard about the old woman. The earth rises higher. I wish to talk of something important, not some old coolie woman.'

Chee Laan gripped the edge of the desktop to steady both hands, refusing to display anger. She pressed a button to stop the music. When she spoke her tone was cool. 'Still the same callous toad, Pao! I suppose you're here for your usual handout?'

He shook his head in pretend wonder. 'What is the matter with you, Sister? You are not a woman but a cash register!'

She scowled. 'Not, however, a hole-in-the-wall cash point. Not for you. Not anymore. So: if it's not money, what do you want?'

'There was a helicopter on the roof,' Pao howled, banging his fist on the table. 'When you were all off getting yourselves murdered. That Devil Sya, the Black Tiger. In a helicopter.' He gestured wildly toward the darkened window. 'He's got a woman with him, either drugged or dead. And—and a monster. He's got a monster with him.'

She saw that he was genuinely afraid, and she laughed. 'A monster? A dragon, breathing fire and smoke?'

'You don't believe me,' he said bitterly. 'You mock. But you will see. I recognized that woman. It's that friend of yours, Miss Thailand, who was going to marry the drowned prince—that girl they married off to that Akha devil, to get her out of the way...'

Pao saw that he had caught her attention.

'What is this about Salikaa, and helicopters? And monsters?'

'The monster is a great hulking fellow. His mouth hangs open. His hands are as big as durians.' In illustration, Pao let his own arms swing loose, slackened his jaw, assuming an expression of mindless, unfocused menace. 'I saw the helicopter land. I was going to run—I thought it might be terrorists!' His voice rose shrilly. 'You were all gone; there was nothing but music on the radio, no news, the way they do when anything happens—just pour out dance music, you know, hour after hour, while they decide what the official line is to be. I knew something was up. I heard a rumble and I looked and saw the tanks heading out from the barracks toward Chinatown, and—oh, gods, he saw me. The demon, the black Akha! And he forced me to open up one of the private rooms on the penthouse floor, for VIPs, the family...and he's here, in the hotel!'

Chee Laan leaned back in her chair, stiff with bafflement and the firm desire to keep her wits. 'Pao.' She studied him as though in the past few minutes he had suddenly become an entirely different person. 'Why are you telling me all this? *Tsu mu* has returned; why aren't you telling *Tsu mu*?'

'Oh, yes, the all-powerful old woman! Damn the old woman—and damn you, too! Well, I did tell her. Small thanks I got!' Pao slumped in a carved chair. His heavy body scattered the fuchsia silk cushions to the floor. He glared at his sister, blaming her for whatever had caused him so much aggravation. She saw then that he was drunk, and that his drunkenness was about to explode in frenzied rage. But she couldn't help being alarmed by his news, and she rose, pacing the carpet, thinking fast.

'Is *Tsu mu* safe?'

He snorted, spluttering slightly, plucking at his rubbery lips with wine-stained purple fingers. '*Tsu mu* will survive. That old woman is made of ice. Nothing moves her. I tell her that devil Sya Dam is on the roof with a helicopter and a monster, and what does she do? Orders me about like a market coolie. "Pao, send the servants to fetch Honourable Colonel at once!" And then what am I to do?' He broke off and gazed furiously at his sister. 'I am to go check the vintner's accounts. I am not permitted to hear her business. She and the Tiger, they make conspiracies and plots, and me, I am a lackey, sent to check the damn wine bill!'

Chee Laan looked at him. 'If our grandmother told you to go and check accounts, do it!' He glowered, squinting furiously at her. He fumbled at his pocket and produced a bottle. She swooped in and seized it from his hand. 'No! No drugs! No more booze! For once in your life, Pao, face your responsibilities, and face them sober. This is serious!'

'Give me that!' he shouted, his face purple. She held it away, taunting.

'Shall I tell *Tsu mu*? Shall I show her that you can only function with the poppy-sleep?' He halted and glowered, seeking a means of escape. His eyes returned to the bottle, which she held just out of reach. 'Go. Check the accounts—check them very carefully.' She stood up to indicate dismissal, ignoring his claim, as oldest son, to her deference. She was trembling. Pao might be fat and flabby, but she had not forgotten his bouts of insensate violence. She was wary, even now. Some memories never died.

Still shaken by what he had seen, Pao shambled toward the door. In the doorway he looked back at her, slack-jawed, questioning, but finding no words. She considered how ugly he was. He looked like their father. She shuddered.

As the door closed behind him she placed the bottle in her purse and took the elevator down to the lobby. Her grandmother's office was in a suite off the lobby, next to Chee Laan's old, smaller office, where some of her things, including changes of clothing, had not yet been moved to her new quarters. The offices were next to the smaller rooms used by the hotel staff; thus, a watchful eye could be kept on both the highest and the lowest levels.

Chee Laan did not approach her grandmother's office but entered the adjacent staff sitting room. Finding it vacant, she locked the door behind her and moved softly to the listening panel in the wall. Sunii Lee herself had installed it. It was useful, she explained, to be able to check on employees. Disloyalty was a contagion which must be eradicated at first appearance. Chee Laan pressed her ear to the thin panel, then froze, hearing her grandmother's voice. As she listened, she felt her loyalties eroding, her old life crumbling around her.

'Why bring the girl back?' Sunii's tone of cold anger shocked Chee Laan. 'Your people condemned her to death. Why make trouble? Why not leave matters to take their course?'

'Really, *Khun* Sunii,' a man replied, his tone rich and deep, and profoundly scornful. With a shudder, Chee Laan recognised the voice of Sya Dam. He laughed, a snort of disgust, bitter as bile. 'Condemned, yes—by the Akha!'

'Condemned for killing her husband. For which crime Thai law, too, would condemn her.' Sunii's voice tone stung like a whip. 'What use is she?'

'I need to discover the depth of the king's feelings for her. If it was more than a mere passing fancy, she is potentially extremely useful. And otherwise, she will be easily disposed of.'

In the pause that followed, Chee Laan sensed the tension, imagined them staring at each other, neither willing to concede, weighing each other like wrestlers.

At last Sunii said, 'As to that, well and good. But why bring that thing, that thug, here?'

'Archin is a simple fellow. It is that very simplicity which makes him invaluable. He has served us well. Archin has done more than you know.'

'He may be useful and obedient, but his stupidity is dangerous. The attack on this so-called environmental expert, this Raven, for instance.'

'Nothing was ever proven. There was no publicity, either.'

'No, and that is fortunate, because we cannot afford publicity. Thanks to the quick thinking of the American general, a disaster was averted. It was unfortunate that my granddaughter became involved in the sordid business, though. That should not have happened.'

'One might have thought you of all people would have welcomed the timely removal of Raven. Given your views on miscegenation.' He paused. Chee Laan realised, with a stab of anger, that he was talking about herself. 'Raven poses a threat for other reasons, as you know. The man masquerades as an absentminded professor, but I am reliably informed that he is a spy—a very dangerous man.'

There was silence on the other side of the panel. Chee Laan wished she could see their faces, read their expressions. Her chest throbbed. She steadied herself with a hand on the wall, wishing she could press herself through it and emerge, invisible, on the other side.

'My views on miscegenation?' Sunii's voice was still and clear as silk stretched taut.

His voice, in reply, had a studied casualness. 'I have always found it curious that you, especially, should entertain such strenuous objections to alliances as, for instance, the relationship between your esteemed granddaughter Miss Chee Laan and this *farang*.' He paused again to let this sink in, then continued softly, his voice purring deep in his barrel chest like a great engine idling. 'That you, of all people, should object…'

'What do you mean, me of all people?' she demanded. There was a high note in her voice, both challenge and panic, and her words were quick and sharp.

'One cannot ever blame women.' Sya had adopted a lighter, musing tone. 'Does not your sage Confucius say the saddest of all fates is to be born female? Weak beings have to embrace expediency. There are ladies, I hear, who even managed to stifle their revulsion toward East Ocean Nippon Devils, seeking advantage in…' The pause was heavy with insult. 'Certain friendships.' He continued with an undertone of menace. 'Such alliances may have unforeseen consequences. Well-known local businessmen, pillars of the community, yet fatally flawed—who are now gone to their ancestors.' He sighed piously.

She burst out, her voice tight with accusation: 'You were not told to kill him! Why did you have to kill him?'

'You requested my help. Your son was robbing you, destroying your empire, dissipating your life's work. You told me so yourself, madame,' he countered coldly.

'You did not need to kill him!' she cried brokenly. Chee Laan trembled at the pain in her voice.

'There was no other way,' Sya reasoned calmly. 'Not to save face, and ensure the problems did not recur. Your son has joined his paternal ancestors. Not, perhaps, after all, Cantonese tycoons murdered by the Japanese, but instead those very warriors from the East Ocean islands…'

There was a fragile silence, delicate as a spider's thread. Then Sunii spoke, her voice little more than a whisper. 'Who else knows this?'

'Not many. Be reassured. Certainly, your granddaughter, at any rate, has no idea her grandfather was Japanese!'

'You can prove nothing!' Sunii said loudly. Then she switched tacks. 'My granddaughter would never believe it. My grandsons are strutting fools like their father and his odious, bowlegged bantam-cock of a father before him. Chee Laan is loyal to me. That is all that matters.'

The eavesdropper, engaged in an act of shame, blushed to hear herself commended.

'I am sure she is,' Sya replied smoothly. 'Rest assured, I shall not be the one to tell her. And do not concern yourself with this man Raven. He has cheated death for the last time. He and I shall come face to face one day, and one of us will not survive that encounter.'

'You will not find me ungrateful, Colonel.' Chee Laan shivered at her grandmother's steely tone.

There was a smile in Sya's voice as he said, 'Indeed! I have a certain respect for your granddaughter. She has brains. There are few women I admire. Yourself, of course. And the Princess Regent. It was she, you know, who contrived this marriage with my late cousin for this bitch thing I have brought here while we decide what is to be done with her…'

'I had wondered,' Sunii murmured. 'Yes, I had wondered about that.'

Sya chuckled. 'I informed Her Highness that I discovered the young king disporting himself with the bitch. We agreed that a speedy marriage was the best solution—in view of possible future developments, you understand.'

'But the woman, Salikaa…there was already a fiancé, so I understood.'

Sya sighed, as if in genuine sorrow. 'Yes, poor young Prince Toom. One of the few acts I have genuinely regretted in my life.'

'That was you? The drowning?'

'How strange that you should need to ask. He did not suffer. The training offered to BPP specials is excellent. His neck was snapped before his body was placed in the yacht. Then it was capsized. Very neat.'

Chee Laan shivered. Weariness dragged at her limbs. She had hugged her commonplace little love to her breast like a child burying her face in a soft toy, while all around her was an adult world of chaos and malice. Infatuation had made her both deaf and blind. It was unforgivable. Despite the flame shrivelling inside her chest, she went on listening.

'Why such an elaborate remedy? Would it not have been simpler merely to bring forward the date of her wedding to Prince Toom?' Sunii asked, in a measured tone.

'Alas! I had no room to manoeuvre. You see, I was not alone when I discovered the young couple—Prince Toom was with me. And there were others. Toom himself saw me hustling His Hot-blooded Majesty into his pants.' He paused. 'Toom broke down.'

'Unfortunate young man.'

'Foolish puppy! The king has had the good sense to keep his mouth shut, whereas Toom could not have held his tongue. That is the way with these liberals when they imagine themselves injured. They squeal like stuck pigs. He had to be silenced. The earth rises higher.'

'How long do you expect me to keep that thug here?' Sunii demanded.

'He will guard the girl while I attend the official banquet at the Summer Palace.'

'Ah, yes! The royal recognition of the new cabinet. New lamps for old!' Sunii laughed mirthlessly. 'Honouring the gallant officers who put down the Chinatown massacre.' Her tone sang with the bittersweet sting of ancient resignation. 'Well, keep your pawn. I wish you success. I hardly think, though, at this stage of the game, that she will succeed in crossing the board and returning as a queen. Once, such a thing might have been possible, who knows? But the end game approaches, Colonel.'

Now it was his turn to demand explanations. 'Meaning?' His voice was sharp.

'Meaning, already the inquisitive have been probing into my financial affairs. Our bank security I regard as impregnable, but somewhere there is a leak. If the provenance and destination of those funds were to become common knowledge…'

'How could that happen?' He was patronising her now, as though she were no longer an equal, but a little woman who was overreacting and required soothing. 'The sums were brought into the country well camouflaged, and introduced through the bank's Hong Kong branch. I shall be making the agreed withdrawal in the near future.'

'I am still surprised you need so much money to bribe those people. I should have thought they would have been willing to do anything to prevent our enemies from joining forces—to strike a blow for face, for honour, without the necessity of payment. It is, indeed, a point of honour to prevent this betrayal! It is what the last of the Kuo Min Tang have dreaded all these years: the recognition of Mao's bandit regime, those communist murderers! After all the fine words spoken by Westerners, all the assurances they have given Taiwan! It is true, they are deceitful barbarians!'

He laughed. 'Once upon a time, the descendants of the warriors of the last Chinese Nationalist stand would have acted from pure motives. They would have intervened to prevent this unholy alliance with the Western powers.'

'Yes,' she said, more matter-of-factly. 'What does it matter, after all, bribe or no bribe? So long as that aircraft is prevented from taking off and the treacherous *farang* delegation never reaches Beijing.'

'Indeed,' he said, 'my sentiments entirely. So we proceed? '

'We proceed.' Sunii paused. 'Of course, to me, you realise, the Middle Kingdom is home, no matter what villains are in power. One's bones yearn for that soil.'

They moved away from the panel, and Chee Laan heard no more. Trembling with adrenaline and rage, she sank slowly to her knees on the polished floor. Her grandfather was no Chinese martyr, but an East Ocean Devil, a Japanese oppressor. No wonder her father and brothers were ugly, bowlegged creatures! Did she have a sinister Nippon look, too? She had been kept in the dark about her origins, and about so much else. Resentment against her grandmother choked her, even as she recognised that she was Sunii's creature and creation. Pruned, trained, stunted as a bonsai tree, she would go on living in that shape. She could never learn another way of being.

And her grandmother was in league with the declared archenemy of the Chinese, the Black Tiger, Sya Dam—and had as good as given her blessing for Raven's murder.

Chee Laan grimaced in the silent room, pondering how such an unlikely alliance had ever come about. But it was clear enough: Sya was an outsider, like Sunii Lee. They were both preoccupied with ambitious schemes, and had recognised the potential usefulness of a powerful alliance. Their cooperation was born of expediency, nothing to wonder at.

And who had Sya commanded to prevent a plane from taking off, the plane carrying a Western peacebroker to Beijing? The 'broken promises of the barbarians' must mean the United States was about to recognise Red China. Chee Laan knew Tsu mu would be bitter about that, for her sympathies lay with the nationalists of the old regime in Taiwan. Her hatred of the communists was implacable. Chee Laan realised that this was the information Raven had been waiting for: the secret plot to sabotage the reconciliation mission. She knew she must tell him immediately and warn him of the danger; she would no longer hesitate or wait to examine her loyalties.

But first, there was Salikaa—what had Sya said? A prisoner in the penthouse suite, guarded by a monster? Easily disposed of if the time came? Here, at least, she was not helpless.

Chee Laan emerged from the staff quarters and glided through the crowded lobby, hoping none of the employees or guests would recognise her. Most of the front desk staff were Chinese, keen-eyed and intelligent. For hostess and domestic work, Sunii employed the charming, malleable Thais, but for bookings, accounts, and discouraging undesirable customs, it was Chinese. Fortunately, the staff was busy, and they hardly glanced at Chee Laan. She moved smoothly, with small steps, keeping her eyes on the carpet ahead of her, forcing herself to conceal her agitation. Her tastes in clothes were simple, inconspicuous; in her white blouse and dark trousers she could pass for a maid, especially walking just so, close to the wall, looking down modestly like small person.

She reached the elevator and stepped in, pressing the button to close the door quickly before anyone could join her. Safely back in her new suite, she slid into the executive director's chair. She pulled the phone toward her across the desktop, disturbing coloured brochures and stiff invitations still in their envelopes. Fashion shows and soirées tumbled noiselessly onto the thick Chinese carpet. Chee Laan held the phone but did not lift the receiver. She needed to think hard before she spoke to Raven. She curled her bare feet beneath her on the scarlet silk cushions of her carved dragon chair. The double thickness of doors and windows, the hum of the powerful air conditioners, created an enclosed micro-climate. As she urgently clutched the phone, Chee Laan's eyes roved the rich room, seeking solace. She had chosen the decor herself. The joss sticks she had lighted glowed before the Khmer stone Buddha, hacked off from a wall in Ankhor Wat and smuggled to Bangkok in an infantryman's backpack. The gilded full-figure Bangkok Buddhas sat gravely in their wall niches. Their calm, static poses were at odds with her disordered state of mind. She was startled when the phone she was holding shrilled loudly with an incoming call. When Salikaa's voice came through loud and clear Chee Laan almost dropped the phone in astonishment.

'Is this room service?' Salikaa's voice was studiously casual, with a touch of the old hauteur.

'*Chai, kha.* Yes, madame,' Chee Laan replied. *She knows damn well this number is not room service, but my private office*, she thought. 'Salikaa! You're not alone? You can't talk freely?'

'Correct. I wish to order food.' She still had that distant, imperious tone.

Chee Laan had a sudden inspiration. 'Our menu is French,' she murmured. Salikaa drew in her breath sharply but picked up the hint. Chee Laan wondered about the monster reported by Pao—was he breathing down Salikaa's neck even now? Would some huge hand descend upon the phone set, cutting off this thin lifeline?

'French. Send me up *une boisson soporifique*—better make it beer.' In the background Chee Laan heard a growl of approval. 'There is beer in the minibar. But it is imported beer. I wish for local beer. And bring some rice. You will bring this right away?' Despite the haughty voice, there was a slight stress in her tone.

'I will bring it personally, madame. To which suite, madame?' Chee Laan asked innocently, as though she did not know.

'Penthouse,' Salikaa snapped. The line went dead.

Chee Laan pulled open the top desk drawer and extracted the hotel's master key from its hook at the back. She tucked it into the waistband of her slacks. Fortuitously, she still had the potent somnifers distilled from opium poppies she had confiscated from her brother. There was beer in the office refrigerator, kept for the entertainment of male business associates. Beer and whisky, both Thai and imported, vodka and Bourbon, and also sake. Japanese sake. Chee Laan shook herself. One thing at a time. She would think about her Japanese grandfather in due course, and come to terms with that also.

Probably.

First, she rang Raven. They spoke briefly, in terse, paratactic sentences. She replaced the receiver and took the bottle of liquid opium from her purse. She poured several drops into a clean crystal tumbler. The glass was so deeply incised and embellished that the drops were indistinguishable in its depths. When she added the beer they would blend and mingle, the minute changes in colour seeming no more than the refraction of sunlight in the facets.

Drinkwater Residence, Bangkok

Raven
'Chee Laan!' I said urgently, but she had already put the phone down. I slammed the receiver down too, and stared unseeing at the wall. I imagined her delicate, oblique face, her eyes merry with laughter, as on the river at the water festival. Then I pictured her now, troubled, wearing a worried frown. I'd feared for her since the Chinatown riots, where her old *amah* had lost her life. There would be more bloodshed; violence lay thick in the air, and there was nothing I could do to keep her safe. I was an inexperienced Galahad, and Chee Laan Lee was a very stubborn young woman.

Blinded by my own selfishness, I had never felt especially protective of my fellow human beings. I'd pretended my lack of gallantry was a reformed chauvinist pig's respect for the independence of modern women, but if the truth be told, I'd just never cared enough before.

I recognised that Chee Laan was an independent woman, as independent as any I'd ever met—yet she appeared more vulnerable, her bright courage merely the prideful recklessness of youth. Legionnaires see a lot of that; it leads to many needless deaths.

I had told her little about myself, to protect her from becoming embroiled in an enterprise, which was certainly not devoid of risk. Neither had I elaborated on my relationship with Angel Fleischer, for some things are best forgotten.

But the conversation she had overheard between Colonel Sya and her grandmother must have indicated to her the extent of my involvement, and the dangerous man I was dealing with. Much had now become clear to me. The image of the lonely airstrip in the northwest, where I had gone with van Hooten, flashed into my mind. Methodically I made an attempt to piece together what I knew.

Even then I had suspected, through van Hooten's edginess and the occasional veiled reference, that the airfield was to be used for a secret mission of enormous significance, but it was impossible to guess by whom, or for what purpose.

It was evident that any mission from that desolate place could not be military in nature. The U.S. Air Force operated five major bases in Thailand, all of which were closer to the theatre of hostilities and more favourably situated to strike across the Cambodian border into Vietnam.

If the mission was not military, neither was it likely to be related to the opium traffic, for van Hooten was clearly not concerned that I was aware of those peculiar local activities. Even before Chee Laan's phone call, I had already concluded there was only one other possibility. The operation planned had to be a top-level diplomatic mission involving major players. It was self-evident that, if the Americans had determined to open a dialogue with Mao Zedong and Zhou Enlai, they must bring in a statesman of the highest rank.

It was the only logical conclusion: the Americans wanted to break down the door to Mainland China at last. The more I thought about it, the more certain I became that the only person who might be capable of achieving such a coup, in the terms of international diplomacy, was the Secretary of State, Henry Kissinger.

They would have to bring Kissinger in to broker a deal with Red China. They would need to fly him out at night from an obscure rural airstrip in a friendly country, in deadly secrecy. There could be no preemptive rumour-mongering. If the operation was to succeed, the world must be presented with a *fait accompli*. As I followed this line of reasoning, I surmised that even the State Department was probably kept in ignorance of the plan. It reeked of the CIA acting alone. I had no proof, but I had long suspected that the CIA had been backing the Kuomintang-controlled opium convoys from the Golden Triangle for decades. After all, they knew the area like their own backyard and had numerous operatives on the ground, as well as invaluable local contacts.

At last I began to understand as well why I, rather than an American citizen, had been entrusted with this mission. If the State Department were as yet unaware of the planned operation, deploying U.S. citizens would have been a risk. My mission was to report on signs of instability within Thailand, any turbulence which could endanger Kissinger's delicate diplomatic endeavour, and I was to make my reports to London, where the information would be assimilated and digested, and then relayed—as much of it as was deemed politic—to the Americans.

I had filed my account of the Chinatown riots and the shooting of the demonstrators, but there had been nothing to link those events with the kind of general unrest that the grey men in London feared. I had been kept in the dark about who would reap the benefits of what information I gleaned, as well as about the true nature of the mission I was supposed to carry out. This made me feel mistrusted and marginalised, even while I told myself that this was a well-known characteristic of such cloak-and-dagger endeavours. At least now I too was alert to the fact that their great master plan was known to dangerous people who would seek to thwart it, at whatever cost. I could not suppose for one moment that Sya Dam and his underlings would hesitate at sabotage, or even murder.

Like many of my generation, I had a healthy distrust of the whole breed of politicians and diplomats as a matter of course, but Kissinger commanded my grudging respect. Time was of the essence. There was no mistaking the urgency in Chee Laan's voice. I thought of her, and I knew the sooner all this was over, the sooner I could pick up the threads of my real life again, and discover what I had to offer a young and beautiful heiress, and what, if anything, she would accept from me.

Mechanically, I started to pull on my shirt. A blast of arctic air from the humming vent on the wall above the bed reminded me that you could catch a chill as quickly from air conditioning as from winter soakings on that wet coast of my childhood, which at the present moment seemed unimaginably remote. I found it hard to believe I was doing these absurd James Bond things again, strapping a knife to my calf, placing an automatic in a shoulder holster, patting it into place before putting on my jacket. I had been used to performing such actions once, long ago, in another life, and my hands carried out the tasks automatically. Yet for too long my existence had been comfortably humdrum.

By the time my report reached London and wheels were set in motion, it would be too late to wait for authorisation. Sya Dam had to be stopped, and I knew only one way to achieve that end.

I closed the door softly behind me and left the air conditioner running, reflecting that I would need a cool refuge when I returned.

If I returned.

Rachanee Hotel, Bangkok

Carrying a small silver tray upon which reposed a glass and a bottle, Chee Laan emerged into the corridor of the penthouse floor and noted with relief that it appeared deserted. Purple silk curtains were drawn across the glass walls from the floor to the high ceiling. The sun blazed against them with an amethyst glow. She hesitated for a moment outside the door of the penthouse suite to adjust the weight of the tray. The trembling of her hand caused the bottle and glass to chink against one another. She told herself sternly that it was because she was unused to carrying trays, not because she was afraid. All the same she took a deep breath to steady herself. There was no going back now.

She knocked twice, the soft, discreet knock of a servant. From the other side of the door she heard a growl, close to her ear.

'Leave the stuff outside and go!' The rough voice was slurred, as if the speaker were drunk, or afflicted with a cleft palate. She set the tray down outside the door and hurried to the corner of the corridor. There she made a fortunate discovery. She could see the door clearly in the wall mirror, but anyone standing in the doorway of the suite would be unable to see her, because the view was obscured by a full-length, gold-painted statue of a *dephanon* angel.

The door opened cautiously. A shaggy dark head peered out. Huge hands gripped the tray and lifted it out of sight. The door was kicked shut from inside. Chee Laan strained to catch any sounds from the suite, but all she could hear was the hum of the air conditioning. She closed her eyes, trying to turn her thoughts inward, breathing deeply. So deep was her moment of meditation that she did not hear the lock slip back or soft, quick footsteps approaching over the thick carpet. Then Salikaa was at her side, stroking her arm. She wore nothing but one of the hotel's peach-coloured bath towels, folded like a sarong over her bosom. It took Chee Laan a mere second to secure the door from the outside with the master key.

'Only another master key can unlock it; turning the knob on the inside will not release it,' she whispered. 'But it's not safe up here; we could be trapped. Quick!'

Salikaa reached for her hand. Together they ran through the violet light of the purple corridor and into the waiting lift. Chee Laan pressed the button for the ground floor, keeping her finger pressed down hard so the descent could not be interrupted.

When the lift stopped, they alighted and sauntered casually through the lobby, negotiating their way through the designer seating and the potted palms among the brightly dressed tourists and their mounds of luggage. Chee Laan led the way into her old office and locked the door behind them. They sank to the carpet, staring at each other. Then Salikaa threw head back and began to weep, her tears falling between gulps of hysterical laughter.

Salikaa

If you want to know the truth, things started going wrong with that man Fleischer, back in Normandy. I didn't trust that mother from the outset, from the moment he rolled up at the convent gate in that shit-can of a jeep to drag the three of us off for our holiday from hell on his so-called training course. Some training course—mud, blood, bad food, bad hair, a real bad scene. He was a smartass, Fleischer, who seemed to know way too much for my liking. Vichai always said that. 'Never trust a guy who knows too much.'

Fleischer knew all about Vichai, or thought he did. He certainly knew about Chee Laan's grandmother, and that Pim was not just a princess but a committee member of SWORD.

During that first jeep ride, I put my hand on Fleischer's thigh, and he was mad as a hornet. I laughed in his face. Not so clever after all—one of those wankers who pretend to be immune! And then, that other time, when we stood together in the downpour, the night the boot nails had carved up Chee Laan's foot, and Fleischer groaned and hauled me against him, then I knew for sure, and I laughed again. He hit me then, burst my lip, and I laughed even harder. But I had allowed him to get too close and learn too much. I had exposed my flank, you might say—you might indeed. He thought he had something on me then, the bastard!

Then, later, after I won Miss Thailand, got myself engaged to Pim's brother, Toom, and was about to become Princess Salikaa, Fleischer resurfaced. He crawled out of the sewer like a rat and started to send cryptic little messages about what he knew, and who he was planning on telling. It just had to be stopped. There was nothing else for it. So I told Tamsin. That was enough.

Tamsin had lots of friends—people like Tamsin always do, though friends become enemies overnight or even over a single drink. Through his chums, Tamsin discovered the plan to blast a hole in the Lee Bangkok Bank during the Asian Rally, and that one of the men involved was an explosives expert called Fleischer who had come to Bangkok, officially to work at the American Embassy.

Tamsin brought me a Polaroid he'd taken outside the Mandarin Hotel and, though the man was dressed like a sober citizen and not in filthy combats, I recognised him at once. The great thing about Tamsin was that he did his own logistical thinking. I merely had to identify Fleischer as the target, and indicate that his existence had become irksome to me. Then Tamsin said, 'I'll take care of it, Salikaa, sweetie,' and went off quietly to do just that. I liked that about Tamsin.

Tamsin was the best minder you could ever have. He was wildly attractive—I never could endure being around ugly people, any more than Tamsin could. We knew we were both gorgeous. Tamsin was an amusing and reliable little darling, and we got on like a mortar and pestle. It was too bad he never came back. I really missed him.

I suspected Sya Dam, that black Akha devil, engineered Tamsin's disappearance, and just before I was packed off to marry that depraved animal, Vasit, I was proved right.

After Sya found me cosying up to young King Vajah, he locked me up, guarded by a couple of strapping peasant nurses. They pumped me so full of drugs I didn't know what day it was. Then Sya arrived, grinning like a split melon, carrying a big bunch of flowers. 'Welcome to the family,' he said. 'You're going to marry my cousin. Congratulations!'

'I'm not marrying any stinking tribesman!' I spat at him, full in the face, and while he wiped my spittle off his chin, I said I'd rather be dead than marry any black Akha. 'I am not without friends!' I said, trying to sound more confident than I felt.

'It's married or dead. Dead can be arranged too, little lady,' he gloated, 'And you are mistaken. You have no friends left.'

'My guardian is Vichai the Bandit,' I said. 'Vichai, who has the heart of a leopard, who eats little police colonels for breakfast!'

He threw back his head and brayed like a donkey. 'Your bandit with the iron stomach just got indigestion!' He handed me a newspaper clipping. One glance told me everything. Vichai was dead. The enormity of it stunned me. I could not understand. But one look at Sya's savage face was enough; my resolve to survive and seek vengeance was born in the moment of his triumph.

'You cowardly bastards! You lured him, ambushed him! You must have tricked him! Nobody was smart enough to take Vichai!'

He shook with mirth. I wanted to kill him. 'Maybe someone told Vichai that Miss Thailand, the future princess, wanted to meet with him.'

When I understood what he'd done, I was dizzy with rage. They had tricked him, cut him down in cold blood. I can't forget the pictures, or those ridiculous headlines: *Notorious Communist Terrorists Eliminated!*

'What total bollocks!' I shouted. 'Vichai was just an ordinary bandit! He wouldn't mess with filthy politics! He was no more a communist than a water buffalo!'

Sya just shrugged. 'What's the difference? He's dust. Here's another late friend of yours,' he said. 'They certainly seem accident-prone.' He showed me a picture of Tamsin then, and as I stared at it, he studied my face and laughed.

Tamsin was stiff by the time the picture had been taken, but Sya offered to show me others from when he wasn't quite dead. You could see what Sya's people had done to him. It made me furious, the thought of the agony Tamsin must have endured, the disgusting, obscene things they had done to him because of his sort.

Sya saw I was appalled, and he grinned. 'So now you know what to expect!'

I clawed at his face; he seized my hands and forced them down. He was so strong I thought my wrists would snap.

'Calm down, wild cat!' he mocked. 'Now, instead of a prince, you will bed an Akha. Never fear—you still enjoy some measure of the royal patronage, and you will have a more splendid wedding than you deserve!' I was to take that half-witted whore Pawn as my 'lady's maid'—living among the Akha, I was to be attended by a 'lady's maid'!

And a dreary pathetic object she was, too, snivelling about her baby, quivering with terror, squeaking and wetting her pants like she was a mouse caught in a trap. Since she'd been inflicted on me, I insisted on making her useful. After that first experience with my brute 'husband,' which even now I can't recall without retching, I made sure there would be no repetition. Every night I pressed the poppy-sleep on Vasit, and he was not reluctant to accept. He gulped it down in mouthfuls, like a landed fish drowning on air. When he was too drugged to tell the difference, I sent Pawn to his bed in my place. When she protested, I showed her my nails and demonstrated how easily I could scratch her eyes out. She never doubted I meant it. She knew I would have done it and nobody in that village would have cared. Most of the women endured worse.

I'd always been in a hurry. Maybe it comes from being brought up among people who don't live long. There's a lot of living to cram into a short span, and you become obsessed out how little time is left. The life of the average bandit is about thirty-five years. In consequence, I'd only ever concerned myself with things that were profitable or made me feel good. You can say that's bandit's philosophy, too, but I would bet the rest of the world's not that different. I learned French because there was some point to it. Folks take you for an educated lady when you spout French. Even those snobs at court were knocked sideways by my French. Nobody would respect me for learning Akha, so I didn't bother. But Pawn had the whore's aptitude. She'd already learned a few stock phrases in English: 'Lovely GI, you numbah one, you like party!'—that sort of rubbish. A woman like Pawn will always find a weak spot and gnaw her way into someone's life, like a rat. She started chatting with those dour, downtrodden Akha women, all about babies and menstruation and girlie stuff, and soon she was jabbering away like a mynah bird. Then she started looking at me in a nasty way, as if she knew some great secret I didn't. Of course, low women can never really keep a confidence of any kind. Sharing privileged information gives them a momentary illusion of power and importance.

I'd had enough of her hints and glances, so one day when we were alone I twisted her arm behind her back and pushed her wrist upward, toward her neck. I could hear the sinews crack and she began to shriek.

'Shut up,' I said. 'Tell me why you've gone all secretive.'

'I don't know what you...ow!' Her lie ended in another squeal as I cranked the angle up a little. I braced myself against her, placing my knee in the small of her back. She tried to claw me with her other hand but failed.

'The truth, now,' I said. I can be very patient, although most people will claim the opposite.

'All right!' she gasped. I relaxed my grip a little, to encourage her. 'They're going to break out.'

'Who are?'

'The Akha. All the tribes.'

'A pack of nomads!' I snorted dismissively. 'Clueless, befuddled savages!'

'But they have a leader! Sya Dam will lead them!' I dropped her arm then and stared.

'You can't mean it.'

She took on that cunning expression I detested. 'Do you think the men cheer him because he spouts government propaganda? He's planning a rebellion. They'll massacre the Thais, and you'll be the first! They hate you—even the people here think you are a witch!'

'I'm so pleased,' I drawled. 'I could never respect myself if I thought I enjoyed the affection of this lot! But you're Thai, too, Pawn, or had you forgotten?'

'Oh,' she smirked infuriatingly, with a superior little chuckle, 'they won't murder me. They like me!'

I gave her a black eye for that piece of cheek, but it was far insufficient as retribution for her impudence. When Sya told me what the tribe intended to do to me, after I rid the world of the insect Vasit, I looked him in the eye and I told him I knew all about his tribal revolution. I made sure to tell him where I got the information from.

If he was going to kill me, I thought Pawn might as well join me.

Sya thought I was unconscious when he ordered his ape Archin to pull me out of the grave, but I wasn't; I just kept my eyes shut and made no sound. They don't know I'm aware that they killed Pawn and laid her in Vasit's grave in my place. By this time nobody will be able to tell the difference, anyway. Or care, either way. I certainly don't.

When Sya kidnapped me out of the pit, I lay in the back of that jeep listening to Archin grunting and snorting like a pig. I knew what Sya was up to. He was going to pretend he'd saved me from the tribe's vengeance in order to bring me before a Thai court to be tried for murder. He would take me to King Vajah, to discover whether I still enjoyed the king's affection. If I had fallen out of favour, I would be thrown in jail to await trial for killing Vasit. I could never be brought to trial, of course—I'd be left to rot forever, like other inconvenient individuals. Thai prisons were crammed with people like that.

I was convinced this was what Sya would do, because in his circumstances it is just what I would have done myself.

Throughout the helicopter ride, I was sure we were bound for Hua Hin. But then we suddenly landed—far too early by my calculations. I could see the glimmer of a city's lights and knew it had to be Bangkok. Archin was left to guard me and I lay very still, even though the floor of the helicopter was hard and uncomfortable and I had a great urge to change my position and seek relief. It was disconcerting, being guarded by Archin. He prowled round me, sniffing and pawing at my clothes like an animal. I knew it was only his fear of Sya's reprisals that kept him from seizing me there and then. I looked a wreck, hardly an appetising morsel, but I don't suppose Archin had much discrimination.

So I kept my eyes shut, my face without expression, and hoped Sya would return soon. I thought of my parents, whom I'd never known, never had a chance to know, because this animal had murdered them when I was born. Vichai told me that. Vichai knew every celebrated criminal in the country. He'd employed most of them at one time or another, but he said he drew the line at employing Archin, a psycho. By all accounts—that is, by Vichai's account, for he was my only source of information—they were losers, my *paw* and *mee*. But when all's said and done, they were my parents, and because of Archin, I'd never even had a chance to say hi. I resented that like hell. One more item on the bill.

As I lay there, I could sense Archin's growing excitement. He spluttered; his drool trailed over my face, and I longed to wipe it off but didn't dare raise my hand. Then Sya came back and barked his orders, and Archin set off again, lugging me over his shoulder like a sack. I let my limbs hang lifeless.

He brought me inside and threw me down on a big, soft double bed. He was still grunting and wheezing with excitement. Then he finally lost control, even though Sya was there, and threw himself on top of me, crushing all the breath out of my chest. The next moment, he was lifted off and fell heavily to the floor. I could breathe again. For a moment that was all I could think about. In my relief I sat up and opened my eyes.

Sya Dam was standing over Archin. He must have picked him up bodily and thrown him down. Sya had to be as strong as a tiger—Archin weighed as much as a jeep. My rib cage couldn't forget that weight.

Sya turned his attention to me. 'So,' he leered, 'the Sleeping Beauty awakes at last!' He let his eyes roam over me insolently. I was still wearing that revolting tribal dress, embroidered black with silver pieces. I'd been sick on it, when I was lying in the grave. It was covered with earth still, and it stank, as did my legs and my hair. My face was streaked with dirt. I had almost been a princess, and I loathed Sya Dam more now than ever, even more than I hated Archin. I stood up and I faced him.

'What are you going to do with me?' I demanded.

'You?' he mocked. 'What should I do with a freak like you?'

'The king loves me!' I yelled.

'The king? A callow boy who has led such a secluded life he takes a mynah for a peacock? You were a new toy, a plaything.'

'He wanted to make me his queen!'

'And then what? Supposing you managed to keep the ignorant young cub dangling until he braved the outcry and made you queen. Queens are not mere ornaments—they are breeding machines. What would you have done when you couldn't put it off any longer? Raided the Khlong Tooey orphanages?' He stared at me contemptuously. 'Oh, go and clean yourself up. The odour grows offensive. Even,' he paused, and his eyes were bitter, 'to an Akha!'

It was like a rebirth. I stood under the showerhead with the water on full and let it cascade down over me for ten minutes. Even when Sya and his henchman banged on the door, I ignored them, letting the filth drain away, luxuriating in the hot spray before I even got around to brainstorming about what to do next.

I already knew where I was. I did not even need to read the name *Rachanee Bangkok* on the big fluffy peach-coloured towels, tastefully embroidered in a darker shade. You have to hand it to the Jeks, they have good heads for business. Nobody was going to steal one of their towels if they could help it!

They say smell is the most vivid sensual trigger of memory. Perhaps it's true. There's a special smell, compounded of gun grease, metal, whisky, and betel that brings Vichai back to life. In this bathroom, the free toiletries conjured up the image of the person I surmised had been responsible for their selection: Chee Laan Lee, heiress to the Lee millions, and my good buddy. She too had a good head on her shoulders, and she was 'cool-hearted', which we Thais consider an admirable quality. If I could get a message to Chee Laan, there might be a chance of escape. I had made up my mind that the only way forward was to get to the king before Sya did, before that venomous toad poisoned Vajah's mind against me. I needed to take control. If I could see Vajah alone, I could get him to listen to me, and discredit Sya. Then, although all might not be as rosy as once upon a time, my prospects would certainly improve a thousandfold. I might salvage something from the wreckage after all.

When I emerged, Sya had gone. The big brute Archin squatted on his hunkers, staring fixedly at the bathroom door like a dog waiting for his dinner. I wore only a couple of big peach towels, one wrapped like a sarong, the other wound about my head in a turban. Archin's bloodshot eyes were popping out of his head.

I pointed a finger down my throat. 'Eat rice? Drink nice beer?' I spoke in a tone of bracing joviality, as you do to dogs and children. The monster's eyes gleamed. 'Ring for rice, ring for beer,' I proposed, briskly stepping over to the telephone. Fortunately, the hotel's Hospitality and Public Relations Department's number was listed on a crested pad by the telephone, along with every other service, from shoeshine to car hire. I prayed Chee Laan would be at her desk. I had no idea what the time was. When I heard her voice on the line I felt like shouting for joy, but I struggled to keep my tone neutral. Archin was watching me warily. I knew if I made one false move he would launch an attack. Sya would not risk leaving me alone with Archin for long—he might return at any moment.

Her alert, guarded tone told me Chee Laan was alarmed and primed for action. I just hoped she had immediate access to some drug that would render Archin unfit for combat within the space of few minutes—these Jeks have cupboards full of nostrums for every conceivable ailment, and besides, Chee Laan's brother Pao was a junkie. The question was whether she could find something in time. But she did, the little jewel.

I couldn't believe my luck when Archin tilted his head back and tipped the beer down his throat like a man hosing gas into a truck. Whatever was in that beer, it was the real stuff. Within seconds he let out a snore, shunted himself onto the bed, and sprawled there inert as a log. I didn't hang around to kiss him goodnight.

When Chee Laan and I finally made it to the staff office, I collapsed on the carpet and just lay there, laughing. Maybe I even snivelled a bit. Nobody had glanced at me more than once in the lobby. All these luxury hotels have health clubs and spas—they probably thought I was some dimwit who got lost on the way to the sauna. Most of them were *farangs*, anyway, and *farangs* don't notice much.

I looked at Chee Laan. I'd seen her in this mode before: damaged, bruised, yet quietly resolute. But there was a new wariness about her, and the resilience of self-knowledge that comes from surviving a tough time. I remembered her pale set jaw as she trudged through the French mud with her boots oozing blood—Chee Laan, my fellow survivor.

'I need to get to Hua Hin,' I said. 'I have to get to the king before Sya does—get in first, force him to listen to me.'

'You think Sya plans to confront the king?' She nodded pensively, biting her lip. 'Yes. That would be the perfect alibi. He would be at the other end of the country from Mae Sod.' I had no idea what she was talking about, and had no time to ask. She tugged open the door of a built-in cupboard, revealing orderly rows of garments. 'I keep changes of clothes here for when there's no time to go home. I have not yet moved them to my new office. Luckily. Help yourself while I think.'

I found a blue top and a pair of designer jeans that fit and pulled them on. Her taste was more conventional than mine, but I looked all right. I could fix my hair and make-up in the car. I needed all my weapons of war in good working order if I was to carry off my appeal to His Youthful Majesty with success. Then I saw to my delighted surprise that she actually had a flame-coloured evening dress just one I used to own. That colour was always lucky for me. So I dragged it off its hanger and tucked it over my arm, too, planning to change in the car. It seemed a most propitious omen.

'I called Raven,' Chee Laan said. 'He'll be here any moment. There's more going on than you know, Salikaa. Sya's engineering what could be a major international crisis.'

'Oh,' I said, and I tried not to sound as dismissive as I felt. 'If you've called Raven, let him take care of business. I really need to get to Hua Hin now, Chee Laan. It's going to take us three hours as it is.' I didn't know what Raven's interest in Sya Dam was, and I didn't much care. These Westerners were so feeble and indecisive.

She was reluctant, I could tell. She probably wanted to hang around and wait for her *farang* cavalier. I shook her arm and played my ace.

'Please, Chee Laan, dear, you have to help me! There's only you and me left now! Pim's dead! And Vichai, and Tamsin—and Toom. There's only the two of us!'

It was the mention of Pim that did it. I knew, though she'd never said anything, that Chee Laan felt guilty. As if she, or anyone, could have prevented it!

Other people's tender consciences can always be turned to one's own advantage. It's kind, really, because it allows the guilt-bearer the opportunity for atonement. I knew she wouldn't resist.

'Let's go,' she said, sighing. 'My car's in the underground carpark.' We strolled through the crowded lobby toward the lift in a mighty affectation of casualness. Chee Laan smiled, nodded to people, exchanged a brief word here and there—the consummate hotelier—until I was seething with impatience. There was a big group of foreigners in bright shirts, waiting expectantly for their tour bus. 'It's gone half-past,' I heard a woman whine. 'We're gonna miss the elephants.'

I wanted to elbow the people aside and make a run for it through the automatic doors. I should have followed my instinct, because before we could get there Sya stepped out of nowhere and blocked our path. We stood staring at each other. He was in full uniform, carrying a black ox-leather document folder. The zip was not quite closed. Between the grey teeth of the zip, black metal glinted in the light of the lobby's chandeliers. He pressed the document folder against Chee Laan's ribs, staring me down with his languid malign gaze.

'Don't bother looking down, Miss Lee,' he said. 'Your assumption is correct. The discomfort you are experiencing is because I am holding an automatic to your heart. Now, we three will retrace our steps. Ask Miss Thailand here to lead the way.'

'Ask her yourself,' Chee Laan said through gritted teeth, still smiling. Without turning her head, she said to me, 'Run for it, Salikaa. He won't dare shoot me.'

Thankfully, the gods smile on the innocent.

A foreign tourist spotted Sya's uniform and thrust herself at him, rudely knocking his arm away from Chee Laan. 'Are you the doorman? Doorman, would you please go out and check if the Sunburst Tours Coach has arrived?'

Sya bowed. 'Gladly, madame. In one moment I shall be at your service. But first, I must assist this young lady to her suite. She is overcome by the heat.' He swept Chee Laan into his arms and forced a path through the crowd to the elevator. I should have run off then. But I couldn't leave Chee Laan. I needed her to get me to Hua Hin. Plus, we'd have a better chance if we stayed together.

There was something else I'd seen in that crowded lobby, something I'd no intention of telling either of my companions. Behind one of the carved ornamental pillars, I'd clearly glimpsed the foreigner Raven, lunging forward just as the foreign tourist knocked against Sya.

Outside the penthouse door Sya subdued Chee Laan with one powerful arm while he fumbled for a key. She kicked and struggled, but his grip was too strong. 'You need a master key!' she panted triumphantly. 'You can't open it without a master key.'

'What makes you think I haven't got one?' he asked, fitting a key in the lock and opening the door. He kicked it shut and dumped Chee Laan on the floor. In the bedroom beyond, Archin lay snoring, dead to the world. Sya went over and prodded him with his boot. Archin did not stir. Sya set his uniform cap on a side table and pulled up a chair, straddling it. He withdrew the pistol from his document folder and pointed it in our direction. It had an ugly-looking silencer clipped onto the barrel.

'Undress each other!' he commanded. Then he sat back and watched impassively.

I'll say this for Chee Laan: she managed to betray no emotion. She tugged her own clothes, the ones I had borrowed, off of me without even changing her expression. Then I did the same for her, and we stood there facing each other in our underwear, heads bowed, covering up whatever we could with hands that seemed suddenly too small. It was not my proudest moment. Sya, however, smiled, evidently enjoying himself.

The knock at the door startled all three of us.

Sya moved fast. He gestured toward the bathroom with the gun. Naked and barefoot, we stumbled over the thick carpet. He closed the bathroom door behind us. I was still wondering what came next when he whipped out a set of handcuffs and snapped one around Chee Laan's left wrist. He twisted the chain round the steel curtain pole, and secured the other cuff to my right wrist. 'One sound, you all die!' he hissed.

He shut the door on us. The air was heavy with the scent of apple blossom and still hot and humid after my prolonged shower.

We heard voices in the bedroom. 'Raven!' Chee Laan whispered. She strained at the cuff like a dog hearing its master's voice.

'That hurts!' I complained as the chain pulled taut and the steel bit into my wrist.

The voices grew louder. Then there came ominous crashing sounds, then silence. Chee Laan looked stricken. Her eyes burned in her pale face. 'Sya is killing him!' she hissed. I started twisting my hands inside the handcuffs. Fortunately for both of us, I have double joints. There's no such thing, a doctor told me—just very loose articulation, making them suppler than other people's. Still, I can do it. I can also dislocate my toes at will. The pain is useful; it distracts. It was useful when Vasit celebrated our nuptials.

I compressed my hands into the narrow shape of a folded leaf, making my right hand as streamlined as a spearhead and slipping it through the steel ring. I unwound the chain with the empty cuff and handed it to Chee Laan. Wordlessly she wound the chain up and snapped the cuff into the second one about her left wrist.

As I heard Sya leave the bedroom and enter the sitting room, I pulled the bathroom door open a crack, turning the handle softly. I laid a finger warningly across Chee Laan's lips. I had caught a glimpse of Raven, slumped in a chair, his mouth slightly open and his head lolling awkwardly. I have seen plenty of dead people and I was pretty sure I'd just seen another one.

Chee Laan must not see him and start shrieking her head off—or worse still, in a rush of sentimentality, refuse to leave.

His wrists and ankles were bound to the chair. Sya had used the flex from the lamp, which lay on the carpet beside Raven. Its shade had rolled off.

I closed the door and braced my back against it, and then turned to her. She was forcing her arm, encumbered with the bulky steel cuffs, into the sleeve of a bathrobe. Two robes had hung on the hooks behind the door—peach-coloured like the towels, luxury weight. I shrugged into the other one and tied the belt.

'Is there any way out of here?' I whispered.

'I'm not sure. What about Raven?'

'Later,' I murmured. 'If we escape, then we can help him.' She nodded and pulled the door open, gliding through into the bedroom. I followed, remembering she still had that master key. I managed to interpose myself between Chee Laan and Raven; I didn't want her sidetracked.

The penthouse bedroom had heavy silk wall hangings. Chee Laan slid herself neatly behind the drapery and beckoned, and I followed, with one backward glance at the motionless form of Raven, and Archin, still snoring on the bed. Whatever she'd given him, it was potent and Archin was feeling no pain. She fumbled behind the hanging and I heard the chink of chain on metal. A hidden door swung open and we were through to the other side. As she locked the door behind us, I looked around. We were in a mirror image of the penthouse suite bedroom, but in addition to the burgeoning purple silk curtains and hangings, and the same enormous window, this room had a mirrored ceiling, handcuffs, whips, the whole caboodle.

'My father's private room.' Chee Laan glanced about with a moue of distaste.

'Looks like a tart's boudoir,' I said rudely.

She regarded me coolly. 'Just a place of entertainment. My grandmother gave it to him, to keep his games in-house and under control. She understood him well.'

We got out of there as fast as we could, walking purposefully, speaking quietly and casually, as if we were guests looking for the hotel's health spa.

We were dressing in her office when she asked, 'What about Raven? What can we do?'

'Nothing, Chee Laan, if he's in trouble with Sya. We can't act against Sya in this city.' *Especially,* I thought but did not say, *with you wearing half a pair of handcuffs, a pretty Chinese girl who's obviously escaped arrest.* Cops would have orders to shoot on sight, under the circumstances. Since the demonstration and the riots, and a number of fatal accidents befalling members of the royal family, the whole city was on edge; the police force was especially jittery, and fanatically loyal to Sya Dam. And the fallout from the war in Vietnam had made everyone trigger-happy.

'But Sya will kill him,' she insisted, almost pleading. 'It's my fault! I led him into the trap. I told him Sya was here, I told him Sya was planning a coup. He's going to get himself killed, and it's all my fault!'

'Oh, he's not going to get killed!' I said—and I wasn't lying, because for my money Raven was already dead. I had to make her understand that unless we got to the king, there was no hope for me, either, and I was still very much alive, and fully intended to stay that way. 'Raven's probably gone for help,' I consoled her perfidiously. 'You didn't see him, did you?'

'No...' she replied hesitantly.

'Well, then!' I said with an air of triumphant finality. 'He got away!' I could see she wasn't completely convinced, but it kept her going until we reached her car.

Chee Laan's Lotus sports car was a little bomber, and she drove it expertly, gunning the engine once we were clear of the city's chaos and the fleets of samlors, bicycles, and asthmatic Datsun taxis. I sensed this headlong pace was beginning to intoxicate her, but her jaw was set and she had a grim, preoccupied look, so I guessed her thoughts were with Raven. Just so long as she got me to Hua Hin and didn't falter, I didn't care what she did next.

The road ahead shimmered in the heat between paddy fields and palm-fringed villages. Horn blaring, we swerved round the overcrowded buses, listing heavily under the weight of passengers crouched on the roof and clinging to the sides. The flush of evening washed over the sky, silhouetting palm trees and temple chedis with aureoles of pink and gold. Processions of ducks and buffalo under the command of children wearily trudged through the flat landscape, along with a gang of women stone-breakers, returning to their village with pickaxes over their drooping shoulders, the ends of their loose turbans bound about their mouths to keep the dust from their lungs.

I pushed the seat back and stretched my leg onto the dashboard. 'I'd never have fit in, you know. At court,' I said. 'They'd always hate and despise me. And Toom, drooling and whimpering, he got on my nerves!'

'So you never loved Toom?'

'Chee Laan,' I said seriously, 'I've never loved anyone, except Vichai.'

'How about the king?' I was amused by the hint of reproof in her voice. It's usually Thais, not Chinese, who hold royal rank in awe.

'Ah, the king...if he were a peasant, one wouldn't have looked twice. He is handsome in a brooding, coltish way, perhaps. He's bred to pride, brought up to rule, but even so, there's a touch of the rebel in him. I liked that. Not one to grovel, not always wagging his tail and trying to please like Toom!'

My dismissal of Pim's brother annoyed her. Or perhaps the frown meant she was fretting over Raven. This was irritating, because all love does is distract you from more important things. I turned away from her and considered my own troubles. I needed to plan my tactics with the king. Sya would be hard on our heels, desperate to reach the king before I did. My future depended on beating him to it.

'I will not rest until Sya Dam is dead,' I vowed.

Rachanee Hotel, Bangkok

When Sya discovered they had escaped, he regretted not killing the two young women immediately. He was too frugal and opportunistic to impulsively neutralize a potential asset, and he had by no means exhausted Salikaa's potential. As a means of manipulating the young king, she had offered a unique advantage, and she could always be disposed of later, before she had a chance to make damaging revelations. But the risk was high. However, he reflected, killing Salikaa would have entailed the necessity of eliminating Chee Laan Lee also, and that was unthinkable. Grandmothers tended to be sentimental. Sunii Lee was his valued business partner, and such an act would seriously compromise their fruitful cooperation.

Finding his prisoners had absconded offended him deeply. Salikaa on the loose was more than an irritant. Sunii Lee's wrath would have to be endured.

He returned to the bedroom and glared resentfully at his helpless enemy and his recumbent slave. He toyed with the idea of killing Archin in the throes of his haze—as an Akha, he recognised the poppy-sleep. He pressed the muzzle of his gun to Archin's eye socket. The giant did not stir. Reconsidering, Sya twirled the gun around his finger, then slapped it back in its holster regretfully. Archin might still prove useful, and disposing of his enormous corpse would be time-consuming. Avoiding unwelcome publicity to the Rachanee would require ingenuity and bribes better employed elsewhere. Also, Sya wanted Archin to know in his stupid ox heart that there would be no mercy. To fail Sya the Tiger was death.

Now he had the further nuisance of this man Raven. In Bangkok, life was cheap, but *farang* death and disappearance occasioned hassle and could prove expensive. *Farangs* resented the death of one of their own, even scum like drug mules and hippies, garbage anyone should be happy to be rid of. Sya's lip curled. Even for lowlifes, *farangs* sent busybodying, impudent officials armed with warrants backed up by Interpol; they bought politicians and blackmailed them with aid programmes. No, this *farang* had to meet with an accident. Sya considered the layout of the Rachanee, examining its strategic possibilities.

Not too difficult, after all. But it must be done quickly. The foreigner must have a skull of steel, as he appeared to be waking up.

Raven
A heavy brass lamp applied mercilessly to the skull beats any sleeping pill. As I swam reluctantly back into consciousness and pain, I cursed the fat woman in the sunhat who'd blocked the only clear shot I was going to get at my enemy, Sya Dam. After that, I vaguely remembered following Sya and his hostages. There was no sign of the women now, but Sya prowled about me, occasionally peering into my face.

Blood had pooled in my cramped limbs. I must have been collapsed in the chair for some time. He'd bound me with the flex of the lamp. Seeing I was conscious, he brought his face close, a mask of malevolence.

'I hope, Raven, that you are ready to die. It is the time for dying. Your great Mr Henry Kissinger, he too will die. Yes, I know all this! The American general, he thinks himself mighty clever. He will escort the great man to the hidden airport in the northeast, to take off in secret for Beijing. Preparing the way for who knows what—a state visit by President Nixon, perhaps. Rapprochement. Nobody loses face. Trade flourishes. Everybody happy.' He paused.

I kept surprise off my face, feigning a dazed submissiveness I did not feel.

'But maybe not everyone shares this rapture. In Taiwan, there will be unhappy faces. In the northwest, the tribesmen will be pretty sore. Hard men, with long memories, unforgiving descendants of Kuo Min Tang warriors. Expert marksmen.' He adopted a mocking Pidgin English. 'For them, no problem. Those guys shoot your Mistah Big Henry Kissinger right out the sky. Pam!' He leaned along an imaginary gun barrel and took aim at some invisible object on the horizon. 'So—no rapprochement. So sad.'

'But you hate the Chinese,' I mumbled stupidly.

Sya chuckled. 'The Jeks are outsiders. Like me—like all Akha. We are allies in a common cause. We don't need to go to bed together to work together.' He laughed mirthlessly. 'We screw each other, whichever way.'

'Tribal rebellion?'

'I want respect for my people. For this, we need money. The Chinese have money. So we trade what we have. Sunii Lee *taitai* dreads rapprochement with Red China. She has too much invested in Taiwan. She does not care for communists. Also, she has skeletons in her closet. Communists are very narrow-minded people. So I arrange matters to Sunii's liking. She, in turn, bankrolls my rebellion.'

'Civil revolt threatens business interests. Surely the Lee family wouldn't want that.' I was playing for time and he saw that, yet in his arrogance he indulged me.

'For those in the business community, even national emergencies can prove lucrative, with the right foreknowledge.'

'Fostering rebellion? The loyal Black Tiger?' I feigned incredulity.

Sya smiled. 'Ah, loyalty! A wise man learns to prioritise his allegiances. And I, Raven, am first and foremost Akha. Once, it is true, I almost repudiated my roots. But then I saw what the Akha would become: like the Meo, the La-wa, the Lahu—exhibits in the Thais' human zoo.'

'Even if you arm the tribes, the Thais will call on their American allies for help. And they will get it. America will need her Thai airbases, even when the Vietnam War is over.'

He gave a snort of laughter, flaring his broad nostrils. 'The Americans will abandon Vietnam!' The true fanatic now, he seemed bent less on killing me than on convincing me.

I grunted. 'Don't underestimate them. Americans are brave, well trained and well armed. The Akha will be slaughtered.'

'Better dead, perhaps, than stuffed in a museum!' said Sya, with glib *braggadocio*. He looked at his watch and sighed. 'Too bad. No more time to chat. Perhaps after all you are not a stupid man, for a *farang*. Raven—Black Bird. But unfortunately for you, I am pressed for time. Now get up. Hump that chair with you to the lift.' He flung a bed cover over my knees. Seizing the chair-back, he moved the legs forward side by side, pivot and twist, until we reached the elevator. He was as strong as an ox. When the lift arrived, empty, he manoeuvred me into it and pressed the button. I struggled with my bonds but Sya had knotted the flex too tightly; all I achieved was searing my wrists and ankles with the wire. Sya watched the numbers light up in the panel as we descended. I tried to hurl my weight against the emergency stop button, but he anticipated me.

'Accept your fate,' he said. 'Do not anger me. Let us make our farewells with dignity.' The doors slid open, revealing the crowded, noisy, steam-filled kitchen, a vision of Dante's *Inferno*. Sya stepped out. 'Goodbye, Dr Raven. We will not meet again.'

He bent his neat-cropped head in an ironic *wai*. The doors closed behind him. The lift began its ascent.

Then I heard the sound of the doors just below being forced open. The lift jerked to a halt. I heard unidentifiable sounds, and the smell of something burning assailed my nostrils. Scorching heat rushed up, enveloping me. As thick black smoke plumes began to permeate the narrow steel box in the wooden shaft, I realised at last what Sya had done—and I began, far too late, to scream.

Sya had pressed the button for the second floor. The elevator, with its helpless prisoner, was rising again. Sya stood beside the elevator shaft and glared around at the kitchen. The place was hopping, chefs shouting, the full complement of the staff rushing about. Nobody noticed Sya. At the closest workstation to the elevator, a young sous-chef was cooking a clump of green samphire in a smoking wok. Sya thrust him brutally aside. In one smooth movement he dropped a lighted match into the hot wok, which exploded into orange flames. The boy cowered, screaming, as Sya forced the doors to the elevator shaft open and hurled the blazing wok into the wooden shaft. In a final flourish he scooped a cup of water from the sink and tossed it into the flames.

The fire regurgitated a great fireball; the oil spattered wide, sparking off small tongues of flame that licked hungrily up the wooden pillars. The Chinese kitchen workers were already running for their lives, howling, scattering food and utensils. Terrified, the chef tore off his tall white hat and coat, recalling his cousin, a cook whose wok had recently caught fire at the Imperial Hotel, causing the deaths of three kitchen staff and roasting a family of six in the elevator. Frenzied relatives of the immolated had caught up with the cook in Lumpini Park. Only police intervention had prevented a lynching.

In his blind panic, the Rachanee sous-chef failed to see the burly uniformed figure before he collided with him. Sya tugged the white coat up over the sous-chef's face and elbowed him viciously in the kidneys, sending him reeling headfirst into the corner of the kitchen counter. The man struck his temple, fell to the floor, and lay still, blood pouring from the wound.

Sya stepped over the body, seized a meat cleaver, and stood in front of the open elevator doors, surveying the raging inferno within the shaft. Smoke and flames were writhing in the vacuum. Satisfied, he allowed the doors to slide shut and ran through the smoke-filled kitchen to the staff stairway. He ignored the stairs leading up to the lobby, heading down instead into the underground garage.

His unmarked military vehicle stood out amongst the limousines. It was serviceable, but he needed more speed. He wrenched open the rear door, tossed aside the canvas cover, and dragged out the powerful motorbike hidden beneath. Swiftly, he donned gloves, goggles, and leathers. Once astride and swallowed up in the city traffic, anonymous in his gear, he let the engine rattle along while he listened attentively for the sirens of the fire department.

It had taken the fire engine three-quarters of an hour to arrive at the Imperial Hotel, by which time everyone trapped in the building was lost. Sya shook his head sorrowfully. The fire chief had been entertaining his mistress when the fire broke out and could not be disturbed. He alone was authorised to commission the fire engine. Ultimately, no action would be taken against him; his wife was the principal mistress of the mighty Field Marshal Praphan.

As for those who found themselves trapped in the elevator: to seek refuge there in the event of fire was foolish. People should make their way without panic to the nearest exit, not leap into elevators. The Rachanee kitchen staff, too, had clearly been negligent. If there were casualties, they had reaped the wages of sin.

Sya sped up, making for the southbound carriageway, revelling in the rush of air, freedom, and the sheer joy of being alive.

Raven

The whole kitchen below me must have been ablaze. The heat in the elevator was overpowering, and noxious fumes pouring up the shaft made me gag. I knew I could not survive here for long. In its wood and steel shaft the lift had become a roasting tin. The oil in the wood of the chair under me smouldered into secondary ignition. The flex that bound me was melting, and though the copper wire burned into my wrists and ankles, the heat made it malleable. Suddenly I found I had greater freedom of movement. I struggled like a madman to bring my body weight to bear as best I could. One lucky twist and my hands were free. I pulled the knife from its hidden sheath and cut though the molten wire.

My face felt seared as if by a blowtorch. I scrambled onto the disintegrating chair, ignoring the pain in my fingertips, and probed the ceiling until I found what I was looking for: the emergency panel in the roof of the lift. Sliding the tip of the knife behind it, I found the release button. As the chair finally gave way under me, I jumped, clawing and heaving my way through the gap onto the top of the cage.

It had jammed about four feet below the doors leading to the next floor, which I surmised must be the lobby. Sya had forced the shaft doors in the kitchen and jammed them open. The elevator, its electronic brain hopelessly confused, had malfunctioned.

I seized the taut elevator cable in my burned hands; gritting my teeth, I attempted to swing my legs up and kick the doors to the lobby. My legs seemed to be made of lead. My bloodied hands were losing their purchase. I leapt as high as I could, gripping the cable, and swung myself up until my naked toes found the ledge of the doorsill. I released the cable and thrust the full weight of my body against the doors, clinging with slippery fingers to the narrow doorframe.

Without warning, the elevator doors slid open. Accompanied by a choking cloud of smoke, I tumbled out, charred black, bleeding, and breathless, into the hotel lobby. I fell amid a panicked crowd, huddled together like a terrified herd, staring and gesticulating at the fumes rising from the stairwell and from the elevator behind me. Firemen were manoeuvring a powerful hose on a wheeled cart down the stairs to where the kitchen must have become an inferno. I should have known Sunii Lee would have her own private emergency services. Behind me, the charred remnants of the ruined lift I had escaped from gave a violent lurch and plunged down the shaft. There was a distant crash.

As people began to recover their nerve and craned forward to gape, I took advantage of their distraction and hurried off to beat a quiet retreat.

I had no time for explanations. I needed to make all possible speed.

Bangkok is accustomed to the extraordinary, familiar with freaks of all varieties. Unusual sights arouse little comment in Bangkok. Nobody stopped me on the street, despite the kenspeckle and villainous figure I must have cut, limping and lurching with the haste of my errand, smoke-blackened and bleeding. I must have looked like the lowest kind of human flotsam.

I stood on the edge of the street and hailed a passing samlor. The driver, a toothless, wizened sage, was unabashed; he appeared delighted that I accepted his exorbitant first price without quibble, just told him to get me to my destination. He welcomed me like a long-lost and wealthy brother. His chugging machine weaved in and out of the traffic like a hazardous fairground ride. I was too dazed even to cling to the sides and in consequence rattled about like a rotten nut in its shell. It was a relief to both of us when we arrived at the gate and I disembarked. I stuffed every tattered note still in my pocket into his eager, grubby hand.

Then I surveyed the portals of the American Embassy, which looked more like a fortress than a stage of diplomacy, exuding an air of closed and ponderous watchfulness. A respectable stone building, but with the usual trappings: a high spiked wall, formidable iron gates, and a Marine who could have stepped out of a recruiting poster. His pink chin was tilted aggressively. Barefoot and begrimed as I was, I refused to be intimidated when he blocked my path.

'Your business, sir?'

'I must see the ambassador.' I schooled impatience out of my voice.

'Sorry, sir. The United States Embassy is off limits to unauthorised personnel.'

'Look,' I said patiently. 'I have information regarding a potential international emergency. It would be advisable to allow me to pass.'

The boy was wavering. Perhaps my measured tone, or the drawling aristocratic English accent I employ for such encounters, impressed him;

but as he squinted down at me and caught sight of my battered and bloody wrists, the blood which had trickled down from my ankles to cake like rust my bare, grimy feet, his initial distrust returned.

'Please don't make trouble, sir!'

'I've no intention of making trouble. My name's Raven, I'm staying with the Drinkwaters—I'm a friend of General van Hooten, of SEATO. It is imperative I speak with the ambassador on a matter of great urgency.'

At that moment, two more soldiers appeared and, half-lifting me so I had to tiptoe not to fall on my face, marched me across the gravel drive, up two stone steps, and through a side door, ignoring my protests.

I found myself in a small, windowless room. They deposited me onto a narrow bed, turned about, and left. The door slammed and I was alone with my indignation and the chugging air conditioner. I looked round for a washbasin and somewhere to relieve myself, but the room offered nothing.

I fretted silently. The guard had seemed to recognise my name—or had I imagined it? I hammered on the door. It had not occurred to me to question Sya's account of the threat to Kissinger, as it fitted too well with events as I understood them. Sya's impassive delivery made it all too plausible. I was convinced he had taken Chee Laan, possibly as a hostage, and these thoughts overwhelmed me. I drummed my fists on the door, shouting spasmodically now, breathless with effort, my lungs still affected by the fumes I had inhaled in the fire.

When I was exhausted, I lay on the bed, despairing. The weight of the building seemed to press upon me. The moment for amateur heroics was past; I needed the assistance of the established order now to tell my tale of national peril, to protect Chee Laan. As I sat on the edge of the bunk and buried my head in my hands, I became aware of a cool blue eye regarding me through the observation port in the door.

I sprang to my feet. The eye disappeared, and the peephole cover fell into place. I waited, but there was no sound, nor did anyone twist the handle of the locked door. I sank back into the bed. Sometime later, the peephole was flicked aside once more, and a very different eye observed me—a lustrous, dark eye.

Laila Drinkwater's deep-throated cry of indignation jolted me out of my despair. 'Open this door at once! Of course this man is my houseguest—my dear professor, Dr Raven! Why have you locked him up like a criminal?'

Bolts rattled and shot back, the door swung open, and Laila burst in, golden jewellery jangling, black eyes flashing. 'Raven, you poor, dear man!' She seized my hands, then stood back and studied me. 'No wonder these imbeciles took you for a criminal! Such a state you are in!' She brushed ineffectually at my clothing.

'Laila! Thank God! Where is van Hooten? It's extremely urgent! Can you get hold of him?'

She shook her head. 'I'm sorry, Raven. That is not possible. He went out of town. But the ambassador is here, and he suggested they send for me, to identify one mysterious English tramp claiming to be staying in my house! It is better you speak to him. First, though, we should clean you up. Then Ambassador Morgan will see you.'

I shook my head. 'The ambassador will have to take me as he finds me, Laila. What I have to tell him is an international catastrophe in the making.'

Dwight C. Morgan, Minister Extraordinary and Plenipotentiary, Ambassador of the United States of America to the Royal Court of Thailand, proved to be a spare, silver-haired Bostonian. As I was ushered into his office, the ambassador rose to greet me with an expression of courteous concern on his handsome features. Behind him, on the wall, Richard Nixon and the First Lady were pictured disembarking from Air Force One, Nixon's hand extended toward the figure of Ambassador Morgan in much the same gesture of welcome. I glanced from one to the other, and felt a momentary relief that I was dealing with the patrician before me rather than the man in the picture.

'Dr Raven! Please do sit down, sir, sit down! My apologies for the misunderstanding, it has all been sorted. Now, my dear sir, what can I offer you by way of refreshment? You've had quite an ordeal. A fire at the Rachanee Hotel, I understand—terrible business. Fortunately there was no loss of life on this occasion.'

The ambassador gestured toward a sofa upholstered in heavy, thready Thai cotton. The interview was to be informal and professional. I found this marginally encouraging.

'A little fortification?' Morgan opened a cupboard in the desk and took out a bottle and two glasses. He poured the bourbon expertly, a two-finger measure exactly. 'Now.' Morgan sat back in the sofa, nursing his glass, and studied me amicably. 'It seems you've learned our little secret, that the Embassy has been entertaining a distinguished guest. Dr Kissinger has indeed been here—I won't say incognito, because that would be impossible, his name and his face are well known throughout the civilised world. But he's keeping a low profile. No official engagements, no announcements.'

'I know what he has come for,' I said.

Morgan smiled broadly. 'He has come to see how the war progresses. That's obvious.'

'So he wasn't planning on a trip to Red China, from Mae Sod airstrip upcountry, off the record. Is that right?'

Now Morgan frowned, the easy smile abandoned. 'The State Department has no knowledge of such a trip. Let me state that quite categorically. No such information has been received. What would be the objective?'

'Making smooth the path for him that shall come after,' I suggested, and waited for his reaction. I sipped the bourbon. It was as good as I'd hoped. But I was puzzled by the ambassador's bewilderment. I could have sworn it was genuine.

'You are suggesting…' Morgan tapped his fingers on his glass, contemplated the brownish liquid, 'that Dr Kissinger is undertaking a preparatory visit to Communist China without the knowledge of the State Department?'

'Yes. I also have information that this intelligence has been compromised and that if Dr Kissinger were to undertake such a mission, he would meet with an accident. It is possible that his plane would be shot down over the jungle by disaffected elements in the locality.'

Morgan stared at me with a sparkling ice-blue understanding. Apparently convinced, he rose and lifted the receiver of one of the telephones on his desk. 'Henry?' He spoke with a low-voiced deference, despite the familiarity. 'This is Dwight. Good morning.' He paused and looked at me, as if there were some point he were trying to make, some confirmation he sought. 'Henry, this trip of yours. Stormy weather forecast. Suggest you postpone. And Henry? Can we talk…?'

The reply was brief and sharp. Morgan held the receiver away from his ear, nodded, and replaced it softly. When he looked back at me his handsome face had tightened and the gleam of the blue gaze had dulled. He appeared tense.

'Dr Raven, I feel you are owed an explanation. May I suggest you take a shower and we eat some brunch together? I'll send a car for your effects. Mrs Drinkwater will assist us, I feel sure.'

'There's something else I must tell you.' I chose my words carefully. 'Two young Thai women were present at the Rachanee with me. I need to know that they were uninjured, that they escaped the fire.' I watched the imperceptible twist of distaste that passed quickly as a cloud over Morgan's fastidious countenance.

'It can be pretty hard to keep track of these ladies,' Morgan said coldly.

I answered, equally coldly, 'One of these ladies is the granddaughter of the owner of the Rachanee, Miss Chee Laan Lee, of the banking family. The other is the former fiancée of his late Highness, Prince Toom Premsakul.'

'Ah.' Morgan relaxed. 'That sort of young lady. You know.' He leaned confidentially toward me. 'Miss Lee's grandmother is the richest woman in the city, probably in all of Southeast Asia! The word is the granddaughter will inherit.'

The thought of Chee Laan's fortune, which I habitually repressed, ambushed me now with irritation. If Morgan noticed my doleful expression, he doubtless courteously ascribed it to my recent ordeals.

'I am hoping they have managed to leave the hotel,' I explained. 'If they are able to do so, I am sure they will be on their way to seek help from their friends.'

'Any idea where these ladies might be headed in that case, Raven?'

'To Hua Hin, to the king. We need to move quickly. They are most certainly in danger.'

'Dr Raven,' said Ambassador Morgan, 'I think you'd better tell me the whole story.'

'I would be happy to get it off my chest, sir.'

Thonburi-Paktho Road, Southbound, Bangkok to Hua Hin

Chee Laan drove through the night like a demon. The handcuff and heavy chain on her wrist clattered against the gear lever and occasionally she cursed out loud, but she never took her foot off the accelerator. The little car clung to the road, bouncing through potholes, veering violently to avoid the occasional sleeping buffalo or pye-dog, or the wrecks of burnt-out trucks. Salikaa at first crouched beside her, grinning through the windscreen, teeth bared, exhilarated by the speed and her driver's reckless dexterity. But she soon grew bored, huddled down, and dozed.

They reached Hua Hin Thonburi-Paktho Road, Southbound as dawn was breaking. The sunrise blushed the fairytale summer palace into a confection of pink barley sugar, and kissed to radiant life the pink and scarlet of roses and hibiscus. The palace of Sans Souci lay like a turreted toy amid its enchanted garden, nestling in a half-moon of wooded compound dotted with the holiday villas occupied by the Inner Circle, and beyond this, the outer half-moon containing military barracks and guardrooms. Along the palace's colonnaded façade, silver waves lapped indolently on a beach as fine and white as table salt. The palace compound was stirring. The raucous awakening of the sacred cockatoo on his perch had in turn roused the sacred elephant in his wooden hut, and the royal doves crooned and caressed in their bamboo cages. The kitchens clattered into life.

Chee Laan drove up to the guard post and the car bucketed to a standstill. The soldier on guard approached. Salikaa rolled down her window and said in her haughtiest voice: 'I am a member of the Premsakul family. Please let us into the royal compound.'

The guard was young and eager to oblige his betters, but he had heard the gossip. He hesitated, at a loss. 'Heartbroken, ladies. *Sia chai*.' He touched his heart. 'You wait. I call someone.'

Salikaa raised her voice. 'Are you defying me? How long do you intend to keep us hanging about here?' She tapped her hand loudly on the side of the car door. The boy pressed his radio to his ear and with his free hand made a placating gesture, entreating them to wait.

Chee Laan chewed on the last strands of her patience for a moment, fighting the surge of adrenaline within her. Then she made up her mind.

'Down!' she shouted to Salikaa. She gunned the engine and the little car shot under the barrier, passing beneath it with only an inch or two above the windscreen, and into the compound, carving up the edge of the lawn. Salikaa only just managed to cower down in her seat as the barrier swept overhead. The guard began shouting and ran a few strides after them, but Salikaa had already pointed the way to the king's private apartments; she had the door open before the car came to a standstill and was racing up the steps, Chee Laan hard on her heels.

Outside the king's portal, two yawning footmen were adjusting their headdresses and scratching beneath their baggy silk pants. They were too surprised to stop Salikaa, who rushed past them, thrusting open the massive carved teak door and disappearing inside.

Chee Laan was slower; one of the footmen seized her by the arm. Through the open doorway she could see Salikaa had thrown herself on the floor before the young king. The startled boy, rudely awakened, was still in his sleeping robe, standing beside his untidy bed. Barefoot and drowsy, his hair ruffled, he had the bemused truculence of any teenager awoken from his slumbers. He stared down in bewilderment as Salikaa clutched his bare feet and panted, gazing up at him.

'Your Majesty must listen to me! Save me, Majesty! They tried to murder me!'

'Salikaa!' the king exclaimed. Then there was silence.

Chee Laan felt the moment imprint itself on her brain. Salikaa and the king stared at each other. The footmen, holding Chee Laan between them, gaped at the Chinese girl with a handcuff dangling from her wrist; they looked at the king and Salikaa, glanced at each other, and then prostrated themselves, overawed.

Before another word could be said, they all heard it—all five turned their heads toward the sound. Several pairs of heavy boots were approaching at a run. Up the steps behind Chee Laan thundered a squad of Border Patrol Police at full speed. They halted briskly and stood to attention. From behind them emerged the figure of Sya Dam, and his presence ripped at Chee Laan's heart.

Sya had replaced his motorcyclist's gear with his uniform and now stepped forward, his formal cap under his arm. 'At ease!' he barked to the soldiers. Then he sauntered forward and bowed to the king's feet. 'Good morning, Your Majesty. I fear we have disturbed Your Majesty's rest.' To the footmen he snapped, 'Hand His Majesty a more fitting robe, and look sharp!' They scurried to obey, throwing a heavy robe about the king's shoulders.

Sya pointed to Salikaa, crouched like a cornered leopard, her flashing eyes fixed on him. She was breathing hard; through her open mouth the points of her sharp white teeth gleamed. She was still clutching the flame-coloured gown she had snatched from the Rachanee. Now, as they looked on, she threw the chiffon dress over her head. Chee Laan caught a glimpse of a smooth golden shoulder as Salikaa removed the blue top Chee Laan had lent her. She eased off her jeans under the skirt, and loosened the band that held her hair.

Fully transformed, she spun round and faced the king, holding her arms out wide. 'Don't say you don't recognise me, my dear, dear Majesty!' she cried, falling to her knees once more. Chee Laan thought she had never been more beautiful, with her vivid face, her cloud of blue-black hair. The king could not take his eyes off her. He drank in the vision.

Sya stepped forward, determined to break the spell, a cruel smile on his lips. 'We should not waste Your Majesty's time with these unworthy matters. This criminal,' he indicated Salikaa, 'managed to escape. Now we have recaptured her.'

'Sanctuary!' shouted Salikaa, feeling her moment of power evaporating. She lunged in a desperate attempt to grasp the king's leg or the hem of his garment. With a visible effort he pulled himself together and moved adroitly out of her reach.

'On the contrary, Colonel. Everything that concerns my subjects concerns me,' he said loftily, and it struck those who heard him that for the first time the teenager sounded like a sovereign, projecting something like the measured dignity and self-assurance dictated by the role. 'You may await me in the great hall. I will join you in a moment. Go now.'

Sya bowed slowly. Then he signalled to his men, and they rushed forward and grabbed Salikaa, dragging her unceremoniously from the chamber. The footmen relinquished their grip on Chee Laan's arms and entered the king's chamber, closing the door behind them. As the soldiers hauled Salikaa, kicking and shrieking, down the steps toward the great hall, Sya turned to Chee Laan.

'You don't need to see this,' he remarked, with affected casualness. 'Why don't you go home?'

'I came here with Salikaa,' Chee Laan replied, walking down the steps. 'I'm not leaving without her.'

Sya's mocking laughter rang in her ears as she followed the echo of Salikaa's screeches and made her way to the great hall.

When she entered, she saw the soldiers standing just inside the doorway, with Salikaa slumped between them. She was no longer struggling. It looked as though the soldiers had nearly dislocated her shoulders. She stood quietly, marshalling her forces for the last confrontation. At Sya's signal a soldier reached for Chee Laan. Furiously she shrugged him off, and he relaxed his hold, but remained standing very close to her. If she made any rash move, it was clear that he would seize her again.

At last the king entered the hall from the other side. Now formally attired, he stood on the steps, looking down at them all.

'Would someone please tell me what this is all about?' he demanded.

'Your Majesty,' Sya said, stepping forward, 'it is simple. This woman is a murderess.' He pointed to Salikaa.

The king studied Salikaa as if he had never seen her before. Reflectively, he said, 'Well, she is very beautiful, whoever she is. Whom did she murder?'

'She murdered her husband!' Sya announced triumphantly. The king shook his head in disapproval.

'Your Majesty,' Salikaa shouted, 'it's a lie! General Sya tried to have me killed. He is a traitor and a murderer!' She jerked her chin toward Chee Laan. 'Say something, Chee Laan! Tell him!'

The king noticed Chee Laan for the first time. 'Who are you?' he asked. 'What is your involvement with all this?'

'She knows the truth!' Salikaa cried. 'She knows what Sya Dam is! Ask her!'

'So you are a witness?' the king said. Chee Laan bowed and nodded.

'In a manner of speaking, Your Majesty,' she said.

'Hm,' the king murmured. 'A witness wearing a handcuff.'

He was nonplussed. They could all see it. He was, after all, only a boy. Nothing in his life had prepared him for this situation. A turmoil of emotions flickered briefly across his countenance before his features composed themselves once more into the mask of regal impassivity. He looked at the soldiers. 'Who is second in command here?' The sergeant saluted and grovelled. 'Arrest both of these accused persons,' the king commanded. 'I will listen to their statements and the evidence later.'

'Your Majesty—arrest the colonel?' stammered the sergeant, looking from one to the other in an agony of doubt.

The king nodded. 'Precisely.'

'Your Majesty!' Salikaa screamed. Sya said nothing. The king turned on his heel.

'Get these people out of my sight!' he said over his shoulder. 'I have not even had my breakfast yet.'

Sya marched out in silence, upright between the soldiers, overshadowing them, although they were tall men, too. Salikaa thrashed about until the strong hands of her guards overpowered her.

Klai Kangwon Summer Palace, Hua Hin

Chee Laan had been kindly received and escorted, after her interrogation, to one of the small villas to spend the night. She had lain awake for much of it, falling into an uneasy slumber a few hours before dawn. She awoke disorientated. Then memory of where she was and why came flooding back. She got up and went to the window and stood contemplating the luxurious view.

In her practical way, she considered her options. Salikaa and Sya were under arrest. She was desperate to start her search for Raven. He couldn't be dead. She'd have known if he were dead.

She had tried the door of her spacious en suite bedroom the night before. It was not locked, but two armed men dozed fitfully outside. Now a servant knocked discreetly—just as Ah Lee once had, in case Chee Laan's spirit had not yet returned to her body from its nocturnal wanderings, causing her to wake up mad beyond any cure. When Chee Laan responded, the servant padded silently in with coffee, toast, and a courteously written summons to come to the guardroom.

The coffee was black as hot tar. Swilling half a cup of the bitter brew, she showered and threw on her clothes, travel-stained and crumpled. When she emerged from the room, the waiting servant silently led the way.

Her interrogators were two elderly princes taking their holiday at the palace. Conveniently, both were judges of the Thai Supreme Court. They showed the most curiosity about Salikaa's huge warder, Archin, and questioned Chee Laan closely on what she knew about Sya Dam's radio broadcasts, but when she admitted that she spoke no tribal language, they lost interest in her.

The Prince Regent entered unannounced, and the judges bowed

creakingly to the floor. He abruptly demanded their decision. With a startled glance at Chee Laan, one judge said: 'He throws himself on Your Highness's mercy.'

The Prince Regent shook his head sadly. 'Personal sympathies cannot interfere with the course of justice. The colonel must face a military tribunal.' He sighed, looking old, his eyes hollow. 'It is a temptation to take betrayals personally, and to forget that they are usually dictated by mere convenience. I confess I have little appetite for vengeance.' He examined his supple musician's fingers, flexing the joints. Then he announced, with renewed resolve, 'I shall not grant audience to the prisoner until sentence has been passed. It might prejudice the course of justice.'

Chee Laan, wrestling with her own betrayals, was engulfed by a wave of surprise and respect.

'Doubtless you will wish to return to your home now, Miss Lee,' one of the judges suggested gently. She understood that her own supporting role in the story was now exhausted. They were impatient for her to leave the stage. But Chee Laan had unfinished business.

'May I see my friend, Miss Salikaa?' she asked.

The dignified old men looked at each other. Then the senior judge shrugged. 'Why not? Just for a few minutes.'

Chee Laan found Salikaa pale but undefeated. Indeed, she appeared to have regained a little of her old hectic animation. She still wore Chee Laan's flame-coloured evening dress. Her hair was glossy and her eyes shone. Chee Laan could not tell whether her exhilaration could be considered a favourable sign. They exchanged *wai*s, then, impulsively, embraced.

'Chee Laan, dear, you look distraught! Your *farang bien-aimé*?'

'I am worried about Raven,' she admitted. 'I'm just praying he managed to get away after his confrontation with Sya at the Rachanee. At least Sya can't hurt him right now.' She looked hard at Salikaa. 'I'm worried for you as well, Salikaa. What's going to happen to you?'

'Nothing, of course. What should they do? Drag me out and shoot me?' Salikaa threw her head back and laughed. 'They'd never dare, because of the king. If I spilled the beans about our little romance it would discredit him. They can't afford that. None of them could survive it. If Vajah topples, they all topple, like a house of cards!' She looked at Chee Laan with the confidence of one savouring personal power. 'Besides, Vajah would never permit it.'

'But you've confessed to murder, Salikaa!'

Salikaa tossed her head impatiently. 'Oh, I shall plead self-defence.'

Chee Laan regarded her dubiously. 'The central government is wooing the tribes in a big way. How could they acquit a Thai wife who admits to murdering her tribal husband? If the tribes got hold of it, it would cause uproar—and Sya would manage to get the story spread, even from prison.'

'Oh, they won't acquit me—they're not complete imbeciles!' Salikaa laughed. 'They'll eventually "allow" me to escape and flee the country. Hopefully set me up with a nice little nest egg.'

Chee Laan studied her thoughtfully. 'You might just disappear. The Chao Phaya River holds many secrets. And once a funeral pyre starts to smoulder, who can say to whom the bodies once belonged?'

Salikaa grinned. Without make-up, the sinews of her jaw were taut. Hers was a strong, determined face. She pressed herself briefly against Chee Laan. Chee Laan had a fleeting impression of embracing a young tamarisk tree, sturdy, flexible, and brimming with sap.

Ignoring her friend's embarrassment, Salikaa rubbed a firm cheek against Chee Laan's and murmured, 'Take my advice, Chee Laan. Marry your big-nose *farang*. Breed a bushel of round-eye babies. Seek new pastures. To remain in this ungrateful country will break your heart!'

Her blue-black ponytail snapped sharply across Chee Laan's face as she turned, like the caress of a cat o' nine tails. Chee Laan's nostrils caught the hot scent of musk. She pulled away from the embrace and said bitterly, 'Didn't you know, Salikaa? My heart is too cool to break. I'm a Jek.' She held out her hands in a gesture of resignation.

They had forgotten the attendant, who now cleared his throat loudly. It was time to leave.

American Embassy, Bangkok

Raven
'In our interpretation of events, Dr Raven, the State Department has reason to be grateful to you,' the American ambassador said, putting down the phone. 'Our distinguished visitor left the Embassy this morning.'

His relief was obvious. He pulled a book from the shelf, revealing behind it a bottle of bourbon and two glasses with ox-leather belts. The glass was dark and full of facets within the smooth surface. The ambassador ran a finger over the leather and sighed gently. 'Italian. Venice—my last posting. Wonderful! Verdi. Michelangelo. I kind of miss that.' He poured, and while he did so, he spoke, still in that measured tone. 'There is a feeling, Dr Raven, that the State Department has been—I don't say *deliberately*, I don't say *kept in the dark*—possibly not put in the picture here. Doubtless for reasons of "need to know." Caution in such circumstances may be understandable. But it is not complimentary.' I replied with a grunt. I hoped it sounded both sympathetic and noncommittal. We raised the Venetian glasses to our lips at the same time and contemplated the moment with solemn reverence, as though partaking of a sacrament. Then the ambassador said, 'Now, is there something I can do for you, Dr Raven, in return?'

'Can you get me a couple of passes to see Colonel Sya Dam in prison?'

Chee Laan was safe, and for me, that was enough. I had no wish to tempt fate myself, but I appreciated that she had scores to settle.

'*Two* passes?' Ambassador Morgan frowned. He twisted his glass this way and that, swirling the liquid. Then he laughed. 'I'll say one thing for you, Raven. You know the value of your favours. Well, leave it with me. I'll see what I can do. One or two folks out there owe me, too.'

———

Everything was different now that I knew she was unharmed. She had driven straight to the Drinkwaters to find me, or rather, to discover if I was still alive. I interpreted this as a sign that my well-being held some importance for her.

My hostess, for so lively a woman, could be discretion itself. She left us to our own devices. We did not fall weeping into each other's arms with shrill cries of relief—we were neither of us given to histrionics. We just stood and contemplated each other for a moment or two. We felt overwhelmed by relief, certainly, and a hint of the self-congratulation experienced by those who have narrowly escaped death; and for my part there was the painful pounding of the heart that told me in no uncertain terms that losing her would have destroyed me. While I stood there like a sleepwalker, she moved closer and delicately examined my battered head with her fingers, soft and cool as petals. She pulled a wry face, grimacing up at me in sympathy.

We inspected each other's wounds. Her wrist was bruised from the handcuffs. The palace locksmith had cut them off, she told me, laughing shakily, running her fingers lightly over my scorched hair and the black flecks that marked the skin of my face like tattoos. When she saw my charred fingertips she drew her breath in sharply and said, 'You saved a great deal of money there, Raven. It costs a lot to have fingerprints eradicated. Yours have been burned off for free!' She raised them one by one to her lips, the way I had once seen a mother kiss a baby's hands.

Chee Laan's eyes sought mine, intense as the first sparks burning in yellow paper. She told me about the confrontation at the summer palace. And then she made her request. She wanted to see Sya Dam. She was adamant.

'It won't be easy,' I objected. 'He's under close watch. The military tribunal has found him guilty of treason and sentenced him to death by firing squad. Amazing—I never thought they'd go so far.'

'Didn't you?' She released my hand and frowned. 'Oh, I did! The moment the Prince Regent withdrew his support, Sya's enemies were just waiting to strike.'

'There's certainly a lot of talk everywhere.' Even I had heard it. 'Talk of betrayal, corruption, ingratitude. Very high-minded.'

'Only Prince Premsakul says what everyone really thinks.'

'What's that?'

'Once an Akha, always an Akha.' Her eyes held me. 'I want to see him nonetheless.'

Security at the jail was tight, as I had expected. I had never imagined that Morgan's influence would be able to eliminate every barrier to communication with the condemned prisoner, and in this I was correct. Perhaps I had not anticipated finding myself staring into the business end of an assault rifle, though, just as Chee Laan and I entered the long, low grey building.

I gently lifted the barrel and pointed it away from my heart. '*Sawasdi krup!*' I said politely.

'No foreign journalist!' The fox-faced young captain wore his cap so far down over his nose that he needed to tilt his head back in order to meet my eyes.

'We're friends,' I said winningly. I held up the box of Olde English Luxury Assortment. 'See? Friends, bringing presents...' The biscuit box was whisked out of my hands and conveyed into the depths of the jail. When it came back five minutes later the cellophane seal had been broken. The lid was askew. Inside, the ruffled paper cases of the biscuits were disordered. But the officer was smiling now.

'Please!' He ushered us into a comfortable room and invited us to sit on cretonne-covered wicker chairs. After a few minutes, Sya Dam strode in, clean-shaven, his uniform band-box fresh as usual. I think Chee Laan had half-expected—I don't say hoped—to find him stumbling in leg-irons like other condemned criminals, but his arrogance was undimmed, and his manner was bland, charming, not in the least impressed by our presence.

He had scarcely sat down when there was a muffled knock and an officer, coughing with embarrassment, peered round the door. He bowed apologetically, but Sya laughed uproariously and leapt to his feet, holding out his arms as if in a fine Chinese tailor's fitting room.

'He has come to measure me for the target,' Sya proclaimed jovially. The officer bowed low before touching Sya's head. Sya lit a cigarette, curving his shapely lips around it. The eyes of the officer measuring him for the target and the shroud were bright with panic, but the condemned man's yellow wolf-eyes, narrowed against the smoke, were only faintly amused.

'Do you want to check body weight also?' he asked, adding, 'I understand that's customary.'

The officer snapped to attention. He saluted smartly and replied in a breathless shout, eyes on the distant wall, 'Beg to inform you, Colonel, sir, only customary to take body weight for hangings. Also garottings. For shooting, measurements only.'

'I see. You need to check at what distance your so-called marksmen can be relied upon not to miss. But then, I present a pretty broad target!' Sya chuckled. Chee Laan's expression was blank with horror.

'Beg to inform you, sir, measuring for painting of target mark, sir. On back of tent, sir!'

Sya drew a deep breath and tapped the ash off his cigarette into his hand. The floor of the military prison interview room was less filthy than most of the cells. He glanced around, and the officer held out his hand. Sya crumbled the ash into it.

'So the great Thai nation is to be denied the full spectacle?'

'Please, sir. Shooting within tent, sir!'

Sya turned to Chee Laan and myself, eyebrows raised. 'Hardly giving them their money's worth, is it? Are they not to be permitted to search my agonised countenance for edifying signs of repentance?'

'No, sir. Anyway, sir...' The officer hesitated, shuffled his feet, wrung with embarrassment.

'Anyway what?' Sya drawled.

'Beg to inform you, Colonel, sir. There's the bag. The bag, sir. They put a bag over the head...'

Sya began to laugh softly and the young officer hastily gathered up his notepad, his yard rule and tape measure, and saluted. Sya returned the salute with parade-ground precision. He turned for a moment to the small barred window, which transformed a rectangle of blazing sky into a noughts and crosses grid. The young man turned back in the doorway and looked at Sya, his eyes full of pain.

'I'm sorry, sir. About the bag.'

Sya did not turn around. He stubbed his cigarette out on the window frame. When at last he turned to face us, he was grinning. He motioned to the biscuit tin.

'I am in no condition to eat biscuits, my friend. I take too little exercise. However, under the circumstances I shall not need to keep my teeth sound for my old age!' He threw back his head and guffawed, amused by Chee Laan's expression of consternation.

'A great loss!' he declared. 'What a spry old fellow I should have made, still siring sons at ninety!'

His mood changed and he leaned on the table, peering into my face.

'Tell your people this. Whoever sent you—' He waved my attempt at protest aside. 'No, no, my friend: it is too late for weaving fairy tales. Whoever sent you, tell them my revolution is coming. Nothing can stop it. Who will stop it? The Americans?'

He gave a snort of contempt.

'The Asian mind remains a mystery to the pragmatic Westerner. Some of you wallow in Eastern mysticism, yet the fundamental concepts of predestination escape you. Others despise us slant-eyed gooks, because of the way we look, or talk, or walk—but we elude them, too, because our mindset is essentially different. Western progress is linear, but Oriental progress is circular. Where these lines meet is mathematically limited. So much for any cooperation and intercultural understanding. Ask her.' He jerked his head toward Chee Laan, who was listening intently. 'She knows.'

'Is murder circular?' I asked. 'The Americans are aware of your plan to assassinate the Secretary of State.' I watched his face for signs of disappointment or rage, but the untroubled countenance remained smooth as a golden egg. I persisted: 'Kissinger will be warned off—he will not use the airstrip in the Golden Triangle. The flight will be rerouted, probably via Islamabad. But Kissinger will still go to Beijing. The bid to pave the way for an international détente will not be abandoned.'

'*Détente*! Fancy word for defeat!' he scoffed.

But I pressed for more, some kind of acknowledgement. 'You understand, Colonel? You will have changed nothing.'

'Oh, but you are wrong. I have changed everything!' Sya said. 'You Westerners have little sense of timing, and none whatever of time itself. For you, everything must happen at once. You do not understand the convergence of destiny.' A soldier entered, saluted, whispered discreetly to Sya. Sya rose and said in English: 'If that aircraft does not appear on schedule, those who wait in the shadows will send word to the La-wa and the Karen that the time has come to rise. So you see, I win either way.'

He extended a hand and pronounced a little valediction, speaking, as far as I could tell, without a trace of irony.

'My death will be the trigger. And now you will forgive me. No hard feelings, eh? We each did our duty, Dr Raven. Miss Chee Laan, I have little time left, and already I have another visitor. She is beautiful, but rather shy...' He stretched out his hand and shook my own, gripping my elbow in a manly fashion, like a Roman gladiator. 'Goodbye. I do not expect we shall meet again. Watch out for my television debut. Fame will find each of us, if we wait our turn.' He wagged a finger in mischievous reproof. 'Patience, Dr Raven. Another Eastern virtue.' Then he swung on his heel and disappeared into the inner recesses of the building, ignoring his escorts.

Laila had provided my gift, the large square English biscuit tin, adorned with garish scenes and containing wafers like pink cardboard and shortbread like Highland granite. It stood forlornly on the little glass-topped table, a discarded toy. The soldier picked the tin up and bore it ceremoniously after Colonel Sya Dam's departing figure.

The Van Hooten Residence, Bangkok

Van Hooten received Dr Pien's diagnosis of his daughter's condition with horror. He resolved that Genty must be removed from Bangkok at once and flown home for treatment. His wife, however, protested. Taylor van Hooten had undertaken another commission in Switzerland, and was not eager to return to the States.

For once, van Hooten imposed his will. He was accompanying a VIP, codenamed 'Cicero', to the northwest, there to liaise with another aircraft and transfer the precious passenger. His wife and daughter would accompany him. From Mae Sod, they would fly to Singapore and then to the States.

But at the last moment, Taylor refused to go. She stated that she had an urgent overseas commission for the Princess, and a flight booked to Switzerland. Van Hooten regarded her grimly. 'Sometimes, Taylor, I could swear the Thai royal family mean more to you than the welfare of your own child'.

'They certainly have more attractive manners,' she said evenly. She turned away, indicating that the matter was closed.

Van Hooten knew better than to argue, but he felt choked with frustration and anger that she had made other plans which she had not deigned to communicate to him until the last minute, thus pushing his own schedule awry. This had latterly become her habit, since she had 'travelled within court circles', as he thought of it. She was no longer content with the lot of the military bride, the acquiescent camp follower, willing to up sticks when her husband's superiors ordered moves and manoeuvres. He had never wanted her to be a doormat, merely accommodating, but she was growing tyrannical, and he resolved to have it out with her when he had dealt with the more pressing problems of their child's health.

'We need to hurry, Genty,' he shouted up the stairs. 'We need to leave right now, please!' There was no sound from above. In the end, van Hooten had to carry his daughter out to the waiting vehicle. She lay in his arms limp as a rag.

When they reached the aircraft they were already half an hour adrift. The uniformed pilot was standing on the tarmac beside it, looking pointedly at his watch and then, shielding his eyes, at the sunny sky. Van Hooten sensed the pilot's irritation and, with muttered apologies, hustled his daughter aboard the small aircraft. For once Genty was no trouble, numb with shock and heavily sedated. He settled her into her seat and took his own. He leaned back, breathed deeply and composed himself to await the arrival of the other passenger.

The pilot returned from a brief but necessary excursion to the neighbouring jungle, buttoning his fly. He consulted his watch yet again, with increasing concern. He resented the fact that he had to fly to some godforsaken paddy field for a rendezvous where he would have to attempt to land on a postage stamp ringed by jungle. Where was this VIP he was instructed to wait for? He shrugged, and, with a last glance at the road, climbed back into the cockpit. His co-pilot looked up and wrenched at his headset.

'Can you beat it? Another goddamn snafu! Urgent message!' he said.

The pilot stared at him, angry and uncomprehending.

'Change of plans.' The co-pilot grimaced. 'Cicero will not be joining us after all. Just some mechanic—big dopey-looking local. Turned up while you were otherwise engaged. Truck just dumped him. No paperwork, of course. Typical! Had to show him how to fasten his fucking belt, would you believe? Just down from the trees! But these other bods still need transporting. Same destination.'

'Control tell us how come?'

The co-pilot sighed in exasperation. 'You know better than that. Never apologise, never explain. Probably a standard case of paranoia.'

'Paranoia or politics. Same difference.'

'Security double-checked the crate? They've had plenty of time to...'

'Yeah. Let's get this turkey basted. I just hope the hopheads have got the landing flares lighted.'

Van Hooten had averted his eyes discreetly when the third passenger entered and took his place in the seat behind him. He had a sense of a bulky figure, and thought ironically that Cicero had wrapped up well for the journey. He heard the seat creak, and as the little aircraft shuddered in takeoff and the engine roared, he felt a large hand coming round the edge of his seat, in line with his neck. His last thought was that Cicero was about to pat him on the shoulder, a friendly gesture; he smiled in appreciation of the great man's camaraderie. He was still smiling when the massive fingers closed around his windpipe.

Mae Sod, Northwest Thailand

In the shadows at the edge of the airstrip, the tribesmen waited silently, standing reverently around their new toy. Their leader's association with the Black Tiger colonel had brought many benefits, but none so amazing as this killing machine which could, they had been told, blow a great foreign thunderbird right out of the sky, or rip through a hundred police jeeps one behind the other. They tried to imagine what that would look like. The weapon could be used to devastating effect to protect their opium fields and trading routes. At first, their orders had been to shoot down a plane for Sya Dam. Now, they were merely to make a couple of corpses disappear. Sya Dam did not like loose ends, or people who knew too much.

Their keen ears caught the distant whine of the aircraft's approach. The landing strip was lighted with flares. Now at last they saw the plane, circling high and then coming lower. For a brief moment they thought it would plunge into the jungle. They obeyed their instructions to the letter, dousing their flares so the pilot would not be able to land. The aircraft hung almost motionless, its engines screaming. A door opened—some claimed later that they had heard cries, but others said it was just the engines. Two bodies plummeted out of the dark sky and struck the earth with a dull thud. Then the plane soared up, and the next moment it was gone, its lights winking as it gained height. The jungle was silent once more.

The tribesmen lit their flares again, located the two bodies, and approached them cautiously, hoping no ghosts were hovering around in the darkness. They examined the girl curiously, touching her pale skin and yellow hair, and acquired a few souvenirs before their leader recalled them sharply to their appointed task.

'Fetch wood!' the headman ordered. 'Black Tiger commanded us to destroy every trace!'

'The Black Tiger is wise!' they murmured approvingly. They brought the wood, cut and stacked in readiness, and the can of petrol from the palm-roofed storage hut, and improvised a funeral pyre. It billowed scarlet and orange, gorgeous as a poppy dream. Hot air and fumes licked their faces raw. They glimpsed each other's gleaming tobacco-coloured cheeks, and their eyes glistened like the jade eyes of idols. When the flames died down at last they wandered, singing, back to the village.

On the way, they passed a shrine, and the more devout bowed before the resident spirit, and placed in offering upon its carved table some metal buttons emblazoned with eagles, torn from the uniform of the general.

Those who had removed Genty's silver chains and her star sapphire rings, however, kept them as payment for the village beauties.

The Premsakul Residence, Bangkok, Thailand

His Serene Highness Prince Premsakul was more agitated than Field Marshal Praphan had ever seen him. Against all the rules of decorum, he greeted the general at his door in person, and hurried him up the carved wooden staircase into the house, glancing anxiously toward the compound gate, which the gardener had shut behind the general's Mercedes with a swift thud.

'Welcome to my unworthy home!' he muttered automatically, with none of his usual bonhomie. Field Marshal Praphan himself was so preoccupied he almost forgot to remove his shoes at the prince's threshold. He had that morning endured a most unsettling interview with the American ambassador, who had learned that an aircraft had been unable to land upcountry as arranged, the landing flares having been mysteriously extinguished at the last minute. More importantly, upon returning to base, other discoveries were made: the stewardess had been strangled, and General van Hooten and his daughter had disappeared. So had the extra passenger—an unknown mechanic. He was described as an enormous man; in keeping with this description, he appeared to have wrestled open an emergency exit and made his escape while the plane was still taxiing to its position on the military runway. Special Forces had been immediately dispatched to the area, and a search of the Mae Sod airstrip resulted in the retrieval of certain objects identified as belonging to the missing persons.

Two Americans had been murdered. Now Ambassador Morgan wanted to know what the Thai authorities proposed to do about it.

The two powerful men, both heavy of heart and of physique, sat opposite one another on the gold brocade sofas. They stared at each other with expressions dark with foreboding. Praphan was the first to break the ominous silence.

'He's behind it, of course,' he spluttered. 'That damned Sya. Now we've got the Yanks breathing down our necks! He's a loose cannon. Never trusted him! Even in gaol, we can't control him! We'll have to go through with it.'

Premsakul nodded thoughtfully, caressing his chin. 'Of course, originally the arrangement was that the wretched chap's execution was to be cancelled at the last moment.'

Praphan nodded, nervously glancing around to make sure no servant was eavesdropping. He had the military man's innate distrust of security arrangements made by people other than himself. 'Eleventh-hour reprieve, courtesy of the intervention of a higher authority.'

'No,' Premsakul said slowly. He licked his lips. 'We cannot possibly stand by him now, General. He has gone too far!'

'He's a mad dog!' Praphan declared vehemently, striking his fist on the arm of his chair. 'He's got to be stopped!'

'I think, perhaps,' Premsakul said slowly, 'all that wild talk about Sya fomenting rebellion could be just what the doctor ordered.'

'You mean,' Praphan demanded, reluctant to relinquish a chance to assert their old rivalry and cause some discomfort to his ally, 'the wild talk started by that charming young thing who was engaged to your late son, Prince Toom?'

Prince Premsakul's smooth brow contracted briefly at the question. 'Precisely so. I thought it fanciful at the time, I confess, but possibly there was something in it after all. No smoke without fire, eh?'

'So you feel the moment has come to…' Praphan left the thought unfinished.

'To withdraw with discretion. Disassociate ourselves.' Prince Premsakul smiled with satisfaction and clasped his pudgy hands comfortably about his paunch. 'Sever all connections. Just the ticket!'

'Precisely!' Praphan smiled as well.

'I'll explain to His Highness the Prince Regent that a reprieve will not be necessary, after all. Sensible fellow, the Prince Regent. He'll understand. He knows when it is politic to understand matters which are carefully explained to him. Care for a drink, old man?' Prince Premsakul clapped his hands for the servant. 'I'd say we more than deserve one.'

Bangkok, Thailand

Raven

I glanced through the newspaper article once more. It was written in Thai, but I could make out the gist of it at least.

Sya Gets Death

A horrified nation will witness today the well-deserved punishment of the notorious Akha tribesman known as Sya Dam ('the Black Tiger', Ed.), condemned to death by firing squad. A tribunal spokesman said: 'We hope this will act as a deterrent to all other would-be traitors.'

Sya Dam, a former colonel with the Border Patrol Police, was found guilty of provoking rebellion among the tribes, taking shameful advantage of the position of trust he enjoyed among the country's leaders. The man who once moved in the City of Angels' most exalted circles will die before millions of TV viewers.

Viewing figures forecasts predict a record audience for this unique event. Already, sponsors are vying for the privilege of presenting to an eager nation Thailand's first televised execution.

Thought for today:
'The wary avoid death; the reckless are as good as dead already.'
– The Lord Buddha
Bangkok Herald, January 2, 1972

For me, mission accomplished. Smith's orders had been unequivocal: I was to get out of Thailand without delay. That decision met with my full approval. I was a man with his own missions now—I would debrief with Smith and meet with Nancy. I would resolve these two situations. I would do some hard thinking about what I had to offer a millionairess. Then, if I dared, I would return and claim Chee Laan Lee. On a snowy charger, we would ride off into the sunset. The stuff of foolish dreams—but dreams I clung to as I stepped out of Chee Laan's car and onto the airport sidewalk.

All flights were fully booked. I settled for standby. Silently, together but not clinging, we waited in the airport restaurant among noisy sprawling family parties.

An old woman had slipped into the lounge past the airport officials to peddle her jasmine leis. Chee Laan dropped a coin on her tray. She lifted a wreath of chained petals and draped it carefully about my neck. 'Bon voyage,' she whispered close to my ear.

She smelled better than the jasmine, of petals and lemons. I wanted to crush her to me and never let go. I reached out to her but she moved out of reach. She leaned away from me, studying my face, her expression suddenly like flint. For a moment, it seemed as though Sunii Lee, her grandmother, looked out of her eyes. Her next words sounded like an accusation: 'You are running away. What are you so afraid of, Raven?'

'You know damned well. I have to—get rid of baggage.'

'Don't bullshit me, Raven!' For a second, the Westernized Chee Laan was there. I reached out to this other Chee Laan, as though she could mediate for me with the new Chee Laan, the terrifying doppelgänger of Sunii Lee.

'All right, I'll come clean. Your grandmother implied to me the wealth you would inherit—that I'd be outclassed. And I knew you would have no choice but to stay in Thailand, to run your empire.' There was bitterness in my tone. 'I'm not a fool; all this is plain to me. This is how it must be—for now. But later—lawyers, administrators—even your own brother. You could delegate to them while you were away.'

'Away? Where, away?' she demanded.

'Well, perhaps, in Europe…'

'Thank you, but I have seen Europe.'

She shook her head. The glossy black hair swung softly against her cheeks. I wanted to caress it, to pull her close, to bruise her baby's mouth with my own. She did not appear to notice my agitation.

'Chee Laan,' I entreated, and said no more, embarrassed by the desperate pleading I heard in my own voice. I could not bring myself to bleat further, defeated by her iron resolve. I loved her, but I knew that would not help me.

'I have promised to drive my grandmother. I have to go now.' She turned away, her face already closed. She did not look back.

Around me the family parties ate and drank and laughed and photographed each other in cheery groups, all grinning. Not a tear-stained countenance in sight. I sat numbly among the jollity. At the centre of the commotion the travellers smiled, proud and embarrassed, weighted down with leis like mine, creamy jasmine studded with red rosebuds like drops of dried blood. The jasmine bore up well, but already the rose petals had a weary, crushed look about them.

Chee Laan negotiated her way back through the traffic, head held high, her eyes hidden behind enormous designer sunglasses. Once she reached the hotel, she hurried up the stairs, the knowledge of Raven's impending departure quickening her steps. She intended to fill the hollow in her heart with the praise and pride of her grandmother. But she stopped on the threshold to Sunii Lee's office, hearing voices within. She moved quickly to the spy panel, walking like an automaton. Her grandmother's voice came to her ears clear as a chime, her tone icy with anger.

'You are at fault, Archin. You allowed that girl to trick you. She escaped because you did not do your job. She ran away, and she told lies to the royal family. Now, because of your stupidity, Colonel Sya will die.'

A growl, not quite human came from somewhere in the room. Suddenly Chee Laan realised that her grandmother was talking to the huge man who had been guarding Salikaa. In her imagination he stood before her, hulking, his mind clouded but horribly purposeful. Chee Laan's ears caught the impatient *tap-tap* of her grandmother's ivory cane on the floor.

'*Lambaak!*' Chee Laan could almost see her grandmother's long, narrow teeth biting the word off beneath strongly muscled lips with a touch of scarlet cosmetic. 'More trouble for me! My granddaughter has become involved in things that should not concern her. That is your fault, Archin.'

'Archin,' mumbled the gravel voice. 'Archin not do again. Archin be good.'

'Yes. Quite right. You will not do it again. You will do one last service for Colonel Sya. Then you will be free. Everything will be forgiven.'

'Archin free, forgiven?' The tone was cautiously jubilant.

'Correct. Now, listen to what you must do.'

'Somebody get...click!' Archin mimicked the cocking of a trigger. 'Somebody die?' Chee Laan could sense his thrill of anticipation. 'Somebody get dead?'

'Perhaps. Now, listen!'

Chee Laan listened to her grandmother's instructions with growing horror. When she heard the big man dismissed and the sound of him shambling out the door, she went to Sunii herself.

Sunii was seated in her dragon chair, lost in thought. She looked at Chee Laan and her eyebrows twitched. 'Well, granddaughter, I hope you heard all you needed.'

'You knew? You knew all the time?'

'Naturally.' She pointed to a chair. 'It is time to speak openly.'

'Grandmother, why are you doing this? Sya is going to be executed as a traitor. Are you a communist? Is he?'

'Do not shout like a vulgar woman from Hunan. Sya is an idealist. I am a pragmatist, but the notion of idealism is not completely foreign to me. I too have grown tired of tolerating these incompetent, racist Thai pigs and enduring those arrogant Western barbarians. How dare such people call the hill tribes savages? Sya is a valuable ally. His motives do not concern me. It will be expensive to save him, but I will do so, nevertheless.'

'Save him? From an execution that is a national television event? Impossible!'

Sunii shook her head, smiling. 'In Asia, if you have friends, you need not die—at least, not in such an undignified manner.'

'Sya's going to die. They've even promised to show the body afterward...'

Sunii lifted a finger like a primary school teacher. 'Correction. A body. They will show *a* body. Does this body need to be Colonel Sya? The uniform! Nothing more!' Sunii Lee settled herself more comfortably in her seat. Her spine remained straight as the chair's ivory-inlaid rosewood back. 'I will tell you what you will see: Colonel Sya walking into the tent. The firing squad aiming at a painted target. The medical orderlies removing the body of a large man in a colonel's uniform on a stretcher. The body will be covered by a sheet.'

'But how...?'

'Few people will notice that the dead man is even more powerfully built than the colonel. The body will be that of Archin. An idiot; a crazed man whom the colonel took pity on and employed for odd jobs.'

'What kind of odd jobs?' Chee Laan knew her tone was harsh and rude, but she could not control it. 'Murder?'

Sunii shrugged. 'What are these terms but mere semantics? Archin, that poor fellow, has few talents. He is already under a sentence of death. Without Sya's protection he will be dead soon.'

'So you will arrange—somehow—to get this Archin killed in Sya's place?'

'I? Certainly not! I should not dream of arranging any such thing. But neither shall I prevent it. The demented creature is fanatically devoted to the colonel. I fear he may well conceal himself in the execution tent, evade the guards—who knows how—with some quixotic notion of rushing to his benefactor's aid. Unfortunately, he may just happen to place himself in the target zone. He may catch a fatal bullet. Nobody would regret such a tragedy more than I. But, as I said, Archin is very stupid.'

'What about the guards? How the hell would he escape the guards?'

'Tsk! The military man has extremely sensitive feelings. A mistake of such magnitude—executing the wrong man—can you imagine the loss of face? Especially with the attention of the entire nation focused upon it. You will find the police and the army regard Colonel Sya with something approaching adoration. There is less racist discrimination in the armed forces than in society at large, contrary to popular belief. A fine soldier is a fine soldier, be he Akha, Chinese, or Thai. The guards will dress the dead man in Sya's jacket. Sya will march out as a member of the execution firing party.' She paused. 'Naturally, his deliverance from death will be ascribed to fate. The colonel's karma simply did not permit him to be gunned down like a common criminal.' She looked at Chee Laan. 'Believe me, everyone will find such a solution entirely satisfactory, even politic.'

'Except, perhaps, Archin.'

Sunii shrugged. 'When elephants fight, the grass is trampled.' They were silent for a while. 'Of course,' Sunii resumed in a matter-of-fact tone, 'if poor Archin is to play such a role, the operation must be watertight. The unfortunate creature can only remember very simple instructions. And we cannot risk getting word to Sya. He must anticipate the worst, right to the end. But afterward…nobody will count how many guards are involved in the dismantling of the tent, which will be done immediately after the removal of the stretcher. The Prince Regent has no stomach for this killing. He wants the evidence torn down as soon as possible.'

'Then why did he agree to it, if he doesn't approve of it?'

'The new cabinet manoeuvred him into it—as a deterrent to treachery. Thailand has a tradition of bloodless coups, but each alteration in the power structure reveals the trend toward increasing violence.'

'And…afterward?'

'Sya can no longer serve in Thailand. And as for myself…' She sighed. Her voice faded to a soft murmur. 'Sya's fall will drag others down with him. Few people know of our association. But if even one person knows, that will be sufficient to discredit me. I cannot afford to be discredited. Not again.'

'By "again", you mean your…friendship…with the Japanese? The East Ocean Devils?'

Sunii's famous slender eyes flashed, black and wicked, the eyes of a much younger woman. Then her anger evaporated. She smiled with soft pride.

'So you knew? You knew, but you said nothing. I am proud of you, Chee Laan.' She relaxed her shoulders in relief. 'You are discreet. You are also obedient. You will not rush into unfortunate associations with foreigners when it is not necessary to do so.' She sighed gently. 'Now I am even more convinced I made the right decision. I am old. All empires achieve a pinnacle and later decline. The Lee fortunes are at the flood. The future may see the turning of the tide, or perhaps a rise to even greater power. But I shall not be here to see it. I am weary.'

She did not look weary. Eternally composed, her every action decisive and considered, there was a new resolve about her, as though she had recognised an inevitability and elected to adopt it.

'I am no longer young,' she said. 'My bones long for my own country, for the Middle Kingdom, the Earth's centre. There, when the time is propitious, the ceremonies must be properly performed. I do not wish to linger in a terracotta tomb, awaiting shipment home.' Chee Laan was about to speak, but Sunii raised a pale hand. 'Yes, I know what you will say: China has changed. But some values survive. Under the Gang of Four, the old ways were derided. But now our culture blooms again. Life has returned.'

She considered Chee Laan for a moment, and for the first time Chee Laan could remember, there was in her gaze the vulnerability of love. 'I will miss you, and only you, Granddaughter. Chee Laan, Precious Orchid. Consolation for sottish sons, churlish grandsons, and fanatical daughters-in-law. I hope your path will run smooth, and that you will not be held to account for this old woman's sins. I hope that, in time, I may live on in you.' In the first and only gesture of physical tenderness she had ever shown, she extended her cool lily hand and touched Chee Laan's cheek. 'Do not allow yourself to be drawn in, to become involved. Not with your *farang*—not with any man. Breed and devour, like the spider. That is our motto.' She removed her hand. 'You grow more like me every day, Chee Laan.'

Even as revolt burned in her throat, Chee Laan bowed her head. Her destiny weighed on her. 'Too much honour,' she murmured. She felt empty, drained of all life. She dragged her heavy eyes up to meet Sunii's, and found them, uniquely, bright with unshed tears.

'Go now!' Sunii said. Chee Laan gave a cry like a wounded animal and stumbled blindly from the room.

She made her way home to the family compound, hardly aware of what she was doing. In her own bedroom, she locked the door behind her, threw herself on the blue-and-gold Chinese carpet, and wept like a child—for her grandmother, for Nat Raven, and for herself. She permitted this excessive expression of emotion because she had already made up her mind that it would be the last extravagant action of her life.

The storm of weeping left her exhausted. She fell asleep with her face pressed to the floor. It was several hours later that she awoke. Her face was swollen and her throat felt raw. She wondered for a moment how she could have slept, but remembered one of Fleischer's gory tales from her time in Normandy. He'd told them that torture victims sometimes fell into a deep sleep, the body's last defence. She roused her stiff limbs and walked over to wash her face in the gold-tapped basin. Then she crossed the courtyard and entered her brother's apartments to witness, with sixty million others, the public execution of the Black Tiger.

Her serenity was complete.

'They'll never have the nerve. They'll never do it.'

But, at the very last moment, the final announcement was made. The kickboxing championships were booted off every front page. The execution was to be public—televised on all channels.

The news plunged the country into an uproar.

It would not be Thailand's first televised execution, of course. Previously, the condemned had always been bit-part players, couriers, bagmen, mules, pawns, losers. Not key figures of national importance. Not full colonels of the Border Patrol Police, and certainly not the man who had been old King Rama's favourite.

Television coverage of the event was promised to be detailed and close up; however, soon people came to realise this was a lie, a crude ratings-boosting exercise. That wasn't the first of its kind, either.

Nobody would be able to see the bullets piercing his head and torso—it wouldn't be a real show. Which only went to prove, people muttered, that you should only believe half of what you read in the papers. The mutterings were loudest among the samlor drivers and sweepers, those die-hard cynics and no-hopers who squatted on building sites and, stoutly resisting the Prince Regent's internationally acclaimed National Literacy Programme, still signed with thumbprints.

And Chinatown laughed, set out its stalls, and, awaiting profitable developments, went about business as usual.

The television announcer, Chee Laan Lee noticed, was certainly entering into the spirit of the occasion. Under the stream of guttural tonal Thai, his breath was rasping, as though they'd thrust the microphone down his throat—as if he, and not Colonel Sya Dam, were the one dying. In an excited torrent the announcer recited the highlights of Sya's career. His enthusiasm was understandable; it was an honour to be selected to commentate on the execution of a man such as Colonel Sya, a royal favourite and much-decorated hero. But what was Sya's tribe, really, but a national scandal, an embarrassing blot on the fair escutcheon of the land. Sya was nothing but a primitive tribesman who had rocketed skyward in a few short years to become a star—although naturally, one could hardly say so on a national network, even though everyone knew it.

Chee Laan listened intently as the commentator recited the glory and the infamy, exaggerating what he knew and embellishing as far as he dared. The camera crew, also, were exhilarated, panning and swooping dizzily above the throng like hunting buzzards.

As for the throng, Chee Laan Lee thought she had never seen such a crowd, neither for the king's birthday nor for the Miss Thailand Pageant. The military parade throbbed the ground, packed and heaving.

'Amateurs! All time zoom, zoom, make dizzy, huh!' grunted fat Pao Lee resentfully, who deplored all forms of physical discomfort. Shielding his eyes from the screen's nausea-inducing images, he dumped his heavy, short-legged body onto the corner of the sofa, wrinkling its pink silk, taking care not to spill the large glass of whisky and lime he grasped in one pudgy hand.

Chee Laan Lee felt rather than saw her brother's sidelong glance in her direction, his small eyes rolling like pinballs along the slitted sockets above his bloated cheeks. She remained intent on the screen. Tensely, she watched in fascinated horror as the camera focused on a small hut rather like a field latrine. Nearby a tent had been erected, as though for a tournament, or to house a chamber orchestra in the event of rain.

The rain was predictable. Each morning and night it poured for exactly one hour, as if someone had turned a faucet on full bore, and then turned it off again quickly, leaving the land hissing like a poached egg.

Chee Laan had seen tents like this elegant, rectangular structure of jackfruit-yellow parachute silk at the garden parties of the *farang*, sheltering the musicians playing Mozart and Schubert and, during the rest bars, using the tips of their bows to flick insects from one another's necks. This tent, though, had strange markings on it, unlike any other she had seen. This was the Death Pavilion.

As if in recognition of her thoughts, the announcer's chatter suddenly stilled. Now the sullen silence of the crowd assumed a tangible presence. Oppressively it permeated the room where the Lees huddled round the big television screen. Pent-up air burst painfully from Chee Laan's chest; she realised she had been holding her breath.

There was a ripple of movement. The firing squad goose-stepped whip-smart into view, slicing a path through the multitude. Before the hut they wheeled and stamped, presenting arms. Now a Buddhist priest swam into focus, enthroned upon a high-backed chair, fanned by a temple boy with a woven rattan fan. The boy knelt self-consciously, shaven head and taut little bum thrust backward, but the priest seemed relaxed, his gaze turned inward, sedate and implacable. Some power flowed from him, neither gentleness nor judgement.

The camera slalomed respectfully over the motionless figure of the priest and then nosed out its true target. It homed in on the kneeling man, dwelt at length on every detail of the colonel's dress uniform, lingered over the gleaming planes of the close-cropped skull, as if contemplating the edifying and disconcerting spectacle of so much splendour and power brought to its knees.

And indeed, reflected Chee Laan Lee, watching it was an object lesson. Viewing ratings were purely incidental. It was irrelevant that such didactic spectacles should titillate the bloodlust of men such as Pao Lee, when they conveyed such a moral impact.

'Get on with it!' Pao gurgled, anticipation causing him to slurp his Johnny Walker. No Mekhong rotgut—foreign imports only for Pao Lee. He slapped the plump arm of the sofa. 'Splatter the bastard!'

Chee Laan said nothing. Pao wondered what was going on inside his sister's smooth, painted-doll's head. Beneath the cool surface, surely there must writhe a snake pit of emotion—and much interesting information. He ached with curiosity. He squinted sidelong at Chee Laan, malice twisting his gut, picturing himself hammering slivers of bamboo up the quick of her nails, shattering that infuriating calm, forcing her secrets from her in a tortured shriek. Some part of him knew the bitch would die first—through pride and sheer contrariness.

'Do calm down, brother,' Chee Laan said. 'You will self-destruct. It will make such a mess.'

Her cool regard enraged him. He shouted, 'You think you are so smart, with your convent education, but you are just a little Chinese girl, a Jek bitch, my precious little sister. Overeducated offal. They should have exposed you at birth, on a mountainside, for the buzzards to tear.' His lifelong hatred twisted his guts. She ignored him, her eyes on the screen.

At last the priest moved. Inclined ceremoniously forward without speaking, he handed the condemned man a lotus flower, swollen but still secret, not yet burst from the bud. The uniformed man bowed his head to the dust at the priest's feet.

In one swift movement Sya rose, clicked his heels together, and turned his face directly into the camera's prying lens. It bounced back, off the planes of his strong features, and there remained an impression of immobilised rage, the image of a treed panther; then the camera shot panned out, as if the close-up of Sya's face had been too shocking.

In the next frame, the condemned officer was distantly marching in step with his armed escort across the parade ground, toward the Death Pavilion.

Chee Laan saw he had now put on his uniform cap, and it was clear what a huge man he was. He towered head and shoulders above his six guards. The ropes of gold braid that adorned his uniform reflected the sun, igniting dazzling black blobs like liquid mercury across the television picture. His bearing was that of a young cadet at his passing-out parade, heart bursting with pride and patriotism, trained to his peak, not a middle-aged man one hundred and twenty seconds away from death and final disgrace.

The Thais' admiration for gallantry, almost equal to their love of pageantry, forced a ragged cheer from the throats of the people standing nearest as the seven men marched into the tent without breaking step. They disappeared from view. Outside the tent the target marks were now clearly visible. They indicated the head and heart of a large man standing inside. The firing squad took up their positions. Their officer bawled an order, and they shouldered arms. Like lovers they laid their cheeks against their weapons, as if embracing the almond-oiled flanks of dusky beauties. Each gun was worth a year's pay. Bearing arms was an honour. Even this unwelcome assignment, which offended against religious principles, brought great honour. Besides, Chee Laan reflected, they knew they were on camera. In the crowded street bars of Chieng Rai and Chonburi, they would be pointed out with gleeful yells by families and mistresses.

They took meticulous aim at the diagram on the tent wall. Their officer barked the command. There followed a feeble crackle and pop, like damp New Year's firecrackers. Chee Laan saw her brother's disappointment at this poor show. It did not sound very effective, certainly not fatal. Surely not capable of stopping the heart of the man who, a moment before, had stared arrogantly into the camera's eye.

But the firing squad had obviously practised hard—at targets, tin cans, falling coconuts. The shots had found their mark after all, burning through the tent's yellow silk at the very spot which must have been the heart of the man standing behind the screen.

Faces shining with relief, the squad sloped arms, about-faced, and marched away. Chee Laan remembered the soldiers from the army camp where she'd made her radio broadcasts, and thought they would keep marching, like clockwork toys, until they ran out of steam, even though they themselves were longing for somewhere quiet where they could remove their boots and caps and scratch themselves and chew a lump of betel.

Pao Lee took a large gulp of whisky and craned forward, riding the sofa like an overweight jockey, agog for horrors.

Now they saw men bearing a stretcher enter the execution tent. Moments later, they emerged, heads bowed under the burden of weight and reverence. On the stretcher reposed the body of a very large man with a black bag over his head. A colonel's gold-braided cap lay on his chest. Before placing it there, someone—a medical orderly, perhaps—had lifted the heavy hands and folded them over the chest in a dignified attitude. But the movement of the stretcher had dislodged the left arm. As the party advanced toward the cameras, the arm, with its colonel's stripes, swung casually back and forth, as though its owner were taking his ease on a hot afternoon in a hammock between two palm trees.

Chee Laan wondered whether Colonel Sya Dam would have appreciated that final gesture of posthumous rebellion. Giving the world the bird one last time. Then she realised with surprise that she did not really know. She stared at the big swinging hand. She had not realised until that moment how huge such hands were, how powerful.

As if at a signal, the crowd, like a wave breaking, began to disperse quietly, avoiding eye contact—a class of chastened children.

'Huh! Not even worth watching!'

Pao flicked off the television set, farted juicily, and spat in the direction of the stainless steel bowl that stood by the sofa leg. He missed. His sister, inured to the social rituals of the male members of her family, refrained from comment. She rose to leave.

'So that's the end of that!' Pao grunted. 'Got his deserts, the fucking rat!

I hope he rots in hell! Well, what have you got to say now, eh? Who said the mighty fucking Colonel Sya was above the fucking law?' He heaved himself to his feet, barring her way with his bulk, determined to provoke some reaction. 'Shooting, number ten!' Pao said, peering into her face. Anger made him slobber. Her nostrils contracted at the sour whisky-and-lime stink of his breath. 'Hanging more better! Hanging number one! More funnier. Wee Willie Winkie, wiggle wiggle!'

Speaking to her in Pidgin English was a calculated mockery. Raising one of his hands with the other, he wiggled the little finger back and forth like a flaccid member straining to achieve erection. Now at last she did turn the head that seemed too heavy for her delicate neck, like a dark peony on its slim stalk. She looked at the twitching pinkie and said in fast, harsh Mandarin, 'I see you have a recurrence of the old trouble, Brother. Rhino horn. Remind me to send you some. Now I have work to do. Piss off and play with yourself somewhere else.'

His own Mandarin was not as good as hers, though he had had more lessons, and had even studied in Taipei on a scholarship financed by the local Chinese community—with a major contribution from the Lee family empire. The empire whose millions she would now control, his fucking little sister. Tears of rage welled in his eyes.

She gave him a sharp prod in the chest that took him by surprise. He flopped into the sofa, his heavy thighs spread wide, his fat face twisted with hatred and fury. The salty drops tickled his nose as they ran down and he sneezed gobs of phlegm onto his sleeve.

'Sya Dam is dead!' Pao bellowed.

'Yes,' she said calmly. 'It was on TV.'

The temperature was one hundred degrees in the shade, but as she walked from the room, she trembled as if with cold. She had seen the evidence with her own eyes. But she, in common with a handful of other people, knew that this charade of an execution was not the end of Sya Dam. She felt a stab of despair, longing to confide in Raven, yet knowing that this was a secret she would never share with him, this man with whom she had shared so much. Raven must believe that Sya had been ultimately defeated. He must leave Thailand in ignorance. There had to be a clean break between them.

For once in her life, Sunii Lee looked out of place as she sat in the back seat of her new cream Mercedes. She wore the simple black pyjamas of a peasant woman; her hair was drawn back tightly and powdered, accentuating the grey, but the huge dark glasses struck an incongruous note. For once, the chauffeur had been relieved of his duties. Behind the wheel, Chee Laan drove in silence. She was meditating on the principle of the cool heart. There would be no more wailing.

She halted at the Thanom Vittayu road junction and a man wearing the saffron of a *bikkhu* climbed into the back seat beside Sunii—and even though Chee Laan knew the massive robed figure was the Black Tiger, she neither turned her head nor passed comment. She sat more stiffly, bitterly aware of his malign presence. But she schooled herself not to react. She knew there was no turning back, now that she had embraced her destiny.

Outside the departure lounge at Don Muang airport, Chee Laan swung the big car half onto the pavement and sprang out, pressing a hundred-baht note into the hand of the uniformed traffic official before he could protest at her unorthodox parking. He bit back his remonstrance and saluted smartly, and got busy helping the two passengers alight. A hundred baht was a hundred baht. Now eager to please, he would have assisted them with their baggage, which appeared to be clumsily packed bedrolls, but the older lady bade him desist, with a gentle smile. He gazed at her, puzzled. Her attire was that of a modest woman, a servant even, but her assured demeanour betrayed a very different status. He watched as she and the male passenger walked side by side into the building, followed by the young Chinese woman who had given him the tip. It was true, he thought, the banknote crisp in his hand. Not all Jek girls looked like pigs. This one was beautiful.

As they entered the hall, Sunii Lee said to her companion, almost jauntily, 'You will ensure that, at the appropriate time, I am wearing this contraption correctly?' He nodded.

'What *is* that thing?' Chee Laan asked, catching up with them and glancing at the bulky roll of cloth.

'This? It is a double parachute, of course. I am unfamiliar with the procedure, but my companion, fortunately, is experienced, and we shall make the leap together. It is known as a tandem jump. I am told the experience is most stimulating.' Sunii Lee's eyes sparkled. 'We are travelling by the premier Royal Thai Orchid flight. The pilot will make an unscheduled detour over the northwest, where we shall leave the airplane by parachute. There, a small aircraft awaits to continue our journey. This commercial pilot, an intelligent and accommodating man, has a private agreement with me. If questioned he will simply say some technical consideration forced the detour. One of the cabin crew has been…encouraged…to open an emergency exit for us. The pilot will continue his route with only minimal delay. For this favour, he will never need to work again.'

'On the other hand,' the man dressed as a monk interposed, an undertone of chilling menace in his soft deep voice, 'had he refused, he would never have needed to work again, either.'

'This is a mad scheme!' Chee Laan exclaimed. For a moment her iron control of her emotions faltered. Sunii Lee stopped and turned to face her. 'Why risk killing yourself?' Chee Laan demanded, fighting to conceal her anger. Her grandmother tipped her head.

'The flight is bound for Switzerland. Passengers arriving off Bangkok flights in every international destination will be under close police scrutiny. Here, in Bangkok, I still have a little authority. Money speaks with a loud voice. Elsewhere, it would be too risky to travel conventionally. But today is safest for us. Nobody will expect us to leave from the major airport. Now, Granddaughter, it is time. I have left everything in order.' She started walking again.

'Shall I ever see you again?' Chee Laan heard the desolation in her own voice.

'The end of filial piety is establishing one's character,' Sunii said. She paused again and regarded Chee Laan long and coolly, as if memorising her features. Then she nodded, a curt gesture that expressed both satisfaction and dismissal. As if by mutual agreement, she and her companion turned away. Helplessly, Chee Laan stood and watched the unusual couple move to join a queue of passengers, the elderly Chinese lady in her black silk pyjamas, carrying her tightly rolled sleeping mat, and the powerfully built monk in his saffron robe, the roll under his arm dwarfed by his size. Chee Laan stared bleakly after them. They did not turn back.

As she turned to leave, her eye fell upon a tall coolie girl dragging a broom along the floor. For an instant, the light glinted on a sharp cheekbone, and the girl seemed familiar.

Chee Laan told herself severely that she had allowed sorrow to unhinge her mind. The momentary illusion might be because her eyes were full of unshed tears. She put up her chin, slid back behind the wheel of the Mercedes with a smile to the guard, and pulled out into traffic. She wanted to go back, to run after her grandmother, appealing, begging even. But such behaviour was unthinkable. She drove on.

The Royal Palace, Bangkok

Salikaa had been brought discreetly from prison to the Royal Palace in Bangkok and imprisoned in one of the guest suites. For two days she had seen only the mute, patient servants and the impassive major domo, and her nerves were strung taut as bowstrings.

'How dare you keep me cooped up like this?' Salikaa slung her silver tray against the wall. 'I refuse to eat until I am granted an audience with King Vajah!'

With weary resignation, the major domo clapped his hands. Two maids scuttled in and began to clear up the spilled food.

'By whose command am I imprisoned?' Salikaa demanded, for the umpteenth time. As usual, the major domo made no reply, his habitual expression of pensive pessimism merely deepening.

At the sound of approaching footsteps, the major domo gestured hastily for the maids to disappear. They sidled out, carrying the debris. The major domo bowed to the rotund figure of Prince Premsakul, who bustled in with a portentous air. He flapped an impatient hand at the major domo and the man tactfully withdrew. Prince Premsakul observed Salikaa's astonished face with a faint smile.

'What's going to happen to me?' Salikaa demanded.

'Much less than you deserve,' the prince replied placidly. 'You will be exiled. You will be escorted to the airport and put on a flight out of the country. You will never be permitted to return to Thailand. His Majesty and Her Royal Highness the Princess Regent have declared their intentions of graciously granting you an audience this afternoon. May I suggest...' He cast his gaze insultingly over her dishevelled appearance. '...that you prepare yourself?'

He pressed his fingertips together in a perfunctory salutation and glided out, leaving Salikaa to her tumultuous thoughts.

The king gave Salikaa a look, a volatile compound of desire and disappointment. The Princess Regent moved discreetly to the window and stood with her back to the room in apparent contemplation of the gardens. Prince Premsakul, escorting the royal couple, had placed a small suitcase ceremoniously upon the low table. He looked prepared to remain, until the king made an unmistakable gesture of dismissal.

Salikaa stared at the king. The spoiled boy had grown up; his personality and bearing had expanded. Now he filled the framework of power that had sat upon his slender shoulders since youth. This young man would not have succumbed so easily to her crude seduction. About him was the chill distance of those born to command—a king at last.

'You deceived me, Salikaa.' King Vajah spoke softly, without reproach, in a measured tone. His voice seemed deeper. Petty imperiousness had been replaced with quiet authority. 'Yet I do not blame you. You cannot help what you are. But our brief encounter has had its uses. My desire for you struck me like a thunderbolt. It was the first intense emotion I had ever experienced in my life, and appeared to me to be irresistible. It forced me to confront my own weakness. It was a salutary lesson.'

He paused. He studied Salikaa's face as though to observe the effects of his words. Salikaa saw he was coolly assessing her appearance. Beneath his objectivity, there was a tremour of self-congratulation as he repudiated that earlier, susceptible self, a humble petitioner to her beauty.

'Our encounter advanced my self-knowledge. I am now fit to undertake the tasks that lie before me. For this, Salikaa, I am in your debt.' He gestured to the suitcase lying on the table. 'For you.'

She bowed her thanks, wondering what he had brought her—gems, gold, perhaps a fortune in banknotes. Once more he studied her face regretfully.

'We are each prisoners of our own fate.'

The Princess Regent turned from the window and moved toward the door. The young king, after a pause, followed. Salikaa was about to fall prostrate at his feet, but he extended a hand.

'Oh, and *Khun* Salikaa...'

'Majesty?'

'Those judges who selected you as Miss Thailand had the right idea, you know. You are the most beautiful of all. My golden lotus, my graceful swallow.'

The door closed quietly behind the royal pair, but not before Salikaa had glimpsed the eyes of Prince Premsakul, hovering by the door, and recognised their gleam of triumph. She listened to the receding footsteps of the royal party. Then, shrugging off a momentary weakness with a stab of regret for what might have been, she turned her attention to the small case still lying on the table.

She snapped up the locks and threw open the lid, and stood staring. Inside, neatly folded, lay the clothes of a servant, and beside them the flame-coloured dress she had worn when she'd fallen on her knees before the king, afire with determination and adrenaline to win back the life she'd imagined.

On top of the clothes there was a large envelope. She tore it open with trembling hands, and sat back, shaking with rage and disappointment. It contained a one-way ticket to Switzerland, and a sum of money so despicably small that Salikaa's first furious impulse was to smash the sealed window, rip up the ticket and the banknotes, and scatter them into the blood-red roses below.

Good sense prevailed. Grimacing, she pushed the notes into her padded lace bra.

Don Muang Airport, Bangkok

Salikaa
As the palace limousine churned along, I stared at the chauffeur's stolid shoulders and the bull neck of the guard who sat in the front seat beside him. I was savouring Vajah's last words. It is quite a compliment to be desired, even briefly, by a king. I looked most unlike either a swallow or a golden lotus at that moment, wearing the black *pasin* and white blouse of a servant. I had been given plastic flip-flops for my feet. Ashamed of my appearance, I had wound a cloth about my head, covering half my face, like a woman from one of the stone-breaking gangs who work on the roads.

When we reached the airport, the guard picked up a suitcase identical to the one I had been given and set off purposefully into the building. I leapt out, seeing my opportunity. Ignoring the shouts of the chauffeur, I hurried into the building through the glass door, still carrying my little suitcase, and mingled with the mob. I could hear the calls of my pursuer growing closer; he had clearly abandoned the car to chase me.

Frantically, I glanced around, and quickly saw, to my good fortune, just what I needed—a sweeping broom, abandoned by a coolie. I slipped off my shoes and seized the broom, dragging it along. I worked my way across the entrance hall, trying my best to look the part of a downtrodden, self-effacing servant and curbing my impatience—lazy coolies never moved at more than a snail's pace. I was still thinking out my next move when I saw something that caused me to crouch down over my bucket and hide my face behind the tail of my turban.

It was the sharp-eyed Mrs van Hooten: the red-haired foreign woman, tutor to Vajah, and the only foreigner at court. Hauteur is infectious, and she'd been at court so long she fancied herself a royal, too. She was arguing with the Thai International representative, clutching a small suitcase identical to the one I had been given. I realized that the guard who had been in the limousine with me must have given it to her. My curiosity was aroused. I wondered what it contained, and why an official had been ordered to hand it over to her.

Throughout her heated dispute with the woman behind the counter, her hands never left the case. She was a woman given to large gestures with her bony freckled hands, yet now she gripped that bag like a life belt.

I knew, like everyone else, that the royal lady tutor enjoyed the Princess Regent's confidence, and that she made frequent trips to Switzerland on royal missions. The official line was that she brought back health and beauty products for the Princess that were too fragile to be sent by post. Pim's theory had been that the Princess Regent dispatched Mrs van Hooten with consignments of valuables from the royal treasure, to be stored in a Swiss bank in the event of a coup. The Chakri dynasty was ancient; their wealth was inestimable.

I hadn't paid much attention to Pim at the time. But now I needed a decent bankroll to get myself launched again, especially when I considered the insultingly paltry farewell gift from the king. I decided to investigate Mrs van Hooten at the earliest opportunity, and, if need be, eliminate her. She was a very irritating woman, and Thailand was finished for me anyway. Vichai always told me killing wasn't such a dirty business as high finance.

Any fool who lifted a hand against Vichai was dead before that hand could find its mark—unless he was tricked. I had long suspected the involvement of that big American, the husband of the ugly red-haired woman who stood before me, gripping her case with white-gloved hands. How the threads tied together.

My arm shook as I recalled this memory, and water from the pail slopped onto the floor and my begrimed bare feet. I moved close enough to hear her flight number.

As I watched a neat little air hostess walk by, humming, tittuping on her high heels and patting her little hat, inspiration struck me. The air hostess wiggled her fingers coquettishly at an airline official, called, 'Switzerland, then three days leave!' and vanished into the ladies' toilet. Poor girl—her death warrant was signed. I took up my pail and shuffled along in her wake.

The adjacent men's toilet bore a large sign: 'Closed for cleaning. Please use toilet in restaurant.' I took it off the men's and hung it on the handle of the ladies' before entering and closing the door behind me. I saw with satisfaction that only one cubicle was engaged. Under its door I could see the stewardess's shoes. I heard a clatter as the girl kicked them off and stepped barefoot onto the toilet bowl to urinate in the Thai fashion. I waited beside the cubicle door. I held the mop handle horizontally in two hands, like a Siamese fighting-stick.

The toilet flushed. I gauged the moment exactly. As she came out I raised the mop handle and struck a blow across her windpipe. She gasped and tumbled backward. Her hands clutched at the air. I dropped the mop and grabbed her hair with one hand. At the same time I flung my free arm round her waist, pressing into her solar plexus. I braced her body against my own and folded it like a jackknife, pressing her face downward toward the toilet bowl. She fought energetically, but my position allowed me to use all my strength without losing my balance. Angel Fleischer had been an excellent tutor.

People think you have to be as strong as a bear to kill another human being, but that's nonsense. You just have to calculate angles and stress points correctly. I performed the twist-and-press movement with textbook precision, exactly as I had been taught. The girl's vertebrae crunched and parted obediently. She slumped in my arms.

In truth, she was more trouble dead than alive, for she was surprisingly heavy. I had to half drag, half push her lifeless body into the cubicle to close the door. Stripping off her uniform, I was gratified to discover that she had been a girl with respect for herself, who kept herself tidy. There was the inevitable slight odour of fear, of course, compounded of perspiration and incipient micturition, the result of our struggle. But there was also expensive scent—these international stewardesses shopped in the rue de Rivoli—and her underwear was matching white lace and spotless. Perhaps she had a rendezvous with some sexy captain, or she was just a nicely brought-up girl.

I locked the cubicle door from the inside—a delaying tactic, nothing more. The body had to remain undiscovered until the flight for Switzerland had left. I kicked the black patent shoes and shoulder bag under the partition into the next cubicle, dropped the lilac two-piece after them, and shinned over the narrow wall.

Still wearing my coolie clothes, the stewardess's clothes safely inside my case, I sold my ticket to a loitering tout. I could see police and guards routinely checking the queues. I knew they would not detain me even if they recognised me; nobody was interested in dragging me back, for they wanted to get rid of me. When the tout insisted, I sold him my passport too. It was made out in the name they had given me, as the wife of that filthy creature Vasit. The first name on this passport was Boonmee. The picture could have been any Asian girl between fifteen and thirty. The tout grunted his satisfaction and paid me handsomely. I insisted on American dollars.

I went back to the restroom and dressed myself in the uniform of the dead stewardess. The clothes fitted me fairly well, except that I was eight inches taller. The lilac skirt stopped above my knees, at a point officially declared immodest by government decree. I tugged the skirt down, feeling relieved that I was bound for a destination outside Thailand. My legs were my best features.

The shoes were tight, though. Nothing to be done about that. Fortunately, aboard the aircraft, stewardesses changed into traditional Thai costume, so with any luck I should be able to go barefoot beneath the floor-length *pasin*, with the added advantage of disguising my height. I rummaged in the stewardess's shoulder bag and discovered a hairbrush, a hand mirror, and some cosmetics. I squatted on the toilet seat as best I could in the tight lilac skirt and applied lipstick and eye make-up, and brushed rouge beneath my cheekbones. The stewardess's tastes were unsophisticated. I smeared babyblue shadow on my eyelids and applied a vile pastel-pink lipstick. I certainly didn't look myself when I'd finished. Barbie goes to Bangkok! I was almost as well disguised as when I was a coolie, and equally repulsive.

I left the cubicle and was about to leave the restroom when another Thai Orchid stewardess marched into the toilet and stared around crossly. 'Why is that sign there? These toilets are not due to be cleaned now. Really, these coolies! Half of them can't read, the others just hang the sign up when they want to smoke!' She looked at me. 'Are you on flight 355, sister?' I nodded. 'Then these are for you.' The stewardess handed me a sheaf of papers. 'Better get a move-on, then. No more time for titivating!'

'Sorry, sister. It's my first flight—I'm so nervous, I've forgotten all my training!' I looked pleadingly at her. She had a sympathetic, round-cheeked face. 'You will help me, sister, won't you? So I don't make a mess of things?'

'Oh, gods, a rookie! That's all I need!' she exclaimed, rolling her eyes heavenward. 'Okay, come on, I'll show you. First off, just stand where I say and collect the boarding passes. Remember, if there are any babies, help to carry them. Anyone out of the VIP lounge, make a fuss of them, okay? Simple!'

As we left the restroom side by side, I doing my best to match her spirited steps in my pinching shoes, I suddenly threw a hand up to my head. 'This stupid little hat really doesn't feel secure. It's going to fall off at any minute!'

'Your hair's too thick,' the other hostess said impatiently. 'It's too long, too. Here, you can borrow this hatpin. I want it back, mind. It's my secret weapon.' She giggled. 'I use it to dissuade Chinese businessmen who've pigged out on the free drinks!' Pulling the jewelled hatpin out of her lapel, she handed it to me carefully. 'Be careful! It's very sharp!'

I skewered the hatpin into my lilac hat, running my finger over its point. It was very sharp indeed.

'Place hand luggage in rack, madame?'

I bent solicitously over the foreign woman, contriving an obsequious grimace. I noticed Chee Laan Lee's foreign lover sitting at the far end of the aircraft, in monkey class. For the moment I intended to devote my attention to the first-class cabin. It was first class all the way for me!

Mrs van Hooten hugged her small case, the twin of my own, to her scrawny bosom as though she feared I might snatch it—which I did, ignoring her furious glare and slamming it into the overhead locker, simpering, 'So sorry, regulations!'

She'd already kicked up a fuss, demanding to exchange her seat between two other passengers for one next the window. The adjacent seat was vacant. The aisle seat was occupied by a dozing Buddhist monk, his shaven head nodding over a holy text.

Once we were safely airborne, I slid into the vacant central seat and fumbled busily with the tray table. 'Madame permit I fix this table?'

Mrs van Hooten sighed. 'Oh, very well. If you must.' She shifted her weight to the other armrest, distancing herself from my endeavours, and stared out the window. I fiddled with the catch on the collapsible table, glancing around to make sure the monk still slept and I was unobserved. I slid the borrowed hatpin out in readiness.

Leaning toward Mrs van Hooten, I pointed out of the window. 'Madame see Golden Chedi, very famous temple!'

She passed a hand over her eyes and snapped, 'I've seen a surfeit of chedis! Haven't you fixed that table yet, girl?' She added, almost to herself, 'Fuss! Typical! Nothing functions correctly in this country. Such *laissez-faire*! They'll starve to death out of sheer inertia. One can only hope the *pilot's* awake!'

I'd had quite enough of Mrs van Hooten. I struck at once, two-handed, right thumb and forefinger pinching her nostrils shut. Forcing her head sideways, I aimed my hatpin. But she struggled like a devil, scratching, biting, and kicking.

It was a bad moment. Then help came from an unexpected quarter. I was shouldered aside. Two powerful hands seized her throat. Mrs van Hooten gurgled, turned purple, twitched convulsively, and died. I looked up from her dead face and encountered the monk's lazy yellow eyes, and I shuddered, thinking I was staring into the face of a ghost. He laid a finger to his lips.

'Sya Dam! But you're dead!'

He grinned. 'Not entirely. I have some unfinished business, but that'll keep until later.' He grinned more broadly. 'British immigration is slack, and its cops go unarmed. Now, Salikaa, my dear, clearly we think alike. Madame's precious haul? Fifty-fifty split!'

'Why should I share with you? If I sound the alarm, they'll arrest you!' I protested.

He grinned. 'I think not. Besides, you couldn't have managed alone. She would still be alive. Still a problem.'

'You win.' I feigned acquiescence, my mind racing.

'Good girl,' he said. 'I have already disappointed one lady today. I saw an old friend board this flight and decided to give him a surprise. Madame Lee will have to do her parachuting alone.'

I knew he must mean Raven—but parachuting? I had no idea what he was raving about, and I told him so, but he ignored me, just barked:

'Now, stewardess, tuck the rug round our friend's throat so she can sleep undisturbed, and fetch me whisky!'

'A monk, drinking?' I snarled.

He sighed. 'It's for the *farang* woman, stupid bitch! Salikaa, I think we understand each other. Should you get any ideas about alerting Raven, you can forget about fifty-fifty. I will kill both of you.'

I had no doubt he meant every word. I nodded.

Fortunately, passengers travelling on to Europe were not required to leave the aircraft at Singapore. I made sure the rug was tucked comfortably about Mrs van Hooten's neck, and the American lady dozed on, as far as anyone knew. The pilot was slotted in appropriately and his report quickly filed, and then the flight was permitted to continue.

I waited until the approach to Zurich before contacting Raven. He was as shocked to see me as I had been to see Sya Dam, but understood the situation quickly when I explained how Sya had murdered poor Mrs van Hooten despite my best efforts to save her, and that I was too terrified to tell anyone else. Dr Raven was stunned. He, like everyone else, had believed Sya was dead, but a peek into the first-class cabin persuaded him otherwise. While I plied Sya with whisky, Raven managed to contact the pilot and convince him to wire ahead and alert the Swiss authorities to prepare a reception committee. I didn't intend to share my spoils. Let the Tiger and the Raven slug it out!

Raven

The last person I expected to see again was the Black Tiger. It seemed he'd followed me out of the grave to enact some measure of vengeance. I could not afford to arouse his suspicions, so I summoned the stewardess—the real one, not Salikaa. Another mystery! She had not explained; there'd been no time. I told the stewardess I had vital information I needed to communicate personally to the American co-pilot, not the Thai captain, concerning safety of the aircraft. I shamelessly threw out Ambassador Morgan's name.

The pilot left the cockpit while the co-pilot and I talked. He was a clean-cut lad, clearly bemused by my tale of intrigue and murder, but agreed to alert the Swiss police. I warned him not to check out the victim. If we alarmed Sya, he was quite capable of going amok, endangering the aircraft and all of us. There was time enough for a showdown when we landed.

Meanwhile, as I speculated on these latest developments, my eyes lingered on the television screen above my seat. It was tuned to World News.

With dawning understanding, I stared, fascinated, as the camera dwelt on the spectacle at Beijing's Forbidden City: the big Westerner posing with his hosts. Pockmarked and smiling, Kissinger dominated the scene, towering over the small, stocky figures of Zhou Enlai and the other Chinese leaders in their regulation grey tunics, their beaming faces awash with a misleading air of innocence. In a flash of insight, I foresaw that soon the Nixons would stand on that same spot to celebrate the prospect of exploiting China's vast potential as ally and trading partner, and I realised, with a sense of shock, that I had been instrumental in saving the life of Kissinger, the peacebroker. Knowing I had played a part in so momentous an event suffused me with relief and a heady sense of freedom, spurred on by a new resolve. Yes, I would burn my boats and return to Bangkok to claim Chee Laan before the Lee Family enclosed her, like the Great Wall of China, and I lost her forever. But first, I would see the Black Tiger to hell.

Zurich, Switzerland

The Swiss police surrounded the aircraft. Salikaa swiftly removed Mrs van Hooten's case, along with luggage belonging to other passengers, from the overhead locker and kept a tight hold of it. She dropped her own identical case into the central seat beside Sya Dam. 'Here's her case,' she whispered. 'Take care of it!' She scurried off with a wink.

The passengers were ushered into the building and isolated in a separate lounge. Airport police began examining their papers. Looking behind her, Salikaa saw police swarm aboard the jet. An ambulance drew up in readiness. Raven was called aside. He pointed out Sya, strolling modestly in his saffron robe, carrying his small case.

The two officers approached him. Without warning, Sya swung the case. The brass corner put out the eye of one of the officers, who dropped to his knees, howling, blood pouring down his face. The other rushed forward, shouting, drawing his firearm, and then everyone was screaming and taking cover. Sya grabbed the policeman's arm, twisted it so the shots struck the ceiling, seized the gun, and smashed the man's arm with a crunch that echoed through the lounge. He wrenched the injured man in front of him.

'Back off!' he shouted, holding the gun to the policeman's head.

At that moment, the aircrew entered through the glass door. The American co-pilot ran forward, yelling. Perhaps he had not seen the gun, or perhaps he was recklessly brave. Sya shot him in the middle of the chest.

Raven had been edging ever closer round the edge of the room. He saw his chance. In the second Sya's gun was pointing away from the hostage, Raven launched himself at Sya's legs in a flying tackle that brought all three men crashing to the stone floor beside the dying co-pilot. Raven, struggling to his feet while the hostage and Sya were still entangled, stomped hard on Sya's outstretched wrist. The gun clattered out of his hand. Raven snatched it up.

At his feet, Sya crouched, glaring savagely, a tiger at bay. Raven kept the gun trained on him as officers dragged the Black Tiger to his feet and slammed him into handcuffs.

Paramedics rushed to tend the wounded. In the scuffle, Sya's small case had fallen open. A woman's gown tumbled out in a cascade of flame silk—the only item it contained. As he was led away, Sya caught sight of the splay of red; he threw back his head and roared with laughter. His eyes roamed the lounge wildly, but Salikaa had slipped away in the confusion. Sya's eyes snapped back to Raven, the fire in those yellow depths burning down to molten embers.

'This isn't the end, Black Bird!' he shouted, his shoulders hunched in menace. He raised his cuffed hands in a grotesque salute.

Raven met his gaze unflinchingly. 'No, Tiger,' he returned, 'but it is almost certainly the end of the beginning.'

Salikaa boarded a bus for Zurich's centre. It was raining; people with upturned coat collars, bustling under dark umbrellas, turned to stare at the slim, exotic figure in the pastel-coloured uniform striding through the drizzle, heels painfully protruding over the backs of her high shoes.

Salikaa made her way to a jeweller's, then to a bank. The grey financial gnomes were disconcerted by their newest client, but they concealed their discomfiture and treated her professionally. Salikaa possessed the only necessary credential: vast wealth, in cash and kind. After her business transactions were satisfactorily concluded, Salikaa entered a luxury department store where, in prettily accented French, she purchased and immediately donned a pair of black boots. She dropped the stewardess's shoes in the nearest trash bin. Then she pulled outfit after outfit from the racks, and bore them off to an unoccupied changing cubicle. The new black silk shirt felt cool and yet warm. The tight black jeans encased Salikaa's lean thighs; the lizard-skin belt exaggerated a slender waist. The Italian boots were soft as butter. Jewellery completed the new look: bulky silver bracelets, rings, and neck chains. The young man who eventually emerged from the cubicle was lean and dark and deadly.

He made for a barber's, where he marched in and sat down in a vacant chair, scorning to queue with other customers. '*Couper!*' he commanded, with a wave of his hand. He indicated his ponytail. '*Tout court ici, ici en brosse!*'

The black mane was shorn. There was so much of it that two apprentices were required to sweep the floor when the barber had finished his work. Salikaa peered admiringly at himself in the mirror. He pulled the long coxcomb he had insisted on through his fingers and demanded gel to maintain its dynamism. He had never before seen himself with cropped hair. It looked dangerous and seriously sexy, and it showed off his cheekbones and that marvellous carved jawline.

As he sauntered down the street, swinging his hips, Salikaa attracted the usual glances of startled admiration, but now both men and women stared. The crowd parted to let him pass. Salikaa began to whistle.

Bangkok, Thailand

Raven

I had survived the brutal process of freeing myself from my chains while in London. It had taken a few weeks, but I had managed it. As soon as I could, I flew back to Bangkok—the short route, over Tashkent. Even so, I passed the flight in a fervour of impatience. In my infatuated naïvete, I could not wait to throw myself at Chee Laan's feet. I could not stop planning our conversation in my head. There were many versions, but in all of them she agreed in the end to spend the rest of her life with me.

As the taxi chugged through the thronged streets, I was infuriated by the tortoise pace. I felt like getting out and running down the road in the heat, knocking down any who got in my way.

I'd calmed down somewhat by the time we reached the hotel. She had told me where she would be. On the phone she did not sound welcoming, or even very friendly. I told myself that she was feeling shy because we had been apart for weeks. Looking back, I realize that I had already lost her.

A page showed me in, and I found Chee Laan seated behind her grandmother's desk. Everything was the same; everything was different. Her cheek still had the lovely curve of youth, but the gold-embroidered black silk pyjamas she wore were austerely conservative. From the little Mandarin collar her slender neck rose like the pale stem of a primrose. But the young girl I loved had vanished: her posture radiated a mature and steely confidence. She sat ramrod straight in the ornate high-backed chair, both her hands reposing on the surface of the desk, and rested her cool gaze on me. The effect was electrifying.

'My God,' I murmured. 'I don't believe it—you've turned into her!'

She frowned at me reprovingly. 'Tea.' It was not an invitation, but a veiled command.

'Tea be damned!' I was aware of my rudeness, remaining standing, looming over her. I flattened my palms against the desk. 'My darling!' I blurted, chilled by her tone, desperate to evoke some softened reaction from her, some acknowledgement of what we had shared. Chee Laan only pulled her hands into her lap.

'Please do not call me that,' she said.

My hopes foundered. All at once, I knew what I had lost.

She watched me silently for a moment. I imagined she was probably thinking how blind she had been ever to love me, if indeed what we had shared was love, and was choked with self-loathing. She studied my hand as if it were an ape's paw and she couldn't believe she had ever allowed it to caress her. She went to press the unseen bell beneath the desk, then hesitated. 'Something stronger than tea, perhaps?'

'I came back for you,' I said weakly.

'Things have changed,' she said.

'Devil take it, Chee Laan!' I burst out. 'I know things have changed! Your grandmother has fled the country. People have been murdered; Sya has been extradited to the States. He's for the electric chair!'

'You are as bad as my brother Pao. I know all these things. I know everything. Raven, please sit down. Take refreshment.'

I still towered over her, angry and bewildered. But her black eyes glittered dangerously. Finally, obediently, I took the chair that placed me slightly lower than her, bowing to the reflection of her power.

'You see,' Chee Laan was choosing her words carefully, 'I am permitted by royal dispensation to inherit my grandmother's property. Though she was regarded as a defector, the terms of her will are to be respected. By gracious intervention of Their Highnesses. Even though I am only a woman,' her lip curled, 'I am preferred above my brother. It was not cheap. But I too have rendered some small service. They owe me. That in itself does not disturb them. But the fact that one day I might remind them of it, that does.

'Raven, in every Chinese business, there are many workers. But do you know who always sits at the cash desk? A son of the house. This is the first principle of the Chinese family.' She paused. 'The Black Tiger promised to help my grandmother escape. He abandoned her. Worse, he never planned to keep his promises; her parachute was tampered with. Sya made sure it never opened. She fell to her death, Raven.'

Her eyes met mine, and their bleak expression froze my marrow.

'I believe the Tiger had unfinished business with you. This is why my grandmother had to die. He deserted her to pursue you.'

I leapt up from the spindly chair. 'Chee Laan, all that is past. I'm asking you to marry me.' I nearly gasped trying to breathe in. 'Please, my love!'

For a moment hope soared wildly in my chest as she rose and walked calmly toward me and stood looking up. I caught the scent of lemon in her hair. She extended a cool hand. I grasped it, bruisingly, like a child gripping a flower too tightly. Her eyebrows lifted, narrow and wing-shaped, like those of her grandmother.

'Do you remember *The Summer Wives of Mount Lu*, Raven?' I scowled, impatient, tired of smokescreens and games. 'A wise scholar knows when the summer butterfly has turned back into a goddess.' I saw that she spoke without irony. I sank back into my chair. 'The Buddha says, "Pull out that love as one pulls out lotuses in the dry season",' she said gently. It was an acknowledgment, of sorts, and one with which I would have to be content.

She studied me for a long moment, eyes roving over each lineament of my face and body, gravely committing them to memory.

'Goodbye, Raven,' she said at last, reclaiming her hand softly. Never has a touch landed harder, like a whirlwind from a butterfly's wings.

I exited her office into a coach-load of tourists crowding the hotel lobby, chattering excitedly. The uniformed bellhop pranced around me expectantly. I said in Thai: 'Call me a taxi, please. Don Muang Airport. Tell the driver no more than fifteen baht.'

The bellhop pulled down one corner of an eyelid to express his unbounded admiration. 'Sirmadame sapeak Thai numbah one, very clever, satay Thailand long time?'

'Too damned long.'

The bellhop, with a look of pained incomprehension, protested, 'But this dry season! Bangkok dry season, numbah one!'

I never saw Chee Laan again. Occasionally her name crops up in the financial pages in connection with the continued expansion of the Lee Empire. Sometimes she is pictured, usually the lone female among the suits in some boardroom; always in control, always smiling. Her face is slimmer and her teeth appear longer. Her resemblance to her late grandmother is commented on frequently by those who remember the great Sunii Lee or have seen the portrait of her which adorns the boardroom of the Lee Banking Corporation. She favours business suits the colour of flame. There's never any mention of a husband, but there is a son, a crown prince, a handsome Eurasian boy—adopted, probably. His name is Sunny Lee, but the reports use his nickname. *Nok Dam*. Black Bird. He was seventeen when Sya Dam was finally executed for good in Florida. He is, apparently, a prodigy, the apple of his doting mother's eye.

Salikaa, of course, has become the darling of the *beau monde*. In less than two decades, he has built a fashion house that eclipses Dior and Balmain. In the exalted circles in which the star couturier moves, he is known only as *Son Altesse*, His Highness. It is rumoured, and Salikaa carefully fosters the legend, that he was born a prince—Cambodian, perhaps, or maybe Laotian. Certainly, his admirers whisper, he is a prince among artists, resoundingly successful and devastatingly beautiful. As his celebrity has increased, those about him have begun to treat him like a dazzling, capricious god.

Our real Highness, Princess Pim, has also achieved legendary status, though sadly she did not live to enjoy her fame—but that is the destiny of a martyr. She is remembered as a pioneer for reform, and her name is honoured far beyond Thailand's borders.

Occasionally, in the elegiac mood produced by much whisky, I glance at the book Sunii Lee gave me, *The Summer Wives*, and think of my own butterflies. None of them were goddesses, not even Chee Laan, though she was remarkable, and bewitching, and I loved her. We played a role in each other's legends, just as Sya and I did. I also feel that I have played nemesis—not just for Sya, but also for Sunii Lee, who threw herself out of a plane to her death, a victim of Sya's obsessive hatred for me.

As for my 'mission', it was successful. In the interim, the United States has recognized Red China. Vietnam officially ended. The society that produced Sya Dam and allowed him to exert his malevolent regime of assassination and terror is changing. But there are always new enemies springing up like dragons' teeth, new battles to be fought. Perhaps that's the way with empires, and society, and wallpaper. You paper over one crack, another appears somewhere else. That's life's banality.

I'm left with just one question, for what gods and goddesses there be: If a man like the Black Tiger comes along only once in a lifetime, why did it have to be in mine?

Acknowledgements

I would like to thank Malinee Chang, who taught me Chinese. Viggo Bruun and Khun Rasomnee, who taught me Thai. Professor S. Egerod, Julia de Felice Davies, and especially Fiona Spencer Thomas, who believed. Michelle Dotter, my US editor. Salikaa, swift swallow, and of course Frederik, who was, as ever, there and there for me.

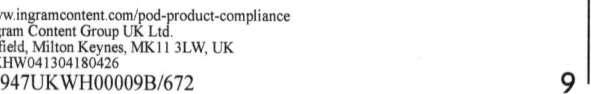